MARRIAGE OF CONVENIENCE

"What you need, Allyn, is a new name and an honorable title, which, whether you believe it or not, the name Manners is in these parts. The wedding must be made public, and it must be soon. I won't demand—how shall I say it?—consummation of our marriage vows. Unless, of course, you insist upon it."

Allyn looked at Joshua unwillingly, standing five feet in front of her, and she could barely conceal her distaste. "You will expect some sort of remuneration for this agreement, I suppose?"

His grin widened tantalizingly. "I take it that means I'm to be deprived of your company. In that case, I think it's only fair. My price is thirty percent of the remaining purses in exchange for my name."

"Thirty percent!" She nearly gagged.

"A bargain, you will find," he replied, his grin fading. "Of course, there will be one additional stipulation."

Allyn stared at him. He had already said he would not demand consummation. What could he mean?

"A kiss," he said, his features now as blank as stone. "One for each day we are married. To be paid in demand, either one day at a time, all at once, or—any other way I see fit."

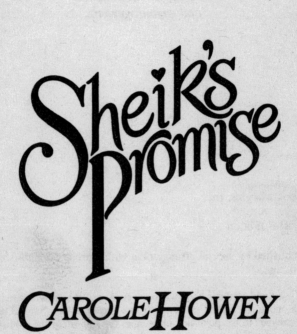

Sheik's Promise

CAROLE HOWEY

*To Bob, for his patience
and encouragement.*

Book Margins, Inc.

A BMI Edition

Published by special arrangement with Dorchester Publishing
Co., Inc.

Printed in the United States of America.

Chapter One

Fresh pellets of gray-brown mud splashed upon Allyn Cameron's riding boots and the already soaked skirt of her abbreviated brown riding habit as her horse galloped through Rapid Creek. She was out of the saddle, leaning far over the chocolate brown colt's perspiring neck as he began his climb to the top of the bluff. She was amazed as always at his effortless stride, and a laugh welled inside her as she realized that she was more breathless than he.

The early morning sun met horse and rider as they gained the top of the bluff. With a fearlessness born of his proud thoroughbred heritage, the colt Sheik plummeted down the steep, treacherous slope, throwing back his equally fearless rider until she was fairly lying along his spine. She gave him rein. The purple-pink sky above her and around her seemed to spin, and giddiness threatened to overwhelm her.

Sheik continued his rapid descent, and his jockey mastered herself. She looked about her at the endless range dotted with clusters of scrub pine, down to the little two-story house where a thin wisp of gray smoke curled from the tumbled chimney, down to where the foreman waited for them with a pale, dumbstruck countenance.

They were on the flat now. The duo streaked past the foreman and Allyn stood again in the saddle as Sheik slowed to a walk. For the first time she felt the damp chill of the April morning and she shivered. The foreman ran up to them, seizing Sheik's bridle. Sheik tossed his head in protest, and Allyn gave the animal a quick pat on the neck before she vaulted from his steaming back.

"Good lad, Sheik," she told him as she landed on the soft ground on unsteady feet. "That was fast, Bert." She turned her attention to the foreman, panting. "How did we do?"

Bert's expression had not changed. Allyn thought, amused, that he looked like one of those wide-eyed Kewpie dolls that she often saw in the general store around Christmastime. She grinned at him.

His gravelly voice was quiet with awe. "I hope the blokes at your saloon'll let me double my bets, love!"

She waved a dirty, gloved hand impatiently. "Time, Bert, time! Don't talk of money right now!"

"A minute fifteen. A bloody minute fifteen! Allyn, this is the fastest damned animal I've ever had the privilege to clock!"

Allyn's sigh became a smile, then a laugh. Then Bert was laughing, and the clouds of steam from their breath joined and evaporated as they embraced one another joyously.

"Missy will be so proud, Bert!" Allyn panted, still giddy from the wild ride. "She's done it! Do you know what this means?"

Bert, to her surprise, grimaced as he lowered his arms.

"It doesn't mean anything until he wins the race," he reminded her, loosening Sheik's saddle cinch.

Allyn did not know whether to scold Bert for his cynicism or thank him for helping her to retain her perspective. Sometimes Bert was as bad as Missy.

"He will win," she chided the foreman, rubbing her arms against the chill. "What is there to stop him?"

"Oh, a hundred things," Bert grunted, lifting the saddle from the patient stallion's back. "That course is a bear, love. You know that. Why, only last week Jamison's prized gelding went lame at the copse. They had to—"

"I know, I know," Allyn interrupted, not wanting to hear the story repeated again. She had heard it all week at her saloon, so many times that she'd finally retreated to her office the previous day and hadn't emerged until closing time. Jamison's gelding had had to be shot. The thought of Sheik's career, possibly his life, being ended on that course by a freak accident left her cold. Missy had worked too hard with the colt. Sheik was her first thoroughbred, her first chance at trying out knowledge gleaned long ago from her horse-trainer father. The knowledge, by all appearances, had weathered the wait well. But Missy had invested too much time and money in the beautiful animal for it all to end tragically in a muddy steeplechase on a fine April day.

Behind her Sheik snorted, as though mocking her sudden dark thoughts.

"You'd best get on back to the house," Bert advised Allyn as they separated. "Missy'll be looking for you. I want to walk Sheik a bit, then we'll rest him."

"How much time have we?" Allyn asked the foreman, flexing her sore shoulders.

Bert glanced up, squinting his eyes against the brightening sun.

"Enough," he answered, "for a rubdown. A rest. A little water, and feed."

Allyn chuckled, trying to shake off her morbid thoughts. "See you inside."

She clapped him once on the back, gave Sheik a pat on the rump, and turned toward the house. She picked her way around the corral, listening to the squish of mud about her boots, avoiding the bigger puddles. There were still traces of heavy, wet snow about, dripping from the birch shingles of the roof. There were mounds of the stuff where it had been shoveled from drifts just so they could get in and out of the four-room house during the long winter. Joining the sounds of dripping water and squishing mud was Bert's faulty tenor shrieking strains of "Barbara Allen" from the stable out back. She smiled and winced at the racket.

Wiping her feet in a soft pile of snow near the door, she noticed the enticing aroma of Missy's cooking. Without a doubt, Missy was hard at work preparing a breakfast of mammoth proportions. Missy Cannon suffered from the delusion that everyone shared her tremendous appetite in times of stress, a habit which resulted in Missy's frank tendency to plumpness. The trouble was that as good a cook as Missy was, one had the inclination to fulfill her expectations. But this morning, at least, Allyn was not about to eat any more than she needed to stave off the hunger pangs.

"A minute fifteen," Allyn sang out as she admitted herself into the dark, tidy house. "We should have named him Linus, Missy. Or Leopold. He has no fear. No fear at all."

She flung herself into one of the hardwood kitchen chairs and began removing her dirty boots. The perky white bow in the back of Missy's crisp apron bobbed as the younger woman ladled out bowls of porridge.

"I just wish this wasn't a steeplechase." Missy's high-pitched voice was muffled by the clink and clatter of her utensils. "One false step and Sheik's career is over before it's begun."

Allyn did not answer her. Missy, being secluded at the ranch most of the time, had not heard about Jamison's gelding. At least, Allyn hoped she hadn't. Missy was enough of a worrier, without adding fuel for her conflagrations. And it would be a monumental tragedy for Missy, both personally and financially, if the promising three-year-old, because of accident or error, was lamed. Missy had trained him for over a year to run the flats, hoping against impossible hope, she knew, that the C-Bar-C might produce a Dakota Derby contender. Missy had never dared to express the ambition that Sheik might go beyond that to Louisville, Kentucky, to make a run for the Roses. "One step at a time" had always been Allyn's motto. And the first step to the Dakota Derby was the Rapid City Steeplechase. Sheik had to win today. They had to win. Or all of that time and money had gone for naught. To say nothing of Missy's self-confidence.

And possibly the C-Bar-C, besides.

Bert and Missy were in the middle of breakfast when Allyn came down the narrow staircase ten minutes later, washed and dressed in a fresh habit, her favorite brown one. She had gotten most of the worst mud off her soft, supple riding boots, and her dark hair was pulled back from her face in a knot at the base of her neck. She slid into her chair, pushing away the bowl and laden plate with a careless but purposeful hand.

"You may as well take half of this away," she said to Missy, a trifle agitated at the feast her friend had set before her. "I can't possibly eat a fraction of it and still keep a light load on Sheik."

"I'm not riding. Ship it over here," Bert volunteered across the table, reaching for her sausage links. Allyn assisted him, scraping the porridge out of her bowl. Missy made a nervous, clucking sound and Allyn glanced at her as she took back her emptied plates. Missy's excitable gray eyes darted between Bert and Allyn as though she were watching a game of lawn tennis.

"How are you riding, speaking of Sheik?"

Bert did not appear to notice Missy's nervousness. He was pouring molasses over everything on his plate with a liberal hand. Allyn nibbled her own hot biscuit thoughtfully, cradling a cup of coffee with a languid right hand.

"Same as the trials," she began, staring into her black coffee. "I'll give him rein at the start, and curb him on those downhills. I don't want him to fall and ruin those splendid knees."

"Or kill you either," Bert agreed with a wry laugh. "That's sound. But what about Coriander? Have you seen her? I hear Boland's got her to—"

"I don't really expect much of a contest," Allyn said, interrupting him with a condescending smile, trying to bolster her own confidence as well as Missy's.

"Allyn, my love." Bert shook his head, returning her smile in an annoying, paternal manner. "Never make the mistake of underestimating your competition."

Allyn liked Bert enormously, but she hated being patronized. She made a face at the middle-aged Britisher across the table, because she knew she could not reach his leg under the table if she tried to kick him.

"You saw his time, Father Caution," she said. "Don't be so bloody ridiculous!"

"Allyn Cameron, such language!" Never was Missy's faint Southern drawl more evident than when

12

chastising Allyn for some breach of decorum. Allyn, seeing Missy's piteous expression, smiled reluctantly and accepted the rebuke.

"What about Coriander, Bert?" Missy pleaded with her foreman, and in typical Missy fashion, not waiting for his reply, turned to Allyn. "Have we a chance?"

Bert gazed at the jockey with expectation. Allyn sighed, looking from one face to the other.

"Have either of you ever known me to champion a losing cause?"

"Yes." Missy's retort was petulant. "Twice. Once was with me and the ranch."

The younger woman left her place and began clearing the table in a loud clatter of cups and dishes. Bert said nothing. Allyn pursed her lips and stared into the dregs of her coffee. She refused to think about the other "losing cause." The C-Bar-C was Missy's sore spot, she knew, although why it bothered Missy that she, Allyn, helped to support the struggling ranch financially, Allyn could not understand. After all, the C-Bar-C was partly hers too: it was only natural that the hard-earned profits from The Golden Wheel, her saloon, should go into the ranch. Missy's pride never failed to irritate Allyn, even though some part of her empathized with it.

The ranch had been Missy's inheritance, a legacy from her father's brother. It provided the perfect retreat for Allyn, who had wanted to break away from her family, and for Missy, who had grown up with her as her maid. But the property had come encumbered by a burden of tax debt and neglect. Allyn had covered the tax debt with her own funds and used what remained to set herself up in the saloon business with the Wheel. She viewed her continuing financial contributions to the operation of the ranch as room and board. Missy, she knew, took a different view.

Carole Howey

"Let's have no more of that," Allyn said, rising. "I'm riding Sheik today, right? That settles any debt, real or imagined, between us. The purse isn't much, but I've bet a hundred dollars on us, and that means . . ." Allyn abruptly jumped to another subject. "How much have you wagered, Bert?"

The older man nodded with a broad, understanding grin. "A month's pay."

"O ye of little faith," Allyn quipped, tapping the foreman lightly on his shoulder with her riding gloves. "You'll be sorry for so small a wager."

"The money's on Boland and his mare, from what I can see," Bert told them, sounding surprised. "If we win, it should be five to one at least."

"You've been talking too much at the saloon," Allyn chided him, wagging a finger. "It should have been ten to one."

"And a place in the Dakota Derby." Missy sighed dreamily, behind them. "Oh, Allyn, do you think we—"

"Yes, I do think we ought to be getting along," Bert said, interrupting her. Allyn shot him a conspiratorial grin. Bert imagined he was fooling the two women when he intervened in a potentially volatile situation, and Allyn saw no reason to rob him of that pleasant delusion.

Bert and Missy went on ahead in the buggy, which Allyn normally drove out to the saloon, and Allyn followed a distance behind astride the handsome, carefully groomed thoroughbred. It was a glorious day for a race, full of promise. Sheik's trot was brisk and spirited, and Allyn managed his lively gait masterfully. She was aware of the critical, even envious stares they were receiving from the few travelers she passed along the trail. These were her neighbors, many of whom had come quite a distance, all with the same destination: Rapid City, and the Steeplechase. Allyn enjoyed their attention and called very civil greetings

14

to all of them, whether she knew them or not. They all knew her, but that was not surprising. After all, she was the only woman from Pierre to Laramie who ran a saloon. And the only woman brazen enough to jockey in the Rapid City Steeplechase in all of its auspicious, seven-year history.

Allyn chucked to Sheik, nudging him to a canter. If the colt fulfilled his promise, his success today alone would bankroll the ranch for another year. If he went beyond that, he could support a dozen properties just like the C-Bar-C. The possibilities were staggering, even to Allyn.

The landmarks of her home of five years sped by them. A thousand times she had traversed this road since she and Missy had first driven down it, after Missy had inherited the ranch, and Allyn was still in awe of the contrast between the vast, wild beauty of the Dakota range and the cramped, crowded city she and Missy had left behind. Now, she could recall her initial horror with some amusement.

The very idea of herself and Missy living on the rambling, run-down spread had been comical, and frightening. But in five short years—or long ones, depending upon which of them was telling the story—with perseverance and hard work, Missy had transformed the dilapidated ruin into a respectable place. Their "Home in the Wilderness," as Allyn liked to put it. For wilderness it was. As endless and full of life as the ocean, the landscape was ever changing, always a different hue or shadow. At first, Allyn had missed the forests of stately oak, maple, and birch trees that had surrounded her home in Philadelphia. She had yearned for the rustling of leaves in the wind, the bloom of azaleas and forsythia in spring, and summers full of white roses as big as her fist. But in the austerity of Dakota's searing summers and brutal, blizzardy winters, she'd learned an appreciation of

15

little things, such as a warm fire with a winter wind buffeting the house, or finding a nest of brave robins under the woodpile. Even the excitement of an annual event such as the Steeplechase took on an added thrill.

As they drew closer to town, they encountered more travelers along the muddy road. Allyn began to feel the resentment of the assorted spectators and competitors whom she passed. It was in the air, as thick as a plague of locusts. People in these parts had always resented the fact that she owned and operated a saloon—a business no lady should even have the right to possess, as far as most of them were concerned, let alone succeed at. And now, adding insult to injury, she, Allyn Cameron, was actually jockeying in the Steeplechase. Allyn imagined their whispers: It was only by connivance that Allyn Cameron was riding in this race, they were no doubt saying. And it would be just her arrogant, uppity way to win it too. Of course, that fellow who rode through here a few years back and worked out at the C-Bar-C had taken her down a peg or two, hadn't he? Took some of the sass and starch out of her, didn't he? Allyn sighed, disgusted with herself. Why couldn't she let Raif go?

"Morning, Miss Allyn. You look fine today."

Bill Boland's deliberate baritone startled her into a blush. He was the nearest neighbor to the C-Bar-C, even though his spread, the Double-B ranch, was ten miles away. Allyn fixed a polite smile on her face, which she then turned upon the tall, hard-built man whose white-blond hair gleamed silver in the morning sunlight. Bill's handsome, rough-hewn features reminded Allyn of a weathered granite statue. He was smiling at her too, atop his dapple gray favorite, Coriander. As usual, the rancher seemed oblivious to her deliberately cordial demeanor. He was a widower in his forties, and it was common knowledge around the area that he was a hopeful, if slow, suitor of his much younger, haughty neighbor. Allyn had been aware of this for months, and did nothing to encourage his attentions (which, spectators believed, was the reason for the suit's stalemate). Allyn liked Bill well enough as an honest, hard-working neighbor, but she was certainly not disposed to marrying him. Besides, she did not love him.

Yet Raif had possessed none of Bill's fine qualities, and she had loved him to distraction.

"Good morning, Bill," she answered him at last, hoping to thrust Raif from her thoughts. She reined Sheik to accommodate the pace of the smaller mare. Sheik protested with a toss of his head, as though jealous of her attention to the lesser breed.

"Sheik looks a might prankish today," Bill offered conversationally.

Allyn did not reply. She looked about her, hoping that he would move on ahead. He did not.

"Who's riding him in the race?" he went on.

Allyn did stare at him then, not even attempting to hide her wonder.

"Surely you must have heard the scandal, Bill," she answered patiently. "I am."

His blue eyes widened. She enjoyed the expression.

"Miss Allyn, you must be cr—I mean, do you think that's smart?" His voice dropped, as though he might be afraid of being overheard.

Allyn restrained her hot words.

"Do you imagine I would take such a risk if I didn't think we could win?" She pronounced each syllable carefully, as if Bill's primary language was something other than English.

She didn't know what it was about Bill that often made her feel so impatient. Once Missy had suggested

17

to her that it might be because Bill treated her with respect and deference. The people of Rapid City had, with few exceptions, never seemed to like her very much, and Missy seemed to think that bothered her. Well, maybe it did. Especially after she had allowed Raif to ride roughshod over her reputation. Bill alone, among all of their mutual acquaintances, had never so much as mentioned Raif's name afterward. She might have been grateful to the rancher for that. Or at the very least respected him. But more often than not, she wanted to avoid him altogether.

"I've ridden rougher trails, Bill," she replied at last, staring straight ahead at the road before her as she thought again of Raif. "So if it's me you are worried about, I advise you to save your trouble."

Bill's already ruddy complexion turned copper at her thinly veiled rebuke.

"Well, I am worried about you," he grumbled. "I don't mean no harm. That's one hell of a course— I beg your pardon. Tough enough for men and seasoned riders, let alone a woman—"

"A woman," she interrupted tersely, "riding a thoroughbred whose simplest abilities far exceed any contenders in this race, present company included. Even if I were the worst rider in the field, Sheik would never allow me to commit an error. So when we win, Mister Boland, you and the other men can give all of the credit to Sheik. I hope that will salve your wounded pride. Good morning."

She nudged Sheik to a canter, leaving the surprised and stung rancher in her wake. Bill Boland watched her ride off into the crowds ahead, rubbing his cheek ruefully. A slow smile finally creased his features. No doubt about it. Allyn Cameron was one hell of a lady, and if she won this race, she deserved it. But of course, she wouldn't. Either way, he decided, win or lose, he would make her his wife.

18

Chapter Two

The sound of water splashing into a washbowl awakened Joshua Manners from a pleasant but forgotten dream, and he stretched his arms above his head as he opened his eyes. It took him a moment to orient himself. He traveled quite a bit, and this town—Rapid City? yes, that was it—was the third he'd been to this week alone. He closed his eyes again, hoping to recapture the dream as well as a few extra moments of sleep. The touch of a warm, wet washcloth on his brow robbed him of both.

"It's late, Joshua," a low, luscious alto voice told him. "You'll miss the race."

He smiled lazily, remembering the night before. What was her name? Lottie? No, Lettie. That was it. He reached for the hand bathing him, without opening his eyes. The hand was warm and plump. He massaged it with a cavernous yawn.

"Get me some breakfast, will you, darlin'?" he drawled. "I could eat a moose."

19

She laughed as though it was the funniest thing she'd ever heard.

"I doubt I even have a steak," she told him, and he could hear her move toward the door. "But I'll do the best I can."

"That's all any of us can do," he mused aloud, more to himself than to her. She chuckled again and closed the door. When he was sure that he was alone, he got out of the bed—a nice, firm, clean one, better than most hotels he'd stayed in—and dressed quickly.

He tied his cravat, gazing out of the boardinghouse window into the busy street below, concentrating again on the business which had brought him to this remote mining town from the governor of this equally remote Dakota territory in the city of Pierre.

Coriander was a filly, not the governor's preference—in a horse, that is. But Manners's own scouts had agreed she was worth a look, based on her showing in a match race the month before at a fair in Lead. In any case, a trip such as this often yielded a surprise or two, which had, on past occasions, resulted in handsome bonuses from the governor, who did so enjoy adding to his stable of the finest racers in the territories, if not the country.

Since arriving in town the previous evening, Joshua had learned of just such a potential treasure: Small-town gossip being what it was, he'd heard the name Sheik on several lips loosened by drink at a local saloon. There seemed to be two camps where the colt was concerned, sharply divided on most counts, yet united in their general disapproval of the jockey, Allen Cameron, who coincidentally owned the saloon. Not wishing to have his assessment prejudiced, Manners left the establishment before hostilities erupted, preferring to seek the comfort of a woman, ideally not one with strong opinions on the upcoming race.

Lettie Osbourne had proven just such a woman, operating a very respectable bordello in the thin guise of a boardinghouse. Mercifully, she was as adequate a cook as she was a bed partner, and his night was capped off by a fine breakfast. When Manners left her house he was sated in all important respects, and anticipating the race with some interest.

Rapid City bristled with fevered anticipation of the biggest annual event the town ever celebrated. It was normally a modest municipality with a population approaching five hundred people, but its numbers swelled to over double that for the race. The muddy main street, through which most of the spectators were passing, was hung with a huge banner, suspended on one side of the street by the Commerce Bank and on the other by the post office, proclaiming "Rapid City Steeplechase," along with "April 1, 1889." The last number in the year had been patched and stitched over many times, and the cloth there was worn and frayed. The citizenry, clad in their best Easter finery, was amassing at the town hall at the end of the street, perhaps a quarter of a mile distant, carrying flags and firecrackers and crying babies.

With a practiced eye, Manners appraised the Steeplechase entries which passed before him as he stood on Lettie's front steps. There were cowhands, young and old, atop sturdy, dependable mounts with no blood to support their owners' faith in their speed. There were young, would-be dandies on newly broken stallions and geldings whose fire and excitability would not translate well to a tortuous race course. He wondered which of them, if any, might be Allen Cameron and Sheik.

"You'll be back for supper?" Lettie, in the doorway behind him, sounded hopeful. He extracted a solid-gold watch from his vest pocket, glanced at it, and replaced it, shaking his head without looking back.

"Not if my business goes well. Maybe next trip."

"I'll be here," she assured him, her tone flirtatious.

Without a parting word, he descended the remaining steps to the sidewalk and began his unhurried stroll in the direction of the mob. He gained the assembling ground in minutes, squeezing through the excited crowd to the rope which had been strung to keep the populace from being trampled to death by twenty unstoppable horses. The mob pressed him annoyingly. Perfect pickpocket territory, he reflected, glad that his own valuables were safe in his breast pocket. He looked about himself, amused. All of these people at best would glimpse but a few seconds of the race, and think themselves well-rewarded. He smiled inwardly at the peculiarities of human beings and trained his eyes to the field.

The twenty riders huddled in a pack, apparently drawing lots for their starting positions. One by one, they emerged like fleas off a dog, waving their slips of paper to supporters in the crowd.

He started, then shielded his eyes against the glare of the sun. That couldn't be a woman! He was so startled that he did not even realize he had spoken the words aloud until the fellow beside him, a middle-aged man with a round, porcine face, addressed him in a raw soprano.

"It sure can be," he told Manners, his tone laconic. "And it is. That's Allyn Cameron." Then lowering his voice so as not to offend the ladies, he added, "The bitch. I hope she kills herself."

Manners allowed the offensive little man's ugly sentiment to slide past him, too captivated by the sight of a woman with a crown of auburn hair caught into a knot at the base of her neck. She was tall for a woman, but she moved with as much polish and refinement as if she were the hostess of a grand society gathering instead of a jockey in the Steeplechase. Her eyes were the brilliant green of fine emeralds, set in her cameo features as a striking contrast to her white skin. Her beauty and refinement could only be products of an aristocratic heritage and upbringing, and seemed to be assets she herself held in magnificent disdain.

Dressed in an abbreviated Western habit, the woman was indeed ready to ride, not watch, the race. She studied the slip she had drawn, then lifted her head and stared his way for an instant, directly at him. He was stunned by the undeniable shiver he felt as she glanced past him to an unknown third party. The features on her pale, arresting face ignited with an unabashed pleasure he felt privileged to witness.

"Missy! Bert!" she called in a clear voice which cut through the noisy crowd. "I've drawn third!"

Manners gripped the rope in front of him, leaning on it for a better view. The striking, attractive woman came closer to him, moving with a grace not found in most women in these parts. She came close enough for him to reach out and touch, although he mastered the impulse to do so.

"Third," she repeated, more joyously than before. Apparently, she then received a reply which satisfied her, for her cool green eyes relaxed into a grin that could only be called smug. She started to turn back. He had to speak to her.

"Good luck, Miss Cameron," Manners heard his own voice say, his tongue finally loosened. She pivoted on her heel, narrowing those captivating eyes directly at him. Her guarded expression told him that she was, at the very least, cautious of strangers.

"Thank you," she responded after a moment, her tone grudging and clipped, not at all like the brilliant, bell-like quality of her remarks to her entourage.

Then she was gone, stepping gingerly through the muddy area to the post. Her careful step made Manners smile. She would, he realized, be covered with mud before this race concluded, whether she finished or not. She then disappeared into the cluster of men and horses.

What the hell was a woman—a lady like Allyn Cameron—doing on the back of a horse in this race? A steeplechase, no less? he wondered. For lady she was. There could be no mistake. It was more than her striking beauty, and her refined, graceful movements. There was breeding in her manner, education in her address. This was a hothouse rose in a desert of tumbleweeds. This was a find!

In a moment, the woman to whom Joshua Manners's immediate attention was riveted was astride a big, fine-looking chocolate thoroughbred, looking as though she belonged nowhere else. Indeed, the horse was a compliment to his mistress's regal deportment. He was a credit to his prestigious breed. He tossed his proud head with spirit and a moving sort of dignity. His heritage was demonstrated in his narrow face, lean shoulders, and long, strong limbs. He was built for power.

He was built to win.

Allyn Cameron leaned over her mount in readiness. Her small, curved mouth was set and her eyes were steeled to the track ahead. Joshua Manners could sense the tension in every fiber of her body. Perhaps, and he was unmistakably pleased by the thought, he would have the opportunity to meet with her at the end of the race and make her an offer on her horse. Watching the determined female jockey, he was certain suddenly that this would be one hell of a race.

Allyn's legs were drawn up tightly under her modified habit, gripping Sheik's flanks like leeches. Her ears strained for the sound of the shot that would start the race, and she could feel the combined energies of Sheik and herself building like steam in a Corliss. Her heart pounded until she thought she would burst, and at the precise moment when she felt she could no longer wait, a shot cracked the air.

Twenty horses lunged forward with enough combined force to power a locomotive. There were shouts and cries, an official madly waving his hands. Allyn was incapable of heeding.

She did not see any of the other horses. Urging Sheik on with wild cries she did not later recall, she pressed forward over the thundering road in chase of the win.

Sheik was a natural jumper. The first hurdle was a gully, a drainage ditch from a mine, lined by a fence designed by ranchers to keep their livestock away from the bad water of the Black Hills mines. A tangle of bramble had grown up around the fence, but in April it merely looked like wiry black webbing. Allyn knew just the spot where she wanted to take the jump. With nineteen horses several yards to the rear, she was able to stay with her plan.

There was a spot where the ground swelled before dropping off into the ditch, where, with the speed Sheik had attained, he could easily span the breach. She rose in the saddle, leaning forward over the regal creature's bouncing sable mane as, without pause, he leaped high and far into space, clearing the hazard and sending a thrill through his rider.

"Good lad!" she breathed, righting her seat as the colt hurtled over the flat field to the next obstacle, hung with red flags.

The other riders were even farther behind by the time they reached the flags. Allyn dared not pause to count the contenders who had survived the first hazard. The second was a cliff-like rise of some four or five feet from the settled field into a copse of trees. This was a dangerous hazard, where an unwise rider could lame even the smartest, sturdiest animal. It was the place where Jamison's now-legendary gelding had met its fate.

Allyn had no intention of repeating Jamison's error. She planned to dismount and lead Sheik up the slope at a spot where the ground had been worn to a narrow path by other such cautious riders. He had given her more than enough of a lead to do so. She reined Sheik, who obeyed graciously, and vaulted lightly from the saddle before the chocolate thunderbolt came to a stop.

Sheik needed little encouragement to follow his mistress where she led, up the steep, muddy, but short incline and into the woods, where she quickly mounted him again. She did risk a backward look then, and saw the riders spread out across the flat, bearing down on the copse, Bill Boland and Coriander leading the rest. The field had thinned. She felt a chill. With a cry and a nudge, she gave Sheik rein and clung to his neck as he cut through the trees like a buzz saw to the third challenge.

Rapid Creek was not wide at the spot, but it was deep enough here and there to necessitate a swim. The early spring thaw had swollen and altered its banks, Allyn noticed with alarm. She was unable to make out her favorite crossing. Sheik, blessedly, was an avid swimmer, unlike his mistress, who avoided swimming when she could. She paused, examining the terrain. A dull, distant thunder reminded her that time was precious. She made her choice, breathed a quick, silent prayer, and guided an enthusiastic Sheik into the swift, dark, icy water.

Sheik was a strong swimmer, but the current was alarmingly powerful. Combined with the numbing cold, Allyn very nearly lost her seat, as well as her grip on the reins. They were carried downstream a ways before Sheik gained footing, but he clambered out, shaking his head. Allyn was soaked to the skin, and freezing cold, with the worst of the course yet to come.

She had little time to review the folly of her decision to ride in the Steeplechase. After another brief gallop, there were two more jumps in quick succession, which Sheik managed gracefully. Then another long stretch of flat, where rider and horse were able to open a greater distance between themselves and the remaining field.

Even through gloves, the reins had become painful. Sheik was strong, Allyn knew, but not even all of their trial runs had prepared her for his indefatigable power. He sensed victory, and he would have it. Missy needed it. Allyn only prayed that she could cling to the saddle long enough for him to claim it.

The final hazard approached. Allyn steeled her failing concentration and flexed her sore fingers once. Then, digging the heel of her boots firmly into the stirrups, she nosed the eager Sheik down, down the tortuous slope, a slope so long and so steep that one errant gesture could send them both tumbling straight into hell . . .

At least three spectators marveled at the effortless stride of the horse and the skill and tenacity of the rider.

The thrill of a hard-earned victory filled Allyn with renewed strength and energy as they tore the ribbon at the finish line. Exultant, she reined Sheik at last to a trot. She looked about herself, expecting the honor due a winner.

There was a tumult in the crowd of spectators. Angry bettors were claiming a false start. Through the crowd, Bert appeared with a blanket over his arm, panting as he ran up and caught Sheik's bridle.

"Grand race, Allyn, but there's been a protest. Seems it was a false start. A firecracker. Some of these chaps are calling for a draw, if not a lynching."

Allyn expelled a hard, angry sigh as she dismounted shakily. Bert applied a blanket to her shoulders and together they watched the place horse, Coriander, cross the finish line.

"That margin," she said through chattering teeth, "is hardly a draw. Walk him, Bert," she requested, handing the foreman Sheik's rein.

The crowd was angry, all right, she decided. Angry not only at her brazen entry, but at her audacity to win the thing as well. Preparing some strong arguments, she left Bert to cool Sheik down as she made for the judges' platform across the square.

She edged through the crowd unnoticed, catching bits of conversation as she went: "All the horses was off the line before the gun . . ." " . . . have to run it again . . ." " . . . must've missed a jump . . ."

She shut the sounds out, unwilling to hear more. She was hurt, she realized, for Sheik. She didn't mind that these people had no respect for her. The feeling was more or less mutual. But to deprive Sheik, and the C-Bar-C, of a hard-earned victory because of some petty resentment . . .

She gained the bottom step of the platform as the mayor called for order. Bill Boland was at the dais with the short, round man, looking every bit as disreputable, after the arduous trail, as she herself did. There was another man with them, whom she recognized at once as the handsome, annoying man who had addressed her prior to the race. Mystified by the unlikely trio, she forgot her quest in her curiosity as to what Mayor Churchill would tell them.

"Ladies and gentlemen," the portly mayor began in his best stentorian tone. "This man"—here, he clapped a beefy hand upon the solid, broad shoulders of the dark, attractive stranger—"comes to us direct from the governor. And he says all the horses started off together. And this man"—here, he performed a similar gesture with the equally tall, golden-haired Boland—"you all know is Mr. Bill Boland, of the Double B. And he says that Sheik, of the C-Bar-C, ridden by Miss Allyn Cameron, ran the whole race, and made every hazard. And he says he should know, because he was eating their dust the whole way!"

The assemblage laughed, except for Allyn. She was too stunned by the import of what was happening before her eyes.

"The results stand," the mayor continued. "The winner is Sheik. Where is Miss Allyn?"

In her soaked, muddy habit, wrapped in a rough old horse blanket, she suddenly felt very conspicuous. Indeed, Bill noticed her, and she watched as a grin spread across his pleasant features. She wanted, oddly, to flee, but her feet would not move.

He came forward, reaching out to her with his big, strong hands, which he clasped about her slim waist, and before she could protest, he had lifted her easily to the podium, setting her between himself and Mayor Churchill. The mayor shook her hand, amid scattered, polite applause, and made a gesture as if to ask her to address the crowd. She shook her head, but leaned close to whisper in his ear. His round, smooth face lit up with an approving grin.

"Miss Allyn says you're all invited to her saloon to celebrate. Drinks are on the house!"

Thus were the protests drowned. The crowd surged toward The Golden Wheel, to the dismay of other saloon proprietors. All insults, real or imagined, were forgotten. Allyn, aching to her core, longed to be far away from there.

"Congratulations!" It was Bill whispering in her ear. "I'm proud of you."

His arm was about her waist. She could not recall his ever having performed so bold and intimate a gesture before, and maddeningly, she was flustered by it. He began to guide her down the steps, but she collected her wits and stopped him.

"I'm a sight, Bill," she told him by way of apology. "Maybe I'll be along later. You go on ahead."

She slipped deftly from his embrace, and he seemed to sense that he had overstepped his bounds.

"I'll see you later then," he said, looking helpless.

He went on. Allyn watched him go with some measure of confusion, but she did not waste time analyzing it. Through the thinning crowd, she saw Missy, Bert, and Sheik. Missy appeared to be crying for joy into the neck of the colt, who seemed ready to run another steeplechase. She could not help smiling at the tableau, and she descended the steps to join them.

"Congratulations, Miss Cameron." Another voice halted her, the same one that had addressed her prior to the race. It was a deep voice, resonant and refined, and it sent an involuntary thrill along her spine. "That was quite a race you ran."

She knew, without even looking, that the intriguing voice belonged to the man who had addressed her by name before the race. His use of her name angered her, yet at the same time she was aware that some expression of gratitude was in order. After all, the mayor himself, fool that he was, had credited the attractive stranger with Sheik's victory. Could she, as Sheik's rider and part owner, do any less?

She turned to face him with a civil, cordial remark, but found, to her dismay, that he was standing a mere three feet away from her, his coffee-colored eyes unabashedly looking her up and down. Painfully aware of her soaking-wet, muddy clothing, hair, and boots, and the mean blanket which scarcely hid them from view, she could only stare dumbly at his immaculate and impeccably tailored black pinstriped suit and gray silk tie. He removed his sterling-black Stetson politely, revealing sable hair which was not dressed in the usual fashion, but was rather overlong and unlacquered. It invited her to arrange it with her fingers. He smiled at her irritatingly, his overly wide but undeniably sensual mouth widening to the corners of his very square jaw, as though aware of her errant desire.

"My name is Joshua Manners, Miss Cameron," he said with an easy courtesy that was no doubt intended to charm her, and indeed, did not miss by much.

Joshua Manners, Allyn sensed, made an impression on everyone he met. The kind of impression he made no doubt depended on the kind of business he had to transact. Men, she suspected, treated him with caution and respect. He was not a huge man, but he was taller than most, and his broad shoulders and lean, efficient physique hinted at the strength he camouflaged beneath an impeccably tailored suit. He shook hands with a firm, commanding grip, she was sure, and his wide-set dark eyes could take a man's measure in a moment.

On the other hand, he had a certain boyish element which women would find irresistible. His features included a wide, sensuous mouth and angular jaw tapering to a faintly dimpled chin that was oddly reconciled to his smallish, turned-up nose. Full, dark eyebrows underlined his forehead like a bold statement, and neatly trimmed yet perpetually unruly sable hair, kept at bay by the crisp black Stetson, completed the ensemble to striking effect.

"I represent Governor Arthur Mellette," he went on in a pleasant, even respectful, tone. "I scout promising thoroughbreds to add to his stables."

Oh, so that was it. She relaxed a little. But only a little. This man obviously recognized Sheik's superiority among a mediocre field, which elevated him in her estimation. But he was altogether too charming to be trustworthy. Thank you for that lesson, Raif, she thought with a grimace.

She arranged her features even as she tried, under his amused scrutiny, to arrange her response.

"How fortunate for us that our governor takes an interest in local events," she remarked, trying for a cool and urbane tone which would match his own. "And how lucky we are that his ambassador has a keen eye." And an authoritative, if not a bossy, manner, she thought, but did not add.

"It was my pleasure to intervene," he enjoined, reminding her—intentionally, she was sure—that she had not yet thanked him.

Her face grew warm, and for the first time she was glad of the mud on her cheeks. She drew the blanket about her shoulders, feeling curiously as though she were naked beneath it. Naked. And vulnerable.

"We are," she murmured, unable for some reason to meet his penetrating stare, "deeply in your debt, Mr. Manners. If you will please excuse—"

"On behalf of the governor, I'd like to discuss buying the animal," he continued as if he had not noticed her attempt to escape. "Of course, I'm sure this is not the best time. Perhaps I could meet you at your ranch later."

Allyn could not prevent herself from staring. Joshua Manners, in her estimation, was coming dangerously close to exceeding the boundaries of common courtesy. It took quite a lot of effrontery to suggest that she and Missy might entertain a stranger at the C-Bar-C, even one from the governor. His boldness rivaled that of another stranger whom she remembered all too well.

"Sheik," she pronounced deliberately, matching his gaze, "is not for sale."

To her outrage, he chuckled and shook his head.

"A bold and ingenuous declaration, Miss Cameron," he countered, taking a step closer to her. "Hard currency, as we both know, is a rare and valuable commodity in these parts, not to be refused without good cause. And in my experience, everything is for sale, if the price is right. Especially in this godforsaken territory."

She wanted desperately to back away from him, but she was determined to stand her ground. Of all the infuriating, self-important, presumptuous characters she'd met during her time in Rapid City, this one beat all for sheer gall. In most cases, of course, Manners might have been right. But that did not, in her opinion, alter the fact that the man was behaving like some boorish political bully. Why, next he'd be threatening her!

"I am afraid," she said, trying valiantly to keep her anger, as well as her fear, in check, "that you have wasted your time, and the governor's. Sheik is not for sale."

Manners lowered his head for a moment, crossing his considerable arms as he pressed a finger against his unsmiling lips. Go now! a voice inside her urged. But for some reason, she remained, fascinated by the powerful allure of this Joshua Manners in spite of herself.

"Your pride is overruling your common sense, Miss Cameron," he said in a quiet voice that momentarily stilled her heart. He was directing his serious, brown-eyed gaze at her in a most disconcerting way.

"And your vanity is overruling your gentility."

33

Her hand went to her mouth even as his stare widened at the insult. For a moment, mortified, she considered apologizing for the words which had tumbled out before she could prevent them.

"My van—excuse me, Miss Cameron," Manners's warm baritone had gone cold as a Dakota winter. "But I bow to you in that area. I never met a woman with any claim to humility who thought she could jockey a thoroughbred in a steeplechase."

His words stung, but Allyn held her head a notch higher.

"In that case, I must pity your limited experience," she retorted, clenching her hands to still their trembling. "And even were 'my' stallion for sale, I don't think I could be desperate enough to deal with a toady for him."

She summoned every scrap of dignity that she could muster and turned away from him. She could not, she thought, recall the last time she had spoken with a man when it did not end in some form of argument. Except, of course, for Bert.

"Are you planning to take Sheik on the circuit yourself?" she heard him call after her.

"My plans are none of your business," she said without looking back. "Good day."

"It's an expensive risk," he shouted after her. "Travel, entrance fees, boarding fees. And if he finishes out of the money . . ."

She had thought of all of those things, and she found it most annoying, not to say unnerving, that the governor's emissary chose to bring them up just at that moment. She dared to turn to him again, as she knew he was several yards away from her at least.

"Your concern for our welfare is touching," she said stiffly, aware that Missy and Bert were now approaching with Sheik in tow. "We have nothing to discuss, Mr. . . ."

"Manners," he reminded, at her hesitation.

Remembering his thorny words, she could not resist a parting blow. "It's evident that you have none. Good day."

Joshua Manners watched her walk away to where Sheik and her associates waited. He cursed his heavy-handedness. He was not accustomed to dealing with women in this business, and certainly not with ladies. In point of fact, he had encountered so few ladies since relocating to this vast wilderness from back East that he had begun to fear he had forgotten how to treat them altogether. He could see, having made a tangle of this conversation, that his fears had been well founded. Watching Allyn Cameron stride off in that filthy, ridiculous ensemble of hers, he rubbed his jaw, which ached as though she had struck him. And damn it, she might as well have. Toady! Was that how she saw him? As she rode off on Sheik followed by her entourage, he tried, and failed, to recall when he'd met anyone as aggravating. Or as intriguing. There was no doubt of it. Her remarks, he reflected irritably, would sting for some time to come. He had allowed the woman to get under his skin. And that was not good.

Allyn began the trot for home, having no taste for the rowdy drinking celebration no doubt taking place in her own saloon. The confrontation with Governor Mellette's representative had shaken her, as much because of the man's obvious obsession with Sheik as because of her own unexpected reaction to what was quite possibly the most attractive man she had seen, or at least noticed, since Raif had left her. For he was attractive, she had to admit, even if he did have dark eyes instead of blue ones, and spoke in a cultured Eastern baritone instead of a Kentucky tenor with the consistency of molasses . . .

Carole Howey

She shook her shoulders. Raif is gone, she recited to herself. He took your love and your reputation and made cinders of them, like a careless child playing in a coal bin. She wanted a hot bath, some dry clothing, and solitude in which to enjoy their victory. It was bittersweet, coming as it did with such controversy, and as a result of the testimony of men. Sheik should have been the uncontested winner. And would have been, she told herself, had he been ridden by anyone else.

Any man, that is.

Chapter Three

"We have a lot of catching up to do, Lucius." Allyn shook her head, surveying the tallies from the previous day. Her generous spirit had resulted in considerable loss for The Golden Wheel. Outside her office window, a cold spring rain was falling steadily, and the room was lit by a single lamp on the desk behind which she sat. Its surface was cluttered with receipts and inventory slips.

"I keep tellin' you, Boss, you gotta water down the red-eye. It's the only way." Lucius was a likable fellow in his fifties whose life's work was tending bar. He was smart, tough, and totally without both hair and scruples. Allyn liked and respected him, but would not trust him as far as she could throw Sheik.

"You know how I feel about that," she told him sternly. "If I can't make an honest dollar, I'm no better than—I don't belong in business. It's easy to make money by cheating. But I have—"

"I know, I know," Lucius interrupted with a laugh,

shaking his head. "You have to live with yourself. Honestly, Miz Allyn, I don't know nobody who beats themself up over what their pa did or didn't do in his life. It's like you always gotta pay for his sins, which, from where I sit, don't look all that bad. So he kept two sets of books. Nobody got hurt, did they?"

Allyn could not restrain a bitter laugh.

"That wasn't all he kept two of," she could not resist muttering, surprised that the memory could still make her tremble with anger and betrayal after so much time. The house on Delancey Street. The young woman, her own age, holding a small child by the hand . . .

"Huh? What'd you say?" Lucius's interrogation called her back to the present.

"Nothing," she replied quickly. She'd trusted Lucius with one secret, but she trusted only Missy with the others. She had been betrayed by trust one too many times. She changed the subject.

"Don't you dare cut the whiskey," she ordered the bartender in a tone few ever argued with. "I mean it, Lucius. If I find out you have . . ." She allowed her warning to fade like the distant call of a lone she-wolf far from her den.

"Miz Allyn, I don't know how you stayed in business these four years," he declared, scratching his bald head with a big paw. "It's a pure miracle."

She sighed at his rebuke, enduring his laughter as she would endure no one else's. He was old enough to be her father, she realized. In many ways, Lucius reminded her of him, especially his ethics. Curious, she often thought. She had run away from her father and his atrocious business ethics and morals, yet in Lucius, she carried him with her always.

"It can't surprise you that much," she sniffed. "You've found ways to steal that would make a magician take notes."

Lucius said nothing. Silence, she reflected, meeting his cool gaze, gives assent. She sighed again. His sins were hers as well. More so, she reflected, because she knew of them and kept him on in spite of them. She was, at last, her father's daughter, she decided, noticing a sour taste in her mouth. No doubt, though, Lucius stole from her too, so perhaps her transgression was also her penance.

"So you'll be going to Deadwood?" Lucius asked, wisely changing the subject.

His question did not surprise her as much as the matter-of-fact way he posed it. As though he expected the response to be affirmative.

"Why, no," she replied, aware of a pang of regret. "Why would you think that?"

It was his turn to express surprise. "You mean Missy's going? And the Limey?"

"Missy is Sheik's owner," Allyn reminded him, leaning back in her chair. "And Bert helped to train him."

"And you manage him."

"I manage this place too," she remarked tartly. "Or have you forgotten?"

"This place," Lucius began, lifting his leg to prop himself on her desk, "runs better without you, and you know it. If you want my opinion, you should be the one going to the Dakota."

"You just want to get rid of me."

"Hell, sure I do." Lucius was forthright about that at least. "But that don't change the facts. And the facts is you belong there, in the thick of things. You got the head for it. And the starch. Missy's no fool, but she'd crumble like day-old cake in that kind of crowd, and you know it. And Bert's a likable enough fella, but don't nobody trust a Limey."

He's right, a naughty, perverse voice inside of her said. Oh, not about Bert, but you know it's what you want. There'll be plenty of action and excitement, both of which were in short supply in Rapid City.

She dropped her pencil onto the miasma of paper-work and rubbed her eyes. Much as she hated to admit it, she wanted to accompany Sheik to Deadwood. Desperately. To watch him run and to see him win. To be among new people, people who lived a different kind of life. Rapid City had become one unending stretch of workaday tedium since Raif had gone.

"Get back to work, Lucius," she told him, and her voice sounded tired to her ears. She wanted to be alone again. Thoughts of Raif tended to bring out the hermit in her. Without another word, her bartender slipped from the room and Allyn sighed. After three years, she still thought about that rake. After three years, it still hurt, more than she could have dreamed possible. True, the pain had been worse during the first few months after his departure, and had subsided to a dull ache, like the perpetual ache of a bad tooth, except it was in her heart.

There was not much she could do to take him out of her mind. He preyed there like a relentless parasite, waiting for any idle moment to make his presence—or more accurately, his absence—felt. She was a prisoner to him. It was a prison of her own making, she knew, but she nevertheless felt powerless to free herself from it.

Work sometimes helped. Yet as time passed, Allyn grew further from her livelihood rather than closer to it. More than once, she wished that she possessed Missy's single-mindedness of purpose: Missy had her ranch and her horses, all of which she mothered and loved with diligence. There was not much to love in a saloon, or in all of Rapid City, she decided forlornly.

She totaled a column of figures, and was interrupted by Lucius's raspy voice on the other side of the door.

"Comp'ny, Miz Allyn."

The figures were forgotten. She lifted her head and stared at the door, feeling her pulse accelerate. It can't be, she scolded herself.

It wasn't.

It was Bill Boland.

Confusion and disappointment fought for precedence in her as the tall widower strode into her office past Lucius, who shrugged helplessly. Bill was wearing a plaid flannel shirt and muddy jeans. He carried a drenched poncho over one arm, which he dropped onto the chair beside the door, and a dripping brown Stetson in his other hand. Allyn was unable to speak for a moment, and Bill took advantage of that fact. He closed the door behind him, shutting out Lucius's curious face, and strode to her desk in a bold step.

He has a lot of vigor for a man in his forties, she thought, watching him.

"What brings you here, Bill?" she wondered aloud, surprised at the natural sound of her voice.

Bill was an attractive man with the kind of solid features that improved as his age advanced. Usually serious, he looked somewhat uncomfortable when he smiled, as he was doing now.

"You might call it business," he began, looking pleased with himself. "Hope I'm not interrupting."

Allyn glanced at her cluttered desk, stifling her annoyance with a rueful grin. "You are. What business brings you to town on such a wet day?"

He sank his tall, solid frame into the worn wooden chair facing her desk and leaned his elbows on its arms.

"First off, I want to tell you what a fine race you ran yesterday," he began, regarding her with a slow appraisal which discomfited her.

She nodded her thanks, uncertainty paralyzing her tongue.

"Second, I want to know if . . ." He hesitated, col-

41

oring. He cleared his throat. "Damn it, Allyn, I want you to marry me."

The office was suddenly stifling. If she had not been trapped, seated at her desk, she might have run from the room. She could only guess at the expression on her face, but she must have registered at least surprise, because her suitor chuckled nervously and rallied.

"What's wrong? You mean to say you didn't know I was getting around to this?"

Allyn steadied herself, swallowing hard.

"I—I don't know, Bill," she managed after a minute. "This is so sudden . . ."

Apparently he took her words as a good sign, for he plunged on.

"Not really," he said. "I've known you for goin' on five years now. I'm a widower for two. I know I'm not the most romantic fellow in the world, and I don't aim to rush you into anything. But the time's come for me to lay my cards on the table. I never met a woman like you. The first Mrs. Boland was a wonderful lady, no mistake. But you're . . . something else. I'm forty-five years old; I got a fine ranch that's paid for, money in the bank, and the best part of my life yet to live. And you're the woman I want to live it with. I hope you'll say yes?"

His crystalline blue eyes burned into her. For a fleeting moment she thought of Raif and his sensuous, caressing gazes. Her cheeks burned as if Bill could read her thoughts. She rose and went to the window to escape his scrutiny.

"I don't know what to say, Bill," she said, hoping she did not sound as strained as she felt. "I don't know what kind of wife I'd be. I can't cook. I'm not much on sewing, or gardening, or anything that makes a good ranch wife. Ask Missy. I—I just can't imagine why you want to marry me."

Suddenly he was beside her, his hot breath making the skin on the nape of her neck tingle.

"I think you can," he said in a low, gentle voice, his two hands turning her shoulders toward him. To her astonishment, he pressed a scorching kiss onto her half-open mouth. It was the kiss of a man who knew how, a kiss which tested the borders of decency. His powerful arms were around her, and her hands were on his arms. She should protest, she knew. Instead, she held onto him. She felt weak, felt herself falling. She had not been kissed that way in years, and it made her want things she had compelled herself to forget.

He stopped, and she could not meet his smoldering gaze. She felt at once excited, surprised, angry, and yes, a little frightened. She wanted him, she confessed to herself. She wanted him to be Raif for her. Could that be enough?

"Well, what do you say?" Bill breathed, still holding her close.

"You have a—quite a persuasive manner about you, Mr. Boland," she managed in a gasp. She fought for breath, for control of herself.

"Does that mean yes?"

He was persistent; she gave him that.

"Yes," she heard herself whisper before she'd intended to say anything.

He lifted her chin with his thumb and forefinger, compelling her to look into his eyes. To her, it was as if he were saying, Look at me. I am Bill Boland. I'll never be anyone else. But of course, he couldn't be. Even if he had heard the gossip years before, it seemed unlikely that he had remembered. Even if he did know of it, he had never mentioned it to her yet, either directly or indirectly.

"You're sure?"

"Yes," she murmured again, trying to stop the small room from spinning.

He smiled faintly in an expression she took for triumph. "When?"

Allyn felt dizzy. She felt a headache start at the back of her neck.

"I don't know." She broke away from him at last, but not far. "Missy's going away. Let me discuss it with her. We'll talk on Sunday."

He seemed satisfied, and he approached her again. She turned her cheek to him at the last moment, not trusting her response to another kiss like the first. Then he was gone.

What had she done? She groped for her chair, found it, and sank into it, dazed. She had said she would marry him. But did she really want to? Well, she did like him. And his kissing, she admitted to herself, feeling hot again. But marry him?

Certainly, there were precedents. People who didn't love each other married all the time. In fact, as she thought back, she could not recall a single wedding she'd been to, or a marriage of any duration, in which love had played a part. Convenience, perhaps. Logic, certainly. But not love.

Mrs. Bill Boland.

She felt indifferent to the name, then sad. She was twenty-five years old, she realized grimly. Raif was never coming back. And, she confessed to herself, she needed a man. Better, perhaps, if she did not love him . . .

A sudden gust of wind challenged the window behind her and she shivered, although the temperature of the room had not changed.

It had stopped raining by the time she left for home. As she drove, the blue-black clouds peeled away, leaving a perfect spring twilight. Bert came around as she pulled the buggy to a halt, and they called brief greetings to one another. She tossed him the reins and climbed down from the seat. As Bert led the horse away to the barn, she strode up to the porch, removing her well-worn riding gloves as she went. Her shoes made a curious, muted thud on the damp planks, muffled by the skirt of her efficient gray poplin suit.

Her old chair greeted her eyes just before she went into the house, like a prospective dancing partner inviting her to watch the stars come out. It was too tempting. She eased her slender frame into the wooden structure, which creaked agreeably. From the vantage point, she was able to watch the last golden wands of sunlight fade from the vast purple sky.

A chilly breeze mustered enough ambition to pry tendrils of auburn hair from her tidy coiffure, obliging them to tease her cheeks. She rebuttoned her collar and drew her arms close about her, shivering, determined not to be driven inside.

She turned her gaze upward and outward, where the evening star pulsed just above the darkening horizon. Idly, her practiced eye selected the familiar constellations: Orion, receding. Sagittarius. Ursas Major and Minor. It had been an evening much like this one that had brought Raiford Simms into her life.

Her world at age twenty-one had found her disillusioned, and more than a little disheartened at the immediate results of her flight from the sheltering bosom of her wealthy Philadelphia family, and seeking something she'd thought she would find by running away to the Dakotas with Missy Cannon, her friend and former maid. She'd been looking for simplicity and integrity. What she found, however, was hard work, lots of it, terse neighbors who lived far away, and an intense, almost crippling need to love and be loved. Missy was a friend and a sister to her, but as time went on, Allyn discovered that she craved more than sisterly companionship.

45

Missy ran the ranch, since she knew about such things. She'd been a child on a working ranch. It was only the untimely death of her struggling father that had brought her to the Camerons first to be a companion for the child Allyn, then to be a personal maid for the young woman. Missy still waited on her to an extent, despite her protests. Allyn used her funds to purchase The Golden Wheel and, as she was accustomed to ordering others around, hired the help for Missy. More often than not, the hands were transients who hired out for weeks or months at a time, with plans no more definite than how they'd spend their pay on a Saturday night. They began to look the same to Allyn until one April night.

A red-golden Southerner, soft-spoken and courteous but by the look of his lean, ragged state on a run of bad luck, appeared on their doorstep one day begging work. It was not hard for her to fall prey to his caressing gazes, the curve of his sensuous mouth when he smiled, or the polite, refined manner he never failed to exhibit. Raif made it quite clear to her from the beginning that he was strongly attracted to her, and it was a matter of but a few weeks before she admitted him in darkness to her bed and learned the ecstasy of being a woman.

As a man, Raif was beautiful, built as she imagined a heathen god to whom virgins would willingly sacrifice themselves might be. His hair was a soft, sunset gold, almost red, and his skin, except for his sun-bronzed face, was fair and covered with the same colored down. His eyes were a sinful sapphire blue, capable of reducing her to a molten mass of want as their heavy lids half-closed in sensuous appreciation.

As a lover, Raif was tender and passionate, skilled and experienced enough to awaken desires few women could know. His very presence was like a drug that never ceased to have effect on her. He created a dependence within her, an addiction to physical fulfillment. Their affair went on for months while he worked in the employ of the C-Bar-C, and Allyn deliberately blinded herself to the rumors which began to spread about her, and to the increasingly apparent fact that Raif, the restless drifter, was ready to move on again. She would not even listen to Missy, who had agonized over the affair from the beginning claiming to have seen through the false bronze god at once.

As a person, he was at best unreliable. He'd talked a lot about grand ideas and fantastic, if not noble, plans, and how he meant one day to be something important. Allyn realized very early that these were nothing more than dreams, as he obviously lacked the kind of gumption such plans required. But that hadn't mattered to her. He loved her.

Or so she thought.

He left as abruptly as he'd come, with no goodbye, leaving a crying hole like the bite of a ruthless predator and much unfinished business with Allyn. Even she was not surprised, not really. Blessedly she had not conceived a child, but she was left devastated just the same, and she was determined never to trust another man with her heart again if she could help it.

Three years later her opinions had not changed much. She did not love Bill, and she would keep it that way, even after marriage. If he had no control, no power over her heart, he could never hurt her, she reasoned. Not as her father had hurt her, betraying her mother in such an atrocious fashion. Not as Raif had. And she was sure she could not survive such hurt again.

The misty Milky Way materialized as the sky changed rapidly to blue-black. It was definitely cold. Shivering, she grimaced and left the chair just as Missy's high, shrieking voice met her ears.

47

"I'm here, Miss," she replied with a yawn. "Outside."

Another cascade of words. Allyn sighed.

"It isn't cold. I'm coming."

The inside of the house was warm, dark, and fragrant with Missy's cooking. Bert and Missy were engaged in some argument or other in the kitchen, and Allyn smiled to herself at the familiar domestic scene, leaving her unpleasant memories on a peg by the door with her cloak. As she entered the kitchen the conversation ceased, as though she had been the topic of discussion. She glanced from face to guilty face with suspicion.

"There's something in the wind, I perceive," she began sternly, trying to keep herself from smiling. "Out with it."

"I can't do it, Allyn," Missy blurted out, sounding miserable. "I'm all nerves. I don't think I'd take good care of Sheik, and the ranch will surely go to seed if I leave it. What can I do?"

Allyn inclined her head in Missy's direction. "What do you mean?"

"Allyn Cameron, you haven't heard a word we've said!" the younger woman exploded.

"That's because I'm not listening to you. Missy, Bill Boland's asked me to marry him."

Missy's anguished whine became a squeal of excitement. "He didn't! What did you say?"

"I said yes," Allyn replied, trying to sound more enthusiastic. "But I have to think about it. I don't want to be rushed into anything."

"The idea of you being 'rushed into' something is too ludicrous to credit," Bert observed, setting to his meal with gusto. "A lot less believable than Missy being a bundle of nerves."

What were these two talking about? Allyn stared from one to the other in perplexed irritation.

"Missy feels that she'll be no good on the Deadwood trip," Bert continued, as if answering her expression. "She thinks, and I agree, that you would be much better to take care of things at the Dakota. I'm going, of course, but if you could spare the time from your devotion to your saloon, Missy should stay behind. You're the one for this task, Allyn. It's obvious to both of us."

Allyn stared. It had been obvious to Lucius as well, and Bert, like Lucius, was no fool. She had wanted time to think about her engagement and, she admitted to herself at last, she had wanted to go on this trip with Sheik. And here were Missy and Bert, holding both of these opportunities out to her.

It was too good to be true.

"Well." She tried to keep her excitement from her voice. "Maybe just this once."

Missy applauded, then flung her arms about Allyn's neck with a squeal. "God bless you, Allyn! I knew you would! I'll be along the day of the race, of course, but Sheik must be there day after tomorrow. Bert's made all of the arrangements. Can you be ready?"

"I'm ready now," Allyn declared, hugging Missy in return.

Joshua Manners settled his long, muscular frame into the big leather wing chair as though it were an ample whore. Cupping his hands together, he declined the cigar that Governor Arthur Mellette offered him.

"What do you have for me, Josh?" the shorter, stocky man behind the rosewood desk inquired, his small, pig eyes darting in a greedy fashion.

Joshua shook his head, remembering the thoroughbred Sheik and his captivating, exasperating mistress. "Nothing, Governor."

"No promising nags?" the older man pursued in a disappointed voice.

Manners pursed his lips. "I didn't say that." He shifted in his seat. "There was a fine-blooded thoroughbred. Wore my eyes out on him. He took the field like he owned it."

"Then damn it, why isn't he mine?" Mellette barked, pounding a small, fat fist on the highly polished desk top.

Manners was not daunted by this show of temper. "Because his owners won't deal."

"Nonsense," Mellette exclaimed roundly. "You know my policy. What did you offer them?"

Manners shook his head. "You don't understand. They were not selling. Not at any price. That horse may damned well be the fastest horse in the country, and those two ladies know it."

He barely got the words out of his mouth when the governor's eyes sharpened, homing in on Joshua's last phrase.

"Women?" he challenged. "Two of them? Racing this thoroughbred?"

Manners nodded, slow and deep. "Women," he affirmed. "One of them runs a ranch, the other a saloon. Businesswomen, you might say."

The governor leered. Joshua thought it an ugly expression.

"Businesswomen, I do say." Mellette stroked his double chin, his voice gone hoarse with lewd suggestion. "But there's only one business for a woman. You mean you didn't appeal to their better nature? Or didn't they appeal to you?"

The governor's ribald commentary had never bothered Joshua before, but he felt a twinge of annoyance with his employer at this moment. "I found her appealing." Manners unconsciously slipped into the singular. "But they talked like tight—" He stopped himself before he said "tight-assed." "Like ladies, prim and proper, and one of them even gave me hell for addressing her by name before we were properly introduced." He chuckled at the memory, against his will.

The governor, by contrast, exploded with round-house laughter. "Gave you hell? Must've been some by-God woman. Unless you're getting too old for this work." He laughed again.

Joshua frowned. He was thirty-three. The governor was fifty. The governor, however, signed his pay voucher these days.

"I expect we'll have another chance at the Dakota next week," the younger man said, as if to change the subject. "Let me study it." He stood up, indicating that the interview was over. "Meantime, I suggest you bank your wagers on Sheik."

The governor followed him to the door, clapping him upon the back with a too-jovial gesture.

"Fair enough. But maybe you should send Red Simms after these 'ladies.' Might be they'd soften up after he showed 'em his stuff."

Manners did not mind the governor's laughter at *his* expense. But he dealt the shorter man a withering look. "I said they were ladies, not trollops," he chided Arthur Mellette by way of farewell, then withdrew, closing the door behind him.

Manners was drawn up short by a presence on the other side of the door that he sensed before he saw. His body went rigid, preparing instinctively for an attack. But that was ridiculous. He was in the governor's mansion, far from the endless intrigues of his former Secret Service life. He forced himself to relax on a deep breath, and found himself leveling the contemptuous, blue-eyed gaze of another of Mellette's retainers, none other than the infamous Red Simms.

"Listening at keyholes?" Manners inquired with as much politeness as if he had inquired after the man's health. "That's a step up for you, isn't it, Red?"

Carole Howey

Red's smile was acid on silk. A brief smolder in his cold cobalt-blue eyes betrayed his anger, to Manners's satisfaction.

"Yeah," he drawled, stretching out his vowels in the Southern way. "Who knows? Maybe one day I'll be carrying slops, like you."

Red openly resented Manners's position of seniority with the governor's entourage, and never made a secret of it. He'd wandered in three years earlier, boasting a knowledge of thoroughbreds from his Kentucky heritage that, Manners had to admit, had been borne out over time. But he was trash, as far as Manners was concerned. Any man who would brag about his sexual conquests the way Red did wasn't worth his spit, even if he did have the amazing good grace to leave the woman's name out of it. Manners had dealt with plenty of petty, hostile underlings in his time, and while he would have preferred it to be different, he never lost any sleep over it. The other men in his charge knew better than to show him any disrespect, either to his face or behind his back. In fact, they had no inclination to do so.

He'd hoped Red would get tired of the job and leave after a short time. That seemed to be his style. He was more talk than action, except, apparently, in a woman's boudoir. But three years later Red was still there, waiting, Manners supposed, for him to give up and go away. His insults were wearing thin after the third or fourth go-around, even with Manners's epic patience. But the governor had a liking for Red, so he stayed.

"Straighten your collar," Manners advised him, then sniffed. "Jesus, Red, you smell like a dime whore. When's the last time you took a bath?"

Red's hands went to his shirt automatically. Then he jerked them away as if annoyed that his extremities had obeyed Joshua's command. His bronzed face

52

went a coppery red and his regular features twisted into an angry scowl behind his prissy little mustache.

"I don't have all day to wait for you to retort to that," Manners said, enjoying the man's rage but hiding it behind a bland expression. "The governor is waiting for you, I suppose. I'm not going anywhere for a couple of days. You know where to find me if you come up with an answer before then."

He took five unhurried steps in the opposite direction before he heard Red hiss, "Damn you, Manners!"

Joshua did not even turn around. "That's an old tune, and you don't even play it so well," he rebuked his subordinate. "Try again later, when you're not drunk."

The hallway was quiet again, the governor's various aides and secretaries apparently being employed elsewhere. Manners quickly forgot Red, and instead found himself mulling over Mellette's coarse jests and recalling the excessively ungracious Allyn Cameron's cold words. He had given more than a little thought to the woman during the days following the race, and he had decided there must be some deeply rooted reason for her wall of ice. He wondered further why he had even thought twice about her, although she had a remarkable pair of green eyes, like luminescent emeralds, and the unmistakable bearing of a well-bred lady. No, Allyn Cameron was certainly worth a second look, he thought, aware of a spark of hope that he might have the opportunity to pierce her wall of ice at the upcoming Dakota Derby in Deadwood.

"Joshua Tecumseh Manners!" Another familiar, husky voice, this time female, intruded upon his idle reverie in a most unwelcome fashion. "Were you planning to leave without a good-bye to me?"

Morgan Mellette, his one-time lover and now the governor's own stunning, hot-blooded wife, appeared in another doorway near the top of the stairs. Or perhaps she had been there all along, watching him approach, and he had simply not noticed her, lost in his introspection. He did not know which. Nor did he particularly care. Their brief, tumultuous relationship had ended nearly three months earlier, shortly before Arthur Mellette had made the scandalous widow from Pierre his second wife, the first having died some years before. Manners paused in his exit. A frown tugged the corners of his mouth as he regarded the undeniably desirable woman.

"I entered without a hello," he observed dryly, unable to prevent himself from stealing a peek at her provocative cleavage in that outrageous scarlet dressing gown she was barely wearing.

She laughed in her melodious contralto tremolo. Morgan, it seemed to him, half-wanted her husband, twice her age, to catch her flirting, or worse. The danger of it ignited her dark, exotic eyes, and made her all the more voracious.

But the governor, her husband, was Joshua's employer. Besides, Joshua never could see the wisdom of carrying on with a married woman, even an exceptionally attractive one, when there were so many unmarried ones eager enough to share their favors with him. Quite simply, it wasn't worth the risk. He turned to go.

"Joshua, wait."

She seized his sleeve, and he stared at her hand for a moment as if it were a tarantula. He met her gaze again, feeling only annoyance in the face of her embarrassingly obvious seduction.

"Morgan, we have nothing to say to one another that can't be said in a drawing room or over a banquet table when you're wearing something beside that careless-cat smile of yours. Good day."

He pulled his arm away with a quick, efficient

jerk and proceeded toward the stairs without look-ing back.

"I hear she wears pants, Joshua," she drawled after him in a teasing whine. "And I know you're used to garters."

Incredulous, Joshua faced her again from the head of the stairs. How had she learned about Allyn Cameron? Or was she just making a stab at the air?

"Properly motivated, a man can accustom himself to just about anything," was what he managed to retort, determined to deny her the satisfaction of his anger. "With the possible exception of another man's saddle."

Her sudden, red-faced outrage reported to him that his reference had not been too obscure, and he smiled to himself as he continued down the stairs.

Chapter Four

The air was cold. Puffs of steam issued from Bert's mouth as he secured Sheik's tether to the back of the buckboard. The sight of it from the window of the house made Allyn pull her gray traveling cloak close about her throat.

"At least it's clear." Missy's tremulous voice echoed her thoughts. "You'll make good time."

"If the road isn't washed out from winter," Allyn felt compelled to add. It was thirty miles to Deadwood as the crow flies, closer to forty by road. Bert had expressed a wish to make Deadwood by nightfall, so they had to get an early start in order to make the trip easy on Sheik.

Unexpectedly, Missy chuckled. "You're starting to sound like me," she chided Allyn, who smiled at the observation. "You're not having second thoughts about this venture, are you?"

"Me?" Allyn was surprised by her friend's question. "Not at all. I'm a little nervous, I'll admit. This will be Sheik's first flat race. We haven't any jockey yet. And—"

"And you're getting married in a month."

Allyn could not refrain from sighing. Bill, she recalled, had not been happy about the Deadwood trip, so she had obliged his desire for an early wedding date as an appeasement.

"Three weeks," she corrected, straining her fingers into her gloves. She did not want to think about the wedding. The Dakota Derby was a week away, and she wanted to concentrate on that. It was important for the C-Bar-C that Sheik make a respectable showing in the race, and now it was her responsibility to make sure he did. She could not let Missy down.

"Allyn, I can't do this to you," Missy exclaimed suddenly, wrenching all of Allyn's attention at last. Her tone was piteous, her pleasant features misery. "You stay home. I'll go to Deadwood."

"Don't be silly," Allyn chided her. "I'm looking forward to this."

Missy eyed her friend, doubt apparent in her gaze.

"Really, I am," Allyn assured her again, even managing to smile.

Missy's dark brow puckered. "I'm beginning to think this whole thing is not a good idea." The younger woman waved her hand as if she were swatting at deerflies. "Sheik's never even raced the flats. This trip and the entrance fees are costing the ranch a fortune. Maybe we should sell him now, before the Derby. If he makes a poor showing in Deadwood, the offer is sure to go down. We could certainly use that money right now, Allyn, with the taxes due and a barn roof that needs fixing. And in a few years, another horse is sure to come along that will measure up to Sheik, and I'll use him as a stud for my mares."

Allyn waited. Missy could not believe her good fortune last year, Allyn recalled, when she'd picked Sheik up for a song at that auction in town. She'd boasted of Sheik's conformation, his lineage, just about everything but his big brown eyes. Sheik was a once-in-a-lifetime animal. On that they'd both agreed.

"Maybe we should contact that fellow from Governor Mellette and ask him to make an offer," Missy went on again, sounding, Allyn thought, less convinced than a moment before. "We're risking so much . . ."

Allyn began counting to herself. Usually, she got to ten before Missy changed her mind. This morning she only reached eight before hearing Missy's familiar sigh of resignation.

"No," the younger woman finally breathed. "Sheik is ours, and we'll take the risks."

"And reap the rewards," Allyn added, forcing confidence into her voice she was far from feeling. "You leave everything to me and Bert, Miss. We'll bring you home a winner." Impulsively she hugged her nervous friend, who returned the fond gesture.

"Be careful," Missy whispered in her ear. "Bill would never forgive me if anything happened—"

Allyn interrupted her with a delighted laugh. "What could possibly happen?" she countered, holding Missy's shoulders at arm's length. "Except that, God forbid, I might enjoy myself for a change? You tell Bill for me, if he's so concerned, he can come to Deadwood and look after me himself."

"He probably would, except Buttercup is about to foal."

Allyn smarted at the thought. Bill, as passionate as he seemed to be, very apparently cared more for the well-being of his livestock than he did for her own.

"Maybe," she retorted, not looking at her friend, "he should marry *her*."

Bert came into the house, stomping the dirt from

his boots on the runner by the door. "All set," he announced, his beery face red from the chill. He directed a look at Allyn. "Where're your bags?"

Allyn pointed to a small valise by the door.

"That's all?" He was incredulous.

"How much do I need for mucking about, Bert?" she challenged him, amused. "Please, let's go. I want to get there by daylight so we can inspect the course."

Within minutes, Bert had stowed their belongings as well as a large hamper of provisions for their consumption en route, and Allyn and the C-Bar-C foreman were perched on the seat waving their good-byes.

"I'll write!" Allyn promised, smiling to ease the butterflies in her stomach.

"I hope there's enough paper in Deadwood!" Missy teased.

Allyn made a face at her, and waved her last as Bert eased the buckboard along the muddy road.

The sun warmed their journey by midday, but provided no relief from the discomfort afforded by the hard seat of buckboard. Allyn tempted herself with thoughts of a warm bath at the hotel upon their arrival. The tedium of the long ride through the Badlands was tempered by Bert's amusing conversation, occasional duets, and the encounters with the odd stagecoach or express rider. Sheik accepted his lot amicably, appearing pleased when Allyn actually rode him part of the way.

Allyn had never been to Deadwood. She asked Bert to tell her about the infamous place, and he seemed amused by her fascination. Situated in the Black Hills as the hub of numerous gold and silver mines, Deadwood enjoyed a reputation as a rough and uncivilized place, a haven for outlaws, miners, immigrants, and various other unsavory elements. It was said that there were more brothels and saloons than there were decent homes, and that the most popular curiosity was the grave of James Butler Hickok, who'd been shot to death in a saloon a dozen or more years before. The original saloon, of course, had burned to the ground in an awful fire after Wild Bill's death.

It was a town like most, Bert assured her, ripe for every sort of vice and corruption. It was a town, he often enjoyed repeating, well suited to its name.

By late afternoon, they reached the fringes of the settlement. Deadwood lay among the pine trees on the side of a hill like a mud pie thrown against a green velvet drapery. Allyn felt her disappointment keenly as she surveyed the disorderly assemblage of clapboard, brick, and canvas structures. Bert deposited her before the Black Hills Hotel, reportedly the finest in town, and drove off to see to Sheik's accommodations at the stables.

The lobby was a small affair, but it offered the first hints of civility Allyn had seen. With a small sigh of relief, she carried her valise across the worn but clean Persian carpet to the front desk of carved, polished mahogany. The clerk was a tall, lean, blond man, fair but weathered, who regarded her with courteous appraisal.

"Two rooms, please, reserved for Allyn Cameron and Albert Emmet. You received our reservation by wire last Monday, I believe."

The man's face brightened with recognition. "You are Miss Cameron?" he asked in a tone which suggested something like amazement. His voice was heavily accented with some Teutonic flavor. "Nils Nilsson, Miss Cameron," he offered by way of introduction. "You own that saloon in Rapid City, *ja?* You win that race?"

Allyn was taken aback by his observations. "I—yes," was all she could manage in the face of her unexpected fame.

"I have here for you some messages." He reached into one of a dozen or more cubbies on the wall behind him and withdrew, along with her key, a fistful of notes. "Room thirteen and fourteen. Up the steps. Sign here. Twelve dollars for all week. I take your bag."

Before she could get out a word, he had gone off. There was nothing for her to do but sign, leave her bills on the desk, and follow him.

Her room was plain, and not large, featuring a bed big enough for two as well as a nightstand, armchair, armoire, dresser, bath, and water closet. It was clean and quiet, for all that its only window overlooked a main thoroughfare. She thanked Mr. Nilsson stiffly, and closed the door without offering him a tip.

Loosening her cloak, she reviewed the notes, curious as to the identity or identities of the senders. One, she was surprised to discover, was from the Governor's agent, Mr. Joshua Manners. She was annoyed to discover that her hands trembled as she opened it. She could not comprehend her disappointment as she discovered that it contained only a brief, formally worded message welcoming her to town. Others were from the Derby officials, requesting payment of various fees immediately. Two, she was alarmed to discover, were crude, mean, and anonymous threats.

Welcome to Deadwood, she thought with a small shudder.

For the next few days, Allyn stayed close by Bert. The pair spent their days at the stable working Sheik and tending to his comforts. They took their meals as modestly and privately as possible, and in the evenings Allyn retired to her room and locked herself in to write long letters to Missy, wondering idly why she had not yet encountered Mr. Joshua Manners. She left Bert free to seek a jockey and entertainment.

She had not shared the threatening missives with him at all. She did not wish to distract him from his own work. Anonymous threats were, in her experience, the work of cowards, amounting more often than not to nothing but words. However, prudence was wise. And she did not like the way the men of this town looked at her, especially the jockeys, handlers, and hangers-on at the stable. There was an ugliness about them which had nothing whatever to do with their looks. They looked at her as though they were starving, and she were a sumptuous seven-course dinner. She avoided their open stares, wondering who among them might have sent the hideous messages.

"Allyn, I've found us a jockey," Bert told her over breakfast two days before the race. "Can we afford three hundred dollars?"

"Huh," she replied with grim amusement. "Can a camel go through the needle's eye?"

Bert was not pleased by her response. "This is serious, Allyn!" he told her darkly. "We only have—"

"I know, I know, Bert. Please keep trying."

Bert grimaced. "Will you be all right on your own for a few hours?" he asked. "I've one more lead to check."

Allyn's stomach tightened at the thought, but she rallied. "Of course," she lied boldly. "You go on. I have to take a walk on down to the telegraph office to wire Missy. I'll meet you at the stable this afternoon."

He grinned at her across the table, and she suspected he was not deceived by her attempt at bravado.

"Chin up, love. They're only men. Not a wolf in the lot. I promise."

She scowled to mask her blush. "Go on with you," she growled at him, shooing him away from the table with a brush of her hand.

The telegraph office was not far from the stable.

It was a small, box-like building attached to the post office. Allyn effected a prepossessed, unassuming pace which, blessedly, attracted no attention as she negotiated the distance. The office was jammed with men, but she was able to squeeze her way to the desk and get her message off to Missy:

"No news. No jockey yet. Working hard. See you soon. Allyn."

Telegraph messages were always so terse. Cost made them so. Everything, she mused, came around to money. She thought unexpectedly about that man Manners and his offer to buy Sheik. Could he have sent those threatening notes? She glanced about the office with distaste. It was full of men who looked ill-groomed and unpleasant. Focused as she was outside herself for the first time, she heard a familiar name:

"Sheik. What's he, a pace horse for one of Mellette's nags?" a voice said. She started. It almost sounded like Bert, trying to advance his gambling prospects by decrying their thoroughbred. But Bert's British accent stood out like silk against burlap, even with his dropped H's. This voice was as flat as the Great Plains. She could not determine its source.

"Mellette will wish that he was," an abrupt, oddly familiar voice responded. "I've seen that colt run a steeplechase, and I guarantee . . ."

Allyn fled the office, not wanting to hear more.

Sixteen hands of chocolate thoroughbred twitched appreciatively beneath her busy brush, the sleek coat shining and steaming. Allyn's song became soft and breathless with the labor, but her serenade went on nonetheless.

"What will you leave your sweetheart, my own dearest one? Ten thousand weights of brimstone to burn her bones brown . . . Sheik, hold still. That's my boy. What fine legs! You're a jumper, lad. Oh—"

Her hand slipped out of the strap on the brush and it fell to the straw beneath their feet. She reached for it, and was startled to see it snatched away by a large, hairy hand with thick muscular fingers like link sausages. Instantly she straightened, and across Sheik's broad back she faced a stranger, a man she recognized only as someone she'd seen about the stables. He had a silly grin on his broad, flat face that frightened her.

"What do you want?" she demanded coldly, hoping to intimidate him.

The man's grin widened. He held the brush up for her to see. "I need this." His speech was slow and thick. She suspected he was drunk.

"It's mine," she told him, meeting his gaze. "Give it to me."

Drunks, she knew from her experiences at The Golden Wheel, tended to follow simple, direct commands when they were delivered with bold authority. She stared hard at the man, trying to recall when she'd seen a less attractive specimen, failing entirely. His offensive smile did not diminish.

"You want it?" he asked her with exaggerated politeness. "Here."

He held the grooming implement out to her, but as she reached across Sheik's back, he pulled his hand away and tossed the brush high over her head and beyond her. She turned to retrieve it, only to find two more men, equally if not surpassingly dirty and ugly, standing two feet behind her. One of them had caught the brush and he was chuckling, an awful, hollow sound. She felt, quite suddenly, like a hapless fly caught in a spider's web.

You have no business here," she rallied, her back stiffening. "Get out. Be on your way."

"Now that ain't very friendly," the third man chided, grinning with half a mouthful of large gray teeth that looked like an assemblage of crooked gravestones in a run-down cemetery. She shuddered at the thought and realized, belatedly, that the fellow had taken a step closer to her. An odor hung about them like a foul old coat. She clenched her fists to still her shaking hands.

"We aren't friends," she pointed out coldly, wishing that she could quiet the hammering in her chest.

"Well, now. That's what we aim to fix."

The first man's voice was behind her. She could not prevent a gasp from escaping as she spun around again. He was not smiling now, and Sheik was no longer between them. The man was close enough for her to smell his breath. He reeked of whiskey and tobacco juice. She felt sick to her stomach.

"Get out," she heard herself say again, but her voice was a shallow mockery of its former self. She was frightened. She tried to remember if she had ever been in a similar situation, perhaps at the saloon, and was stunned to realize that she could barely at this moment remember her own name. She thought of calling out for help, but rejected the idea at once. She had taken great pains to see that she remained as anonymous and inconspicuous as possible. Who would come to her aid? In desperation, she turned to the man who had possession of the brush and reached for it in a quick, frantic gesture. He laughed again, tossing it to the man with the tombstone teeth. He, in turn, tossed it into the air, aiming it for the intruder who stood beside Sheik. She was helpless to do anything except turn to him again, and as she did, she was seized by the waist from behind.

Her ensuing scream was cut short as four pairs of eyes fixed upon a fifth party who held the brush high in the air where he had arrested it on its journey. The tall, dark-haired man looked different in workaday blue jeans, his lean broad-shouldered frame camouflaged by a loose-fitting brown flannel shirt. So different, in fact, that but for the sterling-black Stetson hat, she would not have recognized him. He stood still as a saint for a time, towering over his audience with a stare of deadly calm in his magnetic dark eyes. Slowly, he lowered his arm. It was another moment before Allyn realized that he was offering her the brush.

"Get out of here." He addressed the dumbstruck men in a quiet tone, full of latent power. "And don't ever come back."

The rough, bruising arms fell away from her as if they'd never been there. She could sense the men backing away from her. She was too paralyzed, by fear and fascination, to move her gaze from the tall, angry man before them.

"Aw, Josh, we was only funnin'," one of the other men grumbled, ambling for the door of the stall.

"The lady isn't laughing," was the hard reply he got for his pains.

In another minute, the men had gone without a backward glance. Her rescuer did not speak, but waited patiently for her to take the brush from his hand. She breathed a deep, broken sigh and willed her hand to stop shaking before she reached for it.

"They won't trouble you again," he said to her at last, in a much gentler tone than he had used on her tormentors.

"Thank you," Allyn murmured on a sigh, finding it necessary to look away from him before she uttered it.

His almost magical appearance in her very direst moment of need confounded her inclination to distrust him. The stable was suddenly a very small place, although the air had cleared considerably since the unceremonious exodus of the three men.

"Did they hurt you?" The gentle baritone, which she remembered with such astonishing clarity, was brusque. Its businesslike quality buoyed her own waning confidence. She shook her head twice, but still did not feel equal to his scrutiny, which she also vividly recalled.

"No," she replied, feeling her hands begin to tremble again within the dusty folds of her habit.

Why, she wondered, suddenly diffident, must she always look so shabby in his presence?

There followed a silence which was more than awkward. It was almost painful. Allyn felt her heart beating as rapidly as a caged bird's, as much because of the proximity of this suavely confident and disconcertingly masculine individual standing three feet away from her as because of the horrible events which had preceded his timely intervention.

Perhaps too timely.

She looked up at him quickly, hoping that his expression might betray his complicity in the affair. She perceived a faint smile on his wide, irritating mouth. Anger supplanted the fear she had felt moments before, allowing relief no foothold.

"Mr. . . ."

"Manners," he reminded her, his grin widening, not giving her the chance to forget hers. "I hardly dared hope you would remember me."

She returned his smile with one of her own, an especially nasty brand. "Of course. Governor Mellette's lackey."

Did he wince at that, or did she just imagine it? She must have imagined it, for he chuckled softly, crossing his considerable arms in front of his broad chest. The grooming brush disappeared into the soft folds of her habit.

"How is Sheik today?" he went on. His conversation and accompanying action quelled any hope that he planned to leave.

"Sheik is fine," she replied, incredulous at his presumption. "Mr. Manners, I don't know what you want, or why you are here, but you are not welcomed. Will you please leave, or—"

He interrupted her with a hearty laugh that drew a quick blush to her cheeks. He held up his large, long-fingered hands in a placating gesture.

"Truce! Truce! I assure you I have no evil designs, either on you or your horse. I simply thought you might appreciate a familiar face in hostile territory."

She sniffed disdainfully, forcing herself not to think of the scene moments before his appearance.

"You are hardly familiar to me. And I don't care to alter that fact. I have thanked you for your intervention, and now I—"

"You're having a lot of trouble finding a jockey, I hear."

Manners had gone right on as if he had not heard her remark. He stroked Sheik, who neighed softly and turned his massive head in appreciation of the gesture. Lord, but he was an infuriatingly arrogant man! She stared hard at him, hoping to drive him away with her anger, but he continued to survey Sheik, giving no sign that he'd noticed.

"What business is it of yours?" she said. Her voice faded doubtfully as her indignation and bravado waned. It was, after all, the truth, and she was impelled to acknowledge it.

"None of my business."

Those sable brown eyes which she recalled so well looked suddenly up at hers, meeting them with a directness which forced her to look away in confusion.

"None at all," he said in a light, intimate tone. "Except that it would be a tremendous pity if this fine animal were kept from embarrassing the rest of the field in the Derby, as he's sure to do with the right man aboard."

Allyn found, in his condescending words, the courage to meet his gaze with a measure of defiance.

"What if I told you I plan to jockey him myself, Mr. Manners?" she retorted, hoping her sarcasm matched his audacity. "Would I be the 'right man'?"

"You'd be a fool." Manners's eyes twinkled with amusement, although his wide mouth did not allow a smile. "This isn't Rapid City, and those aren't once-a-year, if not once-in-a-lifetime, riders. Those jockies ride, and win, for a living, and not necessarily on the fastest horse. Even if the officials allowed you to ride, you would probably lose out of sheer ignorance. And besides, you could be killed in the bargain. But as you indicate, it is none of my business."

Sheik snorted and stamped, apparently miffed at not being the topic under discussion. Manners's attention was diverted, and he patted the thoroughbred's neck with real affection.

"A fine horse," he murmured, his angular features softening as Sheik's brown eyes met his own. "I don't blame you for holding on to him."

Allyn did not answer him. His casual words had frightened her. She was suspicious of anyone who came near Sheik, but especially this man, this lackey. How far would he go, she wondered, chilled, to procure Sheik for Governor Mellette? Or for himself? Instinctively Allyn drew Sheik away from him by tugging his bridle.

"Good day, Mr. Manners."

Manners retreated, smiling pleasantly and touching the brim of his black Stetson. "Good day, Miss Cameron."

She followed him with her eyes, watching his lazy, long-legged gait as he strode from the stable and through the corral. She shuddered as if winter had come suddenly to the remote hamlet in the Black Hills. She did not trust Joshua Manners. Those men

who had confronted her obviously knew him. He
might, in fact, have orchestrated the event. She could
be killed in the bargain? She did not doubt it. He was
a dangerous man, she suspected. A man intent on a
goal, like a preying tiger that has chosen its victim
from among the herd and pursues it relentlessly. And
he was pursuing Sheik. Tenderly she patted the colt's
long, silky neck, and the horse nodded vigorously,
pawing the straw floor.

"We'll beat them, my precious," she crooned in his
ear, still looking after Manners, who had disappeared.
"We'll show them all."

Manners strode into the saloon, exchanging unen-
thusiastic greetings with the jockeys and stablehands
he recognized, not slackening his pace to the bar. He
placed his hands on its well-worn ledge, dug the heel
of his vintage boot into the greenish brass rail at his
feet, and ordered a double whiskey. He downed it in
a single swallow and signaled for another. The second
he savored, feeling unsettled as he stared at his face
in the mirror.

Allyn Cameron.

He tried the name in his mouth like the first taste
of a fine wine. Since Rapid City, that name, coupled
with her fabulous horse, had consumed much of his
thought. He had had little time in the last two weeks
when he did not think of her. Riding wildly astride
that powerful beast. Rudely upbraiding him for his
own rudeness. He recalled what he had witnessed that
very afternoon in the stable: those coarse stablehands
buzzing about her like bees around a flower. The sight
had more than angered him. It had enraged him, to
the point that he would, he knew, have taken great
pleasure in killing the man who had held her about the
waist with his bare hands. The knowledge disturbed
him, given his history with the woman and her open

hostility toward him. Her ungracious response neither surprised nor troubled him. Could she really have believed him to be responsible for the ugly business? he wondered, grimacing as he swallowed more of the amber liquid before him. Remembering her caustic words in Rapid City and the blatant distrust in her fascinating green eyes, he knew she could.

She could not be serious about jockeying in the Derby, or could she? It had seemed at the time like a small child's dare, but now he was not sure. Aware that he should be indifferent to the notion, he found himself wondering why she was suddenly so important to him. He knew other women who were more beautiful, certainly more gracious. He smiled to himself at the recollection of her rude remarks on the few occasions when they had spoken. What, he mused idly, would it take to soften her green-eyed glare to a lovelight?

His legs weakened treacherously at the thought. He fancied he heard an alarm sound somewhere, or was that only in his mind? He closed his eyes, then shook his head like an awakening colt.

"A horse or a woman, Josh?" the bartender teased him.

"Both," he admitted wryly, putting up his four bits. He turned away, having settled his accounts. A hot bath, he thought, ambling away into the gathering dusk. And after that, a hot whore.

Bert had failed. Whether he had lost his touch, or was becoming too particular through long association with Missy and Allyn, he did not know. In either case, it was with hangdog dejection that he broke the disturbing news to Allyn back at the hotel.

"My goodness, Bert, what are we celebrating?" Allyn said, greeting him at her door, making light of a gloomy countenance that alarmed her.

Bert did not answer her until she had closed the

door and turned her full attention to him.

"You'd better sit down, love," he began in a tone more serious than Allyn had ever heard him use.

"It can't be Sheik! I just left him an hour ago! He's not—"

"No, no, no." Bert waved his hands. "It isn't Sheik. It's me. I've failed. There's no jockey for us here, Allyn."

Allyn sank back into a chair, weak with relief. "Is that all?" She felt like laughing. "For a moment, you had me frightened."

Bert stared at her as though she had acquired an extra head. "Allyn, love, I don't think you understand me. There's no one to ride Sheik in the Derby for us. We have to withdraw."

Allyn did laugh, perplexing her British friend all the more. "That's ridiculous! I shall ride him." The thought had materialized on her lips. Manners be damned!

"Allyn!"

"Well, why not? I rode in a steeplechase; a derby can't be much different. If anything, it should be easier."

Bert opened his mouth, then shut it again quickly. Her statement proved to him that she knew nothing at all about the skill and knowledge it took to race on the flats against hungry competitors. A steeplechase was one thing. Raw talent, sheer nerve, and a mount with instinct would do it. But there were so many subtleties to racing on the flats.

True, Sheik was an exceptional horse. He *might* have a chance with Allyn at the reins. Wistfully Bert considered the money he could win if Sheik raced and, of all impossibilities, won. He grasped Allyn's hand. "You poor innocent! What you know about racing would fill a thimble. But it just might pass. We have two days until the race. We can practice tomorrow.

I'll teach you everything I know and, bless you, you are smart enough to learn. But . . ."

Would the officials allow a woman to ride? she wondered, certain that the question was on Bert's mind as well.

"Best not to mention it to the officials," she decided aloud. "I'll take some trouble—but not much—to disguise myself. If anyone asks, we'll say that my brother has come to jockey. A. Cameron. I think we can do it, Bert. Anyway, we have to try."

From somewhere came an echo of Manners's warning: You could be killed in the bargain. Well, she thought gloomily, it's a bargain I will have to make.

Allyn's head was so full of racing information on the morning of the Derby, she felt she would go mad. And the worst thing of it, she thought dismally, donning her jockey's jodhpurs, was that she would not be able to think fast enough on the track to use a morsel of it.

She and Bert had drilled for hours the day before at the track. "Lean forward! Tighten your legs! Hold him back! Stop letting your feet stick out, damn it!" Sheik had pounded the track laughing, she imagined, at her bungling, inexperienced commands. After the workout, Bert had looked positively deathlike. He said not another word to her before fleeing to fetch Missy from the depot.

Well, in any case, this was it. Whatever she knew, she knew. Whatever she did not know, God willing, Sheik would. Buttoning her loose-fitting white shirt, she set her mouth in a determined grimace, practicing her manly look. Her stomach growled, reminding her that she was hungry. No breakfast. No lunch. She must weigh in light this afternoon.

Missy came in, wearing a cheery gown of bright yellow, which complemented her ample figure, and none of her usual nervousness.

"You look fine, Allyn. Just tie up your hair, and that's that." Her tone was gay.

Missy had taken the news about the jockey very well. She expressed nothing but confidence in Allyn's abilities, as usual.

"I'm hungry," Allyn grumbled. "Never more than when I can't eat." She belted her distressingly feminine waist, still staring at her reflection in the mirror. "I don't know, Missy," she muttered. "I think I may have put my foot in it this time."

Missy laughed roundly. "Nonsense! You can do it. You can do anything!"

Allyn smiled at her friend's typical confidence in her. Missy truly believed it. It was a tenet which had sustained their relationship since their flight from Philadelphia five years before, when Missy had ceased being her maid and had become, simply, her friend.

"Nevertheless," Allyn asserted by way of a prayer, "if Sheik forgives me for riding him in this race, I promise him a real jockey if we get to the Kentucky Derby."

"Sheik will forgive you. Oh, by the way." Missy turned to her friend on her way out the door. "Bill said to tell you the wedding will have to be put off for a few more weeks. He has to go away on some ranch business. He wanted to come to the Dakota, but . . ." She shrugged expressively, then exited the room like waning sunshine. The room did indeed darken as she left. Allyn supressed a sigh, wondering why she felt like a prisoner granted a reprieve. By rights, she should be angry that her future husband would break such news to her by proxy. Instead, she was aware of a wash of relief. For the moment at least, there was a loosening of the ties that bound.

The afternoon was gray and overcast, threatening rain. Bert stuck doggedly by Allyn's side through the preliminaries. Allyn spoke to no one for fear that her soprano would betray their charade. Every question addressed to her Bert answered, often with some glib lie. She was treated, and behaved, like a deaf mute.

At the weigh-in, Allyn studied the way the jockeys walked and carried their saddles and tried her best to emulate them. She stood as close to Bert as she dared in line, trying not to stare anywhere but up or down. The line was sluggish, and there was much bumping and jostling as they approached the scale. Allyn skillfully kept the saddle between herself and exposure as they queued up to the official.

The terse, balding man with the records did not look up from his desk when they stepped forward.

"Name."

"A. Cameron," Bert responded quickly.

The man looked up with a doubtful expression. "Can't answer for himself?"

Allyn shook her head, regarding him with a scowl, trying very hard to look like a man.

"A deaf-mute. Can't speak a word," Bert supplied in a soothing tone.

The man rubbed his chin in what Allyn took to be a gesture of suspicion. She had the uneasy sense that he was not fooled.

"Cameron, huh? Get on the scale."

Allyn obeyed, standing sullenly on the platform as they toyed with the counterweights.

"One twenty-eight," the weigher yelled in a piercing tenor. Allyn turned from the platform, about to descend, and she caught the amused, derisive grin on Joshua Manners's face. She froze, her eyes widening with terror. The trick was up.

Manners, standing with the governor's jockey, looked straight into her eyes. She felt as if her clothing had been ripped from her and she was standing there stark naked before him. To her astonishment he said nothing. Her horrified stare became a look of pleading. Surely, Allyn thought miserably, he knows what we are up to. Curse him, we're in his power at this moment. If he gives us away . . .

"Next!" barked the man at the table impatiently. Allyn's gaze never swerved from Manners's annoyingly handsome face, nor his from hers. Bert took her arm firmly, unaware, she was sure, of the danger they were in. Her pleading expression blended to wonder as the ever-surprising Manners watched them go without a word.

"Got through that, didn't we, love?" Bert breathed when they were safely out of earshot.

"Purest luck, Bert, purest luck." She was only too aware that Manners could still expose them up until post time. That, she decided, would be in perfect harmony with his cunning character. If he did, she would surely kill him.

The chill in the April air was not the only thing that made Allyn shiver as she huddled herself atop the suddenly enormous thoroughbred. Glancing around at the makeshift grandstand and infield at the crowds of people who seemed waiting, even eager, for Sheik to fail, she was struck and made immobile by the realization that she did not belong there. What kind of brazen fool would put herself up on a prized stallion among professional riders and even dare to think that she might finish? Jockeys who had raced, and won, as Manners had pointed out to her, dozens, if not hundreds of races just like this one? And on top of the crippling sense of inadequacy, there was the sickening certainty that Joshua Manners, agent for Governor Arthur Mellette, would wait until she and Sheik were at the post before exposing her to the officials.

Sheik was being led to the post. Point by point she reviewed the lessons in her head: firm hand, tight legs, lean forward . . . She crouched down over Sheik's neck, hoping to disappear, to escape detection. She clutched the reins in a racer's grip, including a generous lock of Sheik's mane. She recited the commands silently, like a prayer . . .

The gun fired.

The sky exploded. The torrent thundered down like the dozen horses on the field. The rain poured into Allyn's face, blinding her. There was horseflesh beside her. In front of her. Pressing her like a living vise. A hoarse cry arose in her throat urging Sheik on, and everything else was instinct.

Around the turn they were beside the rail and Allyn did not know how they had gotten there. The rail sped by them like a carousel, and Allyn began to feel dizzy. She clutched harder, clung tighter, and prayed louder, and Sheik carried them to the straightaway.

The thunder died away and there was only the steady thrum of Sheik's lightning cadence in her ears. She crouched lower, not daring to glance back to see that the rest of the field was dropping. They approached the final turn, and the others made their drive to the finish.

The track was mired in pools of mud and water. Sheik's every stride sent streams of mud pellets all over his jockey, and Allyn's concentration edged away. The field began to close again on the home stretch, and the governor's horse challenged. Hearing the competitor on her heels, Allyn closed her eyes tightly, pressed her face against Sheik's hot neck, and gave him a nudge and a cry.

Sheik hugged the rail, striding effortlessly. In a single moment, four entities crossed the finish line. Allyn felt something push her foot from the stirrup, and in a moment she was tumbling through space.

Chapter Five

There was a breathtaking bouquet of flowers on the nightstand beside the bed. Allyn's first thought, upon opening her eyes, was a sense of profound wonder that such exotic botanical perfection could exist in Deadwood. Her next perception was that she was no longer riding Sheik, but was in fact lying in her bed in her hotel room.

"Allyn!" It was Missy's soft, delighted whisper.

Allyn turned her head to find her friend rising from the easy chair, setting her needlework on the foot of the bed as she approached. The younger woman's smile was ethereal and confusing.

"You needn't whisper," Allyn remarked in wry amusement, surprised at the weakness in her own voice. "I'm awake."

"Well, I can see that. And as churlish as ever!" Missy retorted fondly. "How do you feel?"

Allyn breathed a deep, broken sigh, closing her eyes again. "Weak. Sore. Unhappy. Missy, I'm sorry I lost the race for you."

"Lost!"

Missy followed her outburst with a cascade of uproarious laughter. "Lost! Oh, you poor innocent! You've been lying there in a state thinking that you— Allyn, would such flowers have been sent to console a loser?"

Allyn grew annoyed at Missy's obvious enjoyment of her ignorance.

"But how—Missy, stop laughing! I don't—"

"Of course!" Missy was generous in her absolution. "How could you remember? You were dumped head-first over the rail, neck and neck with Big Boy. But you finished the race, bless you, and Big Boy was disqualified."

"Disqualified!" Allyn sat bolt upright in her bed.

Missy nodded cheerfully, apparently complacent in her knowledge. "Illegal action by the jockey. He was very clever and would have gotten away with it. But a friend of yours raised a protest and the officials upheld it."

"A friend?" Allyn wrinkled her nose, thoroughly mystified. "Of mine?" Allyn found Missy's sidelong stare most irritating.

"Joshua Manners," Missy purred in a feline way that matched her knowing stare. "He carried you to the carriage and introduced himself to me there. He seemed to take a—a very personal interest in your well-being."

"He's no friend of mine." Allyn sniffed disdainfully. "Did he tell you that?"

Missy purred with delight. "Yes, he did. He was very concerned about you, and I saw no reason to doubt his veracity. Besides, when I told him that the governor's entry had been declared the winner, he excused himself rather abruptly. It wasn't half an hour later that we got word here that you and Sheik had been named the official winners, in spite of your,

Carole Howey

uh, little charade. Can you believe it?"

"That Sheik was the winner, yes. That Manners had anything to do with it, no," Allyn responded tartly, hoping to abbreviate further insinuations. "He has had designs on Sheik since the Steeplechase. I'm surprised he didn't try to buy him from you while I was unconscious."

Missy looked skeptical. "If you ask me, it isn't Sheik he has designs on," she said in her usual blunt fashion. "Anyway, I think you're wrong. I'm sure it was he who registered that protest. Lord knows, it certainly wasn't Bert. He didn't dare show his face after what you two pulled. No, I'm certain it was Mr. Manners. Despite what you say, I think he's most noble. And handsome."

"We have an old saying up North, Missy; perhaps you've heard it? 'Handsome is as handsome does.'" Allyn sugared her sarcastic words. "If you had spent any time with him at all, you would find him to be insufferably arrogant, rude, devious, and—"

"A lot like Raiford Simms," Missy finished for her, matching her icy tone.

"If you must!" Allyn flung back at her, finally losing her composure. "I don't see what he has to do with this!"

"Only that every man you meet seems to merit some comparison to that cad!" Missy retorted, her gray eyes cold. "When are you going to give him up, Allyn? When are you going to allow yourself to trust another man again? You don't trust Bill; that much is obvious. Do you expect to once you're married? Or are you going to carry this with you like a bad debt for the rest of your life?"

Allyn wanted to fling a hard retort at her friend as if it were a stone, but none came to her. Missy, as usual, had placed her delicate finger exactly upon the heart of the matter. She was comparing Joshua Manners

80

to Raif Simms in more ways than one. And she was surprised, and dismayed, to find that the similarities were many. Like, for example, the way that she had wished desperately that he would touch her in the stable the other day . . .

A sudden, brisk knock upon their door terminated the tempest.

"I bet I know who that is," Missy whispered smugly. She called out aloud, "Who is it?"

A now-familiar voice responded, muffled by the door. "Joshua Manners, ma'am. May I see Miss Cameron yet?"

Allyn's face drained of sensation and her tongue cleaved to her mouth. What in the world could he want? Missy turned a triumphant, questioning glance to her, and she shook her head. "Tell him—tell him I'm still unconscious. Tell him I'm—"

"This is the third time he's been here since yesterday. And I'm a poor liar. You've said so yourself. Besides," she added with a prim look, "I want to see for myself if he's all as bad as you make him out to be."

Before a cry of protest could leave Allyn's mouth, Missy had reached the door and opened it wide.

"Mr. Manners! Our most persistent visitor. Yes, she is awake now. In fact, I was just telling her how helpful you have been. Please, come in."

Joshua Manners had stood by the door on two previous occasions, each time feeling relieved when he was turned away. Each time he had, in fact, wondered why he was there at all, and why he had troubled to correct an error in his favor at the Derby. He felt awkward. Almost embarrassed, as he had felt after delivering a jaw-shattering punch to the luckless jockey who had admitted to interfering with Sheik and Allyn Cameron. After that, he had resigned his position with the governor, casting himself adrift.

Adrift, and unexpectedly uncertain of himself at the moment. Why was he harboring a sense of obligation to this difficult, disconcertingly lovely green-eyed lady who had barely treated him to a civilized word? Was he expecting an apology? A thank you?

Now that she was awake, there was no escaping the inevitable confrontation. He removed his black Stetson and handed it to Missy as she closed the door behind him.

He was unprepared for the sight that met his eyes. Used as he was to seeing the rough-and-tumble woman who dressed like a man to ride in derbies and steeplechases, he was startled momentarily out of composure by the fragile, porcelain-like figure propped in bed in a lacy white bed jacket. He approached the bed without speaking.

"Good Day, Mr. Manners. To what may we attribute the pleasure of your call?"

Her injuries obviously had not impaired her chilly address. Manners immediately felt at ease.

"To my concern for your welfare, my dear Miss Cameron," he replied, tipping her a faint grin of amusement. "What else?"

She arched a dark, finely etched eyebrow.

"One might think that you had come to complete the job which your jockey set out to accomplish."

He chuckled at the absurd sentiment, believing she must be joking.

"Assassinating women isn't my style," he teased her, hoping to make her blush. "Besides, as we both know, I could easily have eliminated you from that race had I been so inclined."

"And why didn't you?" Allyn's velvety voice had a hard edge to it which was almost painful to the ear, as if a pair of sharp scissors had been hidden beneath the soft nap.

Manners, wondering at that himself, shook his

head. "It may be as simple as the fact that I wanted Sheik to have the chance to win that race," he said thoughtfully, staring at the white eyelet covering on the bed. "Or as complex as the fact that I wanted you to learn what you had gotten yourself into."

From the figure on the bed came a small, bitter laugh. "And you wanted to ensure that I learned much from your murderous jockey, didn't you?"

So much for an apology, he thought, stunned into meeting her gaze at last.

"Come now, Miss Cameron," he tried again. "You can't really think I engineered that performance just to ensure a victory for our illustrious governor, can you?"

The interview had fallen apart, and he did not know why he was surprised. Perhaps it was because he had so wished she might express a tender gratitude to him. To grant him a glimpse of that softer side that he suspected she sheltered from exposure to the elements.

"Can't I?" she challenged him, shattering his hopes. She no longer appeared soft and frail. "It would have been too obvious to finger us before the race, when you discovered our plan. Much better to have your jockey do the dirty work, and alibi yourself. Don't try to lie your way out of such a shabby little trick, Mr. Manners. We both know you are capable of it."

Manners pursed his lips, avoiding a hot comment which would not have helped. He wondered if a punch in the mouth would. Or a kiss in the same place.

"I am capable of a lot of things," he agreed after reviewing each of these thoughts. "Murder not the least, I assure you. I think we are all capable of it under the right circumstances."

Allyn waited for him to say more. He did not. She regarded him with suspicion. "What are you getting at?"

"Just this." He closed the gap between them and stared straight down at her. "If I wanted your horse for my own ends, I could have him. If I wanted you dead, I would have done the job myself. But"—he touched her cheek with a crooked finger—"you are still alive, and Sheik is still yours." He withdrew his hand, as though he had not intended for it to stray. "And the only thing I've done to deserve the tender treatment you've given me is to make you an offer for your horse. Miss Cameron, what are you so afraid of? Spare me your comments about being the only woman ever brave enough to attempt a derby, which conceit, I hasten to remind you, almost cost you the race. And your life. You are a coward."

"Have you quite finished?" Allyn managed, maintaining her even gaze and arctic tone.

"I have," he returned, backing away at last.

"Good day, Mr. Manners."

"Good day, Miss Cameron."

He seized his hat from Missy's trembling hands and looked back at Allyn again with his hand on the door lever.

"Good luck in the Kentucky Derby. I won't be there to scrape you off the ground again." His stern gaze softened as he addressed Missy. "Good day and good luck to you, Miss Cannon."

In the wake of his exit, the two women did not speak for several minutes. The air was still charged with his magnetism, and it was some time before the effect diminished.

"I think he's magnificent," Missy murmured finally in awe.

"I think he's despicable," Allyn breathed again, shaking. "And I don't trust him."

Missy gave her a queer look. "We have an old saying down South, Allyn; perhaps you've heard it?" she said, mimicking Allyn's own earlier tone, to Allyn's annoyance. "'The lady protests too much.' There's more to this man than you think, Allyn. I shouldn't be surprised that you can't see it; you've always had a pretty narrow view as far as men were concerned. But I don't believe you have seen the last of Mr. Joshua Manners. And I certainly hope *I* haven't."

Savagely, Allyn hurled a pillow at her.

In a day, Allyn was fully recovered, except for her pride, which still hurt whenever she thought about Manners's little speech, which was often. She was careful to give no sign of that to Missy, however, and Bert had no idea of what had transpired in the hotel room. The quartet traveled home complacent in their triumph, with Sheik having returned thirty to one, increasing all of their net worths. The conservative sum that Missy had wagered allowed her a comfortable nest egg: her "dowry," as she laughingly referred to it. It seemed likely to all concerned that the ranch would be the only thing to ever benefit from it. Bert teased Allyn in a loving way about her own dowry, and Allyn, startled, realized that she had barely thought at all about her wedding since traveling to Deadwood.

Finally, on the trip home, she understood why.

She was a coward. Manners had said it himself as he had caressed her cheek. She had been afraid to think about what she now knew was inevitable. She would allow her physical needs to rule her and direct her into marriage, an honest way to ensure a man's arms around her every night. She also knew, with the sense of helplessness which always accompanies thoughts of the inevitable, that afterwards, her free will would no longer exist. After her capitulation to those needs, and to society's tenets, she would be lost. Not because of any restrictions Bill Boland might place on her, but rather because she would forfeit her own self-esteem.

Carole Howey

The buckboard was cramped. She glanced at Bert, and at Missy in the back, neither of whom were looking at her. They were thinking their own private thoughts, Allyn was relieved to note. They had not noticed her introspection. They could not have guessed what she had been thinking.

"You will go along with Sheik to Kentucky, won't you, Allyn?" Thus Bert divulged his thoughts, like a question mark at the end of a long, silent monologue. "After all, you've no idea how long Bill plans to be away . . ."

Allyn curled her lower lip, not averting her eyes from a glorious sunset. "Would serve him right, wouldn't it? Leaving me at the altar that way. Is that what you want, Missy?"

"Huh?" Missy, apparently, had only half been listening. "Oh, Allyn, I wouldn't think of asking you—it's such a responsibility—but—would you? Please?"

Free will was granted parole. Or at least a stay of execution.

"Missy, there's nothing I'd like better," she answered right away, feeling very relieved.

The road home took them through town, where they were surprised to see Bill Boland emerge from The Golden Wheel, looking as though he'd been awaiting their return. A strange, fleeting fear overwhelmed Allyn at the sight of him standing at the threshold, and she was glad that Missy spoke first.

"Well, Bill! Back so soon?"

He grinned his big, sunny smile and Allyn's terror evaporated. She felt foolish.

"Haven't left yet," he admitted, his gaze moving to Allyn, whose face grew hot. "I had to congratulate this handsome young woman. Had to scold her too."

Bert halted the buckboard before him, and before Allyn could protest, Bill had clasped his hands about her waist, nearly spanning it, and lifted her down before him, his rough-hewn features relaxing to a fond smile before he kissed her lightly on the lips. His kiss was gentle and lover-like. Against her will, Allyn felt her body lean into it.

"That was some chance you took, Miss Cameron," he told her, his voice gentle yet chiding.

"I won, didn't I?" she said, allowing him to keep his arms about her waist. "And besides, who was there to stop me from doing it?"

She could sense rather than see a blush creep up his neck, and he laughed, a bit self-consciously, she thought.

"I deserved that," he admitted. "I'm sorry I couldn't come, honey. Buttercup foaled on the day of the race. A fine bay. Looks just like her. Named her Sheba, after Sheik."

Allyn found herself smiling. "Not Allyn after Allyn?"

"That's a name for a daughter, not a horse." His smile widened. "Next year."

His words annoyed her. She could not fathom why.

"And you're going away now?" She propelled the conversation in another direction on purpose.

He nodded, following her lead. "To Laramie. Some ranch business. Nothing to trouble your pretty head about."

She allowed that remark to pass, aware that she was manipulating this conversation for reasons not even immediately apparent to her.

"And you'll be back when?" she went on, sliding her right hand up and down his sleeve. His embrace tightened and he gazed down at her with a warm glint in his eyes that only she, she was certain, could perceive.

"Two weeks, three the most. I'm sorry, honey. I thought we'd be married, but—"

Allyn effected an expression of dismay. "And Missy's asked me to take Sheik on the spring circuit! Heavens,

Carole Howey

Bill, it looks as though it'll be high summer before we take our vows!"

Bill's jaw plummeted. "The circuit! But why can't—"

Allyn gestured to Bill to lower his voice. "Missy asks so little. I couldn't refuse her. Besides, absence does make the heart grow fonder—or so they say." Allyn surprised herself that there was so much of a coquette in her. She felt ashamed. But her improvised performance did achieve the desired result.

"Well . . ." Bill capitulated, managing a rueful smile.

"Allyn, why don't you ride on ahead in Bill's rig?" Missy suggested, breaking into their tête-à-tête. "We'll follow. That way, you all can talk without making us wait."

"Capital idea," Bert enjoined. "All right, Bill?"

Bill looked up as though he had not even been aware of their presence. "Sure," he agreed, and tucked Allyn's arm into his own, leading her to his rig. He helped her in and unhitched the hack, putting his arm around her to pull her close after he climbed into the seat.

Was it his gesture, or the feel of leashed power in the sinew of his arms that triggered the unwanted memory of Raif? She closed her eyes tightly. The buggy bumped and creaked, lulling her into a dreamy state as her body slumped against Bill Boland's . . .

It was Raif there beside her, lean and powerful. She felt the Kentuckian's naked arms tighten around her dream, and she shivered and sighed. The yearning sapped her strength, and she needed him to hold her and to keep her from falling. From fainting.

The rig jolted again, and she was shaken from the treacherous reverie feeling ill. She rubbed her eyes and looked around all at once, not even sure of where she was. Bill glanced down at her, and she remembered. She sighed brokenly, feeling the familiar stirring in her loins that told her that she would need to have a drink tonight before she could sleep, since she could not have Raif . . .

"Cold, honey?" Bill's arm tightened around her, and a low whistle hooted behind them.

"Good thing you two have chaperons," Bert said from several yards back in remonstrance.

Allyn did not laugh. Feeling Bill's strong arm around her, she had a sudden, wild notion. Maybe she would not need whiskey tonight. Never mind that they weren't married. Never mind that she did not love him. Never mind that he wasn't Raif. She knew she needed a man tonight desperately, as she had so many nights in the past, and she was not about to let this chance slip by her.

Missy and Bert climbed down from the buckboard when they reached the C-Bar-C, but Allyn remained seated in the buggy, even as Bill came around to help her down.

"I want to sit out a bit," she said, hoping her voice sounded natural. Missy approached her wearing a stricken look.

"Allyn, it's late!" the younger woman exclaimed, edging toward Allyn so the men could not possibly see her face. Allyn turned a blank look to her friend.

"You go on in, Missy," she said, ignoring the desperate expression on Missy's face. Missy meant well, she knew, but Allyn shook her head. "I'll be along soon."

Missy looked unhappy. Allyn was plummeting headlong into the same mistake she had made with Raif, and she, Missy, was powerless to prevent it. All she could do was hope it would not end the same way this time. The younger woman retreated.

"All right," she mumbled in helpless defeat. "I'll keep a light for you."

Bert drove the buckboard around to the barn, and Missy disappeared after thank-you's and good-night's.

Bill Boland remained, gazing upon his bride-to-be.

"What's on your mind, honey?" he asked, his gravel-hard voice softer than she had ever heard it before. He approached the carriage and leaned on its edge, looking up at her with, she thought, as much innocence as a forty-five-year-old widower could muster confronted with a twenty-five-year-old woman who could barely conceal her passion.

She did not answer him. Gazing steadily into his probing blue eyes under the light of the half moon, she raised her hand to touch his cheek. She felt the roughness of his day's-end blond beard against her palm, and she thought, fleetingly, of Raif's perpetually clean-shaven jaw. Bill's large hand covered hers in an instant. It was hard and strong. She could feel the callouses on his palm and was reminded of its many years of hard work, which it wore proudly, like a badge. Raif had always worn gloves when he worked, and his hands had always been as smooth as a woman's. Smooth and strong, with a most unsettling ability to reduce her, with a touch, to a quivering mountain of want.

She swallowed hard, and remembered that it was Bill Boland before her. She felt for an instant like an adulteress, making love to one man while dreaming of another. It was almost disturbing enough to make her want to stop and run away. But Bill was holding her hand firmly, and his lips were burning into the heel of her hand. He would not be denied now, she knew, gazing into his glittering cobalt eyes.

And neither would she.

She moistened her lips. With a desire that slowly unbridled itself, she slid her free hand up his shirt lapel to the collar, where his fleshy, sun-bronzed neck emerged. In a single movement he lifted her down before him. It had been so long, and she could scarcely believe this was happening to her again, at last.

"Come on," she whispered, not daring to speak aloud. "There's a place . . ."

She took his hand, leading him quickly away from the house, away into the darkness, before she could regain her senses.

The woodshed was nearby, and it was still cool enough in mid-April that spiders and other insects would not trouble them. Bill's hand gripped hers as she led him through the darkness to the small building, empty but for a few logs that would carry her and Missy into the warm weather. The darkness was her ally, for as Bill wrapped his arms about her like living vises and devoured her willing mouth hungrily with his own, she was able to lose herself in her fondest, most impossible fantasy. He became Raif for her, and it was Raif whose fingers tore urgently at her buttons, whose sweet, hot breath teased her neck. It was Raif whose strong arms lowered her gently to the ground, Raif who thrust into her, filling her with ecstasy and his essence. It was Raif, finally, who satisfied her yearning, long denied, for the love he had so abruptly taken away. She wondered afterward, listening to her lover's breathing become quiet and regular in the darkness, where in all the world did that leave Bill Boland?

Allyn did not try too hard to disguise the fact that she had lain with Bill. It was dark as she closed the door on his sleepy smile, and no one was about. She mounted the steps in a soft tread, and was met at the top by the even softer glow of Missy's lamp. Allyn searched the face of the woman before her. That face looked old and taut in the light, like a dried apple. She remembered the look. She had seen it before, on the morning after her first night with Raif. It made her feel every bit as guilty as it had then. She forced herself to meet Missy's sad gray eyes.

"Are you all right?" Missy seemed to gulp the question.

Allyn nodded in reply, edging past the eerie specter. The glow of the lamp followed her into her room. She began to undress by the light of it.

"Why, Allyn?" her friend whispered plaintively.

Allyn fought a sudden urge to cry. "Just because, Miss. Let it be. Please."

Missy was silent. Allyn continued undressing, although her fingers fumbled with the tiny buttons.

"Suppose you have a child," Missy said presently.

The words were like tiny silver pins falling on a marble floor.

Allyn sniffed. "I won't."

"Suppose Bill changes his mind."

"Suppose," Allyn fired back, "I change mine."

"Don't you love Bill?"

Allyn sat on her bed, curling her stockinged toes on the hook rug. She could see Missy's face clearly, although she knew the younger woman could not see hers. "I don't," she breathed, glad of the dimness.

Missy pondered this a moment. "Will you marry him?"

"Probably."

Allyn slid the straps of her chemise off of her shoulders and down her hips.

"Well, that takes nerve," Missy commented, the softness gone from her voice. "It's a braver thing than I could do, marrying a man I didn't love."

"No, it isn't brave at all," Allyn said tiredly, getting up from the bed to put her clothing away. "It's just that—I'm not brave enough to face the rest of my life alone, thinking about—well, you know."

"Raif," Missy whispered, as though the name were an ugly curse.

"Missy, I'm a damn fool," Allyn sighed, throwing her clothes to the floor.

"No, you're not," Missy declared, embracing her suddenly. Allyn, taken by surprise, allowed her to, even cherishing the warmth from the protective gesture.

"You're not a fool at all," Missy went on, releasing her. Her tone became hard and angry. "Raif was the fool. You're the victim. There's something inside of you that you won't let anyone touch since Raif left you. Maybe Bill in time . . ." She trailed off, sensing, Allyn guessed, that her words were unheeded.

"Well." Missy was businesslike again. "You need him. If not him, then someone. He's a good man, and I think you'll do just fine. As long as you don't let Raif come between you."

Allyn felt a bittersweet, stabbing pain each time Missy said Raif's name, as though his name were a knife in her friend's hand.

Chapter Six

The Northern Pacific took them to Chicago, and then they changed trains for Louisville. The journey took nearly four days, what with changing trains, and Allyn had ample opportunity, riding in a cramped and smoky coach car, to regret her promise to venture forth to Louisville. Opportunity, perhaps, but not inclination: The trip reminded her of her love of travel, of seeing new faces and new sights. Her world had been Rapid City for the last five years, and she was reminded that her world was small indeed.

Louisville, on the Ohio River, was set in a verdant valley like a priceless gem. It was late April, and warm enough for dogwoods, azaleas, and rhododendrons to display their full regalia. Even the sight of greening forests filled her winter-bound heart with joy.

The train had barely pulled to a halt in Louisville when Bert disappeared to arrange for a carriage, taking their valises with him. Allyn wished him luck, deeming this to be an impossible feat, judging by the swelling crowds of disembarking passengers. The sight of so many people made her feel very small, and paralyzingly lonely. She found herself all at once wishing for the angular, irritating face of Joshua Manners to appear. The thought both surprised and amused her. But no. He had said that he was not coming to Louisville. Collecting herself, she moved through the crowd toward the livestock compartments where Sheik had passed the trip in the company of cattle. There were not as many people there and she stood by patiently, waiting for the lesser species to be unloaded before presenting her claim check. At last the loaders brought forth the chocolate-brown stallion, leading him down the ramp. Allyn watched in alarm.

The trip had taken its toll on the beast. His large eyes, usually bright and alert, were sunken and veiled. His coat was not groomed, and his movements were as wobbly as a new colt's. Angrily, she sprang forward and seized his lead from the laborer's unskilled hand.

"I'll take that!" she exclaimed, thrusting her claim ticket at the skeletal worker. "You've all done enough damage already, thank you. If this is an example of the care and treatment the Norfolk and Western shows its valuable cargo, then perhaps the president of the company should hear about it!"

The men looked abashed at her shrill words, and could do nothing but mumble apologies and relinquish their charge, trying in every way possible to disappear. As a result she was left alone with sixteen hands of three-year-old thoroughbred horseflesh and a bundle of tack on a busy platform.

There was nothing for it but to saddle up Sheik and ride him out to the track herself. Shaking her head at the obvious neglect the magnificent horse had suffered, she shed her cloak and rolled up the sleeves of her traveling suit. Hampered as she was by her cumbersome clothing, she could not complete the task in any short time. Few noticed the spectacle, for there was much activity, what with new arrivals and baggage claims. In fact, her audience was a total of one.

At what he adjudged a safe distance, by an adjacent baggage car, a well-dressed man leading an ordinary dapple-gray mare witnessed the scene with amused interest. He watched for a moment, chuckled softly at the thought of encountering the woman under unflattering circumstances once again, then thought the better of it and turned away in another direction.

The English saddle was not a sidesaddle, but Allyn was enough of an equestrienne to adjust, and Sheik was enough of a gentleman to allow her. Holding to the main streets, she was able to follow the terse, critical directions of the stationmaster to Churchill Downs in half an hour. She was pleased and relieved to find Bert waiting for her outside the stablemaster's office, wearing a grin which betrayed his amusement at her circumstances.

"Bully for you, love," he exclaimed, clapping his hands. "But—I say . . ." His voice trailed off and his face grew serious as his practiced eye surveyed the animal's condition.

Allyn was too tired to express her anger to him all over again. "Yes, I know; he's in rough shape. I don't suppose you could engage Jack to take him out this afternoon for a bit of light exercise?" she asked hopefully, referring to the jockey Bert had secured for them by wire from home.

The Britisher grimaced, glancing at the westering sun. "This evening, you mean. No, I seriously doubt it. It'll have to wait until first thing in the morning."

As he had half-expected, "first thing in the morning" was not good enough for her.

"Then I'll have to do it myself. To the track, Bert." She masked her weariness with a brisk, light tone.

Bert's beery face registered puzzlement and outrage. He took a tentative step forward and seized Sheik's bridle. "Allyn, you're not going to do this."

Allyn was tolerantly amused. "Don't be silly, Bert. You certainly can't do it, with your back. If Jack Riley can't do it, who else is there but me?"

Bert did not release the bridle. "This place is full of eyes and ears," he warned, sounding truly alarmed. "By now, the press knows you've ridden Sheik yourself. If you take the beast down to the track now, with all the jockeys and riffraff about, they'll make hay of your name and Sheik's in the papers!"

Allyn laughed. "Don't be such an old woman!" She tried to bluff the Britisher out of his warnings. "Who will know, or care, that I've exercised Sheik? We had no problem in Deadwood. Louisville is a big place, and we are but very little people. Why, I doubt if any of them even know who we are!"

She reined Sheik away and was off at a trot to the track, leaving Bert grumbling in her wake, "Ah, but they will, and soon. You'll see to that, love."

She walked, then trotted, then cantered the eager colt around the track a few times, managing him beautifully, keeping a splendid seat. Bert forgot his trepidation and weariness in his joy at watching her, thinking that at least the gossip-mongers could report expert horsewomanship.

Nor was the exercise enough to ease Allyn's mind. She allowed the revitalized Sheik to be led to his stall by a stableboy, and she then proceeded to instruct the lad in the thoroughbred's grooming. He used far too light a hand, she advised him. Sheik's coat twitched, and the animal snorted his agreement.

Bert was finally able to drag her away after she had seen to Sheik's food, water, and shelter, and after she was assured that no one could spirit him away from the watchful eyes of the Churchill Downs security force.

In the carriage on the way to the Legrand Hotel, Bert broke some unpleasant news to her which he had previously withheld because of her preoccupation with Sheik: Due to a clerical error, only one room had been reserved for their use. He had checked around a bit before time compelled him to seek the track, but every room was full. There seemed to be not a vacant lodging in house, saloon, or hotel.

Allyn sighed and allowed her head to drop back. What else could go wrong? she wondered. Why had she allowed Bert and Missy to talk her into this? She knew the answer to that, and changed her line of thought.

"Then let me bathe, change clothing, and get a hot dinner, and I'll go back to the track and sleep in the stable." She was resolute.

Bert gagged. "This is Louisville, love," he managed. "Southerners are less than tolerant of eccentric Yanks. Besides, if anyone was to do that, it'd be me. No, love, I've a more practical solution, and the hotel manager is already working on it. He's inquiring of gentlemen with single rooms if they'd mind sharing their accommodations. He seemed certain we could work it out."

She sighed, feeling her fatigue for the first time. "If you're sure . . ." she conceded, hoping she did not sound too relieved. The notion of a hot bath and a nap before dinner was a welcome thought indeed, but she would not for the world abandon Bert if she thought his plan might fail.

Bert was sure. He shooed her to the room, and the

last she saw of him as she climbed the staircase, he was aiming for the hotel club room.

Bert called for her several hours later, by which time she was thoroughly refreshed, if not revived, and in the midst of scribbling a hasty note to Missy to be posted with the morning mail. At Bert's knock she remembered how hungry she was, and abbreviated her communication with all possible speed.

"Come, love, let's not keep my bunkmate waiting!" he called to her, a trifle impatient. "It's nine o'clock. We're hours behind our time."

Allyn opened her door to him, beaming.

"Supper at last! And I am starving."

"*Specialité à la maison* is a charming little dish called Brook Trout Almondine," Bert volunteered, offering her his arm. He was wearing a new suit he had purchased with some of his winnings in Deadwood. It was a gray wool gabardine, and he looked positively dashing. "My roommate assures me it is not to be missed."

"And are we joining this roommate then?" she queried as he led her to the stair.

"How could I have refused an invitation from the gentleman whose company I'll be sharing for the next week?" Bert retorted in mock reproof. "Although I must confess that, were it for myself alone, I am sure no such invitation would have been issued."

They began their descent to the dining room.

"What do you mean?" she asked, peering into the red, mahogany, and crystal hall.

"Well, quite naturally we got to chatting, and I told him I was in the company of a beautiful woman. A woman of incomparable character, determination, and wit. A woman who—"

"Oh, be still! You didn't!"

"I did," he assured her, smiling. "And Mr. Manners was enchanted. He . . ."

Bert kept speaking, but Allyn did not hear the rest. Her feet had frozen to the stair.

"Who?" Her throat constricted.

"Manners," Bert repeated, his features registering confusion. "Joshua Manners. My gracious roommate. What's wrong, Allyn? For God's sake, let's not stand in the middle of the bloody stair. Dinner, love, dinner! We're hungry, remember?"

Joshua Manners in Louisville. She was flooded with a host of conflicting emotions, prominent among them suspicion and trepidation. Her stomach fluttered annoyingly at the thought of facing him after his scolding in Deadwood. She remembered all too clearly his disconcertingly direct stare, and the gentle, fleeting touch of his finger, like a butterfly against her cheek. The memories triggered a swelling in her throat which she was loath to name. Don't trust him, her instincts told her. In a startling moment of clarity she wondered whether hers and Bert's reservations had been altered by chance or design. In any case, Joshua Manners's presence in Louisville was proof enough for her that Governor Mellette had not yet forsaken the idea of adding Sheik to his stable.

She stared hard at Bert, trying to fathom the depth of his understanding. But he could not know. He had never met Manners, she knew, and Manners probably had not troubled to expand the foreman's knowledge. Now to try and discover what the lackey's despicable little game was. Allyn mastered herself.

"Nothing is wrong," she said tersely, her gaze scanning the room. "I just—I have met Mr. Manners before. Don't do too much talking, especially when you are alone with him. And never, *never* discuss Sheik," she instructed him as he led her between the tables.

"What the devil are we supposed to discuss?" Bert grumbled.

Allyn did not reply. She had just spotted the offending object of their conversation, seated alone at a table set for three. There was nothing outstanding about him, she noticed with some wonder. Nothing particularly stylish about his simple brown vested suit, although it fit his tall, impressive figure like a new glove. Allyn noted several men in the room with features less starkly defined whom she considered handsomer than he. Still, she grudgingly admitted, he was magnetic. He possessed an air of quiet elegance, an indefinable aura which said that he was as refined as he could be coarse. And as always, every time she encountered him, she felt the power, the danger, surrounding him like a white electric current. What was this man? she asked herself for the first time, as his dark eyes met her gaze at last from across the room.

He rose from his seat as she and Bert approached. His now-familiar grin, smug, detestable, played on his overly wide but undeniably sensuous mouth, and his dark eyes sparkled in enjoyment of his own private joke.

"Good evening, Miss Cameron. It is a pleasure to see you again."

His voice was brown velvet, just as she remembered it. It made the skin on the back of her neck prickle annoyingly. She did not return his smile as she took the seat he proffered. "Mr. Manners, if I were vain, I would think that somehow you had engineered this—encounter."

She hoped her true meaning was not obscure. He met her stare as boldly as ever.

"You do yourself an injustice," he remarked, as though it were a compliment.

She was certain his double meaning was intended. Her stare deepened to a scowl, and she felt Bert kick her foot under the table in gentle remonstrance. She glanced at him, but he wisely was looking the other way.

"You are completely recovered from your accident in Deadwood, Mr. Emmet tells me," Manners continued, sinking his lanky frame into his chair without moving his gaze from her own.

Allyn stared into her empty goblet, feeling a blush creep up her neck at the mention of Deadwood. She remembered Deadwood and their conversations, and so, she knew, did he. What else has Mr. Emmet told you? she wondered as she formed an answer for him.

"I sustained no grave injuries. But then"—she aimed what she hoped was a piercing stare at him—"you know that."

"How fortunate," was his oblique reply, and his features gave no clue as to his true reaction.

Bert seemed to sense the tension between his traveling companion and his roommate. He strove for a comment, shifting in his seat, but apparently could find none. Presently the waiter arrived with wine, which Joshua Manners had already requested, and took their orders for dinner. When he disappeared again, Bert found something to say. Unfortunately, it was the wrong thing.

"I've told Mr. Manners all about the C-Bar-C, The Golden Wheel, and all of your successes back home, Allyn." The Britisher effected a light tone, smiling hopefully.

"Yes," Manners agreed as he unfolded his napkin into his lap with a graceful gesture. "I believe congratulations are in order. You're to be married, I understand."

Allyn bit back an angry retort, turning her attention instead to her foreman.

"Why don't you talk more about yourself and less about others?" she flung at the luckless Bert, striving mightily to keep her voice low.

"I see that I'm not the only one upon whom Miss Cameron bestows such gentle words. I am relieved." Manners laughed outright, infuriating her all the more. "Mr. Emmet is obviously proud of your talents. And if I may say, your talents do seem to be quite considerable indeed. I only hope your Dakota rancher can appreciate what he's getting."

If Manners wondered why she blushed at that, he did not ask. Nevertheless, she felt exposed by his remark, as though she and her motives were being held up to public scrutiny. It was a most unsettling sensation. She tried to form a response, but suddenly the waiter reappeared, sparing her the trouble. He made a slight bow to Manners and proffered a flagrantly expensive bottle of champagne.

"The Governor and Mrs. Mellette send you their compliments," he told them, his voice a soft, lilting drawl.

She watched with interest as Manners's smooth, confident expression changed rapidly to something approaching a scowl. She was intrigued, if not amused, by her host's obvious displeasure with the gift.

"Your master has tossed you a treat, Mr. Manners," she prompted him, leaning back in her seat as she rested her gloved elbow lazily on the arm. "How do you show your gratitude?"

Unexpectedly, Manners offered a brief laugh, as though daring her to try to anger him.

"He never treated me this well when he was my master," he remarked dryly. Then, to the waiter, he added, "Our thanks to them both."

The waiter bowed politely, uncorked the bottle, and withdrew.

Joshua Manners turned in his chair, looking for the governor's party. It was across the room, and caught his eye immediately. His former employer nodded and smiled in a typically patronizing way, and his former lover lifted her glass to him seductively. He waved once, forcing a smile to his lips while feeling a scowl behind it. Morgan Mellette, he had discovered, was like her husband. They were both possessive and manipulative, and he had tired of the latter just as he had the former. Morgan, however, was slow to take the hint, in spite of his continued rebuffs. He had never encountered any difficulty in finding beautiful, willing women who would not try to leash him for show and who were not the wives of other men. He turned his attentions to his own party, forcing these unpleasant thoughts from his mind.

"Well," he breathed, all too aware of Allyn Cameron's amused scrutiny. "I see no reason not to enjoy the governor's uncharacteristic generosity. Miss Cameron, Mr. Emmet. Shall we?"

With a flourish he did not feel, he began filling their glasses with the golden effervescence.

Allyn began to rise. Bert's hand shot out like a striking rattler to seize her wrist.

"Sit down, Allyn," the Britisher pronounced in a low, clipped tone. "It would not look right."

Allyn hesitated. Then, to Manners's amazement (and frankly, to Bert's), she did resume her seat. So, thought Joshua, Morgan Mellette completely forgotten. Unlike the horse, the mistress needs a curbed bit. He smiled inwardly, tucking that scrap of information away for future use. He replaced the half-empty bottle into the bucket of ice standing nearby and raised his own glass.

"What shall we toast?" he wondered aloud, his gaze straying to Allyn Cameron's enigmatic green eyes. He was delighted by the faint blush which touched her otherwise white cheeks.

"Luck," Bert volunteered promptly, seeming to find sudden courage. "Our good fortune in finding a gentleman willing to share his room with a stranger."

Joshua granted Bert a grateful glance, but could not prevent himself from returning his attention to the enchanting Miss Cameron. He watched as she raised her glass reluctantly in tribute. As she brought the goblet to her mouth, he realized that her lips were the color of pink rose petals. It struck him suddenly that he would like very much to be the glass she had put to them.

"To Allyn Cameron," he heard himself say, wanting, oddly, to see her blush again. "And her future husband. May you enjoy a lifetime of matrimonial bliss."

She did blush again, more deeply than before, deeper than he would have imagined. He was aware of a twinge of envy of this fellow she was going to marry, whom he remembered only vaguely from the Steeplechase. Funny, he mused, still watching her. He had not taken her for the "blushing bride" type. Still, there could be more to the marriage—or less—than met the eye. Buoyed by the thought, he resolved to learn more of the situation from the blessedly loquacious Bert.

Dinner was, for Allyn, a disaster. At the earliest decent opportunity she excused herself, unable to endure both Manners's penetrating gazes and her own unpredictable responses to them. She locked herself in her room and began another of her continuing correspondences to Missy, trying to blot out the image of Manners's devilishly handsome face in her mind.

He could not know that she didn't love Bill, but his toast had seemed a taunt just the same. What mischief are you up to, Joshua Manners? she wondered, toying with her pen. Perhaps it was a good thing, this rooming arrangement he had devised with Bert. This way, she reasoned, we can watch him, and see to it that he keeps both hands aboveboard. When are you going to trust another man? Missy had asked her. Perhaps it was time to begin, with the engaging, irritating Joshua Manners. Perhaps it was time, at least, to entertain the possibility.

Chapter Seven

Bert's grim predictions had, alas, come to pass. Perusing the *Louisville Times Intelligencer* over a luxurious breakfast in her room, she spotted a front-page editorial about "a certain Brazen Woman" who rode "like a Jezebel through the decent streets of Louisville" astride an "unknown Novice Entry" in the Derby. The editorial's author, none other than the publisher, J. Victor LeWitte, was most persuasive in his condemnation, albeit his participles tended to dangle. Reading further, she was amused to see that she had "wantonly consorted with the Riffraff" at Churchill Downs and had "totally forsaken claim to the Honorable Title 'Lady.' "

Uproarious laughter was her immediate response. What was it Bert had said: something about Southerners and eccentric Yanks? She tore the article from the page and folded it into the vest pocket of her habit to enjoy with her British friend on their way to Churchill Downs.

She was in the midst of a note to Missy when he called for her a half an hour later. He too was dressed for labor. His watery blue eyes regarded her sternly as she opened her door to him.

"I warned you," were his first words. So he had already seen the article. Just as well. She would send it right along to Missy, who would no doubt appreciate it enormously.

"Now look here, Allyn," Bert scolded her in the cab as they headed for the Downs. "You know I want what's best for you, Missy, and Sheik, and I wouldn't be talking to you like this unless I believed it was for your own good. Allyn, damn it, this behavior just won't do here in Louisville. Mark my words, this kind of thing will only do you harm. And if you persist in it, it will only get worse, and the papers will be savage. Please, listen to reason. You have, in one precipitous gesture, brought the wrath of Louisville on your head in spades. This must be your last trip to the Downs for working purposes. You must let the staff take care of Sheik from now on, and start behaving the way Louisville expects you to: going to balls and parties and such."

"That's ridiculous, Bert. Who'll take care of Sheik?"

It was a silly question, she knew, but the truth was she had no taste for the social functions he'd mentioned. The very idea of a formal party left her cold. Indeed, it had been so long since she had attended one that she was a little afraid she had forgotten how to behave at one.

"I will," Bert declared stoutly. "I'll do everything you would have me do, and I'll be only too happy to work from daylight to midnight, if only . . ."

Allyn smiled warmly at the old warhorse. God, but it was a glorious day!

"I know you would, Bert," she assured him. "But think: I can't go anywhere unescorted without setting tongues to wagging. Parties? Alone? Think what that would start! No, Bert, I'm just as well doing what I am doing, in your company."

"Ah, but I've a better solution, love."

He seemed determined to have his way, in spite of her best sweet stubbornness. When Bert exhibited such resolve, she had learned, it was best to allow him his say, after which she normally proceeded after her own fashion. She inclined her head and gazed at him expectantly.

He took a deep breath and plunged on.

"We have an escort for you. One who is far better suited, believe me, to be hobnobbing among society's elite than this old stablehand. His name is Joshua Manners."

Allyn laughed.

"Joshua Manners," she repeated in an exaggerated tone of enlightenment. "Now, why didn't I think of that? I can just see the two of us bickering and glowering at one another from one social event to the next. Oh, that is really too much, Bert. But"—she suddenly had an awful thought—"you—you haven't asked him about this, have you?"

"N-no," Bert stammered, looking abashed at her words. "He mentioned to me this morning that he would be happy to—"

"Thank heavens for that at least," she breathed, feeling only a little faint. "I won't have you throwing me at men. Especially not at Joshua Manners. Even if I trusted him, and I am not altogether certain I do. But the answer is still no."

"Allyn," Bert rallied in a gentle voice. "You know I admire you, and respect you. Ordinarily, I would say to hell with your detractors, but you don't see how important this is—to Sheik."

"Sheik!" She was mystified.

"If Sheik is to be taken seriously on the circuit,"

Bert explained, taking her hand into his, "believe it or not, it will take more than winning on his part. There's a certain obligation on our part if he's to be accepted into the 'inner circle.' You know how these things are, Allyn. Sheik could win all of these races at a walk, but unless you play the game, he's out. And so is the C-Bar-C."

Allyn felt like a frisky puppy that had just run out of leash. Bert was right, of course. She represented Sheik's owner, and as such was obliged to make contacts valuable for Sheik's and Missy's futures. She would just have to trust Bert's abilities in the custody of Sheik, and set about righting the regrettable error she had made the day before, riding Sheik to Churchill Downs. She would have to master her streak of independence for the sake of Sheik, and behave with greater prudence from now on. It was time to put aside the riding habit and don the finery.

"This will be my last visit to the stable until the Derby," she said after a moment in a quiet voice, staring out of the window so she did not have to witness Bert's triumph.

Not one but several engraved invitations greeted her return to the hotel later that afternoon. She had promised Bert she would venture no farther than the hotel lobby without escort, inwardly seething at the unfair restrictions placed on her by social custom. A man could swagger about town any way he chose, but let a woman try and do her duty and there was the devil to pay. It was as though there were a chain fastened to her ankle, with a large and heavy ball labeled "Propriety" fastened to the other end. If she were married, she realized bitterly, and her husband accompanied her, she would be safe from verbal attack. As it was— well, she would, as Bert said, have to "play the game," or suffer society's reprisals.

Marriage to Bill Boland, in the face of all of that, began to seem less and less threatening. Not only would she have the carnal fulfillment she secretly, desperately craved. She also knew that, to a point, Bill was malleable. She would, she suspected, have her own way more often than not. If that meant continuing with the saloon, why, she would do so. Thank goodness Rapid City was not quite so condemning as stuffy, dignified Louisville. Husband or no, a lady managing a saloon would never be tolerable to these Southerners, whose idea of a lady was—well, apparently was something other than Allyn Cameron.

Dressed more respectably in a deep rose gown most appropriate for afternoon, Allyn ventured down to the desk to post her lengthy epistle to Missy. Conversation blanketed the lobby like a downy quilt, abruptly ceasing as she crossed the marble floor.

"May I be of service, Miss Cameron?" The desk clerk's pleasant young features were utterly bland. Allyn realized that the conversation had stopped, and she felt dozens of pairs of eyes upon her like a swarm of insects. She managed, in a whisper, to ask that her letter be posted.

"Of course." The letter disappeared. "Will there be anything else?"

She could not speak at all. The air of hostility about the place was paralyzing. She could not even form a response, or a next move.

"Miss Cameron! I'm glad you're here. There is someone I would like you to meet."

Joshua Manners had magically materialized at her elbow, his urbane, faintly mocking tones cutting the hostilities like a straight razor. Surprise mingled with relief as she beheld him. He was dressed in a superbly tailored vested suit of charcoal gray wool. His only ornaments were a small diamond tie tack, a fine gold watch chain, and the inevitable black Stetson.

111

"Please," he went on, his frankly amused stare prodding her into action. "Come with me."

Bewildered and overwhelmed, she did not resist as he propelled her gently, guiding her elbow, through the spacious, hushed lobby.

"I'll explain later," he muttered sotto voce, his sweet breath tickling her ear. "Just be charming."

"Whom am I to charm?" she wondered, too baffled by his timely intrusion to become immediately angry or suspicious.

"Shh."

He led her to a cluster of lush, stuffed chairs in prominent view, where two matronly women and one balding, thin man sat like elegant statues, monitoring their approach. As though oblivious to the frankly chilly stares cast at them, Manners tipped his hat and bowed to the tight-lipped trio.

"Mr. and Mrs. Foster, Mrs. Pemberly. I would like to present Miss Allyn Cameron, my dear cousin."

Allyn betrayed her surprise at his introduction only by an arched eyebrow. His *cousin?* A moment of silence ensued, and she wondered what might happen next. Like carved stone, Mrs. Foster and Mrs. Pemberly extended graceful, white-gloved hands, and Mr. Foster rose and bowed. Smiling tenuously, Allyn acknowledged the greeting. She and Joshua were invited to sit and join the trio for tea.

Later, Allyn could not recall the conversation at that unlikely gathering. The Fosters and Mrs. Pemberly, she had learned during the course of tea, were among society's elite in Louisville, and by some bizarre happenstance were also well acquainted, in fact seemingly intimate, with Joshua Manners. Determined to learn how such a ludicrous alliance could possibly be, she resolved to ask him at the first possible opportunity. Meanwhile she had followed his instructions. She was charming. She charmed them with her demure conversation and unfaltering smile, never once contradicting Manners's preposterous story about her being a distant relation. Gradually the icy stares thawed, and before long heads were bobbing in approval. At the conclusion of tea, which had more to do with the hour than with the actual consumption of the beverage, the Louisville contingent excused themselves, grasping Allyn's hand warmly, wishing her luck in the Derby.

Allyn, in a daze, watched them depart, conscious of stares of new respect.

"That was relatively painless, wasn't it?" Joshua, still speaking in hushed tones, grinned at her like a small boy who had just played a successful prank. She began, slowly, to recover from the shock.

"Mr. Manners, will you be good enough to explain to me—"

"Keep your voice down!" he ordered, scarcely above a whisper, his dark eyes suddenly serious and alert. "Sit down and let's finish this tea. I will reveal all."

She watched as he resumed his seat with unhurried grace. Aware of the eyes still upon her, she did the same.

"I want to know what entitles you to engage me in your ridiculous pretenses." Her smile, for the benefit of the spectators, did not waver.

He did not smile derisively, as she had been expecting. "Miss Cameron, when will you learn not to suspect my intentions?" he mused aloud. "I'm trying to undo the harm you did yourself yesterday by riding out at Churchill Downs."

"Why?" she challenged him, keeping her voice low. "You always seem to be in the middle of things. You told me when you first met me in Rapid City that you were an agent for Governor Mellette. Allegedly, in Deadwood, you intervened on our behalf against the governor's interests. And after claiming to have left

113

the governor's service, you turn up here in Louisville, in spite of your parting remarks about not being here to—what was it you said? 'Scrape me off the ground'? I demand to know, Mr. Manners, just what business you have in Louisville, and how it concerns me, Bert, and Sheik. And I won't be a party to any more of these charades until and unless I receive a satisfactory answer."

Manners did not answer her right away, but his eyes absorbed her, unflinching, unperturbed. He did not, she noticed, look away or make any other gesture which would make her suspect his response. When he finally did speak, he did not move his gaze, and he chose his words deliberately.

"It's true," he began, edging closer to her so they would not be overheard. "When we parted in Deadwood I had no intention of going on to Louisville. I altered my plans, thinking that a man with my special abilities would find many prospective employers here at Derby time. After all, everyone who is anyone in flat racing is here now. So you see, my reason is a very practical, not sinister, one. I am out of work. I am looking for a job."

"How," Allyn pursued after a moment of thought, "will you find a position if you are busy squiring me about?"

He did smile then, that wide, double-edged smile that for some reason she so mistrusted.

"What better way for me to make my availability known to a society craving my special abilities? Anyone interested in my services will be attending those same parties for which you require respectable escort. So you see, we have a natural alliance."

Allyn could only stare at him in amazement. Circumstances had apparently made then allies of mutual need. It seemed that Sheik's future rested, for the moment, at the whim of this mysterious mercenary

114

who blithely professed to be interested in selling himself to the highest bidder. She, meanwhile, could be condemned by the same society that he courted simply for carrying out an honorable obligation. She managed a bitter smile at life's cruel tricks.

"And is Mr. Foster one of these 'prospective employers'?" she inquired, looking about the room again, unable to endure his smug expression any longer.

"No," he replied shortly. "But Mrs. Pemberly is. And she has maintained an estimable position in Louisville society."

He did not add "in spite of herself," but the implication was flagrant. Allyn mastered a scowl, in fact turning it to one of her most charming smiles. She could always find a smile when contemplating devilment.

"I'm sure that as an employer Mrs. Pemberly would keep you well in hand," she assured him sweetly.

He seemed startled by her remark, she realized triumphantly, but he made bold to reply. "I'm sure that she would like to try."

Before she was able to express her outrage at such a suggestion, he stood up. "A party tonight at The Medfords'. I'll meet you here at eight o'clock." In an exaggerated gesture of courtliness, he bowed, replaced his hat upon his sable hair, and left her to wonder from whence had spawned so arrogant a creature.

The evenings were warm, although it was only early May, and there was a ring around the moon. The celestial phenomenon cast a strange illumination on the sprawling stables of Churchill Downs. A lone figure sauntered across the warming track in a stealthy gait toward the rows of stalls which housed, among others, the Kentucky Derby competitors. The tall, lean silhouette chose the third stall in the third row, inhabited by one sixteen-hand, chocolate-brown thoroughbred,

Sheik by name. Gaining entrance by way of a master padlock key, the figure lit the kerosene lamp upon the shelf and gazed upon the animal.

Sheik snorted, then turned his attention back to his dinner. The intruder smiled to himself and edged beside the trough to loosen the horse's tether.

In a moment he found himself sputtering and bobbing in the cold water, and he realized that he had not tripped. Shaking the water from his eyes, he looked squarely into the business end of his quarry, whose long, silky tail twitched. The unlucky intruder hoisted himself out of the trough, wringing his shirttails. He turned to the thoroughbred with real distaste.

And in the next moment he was lying face first in the straw clutching his groin, watching the stars dance in his head, his mouth open in a soundless scream of blinding pain. It was some time before he could gather himself and stagger out of the stall, abandoning any thoughts of horse thievery that night.

Allyn Cameron was punctual. Joshua Manners added that to his mental list of her character traits, and although it was by no means her most attractive quality, it was certainly an asset in any woman. He took a long draw on the cigar he had recently lit, watching the object of his consideration descend the marble staircase. It was not the gown she wore which commanded his attention, although it was a strikingly simple affair of emerald-green moire which displayed a modest yet provocative portion of her pouting, snow-white bosom. Nor was it merely the cool, vaguely aristocratic expression of superiority on her undeniably lovely features, or the sweep of her rich, chestnut locks into a soft French knot which begged to be loosened by a man's hand. It was, he decided, the spectacle of Allyn Cameron: her grace, her fluid movements, her serenely confident sense of who she was and where she belonged in this world. Stubbing out his cigar in the brass smoking stand, he left the club room, aware of a keen anticipation of having this magnificent, elusive creature entirely to himself for the evening.

"Miss Cameron, you look more than usually beautiful," he said to her as she approached, noting that her expression became immediately guarded, as though he had startled her out of some reverie. "Shall we?"

The intense green of her almond-shaped eyes never failed to intrigue him. The gaze made him wonder what she had been thinking, and even the possibility that she might have been thinking of him gave rise to a host of wonderful, awful sensations within him. He offered his arm as she reached the bottom step. She hesitated a moment, then slipped a gloved hand around his elbow without a word. The warmth of her small hand drew a swelling to his chest.

He had hired a carriage, and it was waiting, with a driver, out front with others hired by hotel guests for the same affair. Against his will and better judgment, he felt a surge of pride as he noted the heads that turned as they passed by. Glancing at Allyn, he found her looking directly ahead, oblivious to, or disregarding, their audience. With a graceful and efficient gesture she lifted an armful of green moire out of her way as she stepped up into the carriage. He held her hand and placed his other hand on her waist, aware that he wanted, very much, to touch her.

Inside, he called sharply to the driver to be off. Allyn sat across from him, her gloved hands folded demurely in her lap.

"It shouldn't take too long to get there," Manners observed, noting the scant traffic in the gathering dusk. "Medford Farm is just east of Louisville."

" 'Farm'?" Her tone implied surprise. It was the first word she had spoken to him thus far.

He nodded, observing the play of light and shadow across her arresting features. "In Blue Grass Country, they're all called farms. Some of the spreads are close to a million acres, and their owners still call them farms. Rather a lame attempt at self-deprecation, wouldn't you say?"

A faint smile crossed her lips briefly, one he recognized. He braced himself for what was coming next. "Still, some of us could profit by the practice, could we not?"

She was delightful. He could not resist a chuckle. "How did Bill Boland manage to woo you, through all of your verbal barbed wire, Allyn?" he mused, shaking his head.

She was scowling, and although the dim light made it impossible to tell for sure, he guessed she was probably blushing.

"I won't discuss my personal affairs with you, Mr. Manners. And I don't recall giving you leave to use my first name."

"You didn't," he assured her. "And if I thought you ever would, I might have waited until you did. But you wouldn't. I figure we passed a few milestones in Deadwood, both in a stable and in a hotel room, which you no doubt recall. So please, call me Joshua. Besides, we're supposed to be cousins."

"I doubt anyone believes that." She was disdainful.

"Why not?" He was unperturbed. "I come from a fine old Maryland family. You come from a fine old Philadelphia family."

"How did you . . ." Her explosion was fiery, but brief.

"Genealogy is very important in this business, Allyn," he allowed after a reflective moment. "And you've never made much of a secret of your background. Don't you read the papers? Everyone knows you're a Philadelphia Cameron. That's why no one's dared to cut you to your face."

He did not add that his diligence was responsible for the press's knowledge of her prestigious family tree. She would certainly resent such an intrusion into her past.

She said nothing, and it occurred to him that she might be afraid. He felt a tightening in his chest and a sudden urge to put his arms around her, which he mastered.

"We're going to make everything right this evening," was what he said softly. "Don't worry."

A quarter of a mile thundered away under the carriage before she spoke again.

"Why are you doing this, Mr. Manners?" she asked him. Her voice was quiet. It made him want to place his arm around her protectively, although he knew he would not. "What is your stake in all of this?"

"You'd best start calling me Joshua," he replied in a lighter tone. "I told you this afternoon. I'm looking for employment. You have to learn to use every means in your power for your own ends. That's not something that comes naturally to most people."

That wasn't quite the whole truth, and it sounded a bit cavalier, even to him. But he had said it, and there was no taking it back. He heard her sigh.

"Then we owe no debt to one another," she remarked coolly. "I see that I can learn much from you in the rather dubious art of using people, Joshua."

His name was like a taunt in her voice, and he silently cursed his tongue. It had been too long since he had enjoyed discourse with a real lady. He had made the same regrettable blunder in Rapid City when he had tried to muscle her out of Sheik. Grimacing, he knew he would have to assess the damage he had done to his own character, and proceed henceforth with greater care. She did not trust him, he knew. He wanted, desperately, to find out why.

Medford Farm was lit without by bright paper lanterns and within by opulent crystal chandeliers. A sixteen-piece orchestra played in an alcove of the ballroom where dozens of richly clad couples already milled about, sipping champagne from fine goblets and nibbling upon savory hors d'oeuvres served by silk-jacketed Negro waiters. Joshua led Allyn along the receiving line, managing the introductions while she handled, masterfully, the small talk. That obstacle overcome, he gently guided her by the elbow into the ballroom, where he was surprised to discover Morgan Mellette holding court among an ever-widening circle of admirers.

She was a handsome woman. Of that there could be no dispute. She was as brilliant as the sun in her gown of golden satin, cut so as to reveal all of her shoulders and more than a little of her very ample bosom, which had the color (and texture, he knew) of firm, ripe peaches. Her black tresses were piled upon her head in a gleaming cloud of French curls, and studded with tiny, sparkling diamonds. She directed her smoky violet eyes at him, and her winsome features softened in invitation.

He turned away, wishing to lead Allyn in another direction, but from behind he heard Morgan's lush, throaty voice beckon him.

"Joshua!" she called, and he could feel the eyes of all of her attendants upon his back. "Joshua Manners! Come over here and introduce your—cousin to us."

He could do nothing but comply with her request.

"She's capable of making a scene," Joshua muttered to Allyn, who stared at him quizzically. "Don't give her the satisfaction."

Hell hath no fury like a woman scorned, he recalled with sudden apprehension as they approached the

Queen Bee, who wore a suspiciously wicked grin. Joshua greeted her formally, using her title, and presented the poised, if somewhat haughty, Allyn Cameron to his former paramour.

"How delightful to make the acquaintance of another of Joshua's cousins," she purred in the fashion of a feline toying with her prey. "Goodness, he has so very many of them! And they are all so pretty!"

"It is more than usually thus in very large, very old families," replied Allyn Cameron archly, a coy smile of her own warning off her adversary. "How very interesting that it should surprise you, Mrs. Mellette."

Two—no, three points for Allyn, Joshua thought, smiling against his better judgment. Her inference that Morgan had no personal knowledge of old families, her condescending surprise, and her pointed use of Morgan's title, as if to say to the woman, cloak yourself in it. It is the only thing of any value which you possess.

Morgan knew she had been lanced. Joshua quickly intervened.

"Where is the governor? Not ill, I hope?" he asked her, forcing a jovial tone which he was far from feeling. He had hoped to make an honorable impression on Allyn Cameron this evening, but introducing her to his former paramour was a big step in the opposite direction, he knew.

Morgan turned her attention to him, seeming to forget Allyn Cameron for the moment.

"Arthur Mellette? Ill?" She laughed, touching his arm in a gesture of intimacy that, he was sure, no one, especially Allyn, had failed to notice. "No. He's off with the other politicians, smoking, drinking brandy, and swapping lies. You know those back rooms, Joshua. You've spent enough time in them."

As well as other kinds of rooms, her bold gaze seemed to add.

Before he could go on, she had turned her attention to Allyn again, this time saying, with a smile, "What a charming gown, Miss Cameron. Moire, isn't it? A durable fabric. And a most suitable color as well. Still, didn't we see you in silks last?"

Charming. Durable. Suitable. Perhaps the three most backhanded compliments one could pay to a lady's dress. "Charming" said "out of date." "Durable" and "suitable" were words out of the text of a mail-order catalogue. And "silks," he was sure, was a reference to Allyn's jockeying in the Dakota. Four points for Morgan.

Briskly Joshua took Allyn's arm.

"Excuse us, please," he said quickly, looking away. "I think that we should—"

Allyn remained still, a serene smile fixed upon her features. "Your gown is lovely as well," she said, faintly mimicking the other's gushing tone. "How unfortunate that you are unable to find a seamstress to fit it properly."

Morgan Mellette was unable to conceal her shock. Joshua fairly yanked Allyn away from the stunned group, holding tightly to her arm so she could not break away from him. He was both alarmed and amused, but it would not do to let Allyn see the latter. He led her straight to the doors and out onto the patio, where it was cool, dark, and deserted. He released her at last and she took two more steps away from him before turning around. Her green eyes flashed with anger, and she massaged the arm he had held so tightly with her free hand.

"What do you mean by introducing me to that—that woman?" she breathed, panting with outrage. "It's so very plain that she entertains more than a passing interest in you! How dare you subject me to—"

"I'm sorry, Allyn," he began, holding up his hands against her angry tirade. "But she spotted us, and there was nothing else I could do. She was rude, I admit. But you needn't have made that last remark. You'd already scored enough points. I warned you she was capable of a scene. I wouldn't have put it past her to start clawing your eyes out right there in the ballroom."

"Huh! I would like to see her try it." Allyn's voice shook, and she tried to brush past him to the door. He took hold of her arm again, pulling her close, close enough to smell her light fragrance.

"No, you wouldn't," he whispered, feeling light-headed in spite of himself. "She's a vicious and spiteful woman, Allyn. You're a lady. I don't care how many saloons you run, or how many derbies you ride. Nothing can change that. Her tricks are as foreign to you as the moon."

"And how," Allyn challenged him, her voice hard as she stared squarely into his eyes, "would you know a thing like that?"

It seemed to him she knew exactly how he would know a thing like that, and at that moment, he realized ruefully, he would give anything to make it different.

"I know," was what he said to her, simply and forcefully. "Now let's go back in there and pick up the pieces. Morgan's influence isn't much in this town. In fact, I'm sure a lot of people will like that she's been taken down a peg or two."

He smiled at the memory of the scene. "You are really something, Allyn Cameron. I can't help but wonder if Boland knows what he's in for."

She started away, although he was still holding her arm and she could not go far.

"I must ask that you refrain from mentioning him," she said in a muffled voice. "I appeal to your sensibilities as a—a gentleman to respect my wishes in this matter."

123

He felt that he had unexpectedly captured a very rare and lovely bird in a silken net. Her plea, oddly and uncomfortably, tugged on his heart.

"You don't love him, do you?" he whispered, before he'd intended to say anything. Or trust him either, he thought.

She shook off his hold and turned an angry stare upon him, which brought him back to himself with a start.

"For the last time, Joshua, the topic is not open for discussion!" she pronounced in a cold, even threatening, tone.

Joshua was unmoved by her anger. Staring into her eyes, inches from his, he had his answer.

It was not long after midnight when Allyn expressed her desire to leave the party. She had been introduced to, and had conversed at length with, a host of prominent families that were eager, it seemed to Joshua, to advance the fortunes of her remarkable thoroughbred. He consented to the departure, sensing her fatigue and relieved to be quit of the place before Morgan could exact a revenge.

Outside, the footman summoned the carriage. In minutes it appeared out of the darkness, and Joshua helped Allyn climb inside. As he was about to join her, he was brought up short by a voice behind him.

"Joshua!" It was Morgan, her tone a stage whisper. "Wait!"

Even as an inner voice told him to ignore her request, some other sense warned him that Morgan Mellette, like a tigress, was not a person to turn one's back to. Without risking a glance at his companion, he complied with her request, even taking a step or two away from the carriage to lessen the possibility that Allyn might overhear their discourse.

"What do you want?" he asked in a low, curt voice.

Her skin, like her dress, glowed yellow in the lantern light of the eaves, and there was an expression of intimacy on her features.

"I thought I made that plain," she murmured, touching his sleeve again as she had earlier.

He felt a frown curl on his lips. "And I thought I'd made it plain that I was tired of this game," he replied wearily. "Good night, Morgan."

Unexpectedly, she laughed out loud.

"Shh!" he exploded in a whisper. "Do you want the whole house to know you're out here?"

"Just one more thing before you go off with your frosty little cousin," she said, ignoring his question.

"What?" he returned with forced patience.

To his utter astonishment she sprang forward, pressing a luscious kiss onto his surprised mouth even as she rubbed her warm, soft body against his. He was too overcome by shock to move. In another moment she backed away, her face a study of smug triumph.

"I'll be waiting," she told him in a clear voice, adding in a whisper, "but not for long."

And she disappeared into the shadows again.

"Is everything all right, suh?" the driver called to him.

His only response was to enter the carriage and close the door. They began to move forward. He thought it best to say nothing to Allyn, against the hope she might not have witnessed the exchange. It was a slim hope, he knew, but it increased as they rode through the night back to the hotel in silence. If that was the best revenge Morgan could devise, he reasoned, then perhaps it was not too bad.

His hopes were dashed, however, upon their arrival when, as he helped Allyn alight, she said coldly, "We will not see one another socially again, Mr. Manners. If I'm to be made a fool of, it can as easily be accomplished by Sheik as by you and some disreputable governor's wife. Good evening."

With those words, she pulled her hand from his and fled up the steps and into the hotel. It was not until then that he realized Morgan's revenge had been aimed at himself, not Allyn Cameron.

Chapter Eight

Allyn turned all callers away the following day, including Bert and an unnamed bellboy who claimed to have flowers for her. She was angry, hurt, and confused, and wanted to share these feelings with no one but Missy. She began her letter at five in the morning, abandoning her futile attempts at sleep, and kept at it sporadically throughout the day, interspersed with periods of weeping and throwing things about the room. Morgan Mellette had won the day, and Missy Cannon would profit with a ten-page tome punctuated by Allyn's tears.

By dinner, she was played out and famished. She bathed and dressed and fixed her hair. It was her intention to slip downstairs to the dining room, find a secluded table, and eat a meal without attracting any attention to herself. This would, prayerfully, be accomplished without encountering either Joshua Manners, who was distressingly omnipresent, or Morgan Mellette.

She risked a stop at the front desk to post her

letter. The clerk was the same one who had chilled her the previous day, with one significant difference: He smiled warmly, greeted her, and inquired after her health. Taken aback, she replied in a polite, if halting, fashion, and was interrupted in her discourse by Mrs. Pemberly, to whom Joshua Manners had introduced her the day before at tea.

After a warm greeting in which the dowager held her hand in her own two knobby ones, the elder woman asked, "My dear, have you dined? We would be delighted to have you join us."

Allyn stammered her thanks, buoyed by the thought of this bulwark of society at her side. The newly solicitous clerk offered to post her letter as he handed her a small bundle of notes and cards. As if on a cloud, Allyn was whisked away by the diminutive and astonishingly vigorous Mrs. Pemberly to her party of ten in a private room off of the main dining hall. The Fosters were there, and they made much over her, as did the others present, whom Allyn did not recognize.

Such attention from strangers bewildered Allyn all the more until Mrs. Pemberly, who insisted she sit by her, whispered in her ear, "You've put that common baggage in her place, my dear. She was very nearly laughed out of Stockard's this afternoon. And it was so cunning of you to keep to yourself today. No doubt we will have to endure her tomorrow at Filson's, but it will be such fun to see her squirm!"

The old woman's startlingly blue eyes twinkled with delight.

Allyn's confusion began to recede. "Are you talking about Morgan Mellette?" she inquired in amazement.

"Of course," the woman replied in amused rebuke. "Oh, Joshua Manners was right. You are quite delightful."

Her displeasure at the mention of his name must

have showed, for Mrs. Pemberly arched a snow white eyebrow. "Oh, my. I've spoken out of turn. Please forgive me. You see, he gave me the impression—that is—"

Allyn was exasperated to find that she was, once again, on the verge of tears. "Mrs. Pemberly, I've a confession to make," she said, barely above a whisper, as the others around them went on with their conversations. "Joshua Manners isn't my cousin. At least, not as far as I—"

Mrs. Pemberly interrupted her with an amused chuckle.

"Pooh! Of course you're not his cousin. I'm well versed in the Mannerses of Annapolis, so I would know. As a matter of fact, he and I are distantly related through his grandmother's sister's husband. He must be very fond of you. His family means a great deal to him."

"You know him well then?"

Mrs. Pemberly sipped at her champagne. "Well enough to wonder why he left a promising career with the government to work for that upstart politician. His own family has had its share of senators and congressmen, although they've fallen short of the governor's mansion. He may yet come to his senses and settle down to a political career. He has the gift for it, and it would certainly have pleased his family."

"They're all . . . gone then?" Allyn wondered aloud, hoping to learn more without sounding too curious.

"Oh, yes," Mrs. Pemberly was warming to her subject. "His mother and father were dear friends of mine, and they've been gone for fifteen years at least. He was an only child, so he was terribly spoiled by them, and afterwards by his uncle. Still, he is a charming lad. Well educated. Quite handsome too, don't you think?"

Allyn changed the direction of the conversation

without answering. "What did he do for the government?" she asked, trying not to appear too interested as she watched the waiters bring silver-domed platters.

Mrs. Pemberly's white head leaned in closer, and Allyn responded with a like gesture.

"Secret Service," the older woman whispered, as though it might be secret still. "He worked at the White House. He took his orders directly from the President."

"The President!" Allyn could not conceal her amazement. "But why—that is, how did he come to be working for Governor Mellette in Dakota?"

"Joshua's uncle was rather a black sheep,"'her hostess replied, waving away a waiter who offered a tray of biscuits. "He'd sown his wild oats, so to speak, in the West. Apparently Joshua took it into his head to see it for himself. I always thought he'd come back. He left a good number of Washington debutantes pining, that's certain."

Debutantes . . . Allyn found it easy to envision pretty young women hurling themselves at Joshua Manners, who was a good deal more attractive than he needed to be. Additional questions immediately came to her mind, but Allyn didn't dare ask more. She perceived that Mrs. Pemberly was fond of Joshua, and she had no wish for news of her interest to travel back to him.

"Will he be escorting you to Filson's tomorrow evening?" Mrs. Pemberly inquired, whittling her fish into tiny pieces.

"N-no," Allyn managed, taken aback by the question. "We've had a—a 'falling out.'"

The dowager seemed mortified. "You don't mean to miss the party!" she exclaimed in a whisper. "You mustn't! It's the most important event on the circuit. More important even than the Derby itself!"

"Oh, no," Allyn assured her, glad for the information, although she would never have dreamed of admitting her ignorance. "I'll be there."

It was difficult, bordering on impossible, to convince Bert of his suitability as an escort for the event. His ultimate capitulation was apparently due to his failure to convince Allyn to allow Manners to perform the duty, but his reasons were unimportant to Allyn. He was going, and she needn't miss it after all.

Bert called for her a trifle late, with the apology that his cravat had misbehaved. Noting his pallor and shaking hands, Allyn could understand why. He looked acceptable in his gray wool suit, and she had chosen a simple yet elegant gown the color of dusty roses. She had no desire on this, the last occasion before the Derby, to attract attention to herself except where it concerned Sheik's welfare. Her reputation hung on a gossamer thread in Louisville. Appearing with her horse's assistant trainer this evening would stretch that thread a bit, but would not be enough to break it.

Filson's was twice as grand as Medford Farm. The grounds were rolling bluegrass dotted with shrubs cunningly sculpted in the shape of animals. The entrance and steps were ivory Italian marble shot with blood-red veins, and the chandeliers were gold leaf and Irish crystal. Bert fingered his collar nervously. Allyn inhaled a deep breath of air perfumed lightly with the scent of blossoming bougainvilleas, and fixed her best society smile on her features to run the receiving gauntlet.

"By God, there's royal blood in your family, love." Bert's voice was soft with undisguised admiration after they had gotten through. "I do believe you'd be at home in an audience with the queen herself."

Allyn stifled a laugh, choosing instead to smile

warmly at her escort, whose color was just returning to his weathered cheeks.

"According to Mr. LeWitte, I wouldn't even be suitable as a footstool for her," she replied, conscious of a slight relief that the first ordeal was over. The next would be dinner and the ball. So far, wondrously, there had been no sign of Joshua Manners.

"Miss Allyn Cameron!" A stentorian tenor jolted her to attention from behind. "How lucky that we should meet at last!"

Turning abruptly, Allyn was surprised, and chilled, by the sight—or rather, the spectacle—of Governor Arthur Mellette and his alarmingly beautiful young wife approaching.

Her first inclination, to turn her back and walk away, was quickly rejected. Certain that luck played little or no part in the encounter, she fixed a dazzling, if predatory, smile on her face and clutched Bert's arm so tightly that he grimaced in pain.

Introductions were carried out. The small, fleshy man grasped her hand and pressed it.

"My wife and I were very impressed with the performance of your Sheik in the Dakota," the governor said in what Allyn took to be his best campaigning voice.

"Yes," she enjoined. "Your man Manners has made it clear to us that you are—"

A restraining hand by Bert softened the word Allyn had intended to use.

"—interested in him." She addressed the governor but stared archly at his wife, who appeared to be measuring her with equal boldness.

The governor did not seem to notice. "Was. Was." He laughed roundly, holding up his hands in a gesture of denial. "I would be frankly uncomfortable in your position right now, what with the press watching your every move, ready to laugh you out of town if your horse is unsuccessful. I get enough bad press being governor without having my stables come under such scrutiny. Besides," he added as an afterthought, "Joshua Manners no longer works for me."

"Oh?" Allyn's surprise, if not disbelief, was genuine.

"No indeed," the governor repeated for emphasis. "He gave me his resignation right after the Dakota. Still haven't figured out why. Speaking of which, have you fully recovered from that bad spill you took?"

Allyn's smile faded. It had been no accident, that "spill," and the governor knew it. She felt Bert squeeze her arm hard, and she barely prevented herself from wincing.

"Oh, yes," she responded in a light, offhand tone. "A trifling thing, really. By the way: our thanks to you and Mrs. Mellette"—Allyn inclined her head in that person's direction—"for your gift of champagne."

Morgan Mellette, in amethyst silk, issued a condescending nod that set Allyn to seething. The governor, still oblivious to the tension between the women, bowed ostentatiously.

"Our pleasure. Manners provided us with several years of service, and we don't hold grudges, do we, dear?" He patted his wife's beringed hand. Morgan, Allyn noticed, did not answer. Instantly, Allyn became wary.

She's a vicious and spiteful woman, Manners had told her.

The Mellettes excused themselves to mingle with other guests. Allyn and her escort were alone again.

"That was the hussy with whom your friend Manners carried on at the Medfords'," Allyn said through her teeth, watching the couple depart.

"I must say, he has superb taste," Bert volunteered, fairly smacking his lips as he followed Morgan's seductive, swaying figure with his eyes.

"Oh, hush! Do you think the governor was lying?"

Allyn managed sotto voce as she and Bert advanced to the dining room.

"About Sheik?" Bert countered, averting his eyes at last. "I don't know. He could still—"

"No, about Manners. Do you think your roommate still spies for him?"

Bert stared back at her with undisguised amusement. She was compelled to look away. "No, love, I don't. You Yanks are a queer lot, and no mistake. Manners, while perhaps not being entirely scrupulous, is hardly the cloak-and-dagger type. Besides, I can't see him spying for such a shady rogue as our governor."

"Perhaps you know best," Allyn replied as if she doubted it. "Dinner awaits. If I can stomach it after that encounter."

There was some confusion with the place cards. A waiter was thought to have dropped them and gotten them mixed up, with the result that Allyn and Bert sat at opposite ends of the table next to unknown parties. Bert appeared alarmed at this unexpected turn of events, but Allyn tried to reassure him with a smile and a wave. Then she realized that Morgan Mellette had intercepted the wave with a look of condescending amusement just a few seats away. Allyn scowled, and immediately turned her attention to her own area.

Her placemate seemed a likeable fellow. He was a short man approaching middle age with a frank acceptance of its tolls, specifically a balding pate and a portly profile. She chatted with him briefly, and then he introduced himself. Her esteem plummeted.

J. Victor LeWitte sat beside her, the same publisher responsible for those scathing, self-righteous editorials which had both amused and confounded her. Decorum being the order of the evening, she gave her name with an icy, reproving stare that dared him to make a remark. He accepted the unspoken challenge with foolhardy bravado, laughing outright, causing that end of the table to freeze in wonder.

"Not the same Allyn Cameron who, according to legend, rode the amazing Sheik to his Dakota Derby victory? My dear, I am in the presence of greatness." He laughed again, shaking his head.

"The only thing of greatness in this company seems to be your mouth," Allyn remarked, determinedly sipping her consomme, aware of the eyes upon her and her loud-mouthed neighbor, who seemed to have had more champagne than was good for him.

"On the contrary! You demonstrate your great boldness in daring to attend this gathering. Why, Miss Cameron, you're a better man than I."

"What you lack in wit, you compensate in stupidity," she replied with what she hoped was admirable civility, focusing her attention on a blob of oil floating on the surface of her soup.

"And what you lack in refinement, you compensate in boorishness."

Allyn faced him, unable, at last, to contain her rage.

"If the *Times* says it, it must be true," she intoned in a sweet way, and with an economical gesture which spoke of much practice in the deed, she overturned his soup into his lap.

With equanimity demonstrative of her breeding, Allyn proceeded about her own meal as though someone else had perpetrated the incident. Meanwhile, the stunned and steaming journalist dabbed and fanned himself as helpful waiters hid their smiles. The surrounding dinner guests took their cue from Allyn's collected demeanor, continuing with their dinner.

Bert heard the commotion from afar and craned his neck in a most crude and undignified way, ready to protect Allyn's honor with life and limb if necessary. Gaining no satisfaction, he began to rise, but was stayed by the calm counsel of Joshua Manners.

"She's quite safe, Bert. She's managing nicely, I'd

say. Let's not add to the scene."

Bert sat down again, frowning at his unsmiling roommate across the table.

"But what's happened?" the Britisher demanded.

Manners was biting his lower lip. "She's just given an editor a hot bath, but it was only J. Victor LeWitte. Nothing to worry about. Your places were not changed by accident, Bert. But I couldn't say for certain who is responsible, so I'd best say nothing for now. Just let it be. She's fine."

"Allyn, love, what could the man have said to induce such—such theatrics?" Bert scolded Allyn as he conducted a turn. Dinner had passed without further mishap, and Allyn was now held captive by her British friend in a lively two-step.

"He tried out one of his columns on me," she answered with righteous indifference. "And I critiqued it for him."

"Pardon?"

"I disliked it, Bert."

"Well, that was pretty bloody obvious."

"Don't swear."

"Apologies."

Another dance was beginning and Allyn would gladly have left the dance floor to abbreviate Bert's reprimand, but he held her firmly and stepped off into the waltz.

"You're aware, of course, that this will be all over the papers?"

"Will it?" Allyn was blasé.

"Of course!" he shouted, causing her to look up at him with one eyebrow arched imperiously.

"Bert, you can't think I'm even a little concerned about that, can you? Not after everything that's been printed. Finally I've done something deserving of some of the titles I've been given. I'm quite relieved, on the whole. Just forget it. The day after tomorrow, we'll be on our way to Baltimore and—by the way, don't mention the incident to your roommate, will you? He—"

"I won't have to," Bert growled in interruption. "He witnessed the entire thing."

Allyn trembled. "He what?"

"Yes, indeed, mum," Bert assured her, grimacing. "He said the change of place cards was no accident."

"*That* I can well believe," she said, feeling embarrassed for the first time without knowing why. "Well, there's no help for it. What's done is done. And," she added, as defiantly as if Manners himself were present, "I would do it again, even if a thousand like him stood and watched. In fact, I would not be at all surprised if he himself were responsible."

She felt an unseen force sweep over her like a wave, and suddenly the all too familiar tall, lean frame dwarfed Bert and tapped him upon the shoulder.

"May I?" the suave, mocking baritone remarked confidently.

Before Allyn could react to the interruption, Bert had slipped away and her hand was taken up by Joshua Manners. Allyn stared coolly as the powerful figure swept her into the waltz.

"If a thousand like who stood and watched what?" he asked with a casual, engaging smile. His hand was cool, yet it made her feel unbearably warm.

"I told you I did not wish to be seen with you in public again. Just what do you think you are doing?" she said, ignoring his question, hoping she sounded stern.

His grin was wide and tantalizing, and it forced her to look away from him.

"Cutting in. Marvelous little custom, that. Allows a man to take a partner who would never have him were he forced to ask her."

"Unusually perceptive," she observed with a scowl.

Carole Howey

"I meant, why? You must know that you are absolutely the last man in the world I would want to—"

"Careful, Miss Cameron. That remark could be taken two ways."

His dark eyes sparkled with laughter, and she could not form an answer rude enough for him. His arm tightened about her waist as he executed a dizzying series of turns. She found herself clinging to him to prevent herself from falling. He was, she admitted, a wonderful dancer.

"There must be a reason why you would choose to dance with a woman who despises you as much as I," she managed after they resumed a slower step. "What have you to say to me?"

"Just this," he replied, bringing his face close to her ear. His breath was warm and sweet against her cheek, smelling faintly of fine brandy. She tried instinctively to pull away, but he held her closer, making her heart beat rapidly.

"Be still, my dear lady!" he whispered fiercely. "Did you know that everyone is watching you? That was quite a scene you played at dinner. I'm sure you are very proud of yourself. But it will be costly."

"What do you know about that 'scene' from dinner?" she demanded, her suspicions renewed.

"Precious little, unfortunately. But never mind that for now. You'll be twice as infamous in the morning, and the papers will be even more unkind."

"What business is it of yours if—"

"Please stop interrupting, Miss Cameron!" His tone then lightened, but he did not loosen his insolent embrace. "You are going to get a lesson in public decorum."

She arched an eyebrow. "The blind leading the blind. How singular."

"Shut up, and stop being clever. This is important. Listen carefully."

138

His grip was painful. She was torn between a desire to leave him cold on the dance floor, a feat that would be Herculean at least in view of the fact that he held her so tightly, and a burning curiosity to learn what he would tell her. The latter spirit won out, and she tilted her head back at an angle perfect for kissing, he noticed, and regarded him with chilly dignity. He grinned.

"You're a smart woman, Allyn," he lauded, daring to be familiar once again. "Tomorrow you must say nothing at all to anyone. As though nothing out of the ordinary happened here this evening. When you dare to venture to the Downs for the Derby, keep Bert handy. Do not allow him to leave your side. You have made yourself trouble enough in Louisville, although I daresay it was warranted."

"Is that all?" she asked in a hostile tone.

"Actually, no," he admitted, steeling his gaze to hers. "While I have your rapt attention, I would like to apologize for the events of the other night."

Just like that.

She mastered her surprise.

"It is of no consequence," she responded, feigning nonchalance. "I am learning to expect no more from you. Anything else?"

"No," he answered, unruffled. "Unless you would give me the pleasure of another dance."

"When Hell freezes!" she hissed through a smile, giving the lie to her indifference as the waltz ended. He sighed melodramatically.

"Ah, well. Good evening then."

He loosened his hold and backed away with a courtly, exaggerated bow, then disappeared into the crowd. She needed to find a chair.

A knock awakened Allyn far later than she had intended to rise. She fell from sleep as from some great height, and she grabbed her pillow to save herself. Again the knock, and a soft voice of the male gender calling her. Reluctantly she pushed herself up from the bed, opening her stubborn eyes. Her hair had fallen out of its bindings and now settled in disarray about her shoulders and face. Her feet found her slippers on the floor and she slid her arms into her robe. She padded to the door, rubbing her eyes, and opened it a crack.

It was a bellboy. He bore a newspaper, a profusion of red roses, a bunch of ragweed, and several notes. Sneezing, Allyn made him wait as she relieved him of each curious burden one by one, beginning with the breathtaking roses. He did not wait for a tip, and that was just as well for him.

Three notes. There first was a cutting scribble and a bill for laundry from the victim of the previous evening's unscheduled hot bath, accompanied by the moribund ragweed. Allyn grinned, planning her response. The second was a note of apology from the Filsons, which seemed to demand a note in kind from her. Allyn opened the third note and read:

"The blush of these petals cannot equal the fire in your face when you doused your unfortunate adversary. It was a spectacle the like of which I never dare hope to see again. I can only thank God, kneeling, that I was not your neighbor, as the original seating demanded, before alteration."

It was signed "J.M."

Allyn threw the roses to the floor and stomped on them, wincing in pain as she impaled herself on exceptionally large thorns.

Chapter Nine

The first Saturday in May was warm and wet-feeling, with a kind of thickness to it like a new quilt, and the blazing sun seemed to be everywhere. Allyn wore white, a simple, slim-cut gown with froths of white lace at the shoulder and on an arc from knee to hem that made her stand out like a water lily on a dark-bottomed lake. Bert had felt somewhat overdressed in his gray wool suit, but one glance around the clubhouse at Churchill Downs more than convinced him he was not. Ordinarily he felt overdressed if he was wearing a neck kerchief, but the rule of the day at this race track was creaseless dove-gray trousers, spats, top hats, and tails.

One glance further convinced him that his duties as escort were indispensable. The wave of hostility was as dense as the Kentucky humidity, but if the seemingly indomitable Allyn Cameron noticed it, she did not remark upon it. Nor did she remark upon Joshua Manners, who was by now conspicuous by his absence. She did suggest they visit Sheik before the race, but Bert restrained her by warning of the ultimate ruin to her white attire and charming millinery from such a mission.

The race card for the day was mercifully short. Racing had begun promptly at noon, and Bert judged a good crowd on hand, several thousand at least. Allyn was the picture of womanly serenity, sipping indifferently at her milk punch, but Bert was sure it was only a facade. At the very least he knew the tension he was feeling had a radiating source outside his own person.

"Allyn, love, are you all right?" He affected a casual tone.

Allyn looked amused. "Of course," she rejoined. "Why do you ask?"

Bert grimaced. "Because you're so damnably quiet. I never quite trust you when you're quiet. Besides," he added, glancing about, lowering his voice, "this mob's given me the shakes. How about you?"

She smiled. "You have been listening to your roommate too much. And I am quiet," she finished, "because I have nothing to say."

"I wish you'd had a deal less to say last night," Bert grumbled. "I feel like I'm in front of a bloody firing squad today. What did Joshua talk with you about anyway? The two of you made quite an interesting spectacle, you know. There was a moment or two when I wasn't certain whether you two were going to kiss or kill one another."

"Go down and place the bets," Allyn suggested, ignoring his question as she produced promissory notes from her sleeve. "To win, of course. I'll watch for Sheik."

"Watch from here." He wagged a beefy finger at her after a moment, deciding against saying what he wanted to say. "Don't go running off. And don't make us any more enemies in Louisville, please."

"I shan't talk to a soul," she promised him sweetly. "Go."

He did. Allyn abandoned her chair and moved to the edge of the balcony, staring down at the empty winner's circle.

Sheik in the Kentucky Derby. Who would have believed it? The long-limbed colt had been brought a long way by his determined Georgian mistress. As a token gesture, Missy had offered Allyn partnership in the colt in exchange for the loan Allyn had advanced to her friend to purchase the animal over a year before, and as a token she had accepted. Never would she have dreamed that the colt would achieve even this. She smiled to herself as she recalled her casual remark to Bert. Place the bets. The notes were worth twelve thousand dollars, and it could all be lost on the run of a horse.

Nothing ventured, nothing gained. That was one of her favorite expressions. Missy was considerably more conservative, but Missy was back in Rapid City. And if Sheik continued his winning ways here in Kentucky, at thirty to one, the thoroughbred could earn her as much as a quarter of a million dollars. A dowry indeed. And if he lost—well, if he lost, she would simply go home. Broke. And in disgrace.

To marry Bill Boland.

The band on the infield interrupted her thoughts with the obligatory Foster tune, "My Old Kentucky Home," and many voices were raised in tribute. In another part of the clubhouse, she saw Mrs. Pemberly and her entourage, misty-eyed and sincere. She looked away, not wanting to catch her eye. Allyn did not know the words to the song. Besides, Dakota was her home, not Kentucky.

Raif was a Kentuckian.

The field of competitors was being led out and

around the track. She found Sheik immediately, and noted with pride that he looked fine. In top form. Jack Riley, the jockey, in green, looked mean, eager, and competent. The little man liked Sheik too, and that was in his favor, even though he had little regard for her. She blew the colt a kiss, and for the first time that day she felt the shivers of anxiety.

"Allyn Cameron."

The male voice behind her had an amused and oddly familiar ring to it. The sound of it severed her concentration. Another malcontent journalist, she decided, frowning. Without granting the new intruder the courtesy of her full attention, she replied to him.

"I'll listen to anything you may have to say to me after the race, sir. Until it is over, please be still. And if you cannot be still, then please leave."

"Allyn, honey! That's no way to talk to me!" The voice, now directly behind her, was insistent.

Impatience kindled a vituperative comment, which prudence doused. Hoping to silence the interloper with sweet demureness, she turned a polite smile to him. That smile froze and cracked, crumbling into an unabashedly shocked stare. There, within arm's length, stood her past, and it rushed upon her like a tidal wave, threatening to flood out reason.

Fond, intense blue eyes whose every dark speckle was etched upon her memory seemed to swallow her with a languor that was paralyzing. The achingly familiar amber face creased into the slow smile that rent her heart, and she felt her own hand at her throat. His full, sensuous lips parted to say something, but time stopped and he said nothing, as though words were superfluous in this moment.

In response, her lips formed his name, but her throat was rebelliously silent, betraying the deluge of emotions which overwhelmed her. Say something, you fool! her conscience taunted her. Do you want him to suspect the truth? That you've been waiting for him to come back to you for three wretched years?

But no sound came forth from her throat. She absorbed him with her eyes, thinking that Raiford Simms looked sparer, leaner, and harder, if that was possible, than he had when he'd left her. He must be thirty, she thought, and the prime of manhood rested upon his broad shoulders like a velvet cloak. His red-golden hair was short and trained back off of his face, and his mustache of the same hue was trimmed unfashionably short but handsomely none-theless. His white linen suit fairly shined in newness, and he brought his long fingers to his waist, showing the lean, efficient build of his torso clothed in white silk. In a treacherous flash of memory Allyn thought of that torso unclothed, and one of those fine, strong hands upon her breast. She felt her strength and her sense falter and she wanted to cry out for help.

"How long has it been?" he murmured in the drawling, seductive tone she knew all too well. He seemed unaware of the effect he was having upon her. Time began to move forward again at a snail's pace. She collected herself to answer him sanely.

"A long time," she managed in a light tone. She knew to the hour.

"How have you been?" he went on.

"Fine. Well. And you?"

How silly is the language, she reflected whimsically. It was patently obvious that he had enjoyed a change of fortune, and was hale and prosperous.

"I've been passing fair," he conceded, and short-ened the span between them. Suddenly Allyn found him in possession of her two cold hands. Had she given them to him, or had he taken them? Surely he had taken them, for she no longer felt a will of her own. The tall Kentuckian looked into her eyes, laying bare her emotions. She blushed in a fever of desire.

"I've missed you, honey," Raif murmured, his honey-eyed drawl washing over her like Kentucky sunshine. "You can't know how much."

Never mind that he had left her, abandoned her, so long ago. Never mind the endless, loveless days and nights in between. She wanted to surrender herself to him. To give herself to him again. To feel his arms around her, and to swear she was his forever . . .

Far away a bugle trumpeted, calling her mind from its distant places to the immediate present. She was safe, for the moment. Tearing away from him, she turned to the track below, where the horses waited at the post like fine, primed dueling pistols. The starting gun fired, and twelve shots issued from the gate. Raif may as well have disappeared.

Sheik and his rider were on the outside, but were off to a strong start. Allyn found herself admiring the prowess of the professional jockey, who kept Sheik's powerful young strides in check as he maneuvered for position at the first turn. As they rounded to the straightaway, the thirty-to-one longshot moved into fourth place, which he maintained along the back-stretch. He rose to third around the final turn as the crowd howled. With a quarter of a mile to go, the chocolate thunderbolt made his move.

In a gloriously unrestrained surge, the Dakota powerhouse broke through, his awesome speed coupled with his unfailing stamina cowing the competition. He crossed the finish line no less than four lengths ahead of the place horse, who seemed to lumber in his wake. Allyn cried out in triumph. Her Sheik! Her champion! Intoxicated with joy, she turned again to Raiford Simms and flung her arms around his neck. Pandemonium roared about them, but he seized Allyn and commanded her with a most indecent kiss. His firm, insistent lips parted her surprised, trembling ones, and she felt once again weak with desire as he held her close.

"I've found you again, Aly," he breathed into her ear, sending thrills along her spine. "And I'm never going to lose you again, never, never . . ."

This was heaven. This was her fondest, most impossible dream come true at last, after three bitter years of abandonment. But how could she believe him? Never say never, the silly old adage clicked in her memory. She clung to him to try to dispel the sudden doubt.

"Allyn!"

She was paged again, but it was Bert's outraged voice, and she recognized it through that mist in her brain. She tore herself away from Raif, feeling suddenly awkward and embarrassed.

Bert did not know Raif. His features registered shock at seeing her intimately involved in a strange man's embrace, but his shock was tempered by the flush of victory.

"Allyn, let's get down there! Sheik's waiting for you in the winner's circle!"

The race. The roses. The purse. The victory. Reluctant, she disentangled herself from her lover's arms.

"I—I must go, Raif." She looked up at him even as her feet moved forward. "That's my horse down there. My Sheik."

Raif reached for her hand. "Stay, Aly," he pleaded in a sensuous whisper. "Sheik can wait!"

Allyn shook her head and pulled her hand away, free, it seemed, from his spell.

"Wait here," she told him in a firm voice. "I'll be back."

"Allyn, stay!"

Something in his tone caused her to examine him in wonder. His handsome features were clouded and

147

distressed. He appeared oddly determined to keep
her there with him, as though she would be lost to
him forever if she went. A knot of fear tightened in
her breast. Why did Raif object to her going down
to Sheik, to claim the purse?

"Allyn, why the devil are you listening to this fellow,
whoever he is? Let's get down there to Sheik, for God's
sake, before the beast gets tired of waiting and leaves
without us!"

Bert's joke sounded strange and frightening in her
ears. Suddenly she was seized by an unreasoning
terror, like a stranger in darkness. Turning from Raif
for the last time she ran, and even Bert was obliged
to catch up with her.

The sea of people all seemed to be going the opposite way, but Bert plowed ahead, clearing a path for
the eccentric, white-clad Yankee woman. How could
the glory of the day have faded so crushingly? Now
that she was no longer with Raif, she felt an uneasi-
ness grow in her. The crowd was impossibly thick to
penetrate. Sheik in the winner's circle. She tried to
think, but her thoughts were hopelessly confused.

The winner's circle was bare. The crowd there had
thinned, as Sheik had not been a favorite, and even the
reporters were edging away. The horse, and the roses,
had vanished. Allyn seized a nearby blue-ribboned
official by the arm.

"Where is Sheik?" she demanded, out of breath.
"Where is my horse?"

"Who?" The man was in a hurry, and did not seem
to understand. "Sheik was the winner, yes."

"Where is he?" Allyn repeated in a shriek of panic,
not caring that several heads turned in disapproval
of the disturbance.

"Led away," the man answered her impatiently.
"Please, madam, I am a busy man."

Led away! Unreasoning panic struck her.

"My horse is gone!" she shouted at the man then, seizing his arm in desperation. "Who has taken him? And where? Sir, I demand that you find him! And the purse? Who has claimed the purse in my name?"

Before he could answer, Allyn turned to the bewildered Bert, weak with terror.

"Get down to his stall and see if he's been taken there," she ordered her foreman, feeling sick. "I'm going to try here."

If one of the grooms had taken Sheik, he would be at his stall, en route, or perhaps at the warming track cooling down. Allyn found herself running in that direction, heedless of the condition and restrictions of her white gown.

The track was vacant. Neither horse nor human in sight. She was rooted by disbelief. Sheik had just won the Kentucky Derby, and now he was gone. Vanished. Someone had simply picked up his reins and ridden him out.

She wanted to scream for the animal as though he could answer her. She wanted to sit right down in the mud and cry. Instead, she ran in another direction: the front gate.

As she approached the entrance, she slowed, panting. Around her she saw traffic of a mundane sort. Cabs were standing, loading and pulling away, and there appeared to be plenty of demand for their services. The cab horses were all a little droopy from long standing, or long work, with only one exception. She could not see him clearly, for he was at the end of a long row, and blocked from view by other cabs, but the animal seemed frisky, even protesting. Moving closer, she could see that several men were trying to calm the fiery, sweating beast even as they secured his tack.

Her mouth sagged suddenly. Right out from under their noses! Without pausing to think she lunged

Carole Howey

toward the cab, crying, "Sheik! Sheik!" as a host of ignorant bystanders stared in undisguised wonder.

The profusion of white organza descended upon the alarmed cab like a snowy maelstrom. With flailing arms and hoarse cries Allyn hurled herself at the trio of strange men who had just harnessed the colt to the cab.

"Help!" she shrieked. "That's my Sheik! My Sheik! They're stealing him!"

Indeed, Sheik neighed in answer, champing and stamping, frisking his head as one wiry man tried frantically to grab his bridle. Allyn began climbing to the driver's seat, pulling desperately at the driver with her fingers. The man held up his arms to ward her off, and a third man pulled her down from behind and thrust her aside. She fell hard to the damp ground, shaken, bruised, still yelling for help.

Several policemen, who had apparently been directing traffic outside the Downs, trotted toward her. Stunned, she watched two men run from the scene, and saw the driver make the mistake of brandishing a whip toward the yoked thoroughbred. Sheik reared, lifting the harness, the cab, and the man high into the air. The driver landed a few feet from Allyn and lay still. The police officers seized and calmed the animal, and Allyn accepted a hand offered to help her to her feet.

"I see that my good advice fell upon deaf ears."

Allyn started. The hand belonged to Joshua Manners.

"Joshua," she whimpered, feeling a sharp pain shoot down her back and into her leg as she accepted his help. "They were—they were—"

"I know." He cut her off so abruptly that she stared at his face in surprise. His features were grim. "And what did you hope to accomplish by going after these thieves yourself?"

His reprimand hurt more than her leg.

"The cavalry was nowhere in evidence," she retorted, rubbing her hip.

"Where's Bert?"

Allyn stared at him again, panting hard. Who was Joshua Manners after all that she should be obliged to answer his questions? His gaze bore down upon her like some fearsome mythical god's.

"Bert went to the stable," she answered him reluctantly, unable to sustain that gaze for very long. "To look for Sheik there."

"Why weren't you down at the winner's circle sooner?" His voice was harsh. "These fellows worked fast, and that was all the delay they needed."

She wanted to strike him for his coldness.

"The reason for my delay is none of your . . ."

She stopped cold, staring squarely into his expectant dark eyes. She could not go on. Raif had been responsible for the delay. Raif had wanted to keep her there with him, away from Sheik. Compelled by Joshua Manners's uncompromising scrutiny, she realized, in a sickening moment of clarity, exactly what she had allowed to happen. Raif had played her for a fool. Again! He hadn't missed her. He didn't love her. He had been after Sheik, and the cad had felt sure enough of her affection to try to keep her off balance while his accomplices attempted to spirit Sheik away.

And the most galling thought of all was that his deception had almost worked!

She could no longer abide Joshua Manners's steady gaze, or his touch. She shook him off, turning her attention instead to the officers, who had restored some modicum of order to the chaos. One of them touched his hat and approached her.

"What's happened here, ma'am?" he asked in a respectful Southern drawl, his features bland.

151

"Three men," she began, controlling the quiver in her voice, "were preparing to drive off with my horse. Sheik. The Derby winner. That's him, hitched to the cab."

The officer looked doubtful.

"Go and examine the horse, Officer." Manners's voice was, as ever, assured. "You'll find that it is Sheik, of the C-Bar-C. And you'd better have a look at the driver as well."

He was doing it again, she realized, at once angry and unutterably relieved. Joshua Manners had completely taken over the situation. It seemed that he was incapable of doing otherwise, under any circumstances. The officer obeyed his suggestion, leaving them alone again, except for the crowd of spectators who maintained a barely discreet distance.

"That dress must have been lovely this morning," Joshua remarked.

He did not laugh, but she could sense the amusement in his voice. Mortified, she looked down. The dress, once white, was now a ruin of brown Kentucky mud. She wanted to die right on the spot, but not before killing Joshua Manners, who had had the temerity to point the fact out to her.

"And what part," she began, feeling her anger swell like a raw wound as she remembered the note and the roses, "have *you* played in this shameful exhibition, Mr. Manners?"

"You're jumping to a wrong conclusion, Miss Cameron." The Marylander met her stare evenly and spoke low enough for her ears alone. "I had nothing to do with this. If you persist, you'll cause yourself a lot of needless embarrassment. It was I who summoned the police, you see. It would be decidedly odd for you to protest my complicity."

Joshua Manners had taken hold of her shoulders with a commanding grip. In his dark eyes, she perceived that his patience with her was ebbing. Her tongue became paralyzed.

"The driver is dead, Mr. Manners," an officer reported woodenly, sparing Allyn the necessity of a remark. "Must've broken his neck when he was thrown."

Allyn felt a chill of satisfaction at his words. She went to Sheik and grasped his bridle, cooing soft words to calm him. She hated herself for what, in her blind passion, she had almost allowed to happen to the animal. And to herself. She was stricken by a near-overwhelming desire to do herself bodily harm.

"Is he all right?"

It was Manners again, beside her. She turned to him and found him examining Sheik with a discriminating eye. She forgot her anger and looked at the thoroughbred, who pawed impatiently at the gravel beneath his hoof. The animal, to her relief, appeared to be fine.

"I think so," she replied, running her hand along Sheik's smooth flank.

He was all right. He bore no signs of ill treatment, and he was as impatient and energetic as ever. Allyn watched as the officers unhitched the thoroughbred, aware that Manners stood beside her, close enough that she could hear his breathing. She was in his debt, again. It was a disquieting feeling.

"It seems I must thank you once again, Mr. Manners," she said, not trusting herself to look at him.

"It's becoming quite a habit with you, isn't it?" he agreed, and she could hear the smile in his voice. Maddeningly, she blushed. Again.

"You'd best have your men lead Sheik back to his stall." Manners was addressing the officer in charge in an authoritative tone. "And call a cab for Miss Cameron."

"Yes, sir."

Before the man could depart, however, Allyn registered her protest.

"What about the others?" she demanded, angered by Manners's presumptive behavior. "Are you going to pursue the ones who got away?"

The young officer pursed his lips and shook his head.

"With all respect, no, ma'am," he replied in his Kentucky drawl. "We will assist the investigation, however. We will question the authorities here at the Downs. We apologize for your trouble, and we'll be pleased to help in any other way we can."

He bowed.

She expelled a hard breath, mastering an urge to slap him.

"Then will you please locate the purse money as well," she requested coldly. "Since you seem unable to do anything else?"

"Allyn, why don't you take a cab back to the hotel?" Manners interjected with such authority that she was obliged to meet his stare again. He was leveling one of those direct gazes at her with which she had become most disconcertingly familiar. For a moment she wanted to heed his suggestion, if only to escape from it.

"Mr. Manners," she began, annoyed at the weak sound of her voice. "Thank you once again for your efforts on our behalf. I believe I can manage from here with no further intervention, however well-meaning."

Joshua Manners could only watch as Allyn Cameron followed the police officers who led Sheik away, a study of dignity in spite of the mud and bruises. He could almost feel sorry for Bill Boland.

When he was not envying him, that is.

Bert was cooling his heels, pacing at the stall. Allyn had bidden him wait, and that was precisely what he had done, although waiting was not one of his strong points. Detached, Allyn reflected that he followed orders well. When Bert spotted the small, dubious caravan coming his way, he dropped his pipe and cantered toward it.

"Allyn! What the devil . . ." His voice trailed off. Allyn was limping, having broken her shoe in the melee. Three stable boys sprang forward to relieve the officers of the Derby winner.

"You may tell the officials that I expect the purse to be waiting for us when we return to our hotel," was the thanks the muddied woman gave to the grim-faced troopers, who took their leave. Bert took her arm gently and led her aside to a stool.

"You'd better sit down, love. You look done in," he told her in a low voice. "What in bloody hell happened?"

"They almost got away with it, Bert," she said through chattering teeth. "They had him hitched to a cab, and—can you imagine? Our Sheik hitched to a cab! And—"

"Who, damn it?"

She stared at him, wondering if he'd become an idiot. "The men," she answered, more than a little impatient. "The thieves."

Bert shook his head, as if to erase her cryptic remarks from a mental blackboard. "Allyn, love, start from the beginning."

Patiently, Allyn recounted her story, from her despair at the warming track to her heated exchange with the enigmatically omnipresent Joshua Manners. Bert listened with somber attention, holding her two small hands with a grasp so comforting that it made her want to cry.

"What did Manners say? Who were the men after all? Did they catch them?" the Britisher persisted.

"He said," she continued, taking the first of his

questions, determined neither to blush nor betray herself, "that the delay at the winner's circle was responsible. Therefore we must assume—"

"That the chap who delayed you was in league with the blighters who tried to make off with Sheik." Bert sighed, sending a stab of pain and remorse through her heart. "I am sorry, love. It's plain the bl—he meant a lot to you."

Allyn scowled in a feeble attempt to mask the truth of Bert's words, and withdrew her hands from Bert's grip, hoping to stem the tide of tears.

"You needn't feel sorry on my account." She met his gaze squarely, although she could see droplets glistening on her eyelashes. "Go and see if you can find him, would you?" she continued, hoping she did not betray her desire to prove that their worst thoughts were false. "I'll wait here for you. I promise."

Understanding showed in Bert's blue eyes. Understanding and pity.

"And if I find him? Shall I have him arrested?" he asked softly.

Allyn set her jaw. "If he's still in the grandstand, yes. If he's out near the gate, shoot him."

Bert's lips smiled, but his eyes were grim. He nodded, and was off. Knowing that Bert's mission was in vain, Allyn watched him go, still fighting back the foolish and futile desire to cry.

"Dear Missy,

"Your horse has caused a great deal of trouble for me. After the victory (a stunning one, I assure you) we suffered a near disaster when three unknown parties and, presumably, a known fourth attempted to spirit away our illustrious thoroughbred in the guise of a hansom cab horse. To add injury to insult, one of the louts shoved me down. I shall claim damages against your purse which, miraculously, awaited our claim.

One thief was subsequently killed when Sheik threw him. It was all very exciting, and we would have been much the better without it.

"The known party to whom I referred was one Raiford Simms(!), whose apparent role in the ghastly joke was to delay me long enough for his compatriots to remove Sheik. Bert could not locate him after the failure of this plot. Nor is the matter closed: No one has been apprehended, and the authorities have reason to believe that the culprits are traveling East.

"There is one bright note, however. Governor and Mrs. Mellette are not attending the event in Baltimore, so we shall have to endure neither them nor their lackey, Joshua Manners. Bert and I have reserved rooms at the Hotel Huntington, reputedly the finest in town. We have engaged the successful Jack Riley for the remaining races, and we agreed that Sheik must have a full-time guard from now on.

"We are off in the morning, and I will be relieved to go. You can keep your 'Gracious South.' The enclosed clipping is all the 'gracious' you could ever want.

"I shall write again soon, and remain,

"Your long-suffering friend,

"Allyn"

Allyn included an article written by J. Victor LeWitte, which had appeared in the *Times Intelligencer* on the morning of the Derby. She sealed it, set the letter aside, and penned her response to the article's sorely injured author:

"Dear Sir,

"A man of your obvious insight into human nature will understand that a woman of my breeding would never pay a gentleman's bills.

"Kindest regards,

"Allyn Cameron"

Chapter Ten

First class was a far cry from coach, Bert reflected, resting his hands behind his head as he leaned back in his seat. A reserved parlor compartment for himself and Allyn in the front car from Louisville to Baltimore had cost three times as much as the longer trip from Rapid City, but it had been worth it. It was far better to relax in the plush seats and roomy solitude, he had quickly discovered, than to contend with the masses in the crowded, uncomfortable coach cars. Besides, what was a few more dollars? Allyn was content to indulge herself in as many comforts as possible, and if it was good enough for Allyn's discriminating tastes, it was good enough for him. Besides, he had reaped a handsome profit from his wagers in the Derby. He had earned all of these comforts with his hard work and his wise wagers.

Allyn, Bert noticed, was unusually quiet and reserved. She spent most of the first day of the trip staring out of the curtained window into the torrential rain, and was seldom outside their parlor. She was unfailingly polite to him, and she always responded when addressed, but did not offer a single topic for conversation, even if he sat silent, reading or napping, for hours. He did not press. He could see she was not herself, and he fancied he could make a pretty shrewd guess as to why. He wished she would say a word, or look at him, or even cry. Something. It broke his heart to think she was suffering in silence over that fellow, whoever he was. And whoever he was, Bert was certain that Allyn Cameron was too good for him.

It was difficult for him to remain closeted with Allyn, though, especially when he realized there was nothing he could do for her. She declined to accompany him to the dining car, electing instead to eat her meals in the parlor. The club car was a welcomed relief to him. It was an exclusively male domain, smoky and alive with raucous laughter. Its contrast to the morose atmosphere of the parlor he shared with Allyn was pronounced. There, he was able to enjoy his pipe, a brandy and free conversation with total strangers who were impressed by his English accent and his free hand with his Derby spoils. When Allyn had retired for the evening of the first day of travel, he returned to the club car for just such relief.

A fine cognac warming in the glass in his hand, Bert wondered about Allyn and the mysterious, red-haired stranger he had seen embrace her in Louisville. Neither she nor Missy had ever made any mention of him throughout his comparatively brief association with the two women. He had heard an occasional whisper linking Allyn to some dark, unforgivable offense, but he had disregarded it as vicious gossip. Still, it did explain why Allyn, by any measure an attractive woman, seemed to demonstrate no real romantic interest in anyone, not even the enormously likable Bill Boland, whom she planned to marry. The poor girl had already lost her heart to a rogue. He stared into the rich amber liquid in his glass, shaking his head.

"I'm told sudden wealth can have that effect on people, Bert."

A black Stetson preceded the fit figure of Joshua Manners into the booth Bert had occupied by himself. Startled but pleased, Bert sprang up, offering his ex-roommate his hand.

"By God, Joshua, it's good to see you! What in bloody hell are you doing here? Sit down, and give me the pleasure of buying you a drink."

Thanking him, Joshua did sit down.

"What were you pondering just now?" Joshua wanted to know, a conspiratorial grin widening his already wide mouth. "You looked like Aristotle contemplating the bust of Homer."

Bert chuckled, not certain of who Aristotle was, and only a little familiar with Homer.

"Just as you said. Sudden wealth. Last week a poor slob of a ranch foreman on holiday in Louisville. This week riding first class with the finest damned cognac. Rather like a fairy tale, wouldn't you say?"

Joshua agreed. "Plenty of interesting ways to spend wealth in Baltimore as well. I know of some fine— well, let that rest for the moment. How is Miss Cameron reacting?"

Bert guarded his response. "Oh." He waved his hand, the one with the pipe in it. "Taking it in stride. Not hard for a woman to accustom herself to money, eh? Now tell me, my friend, what the devil are you doing here?"

The younger man bit his lip with a self-shaming grin. "Still looking for employment, I'm afraid." He ordered a brandy from the white-jacketed waiter.

"Lose much in the Derby?" Bert grinned conspiratorially.

"On the contrary." Joshua winked at him. "Maybe that's why I'm going on to Baltimore. Another payoff like that and I can retire. Still, one must do something with one's time, I suppose."

In the lull which followed, the waiter returned with the brandy. Joshua nosed it. "Was Allyn all right after the incident at the Downs?" he asked.

Bert was startled by the question. He was not comfortable discussing his friend and employer with Joshua Manners. Allyn, he knew, professed to neither like nor trust the man. He himself was disposed to liking him, but Allyn's convictions left him ambivalent.

"She's been a bit—I think she blames herself," he answered, careful not to betray his own musings. "But other than that, she's fine. She's a—she's quite a lady. I have great respect for her."

"I can tell," his companion offered. "She's very lucky to have such a devoted friend." He lifted his glass, and Bert felt his scrutiny. "To devoted friendships."

Bert acknowledged. "To undying friendships," he countered, signaling for the bottle.

Allyn lay awake in her berth, comforted by the ceaseless rocking of the train. Weary as she was, she could not chase the images from her mind. Images of Raif as he had appeared in Louisville. A veritable devil in white. Of herself, desperately trying to maintain her composure, and her dignity, in her ruined gown before Joshua Manners at Churchill Downs. Images of Bill Boland, whom, she was surprised to discover, she could barely recall at all.

She no longer had any perspective on her upcoming marriage. The reappearance of Raiford Simms had negated any clarity or sense she had ever made of it.

161

In the long dormancy of their relationship, gradually the hurt had worn away. The fire of the love she had borne for the scoundrel had been reduced to embers. Just when she had begun to think herself over him at last, back he had blazed like a raging bonfire, and she had been blinded, and burned, by the flame. Blinded, but not quite thoroughly enough to keep her from thwarting his scheme to steal Sheik. But—but he had nearly succeeded.

Even alone in the berth, she blushed with shame at that knowledge. Bill Boland was a hundred times the man her former lover was. Bill was a fine, decent, honest man who would love her and treat her with respect and honor, perhaps even more than she deserved. Bill was a man whose lowest, meanest thoughts could not match Raif's most noble ones for sheer snakery.

But she did not love Bill. She loved Raif. How convenient it would be if only she could transfer all of the intense passion she felt for Raif, the maggot, to Bill Boland. Life, she decided, and love were unfair. And frustrating. And she was powerless to change either of them. If only Raif would change, she thought wistfully. If only he were able to love her as she loved him. But that would never happen. Not now. She was sure of it, and that reality was almost more than she could bear.

How could she care for that blackguard, who cared for nothing but his own gain? She loved him, and hated him because of it. But now, thanks to Raif, she was forced in addition to confront the reality of marrying a man whom she was certain that she could never love.

Allyn was already in the parlor by the time Bert managed to stir himself the next morning. She sat with a board across her lap and, he guessed, another lengthy letter to Missy. She smiled more brightly than she had since they'd left Louisville, and he felt comforted in spite of his headache.

"Good morning, love!" he greeted her, slipping into the parlor. "Feeling better today, are we?"

"I am," she admitted. "Of course, I can't speak for you."

He chuckled ruefully. "I'm all right. Drank a bit too much cognac for my own good last night."

She smiled in understanding and resumed her writing.

Bert debated his next question.

"Allyn," he began, taking his seat across from her. "Who was that fellow at the Downs?"

She stopped writing, but did not look up.

"His name," she said after a time, in a low, deliberate voice, "is Raif . . ." She hesitated. "Raiford Simms."

Bert digested this with the sensation that he wanted to learn more but was afraid of what she might tell him. As though he were impelled to witness the carnage of some grotesque accident.

"You never mentioned him."

It was a prodding remark, he knew, and yet he could not stop himself. Allyn offered a faint, whimsical smile, her eyes vacant. She looked away.

"Raif—was long gone by the time you came to us." There was a long pause. "He worked for Missy on the ranch." She sat very still. "We had—we were lovers." She looked out of the window again, biting her lower lip. "He went away."

He dared not ask more. He felt deeply ashamed that he had asked at all.

"I—I'm sorry."

There was silence in the small room, except for the relentless sound of the wheels beneath them.

"I'm sorry too," she breathed. Suddenly she looked at him, her green eyes as defiant and bold as he had seen them in Rapid City, at the Steeplechase.

"Now you know, Bert. There's more truth than fiction to all of the whisperings about me back home."

Her stare compelled him to look at her, and he prayed he did not look as mortified as he felt. He wanted to be sick, desperately. He found himself remembering isolated moments with her, with Missy, with the ranch hands and townspeople, and pinning this new knowledge into each scene. He had a horrifying thought, and before he could stop himself, he blurted out, "Does Bill know?"

She looked appalled at the question. He was appalled at having asked it.

"The only people who know are Missy, myself, and you. And Raif, of course." Her voice was hard, like the white marble at the Filsons'.

The small room was stifling and unbearably hot. He wanted some fresh air. And he wanted not to know what she had just told him. She smiled suddenly as if she knew what he was thinking. It was a most disturbing expression.

"Have I disappointed you, Bert?"

Did her voice shake, or did he only imagine it?

"Allyn," he managed, his throat tight. "You can never disappoint me. I only disappoint myself."

He excused himself, appalled and ashamed by his reaction to her words, knowing that their relationship would never be the same.

Allyn dozed for a time. In the late afternoon the train made a stop in Morgantown, a small town in West Virginia. Bert excused himself to visit a tobacconist, and Allyn decided to check on Sheik, and to post the letter she had written to Missy.

The first mission was completed to her eminent satisfaction. Sheik was being treated in a manner befitting his name and rank on this trip to Baltimore. Thanks to his earnings in the Derby, the thoroughbred was enjoying a car all to himself and the company of two armed, loyal, and very well-paid guards. Satisfied that the thoroughbred was in good hands, she made her way back along the busy platform toward the post office.

She was startled, and somewhat alarmed, to see the all-too familiar figure of Joshua Manners among the crowd, stretching his long legs and idly lighting one of his long cigars. His presence there could only mean one thing: He was headed for Baltimore, as she and Bert were. But why? she wondered, watching him take a long draw on his smoke. She realized suddenly that she was tucking her hair into place, and she immediately felt foolish. She didn't even want to see the man, much less to impress him. But the post office was beyond him. With sinking heart, she realized the only possible route would take her right past him. Gripping the letter firmly in her right hand, she took a deep breath and moved forward. If she cut him a wide berth, it was possible he would not see her, or that she could use the shield of the milling crowd to ignore him if he called out to her.

She edged her way along the farthest side of the platform, where the people seemed all to be going in the opposite direction. Staring straight ahead, she struggled forward.

"Miss Cameron!" She heard his clear baritone behind her. She tensed and continued, determined not to look around. Suddenly someone slammed into her hard, from behind, knocking the letter clear from her grasp.

"Oh!" she cried, and turned back to retrieve it.

She watched helplessly as the small white rectangle was kicked along, unnoticed by the milling crowd. Allyn stammered excuse-mes and beg-pardons as she chased after it, reaching for it, watching it elude her grasp each time. At last it came to rest, and her hand closed upon it at the same moment as a well-manicured hand she recognized with deep chagrin.

Neither hand relinquished hold as the joint possessors of the letter straightened.

"Good afternoon, Miss Cameron."

Joshua Manners again. His wide, smiling mouth seemed to divide his angular face, and his dark eyes sported their perpetually amused expression. She cast her gaze down, feeling a blush toast her cheeks annoyingly as she grasped her share of the letter more firmly.

"Good afternoon, Mr. Manners," she managed, although her throat had constricted.

She had intended to take her letter and flee, but he held it fast.

"You were about to post this, I believe," he said easily, in an annoying, urbane tone. "Pray, allow me."

With a quick jerk, he pulled the dispatch from her trembling fingers.

"There's really no need to—"

"But it's no trouble, Miss Cameron!" he assured her, slipping her hand deftly into the crook of his arm. "No trouble at all."

There was laughter in his voice. She wished she had not ventured out of her parlor. There was no place to run from him, no way to evade him. She was obliged to walk with him to the post office, her arm in his. As they gained the steps, she tried again to free herself.

"Thank you, Mr. Manners. I'm sure I can mana—"

"Yes, yes, I know. You can manage quite well, thank you. You've been telling me that since we first met. And I do believe you can. But haven't you ever allowed anyone to do something nice for you, just because they wanted to?"

"Of course, I have!" she retorted, then could have bitten off her tongue for answering him so hastily.

"There." He sounded satisfied by her admission, and she hated herself for giving him such an opportunity. "I thought so." He held the door for her. "After you."

She was forced to look at him, although she would have given anything to avoid it. She was surprised to find that he was smiling with his overly wide mouth, but his dark eyes were surprisingly sober. She continued to watch him, nonplussed, as he posted her letter. It was so small a gesture really. And yet she could not deny that there was something very gallant about the manner in which he performed it. Quickly she mastered herself. Joshua Manners was not to be trusted, she scolded herself, monitoring his bold, swaggering stride as he returned to her side. What did the man mean by going on to Baltimore anyway?

"There," he said again, smiling at her, his quest fulfilled. "Bert has told me that you are an avid correspondent. An admirable quality indeed."

She felt a scowl steal across her face. He was employing that familiar cosmopolitan tone of his again, the one she despised for its condescension. Why was it that whenever she began to think Joshua Manners was being nice, he would always spoil it with that infuriating air of disdain?

He offered his arm again, and when she did not immediately take it, he assisted her. She thought it useless, if not impossible, to fight him. The platform was beginning to clear as the passengers re-boarded. He led her back to the train in as leisurely a fashion as if the engineer himself were waiting on his whims.

"I wonder, Miss Cameron," he said at the very steps of the first-class car, "if you would give me the pleasure of your company at dinner this evening. I know you are burning to discover my reasons for going on to Baltimore, and since you are too well bred to ask, I would like to volunteer my story."

He assisted her in, and she considered the merits of such an interesting invitation as he escorted her to her compartment. She administered her most charming smile upon him.

"What a kind invitation, Mr. Manners." She expressed her delight silkily. "I would be pleased to accept. You may come for me at seven-thirty."

He nodded in acknowledgment. Allyn relished the triumphant smile on his handsome features. Unexpectedly, he lifted her hand to his lips and kissed it, not taking his eyes from hers. She was too startled even to blush.

"Until this evening."

The suave baritone became low and shockingly, sinfully intimate. She responded to it outwardly with a nod and a half-smile while inwardly her chest became tight. She watched him stroll along the car in his arrogant gait, swallowing several times. She smiled to herself, slipping into her parlor and planning the engagement.

A basket filled with spring flowers met her eyes as she entered, and Manners was temporarily forgotten. There was a card in prominent view. She opened it and read:

"Although you have no need of my good opinion, you have it nonetheless."

It was signed by Bert.

Bert was happy to forgo Allyn's company at dinner when he learned the reason for her desertion. He was pleased at the notion that his two friends might at last come to terms. When Joshua knocked at seven-twenty-five, he saw Allyn out and wagged a finger at them both.

"Now don't leave me alone for too long," he cautioned them good-naturedly, and received smiles for an answer.

Manners, as usual, looked impeccable in his jet-black dinner jacket. He offered her his arm with the words, "I shall certainly have the honor of dining with the most beautiful woman in the room."

Allyn met his smile with a self-deprecating one of her own. "I hardly think so." She enjoyed her ambiguous remark nearly as much as she grudgingly enjoyed his compliment.

Heads turned as the duo made their way to a table in the corner, where a waiter stood at the ready. Joshua held the chair for her, which she accepted with a smile. He took his place across from her, and she relished the look of self-aggrandizing complacency on his smoothly shaven face.

"Shall we have wine? Or champagne?" he inquired, his sable eyes perusing the wine list.

"Champagne, please," she answered promptly. After the waiter departed with the order, he tilted her an inquisitive look which highlighted his boyish good looks.

"Miss Cameron, you amaze me," he declared with a lopsided smile of wonder. "I didn't half-expect that you would actually accept my invitation, and yet here you are. Do you make a practice of ambushing people that way?"

She smiled back. Now? she wondered. No. Not yet.

"I have been told that, yes."

He dismissed the notion with a wave of his hand. "I'm being unfair. I did not invite you to ask questions of you. I told you this afternoon that I would explain to you my reasons for going on to Baltimore and the Preakness."

Now.

"Mr. Manners," Allyn began lightly, her hands trembling under the table. "Frankly, I don't care why you are going on to Baltimore. I simply came here this evening to thank you for your kind attention in Louisville

169

at the Medfords', and at the Filsons' on the eve of the Derby."

Her voice was growing in intensity, but she could not help it. She stood up, jarring the table as she did so. She paused, delighting in the look of shock on his undeniably handsome features.

"But most of all, for your adjustment of the seating arrangements that evening. And of course, I would not want to forget those lovely roses. Tell me, however did you manage to find ones with such oversized thorns?"

Her only regret over the scene, which silenced the small but crowded dining car, was that she could not see the look on his face as she swept through the car and out of the door back to the first-class compartments.

Chapter Eleven

Allyn took an instant liking to Baltimore, Maryland. Even more than in Louisville, civilization made its presence felt in the lovely brick houses standing in neat rows, scrubbed marble steps, and cobblestone streets crowded with the traffic of cabs, buggies, wagons, and coaches. She was delighted, almost frightened, to see a horseless carriage rattle past them as their cab drew near to the Huntington Hotel. There was a stability about Baltimore, an air of long establishment. She was reminded, with a twinge of homesickness, of Philadelphia.

Bert had promised he would see Sheik safely escorted to the stables at Pimlico and arrange for security there. The foreman had been most distressed at her revenge on Joshua Manners. Neither Bert nor Allyn had mentioned him again during the trip, although Allyn knew Bert spent much time with him in the club car. Without a doubt, Allyn thought with a mixture of relief and regret, Joshua Manners would not trouble her again after her performance in the dining car.

It had been, she knew, quite possibly the rudest thing she had ever done, and she was disappointed to discover that she had not enjoyed her revenge as much as she had expected to. In fact, she felt rather ashamed. He had been so nice, after all . . . But he had engineered the fiasco in Louisville, she reminded herself. Otherwise, why would he have sent that note with the roses? Only the most arrogant of rogues would have confessed to such a deed in so bold a fashion.

It was the half-hour ride through crowded, noisy streets and a variety of neighborhoods that convinced Allyn that she would be able to resume her care of Sheik free from public censure. Any city this big, she reasoned, would surely not concern itself with the activities of one insignificant person, even if that person happened to own the most popular thoroughbred on the spring circuit.

The doorman helped her alight and red-jacketed porters whisked away her luggage, which had increased since her departure from Rapid City. Aside from caring for Sheik, shopping was one of her favorite activities. As she mounted the broad marble steps she was glad to be on solid ground again after three days on a train. All she wanted was a warm bath, bed, and a chance at the Preakness a week and a half away, with no further intervention by Joshua Manners and no further attempts against Sheik.

Joshua Manners. Bill Boland. Bert. Raif. All men. Only one woman in her life wielded as much, if not more, power over her, and that was Missy, thousands of miles away. There was no question, she reflected later as she lounged in the bath, that it was a man's world. And so far, she thought with more than a little pride, she had succeeded well enough.

Two more hurdles: the Preakness and, in New York, the Belmont Stakes. The dark comfort of her room enveloped her like a lovely cocoon, and she yielded to the canopy bed to woo sleep.

She did sleep soundly for a while. She awoke, however, to darkness with no clue as to the hour. Afterwards, she tossed fitfully on the soft, oversized bed, listening to the night sounds in the cozy, dark room. Carriages rolling on cobblestones below her window. A far-off police whistle; the clanging of a distant fire bell. Even when she did sleep, she dreamed that she was awake, staring about the dark, strange room, realizing she was homesick. She longed to sit out in her old chair and stare at the immense, purple Dakota sky in evening. Spring would be bolder by now, she realized. She wondered if the family of bluebirds had returned to nest under the eaves of the ranch house.

She found herself aboard a ship in a dream, sailing across the range, listening to the sound of the oars in their oarlocks. Then she awakened suddenly, starting in the darkness. Was that her door rattling? She roused herself reluctantly to check the lock. Must be careful, she thought. She stubbed her toe as she stumbled barefoot through the pre-dawn light to the door of her room.

It was locked fast. In the middle of a sigh of relief, she saw it.

A long, white envelope lay just inside on the floor, as though it had been pushed in from the hallway. It was unmarked. It had probably been Bert, she decided, who had come in late, discovered that she was asleep, and slipped her a message. With clumsy, groggy movements she lit a lamp and tore open the envelope.

173

Carole Howey

"My darling Allyn,

"It was so nice to see you again in Louisville, but
we had so little time to share. You ran off in such a
rush that you did not hear what I had to say.

"Ours was a warm relationship, and a discreet one.
If Sheik should enter the Preakness, it will be private
no longer. The price of my silence is the unconditional
delivery of Sheik to me. I will contact you soon."

It was not signed, but Allyn knew who had written
it. The letter fell from her hands, and she ran to vomit
in the water closet.

The sun was high. Allyn waited in quiet reflection on
the divan, where she had been since early that morning. She had not gone to Bert directly. The foreman
was rooming with Manners again, this time by his
own choice, and she had no wish to share this dis-
tressing turn of events with the mercurial Marylander.
As early as it was practical she had sent a messenger
to their rooms, with the request that Bert call upon
her as soon as possible. That had been over an hour
ago. She waited, not patiently, but brooding, in the
same position. She was afraid of what she might do
if she moved.

She opened the note and read it for the fifth time,
and this time she was able to restrain her stomach.
Unconditional delivery of Sheik to Raiford Simms.
The price of his silence. He'll cause you trouble, Missy
had warned her long ago. But she had not bargained
for this sort of trouble. She put the note aside again
and stroked the mohair bolster with an idle finger.

In a calculated, detached way, she reviewed the
several possibilities in her mind, none of them including the sacrifice of the thoroughbred. If Raif was
true to his awful word, and she saw no reason for
him not to be, the headlines of the *Baltimore Sun*
would blaze with reports of Allyn Cameron, a scarlet

woman who moved in fashionable circles and raced a prominent thoroughbred. She would be publicly censured, socially ostracized, and perhaps forced to withdraw from the Preakness. In no time word would get back to Rapid City, and she would be finished. There, at least. It would verify what the town had long suspected. The only way to prevent Raif from destroying her life was to give him Sheik, or to kill Raif before he could make good on his threats. But before she could kill him, if she could kill him, she would have to find him.

Another answer, she realized grimly, was to wire Missy. To go home now, and let Missy and Bert take Sheik through these remaining races. She thought about going home, in the light of this new and horrifying day, and she was not homesick. Thoughts of home brought visions not of peace and quiet. The ranch was infernally quiet. Rapid City was tediously peaceful. Home engendered thoughts of return to the sameness of everyday life, where Bill Boland waited to put his brand on her. Where excitement was something one read about in the papers.

Excitement? She sniffed at the notion. Did so ribald a blackmail qualify as excitement? As hard as she thought, she could think of nothing she would not relinquish for the sake of her reputation, with the single exception of Missy's prized thoroughbred. Sheik alone was too incorruptible to be sacrificed to such a shabby rogue as Raif. And for so shabby a cause as her reputation.

A few stray tears ventured down her cheeks. How long must she be called upon to answer for one sweet mistake? she wondered bleakly. And in how many different ways? You must play the game, Bert had told her in Louisville. Even if someone, some man, decides to change the rules in the middle of play. And the stakes.

A knock brought her back to reality. Quickly blotting away the branding tears, she called softly, "Who's there?"

"It's me." It was Bert's voice, quiet but untroubled.

"The door is open."

Bert strode into the room with the vitality of a man half his age, looking fresh and robust from a solid night's sleep and ready to tilt at the new day. He was brought up short, she supposed, by her countenance, which must have been a stunning contrast to cause so abrupt a reaction.

"What is it, love?" he asked, closing the door behind him. "I'd better not stay long, or there'll be talk."

"I wouldn't worry about that," Allyn remarked in a strained voice.

Bert's features registered puzzlement. He approached the sofa in a more cautious step and watched her extend the letter to him. He looked from the paper to her face, and back again. Then he took it from her, just before her hand began to tremble.

Allyn inclined her stare out of the long window, steeling herself against Bert's inevitable reaction. Clenching her teeth against the impending sympathy which threatened to reduce her to tears again, she concentrated instead on the muffin-vendor's song in the street. Thus, she lost track of how long it took Bert to comprehend the note and its implications. The next thing she felt was the pressure of his fleshy hand gripping her shoulder. She closed her eyes.

"Raif," he said, his voice quiet.

She nodded in reply, not trusting herself to speak.

"Well," he began briskly, seeming to sense her mood. "Bloody unchivalrous, I'd say. What do you think?"

Allyn left her seat and moved to the window to

escape his undisguised pity. "What I think is irrelevant." She feigned a cool demeanor. "What will I do? That's the real question. Bert, what can Raif do with Sheik anyway?"

Bert frowned. "With Sheik alone, nothing. But with Sheik and the papers—well, the same as you. Race him, here and abroad. Stud him, or sell him to the highest bidder."

The very idea made Allyn shudder. She said nothing.

"How much time do you suppose we have?" the foreman inquired after a moment.

Allyn shrugged, taking the letter from his hands. "If I were Raif, I would work fast and get out. With that in mind, I have already drafted a telegram to Missy, which I wanted you to see before I sent. If she comes here and I go home—"

"He will pursue you," Bert argued, meeting her gaze with a determination which startled her. "Unless he is faced, and stopped, here and now in Baltimore, that man will harass you all of your life. If not with Sheik, then with money, or something else."

There was a bitter edge to his voice, and his countenance was thoughtful and calculating. She appreciated his practicality.

"Stopped? How?" she asked. "The only ways to do that are to give him Sheik, which would only satisfy him temporarily, or kill him. The first is unthinkable. The second impossible, unless we find out where he is hiding."

Something in Bert's probing gaze made her look away again.

"Who'll pull the trigger if we do find him, love? Do you trust yourself?"

She offered up a bitter smile, sensing that he was aware of her torment.

"After this"—she shrugged, shaking her head—"if I

177

could not kill him, I would turn the gun on myself. But of course, if we can't find him, that is another matter entirely. He's managed to stay hidden for three years, Bert." She looked away from her friend, staring out of the window, where an old woman down in the street below had just purchased a basket full of muffins.

"No, I don't think I could pull the trigger," she said at last. There was a sharp, stabbing pain in her breast as she drew a hard breath. "What am I going to do?"

"The only choice I see right now"—Bert, thank heaven, sounded clearheaded and sensible—"is to play along with him. Perhaps he'll make a mistake, and we can deal with him in the open."

Allyn nodded, daring to look his way again. "That seems sound. I wonder . . ."

"What?"

"Does Raif Simms want Sheik for himself, or for someone else?" she mused, staring at the air.

Chapter Twelve

Joshua Manners worked very hard all afternoon, but his work never took him beyond the confines of the hotel club room. He settled back into a red leather wing chair and extracted a long, thin Havana from his solid-gold cigar case, reflecting on the acquaintances he'd renewed during the afternoon and the varied and interesting offers he'd promised to consider over the next few days. And consider he would. When he was not ruminating on his most recent disturbing encounter with Allyn Cameron.

Much as he hated to admit it, his pride still smarted when he recalled the outrageous spectacle of her exit from the dining car on the train. He had made up his mind to abandon his campaign on the spot, but had discovered, to his dismay, that Allyn Cameron would not be abandoned so easily. Consequently, he'd found himself inviting Bert Emmet to share his Baltimore accommodations. Bert was good company, but his greatest value to Manners was his close tie to the

Carole Howey

monumentally exasperating Miss Cameron.

Bert entered the club room looking, Manners thought, both weary and relieved. He waited until the stocky Britisher looked in his direction, then issued a brief wave. The older man approached, his beery face relaxing into a grin. Like everyone in this exclusively male domain, he wore a suit and a tie and highly polished black dress boots, demonstrating that he had not been out at Pimlico with Sheik. He sank into the chair opposite Manners's own with a big sigh, which suited his stocky frame. Manners signaled for a waiter.

"Allyn have you chasing all over town?" he asked by way of greeting, nosing his own brandy.

Bert grimaced. "I believe we visited every bloody milliner, hosier, dressmaker, and bootmaker between here and the Chesapeake," he sighed, fingering his collar. "Women do love to spend."

Manners nodded his agreement while Bert made a request of the waiter, who bowed and left.

"How about you?" Bert went on. "Any luck?"

There was a false note in the buoyancy of Bert's accented tones, and Manners found himself scrutinizing his friend.

"As a matter of fact, yes," he answered, keeping his voice light. He did not want to talk about himself just now. He wanted to learn what was behind Bert's veil of casual joviality. But he suspected he could not come right out and ask and receive a forthright reply. After a leisurely sip of brandy, a long draw on his cigar, and a moment of watching Bert fidget as he looked about the crowded room for who knows what, Manners spoke again.

"Baltimore suits me. After five years in the Dakotas, I look forward to a little civilization: paved streets, running water, and whores that bathe every day. I like a woman to smell like a woman. What do you

180

say, Bert?" He gave his friend a reckless grin and slapped his arm with the back of his hand.

Bert's alacrity faded to a deep sigh of relief. "I was hoping you'd remembered your promise," he breathed, mopping his brow with his sadly rumpled handkerchief. "I certainly feel in need of some, uh, diversion. Allyn's up napping, and . . ."

He stopped short, his features clouding again. This time, Manners could not help remarking upon his expression.

"And what?" Manners prodded, scrutinizing the older man while maintaining his air of casual interest. "Come on, Bert. Out with it."

Bert looked away, apparently wrestling with a demon or two. He did not, Joshua noted with interest, chuckle or appear sheepish. This was, to the former Secret Service agent, a sign that it was a matter of some seriousness. He watched, waiting for Bert to respond. Finally the older man met his gaze with veiled grey eyes again, biting his lower lip.

"Damn, I have to break my word," he fairly whispered, his voice low and reedy. "But not here. Let's go for skirt first, and I'll tell you all about it."

Joshua's curiosity crested, and he could barely contain it on the short stroll to a little brownstone on Logan Street. The place was by all outward appearances a tidy, respectable townhouse in a row of others, but the similarity ended there.

Inside was a plush, elegantly appointed parlor paneled in champagne satin and trimmed with crystal mirrors and gold-leaf molding. The furnishings were the finest velvet and mohair of the same hue, and the rugs were nothing short of Aubusson. But these things were not the features that resulted in the place's popularity. More importantly, the gentlemen present, a large number, all equal to the room in the elegance of their attire, had a luscious variety of semi-dressed desirable young womanflesh draped over their arms and across their shoulders like ropes of pearls.

"I say . . ." Bert's awed voice trailed off in wonder. Joshua noticed, with some amusement, his friend's wide-eyed gaze taking in the spectacle.

"Decadent colonials, eh?" he whispered in Bert's ear, just as a lavishly overdressed and pleasingly overweight woman sidled up to him.

"Good afternoon, gentlemen," she murmured, her voice a rich alto laced with an Irish brogue. "What's your pleasure? We're busy, but—"

"We're in no hurry," Manners said with polite terseness. "I understand Lucille and Priscilla are still here. We'd like to pay our respects. But that can wait. First, brandy. And a place where we can talk, and enjoy the scenery."

He slipped the woman a bill and she nodded to him vigorously, licking her rouged lips.

"Oh, my," he heard Bert murmur beside him as the woman sashayed off to fulfill his request, gesturing for them to follow.

The room to which she led them might at one time have been a dining room, but now it was set up with a carved oak bar which ran along one wall and several small mahogany tables, each with a pair of leather wing chairs, not unlike those in the hotel club room. She ushered them to a table that afforded them some privacy, and took the hats they offered to her. Joshua watched in some amusement as the woman's smoky, kohl-rimmed eyes traveled up and down his friend's short, stocky frame. Bert seemed embarrassed, yet pleased by the attention.

"Best whorehouse in Baltimore," Joshua remarked after the woman left them alone. A Negro waiter produced a bottle of fine old brandy and two glasses, then withdrew as the men sat down at the table.

"What's on your mind, Bert?" Joshua began, keeping his tone light and politely interested as he uncorked the bottle and poured the aromatic amber beverage. "We may as well discuss it now. I have the feeling we'll be too busy to talk about it later."

Bert grimaced, holding his brandy snifter in his two hands as if for warmth against a sudden chill.

"Allyn wouldn't want you to know," the older man began in a halting way, looking uncomfortable. "And not only because she doesn't trust you. I don't doubt she'd rather die than let you or anyone else hear it, especially after the way she treated you on the train. But damn me, this has gotten out of hand."

Without prompting, Joshua drew his chair closer to Bert's for secrecy. The backdrop of chatter made a suitable cloak for the impending conversation. Joshua surveyed his friend with an alarm he tried not to show. Spunky Allyn Cameron would rather die? The news must be grim indeed.

"Allyn received a blackmail note this morning, under her door. It seems she—ah—had an affair with an indiscreet rogue some years ago. Now the chap is threatening to expose the whole business, unless she turns Sheik over to him, rein, bit, and bridle." Bert shook his head in disbelief. "How Allyn could've gotten herself mixed up with such a rake is beyond me," he continued, but Joshua was only half-listening through the sudden roaring in his ears like distant surf.

Allyn Cameron was flesh and blood after all. Some scoundrel had been the recipient of those loving gazes he had only daydreamed about, and those tender caresses he could only imagine. Some ne'er-do-well had taken advantage of her youth and come back to torment her in her prime, threatening her with that precious jewel so dear to respectable women: her reputation. He frowned. The modus operandi was vaguely familiar.

"Are you listening to me, Manners?" Bert's agitated voice brought his mind back to the present.

"Sorry. What was that last?"

"The man's name is Raif Simms. He made an attempt on Sheik in Kentucky, trying to detain Allyn while—"

"Raiford Simms!"

Bert's alarm at his outburst was real. Manners checked himself, grimacing at his own imprudence.

"Do you know him?" the Englishman asked, incredulous.

"Maybe." Joshua's mouth went dry. "The man I know goes by the name of Red. What's he look like?"

"I—don't—remember," Bert stuttered, looking dismayed. "He did have—rather red hair."

Lightning flashed in Joshua's mind. He deliberately turned his mouth down at the corners.

"Can't be the same man," he muttered, knowing full well it had to be.

Allyn Cameron and Red—Raif—Simms. With what he knew of Governor Mellette's junior operative, it was all too probable. Clenching his fists under the table, Joshua wondered what rewards Mellette had offered the unprincipled scum to acquire the beast in question. Recalling the numerous occasions upon which Simms had bragged of his many and varied sexual escapades, he found himself fitting Allyn Cameron into the sordid picture. He shook his head quickly: He did not want to picture it. There was a knot in his chest even as he thought about it. He tilted his glass and the brandy burned its way down his throat.

Red and Allyn. Closing his eyes, he found the images forming themselves: the alabaster lady and the bronze wolf. The white-clad stranger at Churchill Downs who had held her in his arms, all the while engineering catastrophe . . .

"Gentlemen?"

It was Madam, and she was beckoning the daydreaming Manners and his English friend. Joshua stirred, aware of a disquiet in his stomach which echoed his troubling thoughts. He had, inexplicably, lost his appetite.

"Go on, Bert." He managed a casual tone as he waved his hand at his companion. "I think I'll chew on this information a bit, without distraction. If I'm not here when you're through, I'll just meet up with you back at the hotel."

Bert only seemed distressed for a moment, and soon he was gone. Joshua settled back in his chair and looked around the room, trying to drive away the nagging images which Bert's disclosure had evoked. He watched leering men admire the bevy of sensory treats that were the women of the establishment as though they were cheap but attractive trinkets in a shop window. He knew, quite suddenly, that he would neither gain nor seek solace in that place ever again.

Allyn did not even pretend to sleep. No sooner had she and Bert parted company than she retreated to her room, not to nap, as she had told him, but to slip into her work clothes and run off to Pimlico. It was a short ride by hired cab, no more than half an hour. She was sure there would be more than enough time to slip away and return by dinnertime, to allow Bert some measure of freedom to follow whatever pursuits he cared to. He need not, she reflected, even have to know that she had gone.

Pimlico Raceway was not as grand as Churchill Downs, but Sheik was being treated in a far grander manner than he had been in Louisville. An abundance of funds was largely responsible, but there was a new respect from people these days as well, from track officials right down to stablehands and grooms. Accommodations were similar, but it was obvious to any eye that Sheik was enjoying the fruits of his achievements. Two ostlers tended the vacant stall as the grooms waited idly for Sheik to return from his workout. Pleased and proud of what she beheld, she continued on to the warming track, where her thoroughbred was pounding clay in his usual powerful style. Watching with excitement, she recalled other days when she had ridden the magnificent beast through the fields and roads of home. She remembered Missy's diligence, rearing and breaking the spirited colt.

Sheik was Missy's first experience with a thoroughbred, a flat racer. Her uncle had raised horses for the cavalry, but the army's need had diminished over the years. Missy had always dreamed of breeding and raising thoroughbreds as her father had done, and Sheik was to be the sire of generations of C-Bar-C thoroughbred stock. It was a harsh climate in which to raise flat racers, she acknowledged. But she believed it could be accomplished. Allyn had had her reservations, but Sheik, exceptional as he was, gave her hope. And Missy, having learned her craft well at her father's hands, knew what she was doing.

The chocolate thunderbolt hurtled down the home stretch, pummeling the clay into dust. The run-out brought horse and rider to a halt in front of her. Jack Riley, the taciturn little jockey, scowled at her in greeting. His attitude about women and racetracks had not changed since Louisville.

"Looks as if he's favoring that right hind leg a little bit, Jack," she cautioned the man, observing the stallion's gait. "Let's have a look at it."

Even as the small man alit, Allyn was examining the limb while the placid colt stood steaming. Riley

186

took Sheik's upturned hoof from her hands without comment.

"Where's Emmet?" he asked coldly, without looking at her.

"He isn't here," Allyn responded with deliberate patience.

"I'd as soon wait for him." The tight-lipped jockey dropped the leg unceremoniously.

"And I'd as soon you didn't," she shot back, aware of an intense dislike of the little man. "Mr. Riley, I desire neither your love nor approval, but I do demand that my orders be carried out. Just remember, you are not the only jockey in Baltimore, but this, thank God, is the only Sheik. Now let's take a look at that leg."

"Yes, ma'am." He emphasized her title, then spat a stream of tobacco at her feet.

Despite the chilly wall around the man, Allyn trailed them determinedly to the stable, finding the threat of blackmail invading her thoughts again. Raif was in Baltimore. Perhaps he hung about the stable. Maybe, in fact, he was watching her at this very moment. She shivered and looked over her shoulder.

She would have to wait for his next move.

Don't go anywhere alone, Manners had warned her in Louisville.

And she had come all the way across town without so much as telling Bert where she had gone.

She shook off the feeling of panic that assailed her. Silly, she thought. Nothing will happen. She leaned against the wall, watching the grooms minister to her horse's needs. Sheik's long, silky tail swished from side to side as the brushes massaged him, and every so often his velvety coat twitched over his shoulder or flank. Her arms ached as she thought fondly of the times she had done the job herself. She realized too that if things continued as they had begun, she probably would never have to do it again, unless she chose.

Directing the grooms to look at Sheik's afflicted leg, she turned her attention out into the corral. She was reminded, oddly, of the arrangement in Deadwood, where Joshua Manners had intervened several weeks ago. She could not recall what she had said to him on that occasion, only their second meeting, but she knew it had not been flattering.

What the devil was he doing in Baltimore anyway? She grinned wickedly, remembering what had ensued on the train when he had wanted to explain his presence. Fleetingly she wished she had stayed long enough to hear what he had to say. Of course, she could ask Bert, but then Bert might mistake her interest, and—oh, why bother to tangle things up? Anyway, where Joshua Manners was concerned, she could never be sure of a credible answer.

He had been in Louisville too, despite his earlier remarks to the contrary. She had mistrusted his motives in Deadwood, but now she was no longer certain. Bert liked the man enough to be rooming with him again, and Bert was no fool where people were concerned. She closed her eyes and sighed, pressing her fingertips into the bridge of her nose. It seemed inevitable that their paths should cross, she decided. All she could hope was that there was no hidden evil motive behind the rather boyishly handsome face which smiled too frequently, as though enjoying a private joke.

Sheik's problem proved to be nothing more sinister than a loose shoe. It was corrected immediately, and the afternoon sun was waning as Allyn took her leave of the magnificent stallion.

In a hurry, she was pleased to find a cab waiting outside of the service gate. She climbed in, directing the driver to the Huntington.

It was stuffy in the closed cab, and the windows would not work. The Baltimore climate was humid, and it was warm even for May. Allyn loosened her collar and sat back, closing her eyes.

At half past seven Bert, entirely refreshed, called for Allyn to come to dinner. He knocked softly, lest he attract undue attention, but Allyn did not answer. Thinking her asleep, he knocked louder and called her name in a hushed tone.

No answer.

Panic accelerated in him like new-kindled flame in dry wood. He rattled her door handle and discovered, alarmed, that the door was not locked. He went inside.

The room had been ransacked. Closet doors were open, drawers pulled out with clothing, and other belongings strewn about the room like the wreckage of a hurricane.

And there was no sign of Allyn.

Dread upon him like a wild, preying beast, he ran from the room to find Joshua.

With plummeting heart, Joshua followed his nervous, babbling roommate back to the scene of the havoc.

" . . . left her to nap," Bert was saying, wringing his hands. "What could have . . ."

Joshua stopped listening and examined the scene. To all appearances, it might have been a simple burglary. But this intruder had been looking for something in particular. Allyn herself? No, that was ridiculous. It would take incredible boldness, or incredible stupidity, to attempt to abduct anyone, much less someone as strong-willed as Allyn Cameron, from her own hotel room in broad daylight. It was more likely that the same headstrong woman had gone out on her own, thinking herself immune to the threat of abduction. But where? And what may have happened to her en route?

" . . . and if anything's happened to her, I'll never forgive myself!" Bert finished, near to sobbing.

"Wait for me in the lobby in case she comes in," Joshua told Bert sternly. "I'll be right down."

When he found Bert in the lobby minutes later, the man was pacing the length and breadth of the immense Persian rug in poor concealment of his apprehension.

"Where were you?" the foreman demanded in a hushed voice.

Joshua gave him a reproving glance to mask his own unease. "Getting my protection," he replied as he led the way outside.

Bert looked bewildered until Joshua patted a bulge at his side. His service revolver, he had discovered early, was a remarkable insurance policy. He hailed a cab, and they made for Pimlico with all possible speed.

The racetrack steamed in the dusk, cooling from the unseasonable heat of the day. The odor of horse-flesh and manure was thick, and Joshua found himself wondering again what kind of a woman could endure those conditions for the love of an animal. Crickets were silenced as the men picked their way in a hurried pace across the yards, and the chirping began again behind them as they passed, as though doors were opening before them and swinging shut behind them on creaking hinges. The greater part of him was convinced that Allyn was here, or that she had been here. But the lesser part, the part that was still Secret Service, suspected the worst.

There was a lull in activity around the warming track itself, but the stables buzzed, as much with the large Eastern horseflies as with the evening business of feeding, watering, and grooming. Scanning the path in the darkness for any out-of-place figure that would be Allyn, Joshua grew increasingly anxious as their search yielded no positive results. Their last hope was Sheik's stall, and the information they could get from his grooms.

The lanterns had been lit, and Bert began calling her name in frantic, stentorian tones. He ran ahead, and the grooms and security guard emerged from the stall with confused expressions upon their faces.

Miss Cameron had been there and gone, they said. She had left more than an hour ago. The guard had seen her get in the cab.

Anger and fear fought for preference in Joshua's mind as he pursed his lips in a grimace. How could she be so stupid as to travel about Baltimore as though she were back in that two-horse town she called home? he wondered, wishing he could shake her. Especially after that note!

Further questioning of the grooms yielded nothing. They had not seen, nor could they recall, anything or anyone unusual hanging about that afternoon.

Questioning the cab drivers outside the gate proved fruitless as well. They had just pulled up, and had not been there earlier. Nor did they know who had been there. Clinging to the slim hope that they may have just passed one another, Joshua suggested he and Bert go back to the Huntington to see if Allyn had returned.

It was nine o'clock by the time they got back, and they went straight to Allyn's room. She answered their knock, as serenely as if nothing in the world was amiss. She was slightly pale, Joshua thought, although had he not known about the danger she knew herself to be in, he might not have even noticed.

"Where the devil have you been?" Bert exploded, grasping her arms. "We have been looking all over the city for you!"

"Have you?" She seemed amused. "And me right here all the while!"

Manners said nothing. Looking past her, he could see that her room had been put back in order as though nothing had happened. He scrutinized her, but she did not betray herself with so much as a sigh.

"You went to the stable, though!" Bert scolded her with a shake. Joshua thought he would have shaken her a bit harder. "Why didn't you tell me this afternoon that you planned to go to Pimlico?"

Allyn regarded Bert coolly, and glanced at Joshua as though she wished he would leave.

"Because there's not the remotest hint of a nanny about you." She effected a maddening but passable imitation of Bert's British accent. "Now, what about dinner?"

"I imagine," Joshua interjected dryly, "that you've worked up quite an appetite. Your room was a shambles."

Now she did blanch, but her eyes flashed in anger.

"I'll thank you both to stay out of my room except in the unlikely event that you may be invited!" she exclaimed, all composure vanished. "And I hereby invite you, Mr. Manners, to bow out of my affairs!"

Manners smiled. She was unhurt. "How nice of you to invite me to join you for dinner, Miss Cameron. However I am otherwise engaged this evening. I'll see you later," he said to Bert, and after touching his hat, left the Rapid City contingent to themselves.

"That was uncommonly rude of you, Allyn," Bert chided her darkly after Manners had gone. "That man only means you good. Now just what have you been up to?"

Without a word, Allyn pulled him inside and closed the door.

"I did go to the stable, Bert," she whispered, and he was alarmed to notice that her expression had changed from one of icy haughtiness to honest fear. "And I was"—she hesitated over her next word—"kidnapped."

Bert seized her hands and searched her face. She was trembling, and her hands were like ice.

"I got into a cab, and was taken to some remote place—I've no idea where—and two men ordered me out. They—baited me," she went on, staring at his cravat. "They—they made hideous threats. Then they told me that Raif—Red, they called him—knew where I was and could pick his moment."

"Then?" he breathed, fearing the worst.

"Then," she sighed, "they packed me up in the cab and sent me back here. They said they would contact me soon about Sheik."

"And you're all right?" He held her small, freezing hands tighter.

She nodded as though she did not trust her voice. "You didn't tell Manners about the note, did you?"

"No." Bert felt uneasy with the lie. "But about your room—I'm afraid I became a little frantic when I discovered you weren't here. And that the room had been ransacked. What were they looking for?"

Allyn broke away from his grip. "Sheik's papers, perhaps," she replied, moving toward the window. "Bert, I'm frightened."

His stomach turned to lead.

"So am I, love," he admitted in a whisper.

Chapter Thirteen

High winds and heavy rains altered Allyn's plans the following morning, and meant that instead of escaping to the stables with Bert, or patronizing the shops, she would be jailed in the hotel all day with Bert as her watchdog and endless games of whist and monte. She composed several letters to Missy before breakfast, discarding each one without posting them. She did not wish to relate any of the grim news just yet. Missy was enough of a worrier without providing justification.

She reread her last attempt and found it appropriately bland, uninformative, and dishonest. Each line of it inspired guilt. She was deliberately misleading her friend into thinking that all was well in Baltimore, when in fact nothing could be further from the truth. She prayed that Missy would not detect the lies on the page.

Bert came for her unusually early. She suspected he was afraid that she might try to slip away unless he did, like some truant child. The thought irked her.

The Huntington's breakfast room was crowded, probably because no one cared to venture out into the weather. Allyn requested a table in one of the bay windows which thrust outward into the gray sky and grayer city. It was also isolated from the mainstream, and would provide them with some semblance of privacy.

"Days like this," Bert observed, "bring back boyhood memories of Brighton."

"I thought you spent your boyhood in Paddington," Allyn taunted.

Bert sat down across from her and grinned over the pile of hot biscuits.

"I got around in those days."

Allyn had to smile at him. He was such a character. "I don't suppose you've come up with a plan, have you?" She became serious again as she broached the subject of blackmail.

Bert became thoughtful. "Only one," he admitted, looking away from her.

"Which is?"

Bert inhaled a deep breath, then let it out. "Enlisting the aid of our friend Mr. Manners."

"Out of the question!" she retorted, feeling her cheeks blaze at the very thought. "I won't have him privy to my business, Bert. And I hope I have heard the last of it."

"Not by half, my girl," her British friend fired back, uncharacteristically vehement. "I've learned enough about Manners these last few days to know he's to be trusted, in spite of what you think, and that he's just the man to deal with these scoundrels. Allyn, I wish for once that you would be reasonable. I don't know who put the bee in your bonnet that Manners was a blackguard, but it just isn't so."

Allyn shook her head, feeling a bitter laugh rise in her throat. "What makes you suppose he would even want to help us?" she challenged him, leaning back in her chair. "After the way I've treated him?"

Bert shrugged. "He's a good man, Allyn," was all he said. "I know if we just went to him and—"

"I don't expect you to understand," Allyn interrupted, realizing that she felt weak at the very thought of it. "I want to keep this private. Let's not even discuss—"

"How private do you suppose it's going to be when Simms goes ahead with his plan?" Bert argued, taking his tobacco pouch from his breast pocket. "You won't give up Sheik. You won't withdraw him from the Preakness. And you won't ask for help. Damn it, Allyn, what's left?"

She knew the answer to that. Watching him examine the contents of his pouch, she felt the walls of the alcove pressing in upon her.

Abruptly Bert stood up. "I'm going to the tobacconist," he said in a tone of resignation. "I'll be right back. Don't you budge!"

He was off at a stomping pace.

Not until he had disappeared did she allow herself a heavy sigh. A waiter poured her a cup of coffee with scalded cream, and left the pot. She had been drinking a lot of coffee ever since Louisville, having had some stomach upsets which she had attributed to local water. She was resolved to avoid the beverage unless boiled and brewed. She folded her hands together, bouncing her forefingers against her pursed lips.

Perhaps Bert was right. There was no question that the menace which loomed over them was more dangerous, more imminently disastrous, than anything she had ever faced. There was no question that they needed help. Perhaps, she thought, staring into her cup, they should turn to Manners . . .

Closing her eyes, she tried to conjure an image of the man, and found the memory of his dark, angry eyes in the hotel room in Deadwood. Miss Cameron, he had said then, what are you so afraid of? I think he's magnificent, Missy had said. And how she, Allyn, had humiliated him before all of those people in the dining car! Shaking off those memories, she changed the scene. She was asking for his help, and he was baiting her; demanding to know why she had had a change of heart. What could possibly threaten you so much that you would come to me for help? he would ask. And she would have to avoid those too-bright eyes of his, and tell him.

No. She could not bear it. She would die of mortification. She could not confess her secret to that man. Her face grew hot again, and as she opened her eyes to dispel the vision she had invoked, she felt a rough, bruising hand grip her arm. She was too startled to cry out. She turned to her tormentor, half-expecting to find Joshua Manners himself in possession of her arm. But it was not he.

It was one of the men who had abducted her from the cab. She drew back in alarm, but the large, ugly man held her fast. His strength and purpose froze her with terror and he brought his awful face near hers.

"Get rid of your Limey friend. Red wants to see you tonight." His breath was stifling.

"Red?" she managed weakly.

He twisted her arm in a gesture, she was sure, designed to inflict pain rather than attract attention.

"Raif Simms. You remember him?" The reedy voice became a leer. Allyn cringed. "We'll meet you at Logan and Hughes Streets, at ten o'clock."

A secret meeting. God, did Raif think her that much a fool? She stiffened and tried to pull her arm away.

"I can't possibly—"

"You'd better," he threatened, his fingers now digging painfully into the soft flesh of her arm. "Unless you want to make headlines. Ten o'clock. And bring the nag's papers."

The pain in her arm subsided. He was gone. She wanted to run away, but she was frozen to her chair. The room was growing larger, or she was growing smaller. It was impossible to tell which.

"Friend of yours?"

Joshua Manners, an immaculate contrast to her previous guest in his gray linen suit, sank his six-foot frame into Bert's place. In a languid, compelling gesture, he extracted a cigar from its gold case. Gasping for breath, unable to move or speak, she watched him proceed with the calculated ritual of lighting it.

"No," she managed at last, desperately trying to compose herself. The memory of that man was too fresh, too near. Her heart raced like a runaway train. She reached for her coffee cup, hoping to settle her stomach, but her hand trembled violently, causing the china to rattle. She abandoned her effort and left her hand upon the table like a cast-off glove.

"You look," he went on in that urbane tone which always irritated her, "like a child who's just been caught with one hand in the cookie jar. What could that ugly, wet man have said to you?"

She could not answer him. There was a warm pressure on her hand, the one she had left upon the table. Surprised, she stared at it to find that Joshua Manners had covered it with his own.

"He threatened you, didn't he?" His calm, quiet voice was hypnotic. "What did he tell you?"

The words were upon her tongue. All that remained was to open her mouth, and they would tumble out. She could unburden herself, and deliver the problem to the broad, willing shoulders of Joshua Manners. She would be free, and at peace. Against her will, her gaze traveled up the sleeve of his fine suit, along his shoulder, his angular jaw, and into the unusually serious brown eyes that regarded her keenly, locking her gaze helplessly into his own.

"Why, Joshua! Good morning!"

Bert's voice shattered the spell. Allyn pulled her hand from beneath Joshua's and averted her gaze. It had been a close brush. With salvation, or disaster? She could not be sure which.

Joshua rose to his full height.

"Good day, Bert. Good day, Miss Cameron." The Marylander gave a slight bow, and disappeared from the room.

Bert was unable to persuade Allyn of the folly of her decision to comply with Raif's demand. It was their chance to draw him out, she believed. Consequently, at five minutes before ten o'clock, Bert watched from an alley near the quiet intersection of Logan and Hughes Streets while Allyn waited at the corner, in clear view. In her plainest gray poplin suit, she might have been a menial waiting for an omnibus.

The only bright spot, Bert reflected grimly, was that the rain had finally stopped. The cobblestones glistened, and puddles mirrored the gaslights glowing in pale yellow globes atop black standards along the street.

Bert was certain that this escapade was a big mistake. From his hidden vantage point he was able to survey the entire area, and could be ready to come to Allyn's assistance at any moment. He prayed that everything would work out, although he had no idea how such a coup might occur. The only thing of which he was sure was that if anyone laid a finger on Allyn, he would come out shooting.

He glanced at his pocket watch.

Ten o'clock.

The street remained deserted.

One minute past.

Two minutes past.

Allyn glanced toward the alley, retreat written all over her face.

Three minutes past.

A closed cab clattered on the wet cobblestones, pulling to a halt before her. Bert watched, straining to hear the exchange between the driver and the lady. No one emerged from the cab, and for a moment he thought it might be a false alarm. Then, to his surprise, Allyn reached for the door and, with nary a betraying glance over her shoulder, opened it and climbed inside.

With catlike agility that belied his dimensions, he bounded after her, swinging unobserved onto the baggage rack behind.

It was dark in the cab. The windows were covered with black paper, like a hearse. Allyn did not explore its interior, electing to sit by the door, which she closed firmly. The cab jolted to a start, and she was assailed by panic. What if Bert had been unable to follow her? It was too late to worry. She folded her hands tightly in her lap, hugging the corner, trying to make herself as small as possible.

The journey seemed long and slow, full of turns and pauses. Even had she been familiar with Baltimore, she would not have been able to discover the direction they were taking. Praying that Bert had somehow followed, she willed herself to remain calm. She would need every shred of strength and sanity to get through this night.

She had no idea how long the ride had lasted by the time the cab jerked to its final halt. She reached for the door latch, then withdrew her hand, waiting, challenging someone to instruct her. Presently the creak of old leather and weathered wood crying for oil and the sudden listing of the cab told her that the driver had gotten down. She could detect no other sound or movement.

"Get out." A sharp, unfamiliar voice inside the cab nearly scared her out of her skin, and she wanted to escape proximity to the disembodied voice. She seized the handle again and threw the door open, falling out of the cab and onto the dirty, sharp stones of a dark and cavernous alley. Neither the driver nor the phantom in the cab offered her any assistance as she slowly got to her feet.

"That way." The phantom emerged from the cab behind her and gestured into the black throat of the alley. She still could not see the man's face. She was not even sure she wanted to. She began to comply with the order when suddenly, from some unknown source, she summoned a bit of bravado.

"Just a moment! Who—"

"Move!" the voice snarled again, forcing a hard, blunt object, probably a gun, into her ribs for emphasis.

The bravado was quickly extinguished and she did as she was told, clumsily negotiating the stones in kid pumps. There were two sets of footsteps following her, aiming her toward a dim light at the end of the alley. As they drew closer, the light became a doorway.

The door opened at their approach, as though someone had been watching for them. She wondered, her heart hammering, if it might be Raif himself. Without waiting to be told, she entered the brick building, her captors following close behind her.

The place appeared to be a tack room for a livery stable, or some sort of warehouse. Row upon row of bridles and harnesses hung upon the walls in various degrees of disrepair. Casks and barrels had been put to use as furniture, holding dim and dirty lanterns which afforded an eerie amber light to the stuffy, small room. At one end was an archway leading, she supposed, to another room, but it was too dark to see. Could they have brought her to Pimlico? Her instincts told her no, but there was no way to tell for certain.

"Siddown." A third man emerged from the shadowy archway. He was fleshy and solid, like Bert, and possibly as old. He was also grinning. The expression sent a chill through her.

"Where's Raif?" she demanded, her voice surprisingly calm.

"You'll see him soon enough. Sit down." For emphasis, the man placed a weighty hand on her slight shoulder.

The phantom from the cab swaggered toward her, swinging his leg over one of the barrels to use it as a stool. She could see his face now, and she wished she could not. It was an unpleasant face, scarred and pockmarked, as though the man wore his ugly deeds upon it like proud badges.

"He wanted us to keep you company for a little while," the man began, his dirty, large hand pawing at her cheek. "And get a few things straightened out beforehand."

Allyn jerked her head away from his intentions and glared at him, contempt overcoming her fear for the moment. "Such as?"

"Red knew you'd rather die than be shamed."

Allyn shuddered. Did all of these men know about her and Raif? It appeared so. But that suddenly seemed so trivial, in light of the fact that they now had her completely at their mercy, with no help apparent from any quarter. She realized, all at once, that she would not be allowed to leave here without yielding Sheik as payment. Oh, why hadn't she listened to Bert? To Manners? Pretending to ignore the man's remark, she pursued the question again.

"What 'things' need straightening out?" Her voice was cold and hard as she forced her dread to one side. "I understood this was to be a meeting. I have no intention of relinquishing Sheik."

Her small audience rewarded her with a moment of baffled silence. Then the stuffy room erupted in hooting noises which sounded like grotesque, chortling owls.

"Talks fancy, don't she?" The third man, who had not spoken before, poked his companion the phantom in the ribs with a grisly chuckle.

" 'I don't have no intention,' " the phantom mocked in reply, turning up his flat nose.

"Fools!" she hissed, rising, anger now replacing her fear. "Cretinous imbeciles! I have nothing to say to you. Take me to Raif Simms!"

So I can kill him, she thought, with my bare hands if necessary.

"Red'll see you in his own time, sweetie." The man who had met them pushed her back into her seat none too gently. "Meanwhile, I'd reconsider that attitude, was I you."

"And are the three of you supposed to frighten me into agreeing to the terms?" She mustered a doubtful, haughty tone.

"Well . . ." The man on the barrel stood up and came closer, nursing a leer. "Red gave us a free hand on that point."

There was no mistaking his meaning. Feeling faint with revulsion, she shrank back into her seat.

"Nothin' like a good girl gone bad, I always say. And according to Red, you were some kinda good."

The phantom's voice was reedy with hunger. "How'd you like to give me a taste?"

Shouts from outside distracted him. Allyn breathed again.

"Sounds like Harry's back. Open up!" he barked at the man who had driven the cab, who did not look pleased at the tone of the command, but obeyed nevertheless.

Sure enough, there were more of Raif's men outside. Allyn recognized the first man through the door. It was the same man who had interrupted her breakfast that very morning. She knew the next one as well. Her heart hit the floor. It was Bert, glowering, subdued, and deprived of his side arm. A third man held him at gunpoint. There were now five men, besides Bert, in the stifling room.

Harry, her breakfast visitor, said no word of greeting, but made straight for her with a look that paralyzed her with fear.

"I told you alone!" he bellowed. From nowhere, his hand caught her on the side of her head with a powerful blow, sending her rocketing to the floor.

"You bloody—Allyn! Are you all right?"

Allyn heard Bert's struggle to come to her aid, but she was fighting to remain conscious and could not answer him. Her senses reeling, she was slow to pick herself up from the splintered floor. She struggled to her feet, trying to stop the room from spinning. Feeling nauseous, gasping for breath, she turned in time to catch a curt nod from the phantom, who had taunted her from the barrel, to Harry. The latter, in a swift gesture, pulled a hunting knife from his belt and, with savage force, turned and thrust it into Bert's midsection.

She was compelled to watch. Bert slowly crumpled, his surprised features contorted in pain. The murderer withdrew his weapon, and his hand and sleeve were drenched with blood. Bert's blood. With a cry she moved toward him, but was jerked back by a rough hand on her arm.

"You shoulda played straight with us," the phantom growled. "Harry don't like to be tricked. Dump him in the bay," he ordered the man who had brought Bert in at gunpoint. "You help him, Sy. And get back here plenty quick, or there'll be hell to pay."

Numb with horror, she watched the two men hoist the lifeless, suddenly clumsy form of Bert Emmet over Sy's shoulder, covering him with a filthy tarp. She felt sick.

"We're gonna take a ride to the stable," the phantom was saying as they hauled Bert out of the door. "Red is there now. As soon as you get the nag past your people, we'll take him and the papers, and let you off somewheres out of the way. We'll be long gone before you can talk."

This is where it ends, she thought, still dizzy with horror. The feeling was leaving her legs, like death, and she felt as though she had been in the stifling, stinking room all of her life. She thought of Bert, his life's blood wasted in a watery, unmarked grave. She thought of never seeing his beery face again, and the pain of it almost choked her. Before she could think, she was being trundled toward the archway, beyond which she could now see a closed carriage. She knew that these men had no thought of releasing her, even if she did turn Sheik over to them. She was doomed to follow her luckless friend to the bottom of the Chesapeake.

Impulsively she lunged forward, catching her escort off guard. A few wild, running steps took her near the door before she was tackled to the floor with a force that knocked the wind out of her. Gasping for breath, she clawed the floor and grabbed for a hold as she was dragged backward. Still struggling for air, she brought her hands down and beat upon the head of her captor, now inches away from her face. That act was her undoing.

A second man pinned her arms to her sides, and the two of them jerked her roughly to her feet, cursing and swearing.

"Hellion, this one. Red was right." The words stabbed her. "D'ya think we might . . ." His voice trailed off.

The phantom took a long, leering look at her and rubbed his dirty, unshaven chin with a greasy hand. Allyn squirmed desperately.

"Better not," he advised. "Got too much fight in her for me. I like my women tame."

"She'll tame quick enough when you show her your stuff," the first man argued.

Allyn sent a shin-splitting kick in his direction, and he howled in pain. His cry was abbreviated by a resounding crash on the door. Startled, encouraged, Allyn looked toward it, waiting for the next moment. And in the next moment, a second crash brought a tall, powerful figure into the room whom she recognized at once.

Joshua Manners wasted neither time nor words. With a drawn .45, he encountered no argument.

"Good evening, gentlemen." His urbane, arrogant tone stirred irritation in her. "I'll relieve you of this lady." He motioned to Allyn without looking at her, and the bruising hands fell away. She nearly fell down as they let her go, but she steadied herself.

"Spread-eagle, against that wall." Manners ordered the men to the back of the room, past the carriage.

What the devil was he doing here? Allyn wondered as she watched her former captors comply with Joshua's crisp commands. She could not deny that, once again, she was unutterably grateful for his timely intrusion. She riveted her eyes upon him, aware that she too awaited his next orders.

His self-assurance fascinated her. It seemed to her that he had been handling situations such as this all of his life. His long-fingered hand held the gun with confidence, even after the men were assembled in that ridiculous fashion against the wall.

"Where's Bert?" she heard him ask in a clipped tone. He did not take his eyes from his hostages. It was a moment before she realized he had spoken to her.

"Dead," she heard herself respond, in a tight, unnatural voice that she did not at first recognize as her own. She tried to speak again, to tell him the story. But all she could say was, "Bert's dead."

She fell to her knees. Manners started, glancing at her, trying to determine the extent of her injury. In that moment, one of his captives sprang forward and grabbed his gun arm. Caught unawares, Joshua cursed his stupidity as he landed a left hook on the luckless fellow's jaw. By that time, however, the remaining two had joined the attack.

The gun was knocked from his grasp, and all he could do was hope to keep these two busy enough so neither of them would find it. His advantage was his height and his skill, although weight was a considerable edge for his adversaries. The punches that landed threatened to rob him of consciousness, and that, he knew, must not happen. If he were to lose consciousness, he knew he would never regain it. And Allyn would be as good as dead as well.

One of the two remaining assailants fell with the delivery of an uppercut from Manners's right fist, and did not get up again. Staggering, Joshua swung at the other man, who was already retreating, with only the force of momentum. The man swayed, then toppled, slowly and heavily, like a felled oak. After he crashed, the room settled into an eerie quiet. Manners straightened, breathing hard, wiping a trace of blood from his lip with the back of his hand. He glanced around the room at the prone bodies, briefly thanking his Maker. He looked in Allyn's direction again, and saw that she was pushing herself up on her arms. He crossed the floor on increasingly steady legs and knelt down beside her.

"Are you hurt?" he asked.

Her eyes met his. They were tired eyes which had seen too much that night. There was a sizable bruise on her cheek and temple, but she shook her head. He wanted to lift her into his arms, but he doubted he possessed the strength for such an act at the moment.

"Come on, Allyn," he beckoned her, offering her his hands instead. "We have to get out of here."

To his surprise, she relied on him heavily for support as she stood up. After she made it to her feet, she held his hands, clutching him as though terrified to be left alone. Her green eyes were like a waif's: wide, frightened, and sad. He drew her close to his breast. He had never held her before, he realized, stunned by the power of the emotions she drew from him. Magically, she did not protest. In fact, she buried her head in his chest at once, sobbing "Bert" ever so softly.

She'd watched him die, and she had never seen death until that moment. He knew what that was like. Empathy made him crush her in his arms and croon to her softly, burying his face in her soft, abundant hair.

"It's all right, Aly," he said in a whisper, inhaling the sweetness of her sorrow. "Everything will be all right."

Her sobs quieted, and the shuddering of her slender body ceased. She was, he knew, bringing herself under control. In a moment Joshua felt embarrassment holding her so close, and his arms awkwardly loosened themselves. He found himself wondering how the woman could make a man feel so confident one moment and so callow the next. She pushed him back and his arms fell away from her. In a moment she raised her head and met his gaze squarely, her green eyes emotionless.

"I'm ready, Mr. Manners. Where must we go?"

He felt oddly relieved. She seemed herself again. Formal and remote. Someone he knew how to deal with. He glanced around the room to look for his gun, but more, so he did not have to sustain her gaze.

"Out of here," he told her, unwilling to think beyond escape. "Raif's friends will be back at any time."

He stooped to retrieve his weapon, and as he straightened, he noticed her staring at the floor. Following her gaze, he saw a splash of dark red, like spilled claret, on the floor near where she stood. He saw her catch her breath. Her narrow shoulders shuddered as the pain seized her again, the knowledge that Bert was gone. Murdered. Her eyes met his slowly.

If she looked at him that way any longer, they would never get out of there.

"Allyn," he urged her softly. "We have to go. Quickly."

He took her arm with firm authority.

He pulled her along behind him through the door and up the long, dark alley, and she gave him no resistance. The rest of the Simms contingent, he suspected, would return at any time. He maneuvered her through the narrow passageway, careful to stay in the shadows, keeping his eyes trained on the light from the street lamps ahead of them. He brought his free hand up to his mouth to wipe away fresh blood. Three had been a handful. Two more would be impossible.

Two more would be deadly.

Glancing back at Allyn, he whispered encouragement.

"Hold on, Allyn. We're almost—"

Before the words were out of his mouth he saw not two but four burly silhouettes at the mouth of the alley. He drew Allyn up close behind him and watched, his heart pounding in his chest.

"What is it?" she demanded in a whisper.

"Shh," he advised, not averting his stare.

Chapter Fourteen

The figures idled, seeming to pass time. Perhaps, Joshua hoped, they were merely locals, out for a night of fun. But more likely they were part and parcel of the Simms gang.

They continued to wait at the mouth of the alley. For what? Joshua wondered. His groping hand found a narrow recess, and in he slid, shoulder first, pulling Allyn up close as he looked over his shoulder at the sentries.

The woman wriggled in his firm embrace, and he turned to her, even managing a fleeting grin.

"Stop struggling, my dear," he whispered. "I confess, under other circumstances, I might take advantage of this compromising situation. But things as they are, your honor is quite safe."

He met her angry, frightened stare without smiling. She looked down, unwilling, he guessed, to meet his close gaze. He could sense rather than see her embarrassment. He turned away from her again, peering back up the murky alleyway, saving his amusement

Carole Howey

for a later, more convenient time.

The quartet had sprung to life. Two of them had sauntered into the alley, and were even now only a dozen feet away from where Joshua and Allyn stood. Joshua wanted to escape quietly, without use of force. The predicament offered its own solution.

"Follow my lead," he muttered low to Allyn, and before she could ask him to repeat it, he moved around to press her into the hollow between the dank brick wall and his body. He heard her gasp, and she turned her face away from his.

"Come on, darlin'," he said in an overloud, slurred voice. "D'ya think I brought you out for th' night air?"

Thus did he make the men aware of other presences in the alley. He heard their snickers, and knew he had succeeded. So far. Allyn turned her outraged face toward his, and he knew she was about to protest. Manners, hoping both to preempt her remark and to make the scenario more credible, quickly covered her mouth with his own.

He realized, forcing his kiss onto her sweet, salty lips, that he had never kissed her before. His kiss followed her writhing, futile attempt to free herself from it. It was a kiss hot with the fever of fear rather than desire, and her protest was soon quelled by his persistent, if not desperate, passion. As the sudden light from a lantern made shadows on the wall at her back, his plan was illuminated to her and her resistance ceased. When he was sure she would not cry out, Joshua finally released her from his kiss and turned from her, shielding his eyes and Allyn's face from the intruders with his arm.

"Whatsamatter? Go find your own piece!" he growled in the same loud voice, holding her tighter. The two men—now four, the first two having been joined by their comrades during the commotion—

chuckled in what Manners hoped was misdirected understanding.

"Take her to bed, friend," one of them advised Manners. "A alley's no place for a, uh, lady."

That remark brought guffaws from the party of men. Allyn started to say something, but he stopped her with a look of warning.

Grumbling under his breath, he took Allyn firmly by the arm, careful to keep her faced away from the men, and they stumbled out of the alleyway, free but not yet safe.

The night reached out to them with pawing hands. Allyn stayed very close to her rescuer, a phenomenon Manners found bitterly amusing. It had taken Bert's death to force her to turn to him. A man had had to die, and a damned fine one at that. Suddenly he was angry with her. How dare she gamble with, and lose, another life to her own pride? Her own vanity?

He flitted with catlike agility from corner to lamppost, alcove to gutter, to the end of the block, where his cab waited for them. It loomed before them, a black silhouette, a huge, ebony bird priming for flight. He drew her up and pulled his hand from her grip. He closed his hands around the soft, yielding flesh of her arms, training her wide-eyed, frightened stare to his own uncompromising one.

"You're going back to the hotel. Go to my room. When they know you're gone, they'll be coming to yours. Here's my key." He dangled the object before her like a trinket.

"Your room!" she protested. "But how will that—"

"We're talking about your life! You pick a fine time to start concerning yourself with public opinion!" he told her fiercely, shaking her once for emphasis.

She gulped. Then she nodded. And he knew she was not herself. Well, maybe that wouldn't wear off by the time she got back, he thought, satisfied, and

213

she would follow his directions. He released her and unlatched the cab door.

"Wh—where are you going?" she murmured, her forlorn gaze searching his face.

He regarded her with a softening gaze. Why was she so damned lovely? Of its own accord, his hand reached toward her face, wanting to touch her cheek, to wash away the pain and memory of Bert's murder . . .

He straightened, reminded of his task. "To Sheik."

"But what about Bert?" she sobbed, and he mastered a sudden, almost crippling desire to take her into his arms again.

"It's too late for Bert," he said roughly to overcome the swell of emotion that caught him unawares. "These men want Sheik, and they won't waste any time. Now go, or I may be too late."

She seized his arm. "Let me go with you!" she pleaded then. "I—"

Inexplicably, he wanted to strike her. "We're wasting time!" he exploded. "Get in!"

Allyn lowered her stare and swallowed hard again. She stepped up into the cab with his assistance, and he slammed the door.

"Back to the Huntington," he told the driver, handing him a ten-dollar gold piece for a two-dollar fare. "Day before yesterday."

The driver was gone before the last word was out of his mouth. Manners watched the cab pull away and heaved a sigh of relief.

It was a mile to Pimlico, and he negotiated the distance on foot. As he expected, Red had sentries posted at the front gate, so he detoured around the back and climbed the ten-foot fence designed to keep such as him out. Falling hard to the ground on the other side, he decided his climbing days were over. Sure that there were no internal injuries, he limped unchallenged through the dark toward the row of stalls housing the fabulous but troublesome Sheik.

The stables were quiet. There was a lantern lit at either end of the row. He slipped around the side, his gun drawn, ready for the worst. He heard a click at his ear.

"You'd better have a damned good reason to be sneaking around this stable with a drawn gun, mister."

He relaxed. It was Sheik's guard.

"Would you believe me if I said I did?" he countered, throwing his side arm ahead of him into the circle of light on the gravel.

"Nope," the older man admitted. "Follow that gun and stand over there with your hands up."

Holding his hands obligingly in the air, he did as he was told. Secret Service had trained him well.

"That's far enough. Don't move, if you know what's good for you."

Manners stood in the center of the light, which also encircled Sheik's stall. Craning his neck, he could see that Sheik was safe and sound inside, placidly munching his feed and swishing his voluminous tail. The guard, an older man of rather nondescript plainness, rang a bell that clanged through the compound like gunfire, disturbing the clammy stillness. He regarded his captive with obvious distrust.

"Who's on duty?" Manners asked congenially.

"Shut up," came the gracious response.

Joshua pressed his lips together and waited quietly thereafter. In a few moments, three Pimlico security guards appeared. Manners sighed with relief, recognizing one of them as Dan Hargan, a long-time acquaintance of his.

"Josh Manners!" the tall, rangy Hargan exclaimed upon gaining the stable. "Turnin' horse thief this late in life?"

Manners grinned ruefully, lowering his stiffening arms. "Looks that way, doesn't it?" he agreed. "But no. I'm—Allyn Cameron sent me. She had reason to believe that someone would make a try for Sheik tonight."

"That's why she hired *me*," Sheik's personal guard grumbled, holstering his gun at last.

Hargan frowned. "Now that is funny," he mused, shaking his blond head. "Must be something to women's intuition. As it happens, a couple of fellows've been waiting around the front and side gates since about ten. Said they were expecting Miss Cameron."

"Did they give their names? Are they still there?" Manners fairly leaped at the information.

"They're there, all right. Or they were last we left there."

"I saw the men out front," Joshua informed him. "Let's take a walk to the side gate. I want to have a look at them."

Leaving Sheik and his guardian with an additional sentry, Joshua went with Dan Hargan.

Approaching the side gate through darkness gave the duo an advantage. The two men who waited outside stood in the fringes of the lamplight. Joshua was satisfied that Raif Simms was one of them. With a restraining hand he halted Dan and addressed him in a hushed voice, his stare trained on Raif.

"Have you ever seen them before tonight, Dan? Especially the carrot-top?"

Dan shook his head, not moving his gaze from the pair, as though making sure of his answer.

"Nope. But that don't mean nothin'. I'm only here at night. Do you know him?"

Manners did not answer him right away. He was remembering a moment in Louisville, not long ago, when he had last seen the red-haired man who was at this moment trimming his fingernails with a hunt-

216

ing knife. In Louisville, the man had been wearing a white suit, a carefully groomed mustache, and a woman in white who had melted in his embrace. Now the same man wore blue jeans, a Stetson like his own, a dark green kerchief around his ruddy neck like an outlaw, and no loving woman whom he had betrayed. Manners bit his lip, ruing the fact that he had not recognized his former subordinate then and there, and trying to comprehend the kind of a man who could love such a woman and then torment her with it. Had Dan Hargan not been there with him, standing by his shoulder, he would have taken great pleasure in putting a bullet through the miscreant.

"Yes, I know him," he replied finally, still not taking his eyes from Raif. "You'd do us a service if you'd give me back my gun and let me approach them. Miss Cameron would be very grateful."

"I'll do more than that," Dan assured him in the same whisper. "I'll cover you from here."

Joshua appreciated the support, even though he suspected that it meant that Dan doubted his word. Holstering the gun, which Dan had returned to him, he sauntered toward the gate a few yards away, making no further pretense to secrecy.

Raif and his man looked up at the sound of his approach. Manners had an idea of the kind of reception he would receive from these men, and it would not be a warm one. He had never cared for Red, and he knew the feeling was mutual. He kept his eyes steeled on the red-haired scoundrel, who peered in his direction in the steaming darkness.

"Harry?" the Kentuckian called in a faint drawl, sheathing his blade. "Is she with you?"

Anger simmered in Joshua. Red was so certain of the success of his plan! Hovering on the fringes of the light, Joshua opened his own line of commentary.

"Red, I always thought you were a low-down,

scheming bastard, and now I'm sure of it."

His tone was that of a resigned parent rebuking a much-erring child. His audience drew their guns and circled, their backs to one another. Raif furrowed his amber brow in curiosity.

"Manners?" he asked in a perplexed way, half to himself.

"Tell the governor," Joshua continued from another position, ignoring Raif's question, "that one of your sewer rats murdered a man tonight. I wonder how pleased he'd be with your methods. But tell me, Red, are you putting yourself through all of this trouble for Mellette? Or is it for yourself?"

There was an explosion of fury on Raif's face when he turned in Manners's direction but, Manners was grimly amused to note, he was not stupid enough to open fire. Unfortunately.

"That's what I suspected," Joshua remarked, from yet another position. "When he finds out, you're buzzard meat."

A shock of fear slashed the red-haired man's features. Then a thin, anemic smile skittered across his lips and he raised his gun and shot out the lamp above him.

There was something cool and wet upon Allyn's face. In her dream, it was Sheik's tongue. She reached up to brush it away and caught firm hold of a wrist. Her eyes popped open, but she was not fully awake, and she thought for one terrified moment that she was about to be seized. She twisted away, uttering a groggy cry, and sat up just as a calm voice steadied her and two large hands were laid reassuringly upon her narrow shoulders.

"Take it easy, Allyn. It's only me. Joshua."

Her eyes focused in the darkness on the smiling eyes and wide, unsmiling mouth of her rescuer.

"What's happened?" she demanded, supporting herself on one elbow while seizing his arm with her other hand. Gently he pulled away from her grip and pushed her shoulders back against the pillows again.

"It's four in the morning," he began. "You're in my room. You have a nasty bruise on your head. There was nobody at the stable. Sheik is safe, and . . ." He paused, lowering his voice. "Bert is gone."

Allyn sank into the bed. Would morning never come? Would this nightmare never end?

"Tell me. Everything," she managed weakly, certain she did not really want to know.

"Not now, Allyn," he told her. "Wait until morning."

She slipped back into sleep.

With almost criminal stealth, Joshua brought the covers up to her rather dirty neck, patted her cheek, and retreated to the easy chair at the foot of the bed, sinking gratefully into its yielding softness. He settled back and lifted first one, then the other booted foot slowly and carefully onto the foot of the brass bed, folding his hands behind his head. Watching her with some contentment, he allowed the events of the evening to replay themselves.

He yawned cavernously, remembering those things he would never tell Allyn. It was best she did not know what had transpired between him and her former lover. It was best, he thought, that she did not know he knew Raif at all. Grimly, he realized he would have to keep secret from her the fact that he knew about her affair until revelation could be useful. Some good might yet come from the rather sad, sordid business, and if he could stay awake long enough, he might succeed in finding it.

All at once he found himself smiling at the memory of the alley. Her obvious indignation. Her attempts to free herself from his grip. The taste of her mouth and how he had, admittedly, enjoyed their little scene. A most convincing charade, he decided, sliding his finger over his lips. Lovers. Lovers in an alley. He stifled a laughed at the notion. Wouldn't that have made a headline? Allyn Cameron and Joshua Manners . . .

Suddenly, quite by accident, he stumbled upon a plan.

Chapter Fifteen

Joshua Manners was asleep in his clothing in an easy chair, his feet, still booted, crossed in a relaxed fashion upon the foot of the bed. His handsome, animated features were peaceful, and his expansive chest rose and fell with each shallow, regular breath. She was in his room, Allyn realized. His and Bert's. The thought triggered her memory of the previous night's grisly events.

Bert was dead, she recalled, and she gasped at the recollection. The brute callousness of the killer as he thrust his broad hunting knife deep into Bert's abdomen. The crimson blood that spread a stain on Bert's shirtfront and the killer's sleeve. The expression of pain and disbelief contorting Bert's pleasant features . . . She shuddered, wishing to shut out the images.

But she could not.

There was a web about her, she sensed, and each futile attempt to struggle against it merely entangled her further, and attracted the attention of the deadly spider.

She flung the damp washcloth from her cheek and sprang up from the bed, feeling trapped. Her host stirred as she crossed to the room's only window and clutched her arms about herself. Behind her, she heard him yawn. It was a lusty, resonant sound, full of life. She heard the creak of his chair, and she knew he was stretching. She could almost see, in her mind's eye, his long, solid frame expanding like some predatory beast in his prime, awakening to the hunt.

God, how she hated him! How she hated his arrogance, his wit, his mock courtesy! How she despised his smug grin, his penetrating dark-eyed gazes, his lazy, calculated gestures! How she resented his utter lack of responsibilities, and his liberty to carry on in whatever way he chose, without concern for the welfare or reputation of himself or others!

Suddenly she had to leave the room. She could not bear to be with him for another moment. She turned to the door and took two steps toward it before she was halted by the sound of his voice.

"Where are you going?" he inquired in a lazy but pointed tone.

She could not bring herself to face him, so she spoke to the door.

"I need—some fresh air," she breathed, feeling his gaze upon her back like a pair of gentle hands.

"Open the window," he advised, yawning again. "Someone is after you, Miss Cameron, and if I may say, you're a pretty easy target."

Someone . . . Raif. Her face grew warm. Did he know about Raif? Or had he merely been curious and followed Bert last night, once again interfering in her business? There was no way to know, short of asking him. And that, of course, was unthinkable.

"I don't recall appointing you as my jailer," she retorted coldly, still not looking at him.

There was a rush of air and he was behind her. She felt his strong hands on her arms and he turned her to him, his features dark with rage, inches from her own.

"Now you listen to me," he breathed in a low, dangerous tone. "And listen good. Because I'm only going to say this once. You killed Bert last night in that tack room, as surely as if you put the knife in his gut. You were out of your element with those men, and you knew it. But you went ahead anyway and sacrificed Bert's life to your own arrogance and vanity, instead of going to the authorities, or asking me for help. You're a smart woman, Allyn. Too smart for your own good. But you don't have one lick of sense when it comes to doing what's best for yourself or for the people who care about you. What do you plan to do now?"

The question took her by surprise. The fact was, she did not know. His features blended to disdain.

"See what I mean? Well, I'll tell you, Miss Cameron, and it will be the last thing I'll ever do for you unless asked. I promise.

"I'm going out to report to the police that Albert Emmet is missing. I'll say that he mentioned meeting with some men last night, and hasn't returned. It isn't likely his body will turn up. Not in any recognizable form anyway. But this way we'll both be covered if it does. Other than the fact that he had this meeting, we know nothing about the situation. Did anyone see you leave the hotel last night?"

She shook her head. They had gone out at a service entrance, and had been fairly well disguised. The lobby had been deserted when she returned.

He seemed satisfied. He released her, and she took a step backward.

"I'll be back in a few hours. You are welcome to

stay here in my room and wait for me. If you choose not to, that's fine, but understand that our association is then ended, unless you come to me."

He stared hard at her for a minute. It was as though he were boring holes into her with his eyes, obliging her to look away. That seemed to satisfy him, for he turned from her and strode out of the room, slamming the door behind him.

She stood for a time in the center of his room, waiting. Waiting for a revelation. Then, because she sensed the spider about to entrap her, she fled.

Soaking in a warm bath in the privacy of her own room hours later, Allyn reviewed her actions. Our association is ended, Manners had said. Good, she thought, but was surprised at the lack of conviction behind the sentiment.

Much as she hated to admit it, Joshua Manners had been her safety net as far back as Deadwood. No, even in Rapid City. After all he, along with Bill Boland, had confirmed Sheik's victory to the officials. Then his interventions in Deadwood and, of course, Louisville . . .

She thought of going on alone, without Bert. She thought of facing the contempt of society and the humiliation when Raif carried out his threat, as he was sure to do. The thought left her as cold as death. She thought of Bert, lying at the bottom of the bay, or in some hungry shark's belly. She thought of Missy, who had to be told. Missy, who had sent them off a month ago with high hopes and unquestioning confidence in her. She thought of Sheik, the noble, extraordinary beast, who deserved a chance to win the Preakness and the Belmont, and to make his detractors eat their words.

She emerged from the tub and toweled herself. What was she to do? Even after Raif exposed their affair, she would be foolish to believe there would be an end of it. Raif was after Sheik. Raif had plans at which she could only guess, and the men and resources to carry them out. She had only money, herself—and Sheik. And the dreadful certainty that those things would not be enough to protect them.

She dressed in a freshly starched white linen blouse and blue poplin skirt, and she noticed that her fingers trembled as she manipulated the buttons. Her throat tightened as though her neck were in a noose, rather than a collar. She needed help, she realized at last. Desperately. And there was only one person with whom she had established any sort of relationship, and even though it was not a very good one, she had no choice but to impose upon it if Sheik were to continue racing.

Brushing her long, chestnut hair, she realized she was no longer sure of anything but Sheik. He had to run the Preakness, and the Belmont. She owed him that. She owed it to Missy, and to Bert, considering she had so badly bungled everything else. And now, there was but one hope of realizing those dreams.

She needed Joshua Manners.

Before her pride could rise like a phoenix from the ashes of her devastation, she made the pilgrimage to his room, praying he had not left Baltimore yet. Before she could summon the myriad of reasons why she should not ask his aid, she knocked quietly on his door.

"Yes?" came the clipped reply from inside.

Her relief at finding him there was tempered by her distaste for what she was about to do. In answer, she knocked again.

"What is it?" The voice inside was a trifle more impatient.

She tried to speak, but could not call out in reply. Instead, she knocked once more.

Carole Howey

With a rush of warm spring wind the door opened, revealing the tall panther of a man. He wore no jacket or tie, merely black creaseless dress trousers, a blindingly white shirt to which he had not yet applied a collar, and black boots with a high shine. Allyn watched as his impatient expression became one of surprise.

"I'd like to talk with you, Mr. Manners," she began simply, keeping her features bland. "May I come in for just a moment?"

He did not reply for a full minute, which passed to her like a day. He seemed to be measuring her, weighing the import of her call. She was determined not to betray her nervousness by so much as a flicker of her gaze. He must not suspect such weakness, or he would surely use it against her. After an eternity, he stepped aside and ushered her into his room with a sweep of his hand.

Glancing around the room, Allyn discovered that he had been in the midst of packing Bert's belongings into a box. The box was a small crate. It oddly resembled a coffin. Allyn swallowed a dry knob in her throat: It would be the only coffin Bert would have.

"What's on your mind, Allyn?" Manners's quiet baritone had a respectful edge to it, despite his words, as though its user was loath to disturb her thoughts.

"Bert," she responded faintly, touching the tarnished sterling flask she had so often seen pursed to the robust Englishman's lips. She turned toward Joshua, but did not meet his gaze or shorten the distance between them.

"I wanted to thank you for all you've done," she began in recitation, clenching and unclenching her fists. "And to ask you—if I might impose upon your—upon your evident good will."

Joshua's well-manicured hands rested at his waist, his long fingers tapping on his belt. "You use a curious choice of words, considering your opinion of me."

The words were hard. The tone was not. Allyn winced obligingly. "I realize I haven't been quite fair to you. I treated you badly on the train, and I hope you—won't hold that against me."

"You know, that's something I never did understand," he remarked in a tone of wonder. "You said something that night about a note, and roses."

Allyn felt the color leave her face. He had no idea what she was talking about! Morgan Mellette, she recalled him saying, is a vicious and spiteful woman . . . Could the governor's wife have been the architect of that entire calamity after all?

"I—" She swallowed an unexpected lump in her throat, then went on. "I was led to believe that you— that you had been responsible for—"

She could not go on. How could she have allowed herself to be so duped by that woman's devious plans? Her cheeks grew warm, and she stared fixedly at his watch chain. It would be an effort to keep any pleading tone from her voice.

"I know now that I have misjudged you. And I am sorry." She met his gaze at last, and was disconcerted to find an unpleasant glint in his eyes.

"You have chosen a convenient moment to change allegiance, Miss Cameron. You know, I trust, what a bad light that sheds on anything you might ask of me?"

His expansive chest, camouflaged in white linen, heaved in short, panting breaths, like a fighter's. If he did not stand between herself and the door, Allyn might have chosen that moment to flee. She caught her breath and swallowed hard before rallying to parry and riposte.

"Bad or good, it cannot be helped now, Mr. Manners. I can only make my request. It will be your decision in the end."

She refused to beg. The glare in his face softened.

"Very true," he conceded, retreating to a relaxed posture on his bed. He crossed his hands behind his head, leaning back against propped-up pillows, monitoring her with a piercing scrutiny. "Pray continue."

She wished that he had not sat down. It made it impossible not to look him in the face. In order to avoid it, as was simple when he stood since his height would have allowed her to stare at his chest, she would either have to hang her head and stare abjectly at the carpet or raise her neck and observe the chandelier. Neither pose would suit the earnestness with which she must make this request.

"Sheik is to run the Preakness on Saturday," she began, frightened by the cold look in his eyes. "And the Belmont Stakes in two weeks in New York. Since I am—alone now, I will require the benefit of an escort."

"Why?" his taunting voice challenged. His expression did not change. He seemed determined, she thought, to make this as difficult for her as possible.

"To safeguard my reputation, of course," she said in a choked whisper, feeling her face grow warmer.

"How convenient a reputation can be," he wondered aloud in a snide tone. "You cared so little for it when you deserted me at dinner last week."

"I knew you would throw that up at me!" she hissed, wanting to strike him. "How dare you, after what you—" She stopped, before she did further damage to her cause. Pride did not go down easily with her choking swallow. Her next words were gentler.

"I'm sorry," she managed, unable to meet his piercing, predator's gaze. "It was not a nice thing for me to have done."

"Or ladylike," he added instructively.

"Or ladylike," she echoed, utterly subdued.

Manners smiled, and the expression made her want to smash something into his face.

"You are delightful, Miss Cameron," he fairly chuckled. "What could possibly scare you so much that you would come to me for help?"

She swallowed hard. He was coming dangerously close to wringing the truth from her. She tried to ignore the question.

"Mr. Manners, surely you understand that I must be properly escorted here, and in New York. Along with my life, and Sheik's, I must think of my—reputation." The word escaped her in a whisper. "What little there may be left of it, after managing my horse, and conducting a private interview with you here in your room."

"And," he added silkily, scratching his cheek with a lazy forefinger as he played his trump card, "after Raif Simms is through with you."

Reality struck her with the force of a screaming comet. Her humiliation was complete.

"You knew!" she gasped, strangling, choking on her fury and embarrassment, struggling to assimilate the fact of his knowledge, and the thoroughness of it. This piratical mercenary, who sat enthroned upon his bed like some leering Mephisto, knowing that she had lain with a man and had had an affair. It was beyond endurance.

"Bert told me. Come now, Allyn, don't look so shocked. Do you think I give a damn whether you've slept with one man or a hundred?" His brown eyes were really unpleasant, relishing the spectacle of her devastation.

"You detestable cad!" she breathed, looking away. "You knew exactly why I came to you, but you made me jump all the hoops. I hate you!"

She made a move to sweep from the room in a limping mockery of the dramatic exits for which she was known, but in a single, swift movement he was on his feet, grasping her arm with a firm, bruising grip.

"Don't be a fool, Allyn!" he said brusquely, shaking her. "The moment you walk out of that door, all of the satisfaction you get from your grand exit will be a thing of the past. Yes, I did know why you came to me. But I'm a firm believer in humility, and you've had it coming to you. If you expect to finish the Triple Crown, you'll need my help to do it, and if you hadn't been so arrogant from the start, you might not be in trouble now up to your pretty neck!"

"Unhand me!" she demanded, shaking off his grip. She did not, however, make any further attempt to leave.

Manners smiled acidly. "Good. I see that you do have sense, in spite of your tender sentiments. Shall we dispense with the melodrama and discuss our strategy?"

Allyn hesitated. Were it not for Sheik, and her own desire to finish the Triple Crown, she would have taken the chance to tell him to go to hell. But under the circumstances, she knew that would be suicide. She desperately needed an escort, not only to safeguard Sheik and her reputation, but her very life as well. Walking out now would be throwing that chance away with both hands. She retreated from his square, too-close gaze to the whiskey decanter on the dresser. He already knew her worst. There was no point in further pretense.

"What do you propose?" she asked, aware that she would agree to anything just to be quit of the room. She poured a thin stream of amber liquid into a glass.

"You will need more than an escort to hide behind once Raif carries out his threat."

"Perhaps an army?" she suggested caustically, allowing herself a bitter chuckle.

He shook his head. "You will need a husband."

She sipped the liquid, then gulped it like a glass of lemonade. "Bill Boland couldn't possibly come—"

"I wasn't speaking of Bill Boland," Joshua said with deliberation.

His intention was obvious. She faced him, stricken with shock and revulsion. Her glass fell to the floor with a crash. "You mean *you*—"

"I'll sacrifice my bachelorhood, yes." His uncompromising gaze bore down upon her.

She hiccuped. "I'd as soon marry Sheik."

Manners grinned derisively. "Sooner, no doubt. But Sheik can't protect you. Bill Boland wouldn't understand. Or if he did, he would probably break your engagement. Besides, there's no time. What you need, Allyn, is a new name and an honorable title, which, whether you believe it or not, the name of Manners is in these parts. The wedding must be made public, and it must be soon. I won't"—he paused, grinning sourly—"demand—how shall I say it?—consummation of our marriage vows. Unless, of course, you insist upon it. That way, we can annul the marriage after the Belmont, and you can go back to your Dakota rancher, if you can explain yourself to him."

Allyn looked at him unwillingly, standing five feet in front of her, and she could barely conceal her distaste. "You will expect some sort of remuneration for this arrangement, I suppose?" she inquired in her most sarcastic tone.

His grin widened tantalizingly. "I take it that means I'm to be deprived of your—ah—company. In that case, I think it only fair. My price is thirty percent of the remaining purses in exchange for my name."

"Thirty percent!" She nearly gagged.

"A bargain, you will find," he replied, his grin fading. "Of course, there will be one additional stipulation."

Allyn stared at him. He had already said he would not demand consummation. What could he mean?

"A kiss," he answered her unasked question, his features now as blank as stone. "One for each day that we are married. To be paid as I demand, either one day at a time, all at once, or—any other way in which I see fit."

"That is the most outrageous, most insulting thing I've ever heard!" she retorted in an enraged whisper, her face growing hot at the idea. "I won't do it!"

Manners shrugged, still not smiling. "Good luck then, Miss Cameron."

He turned his back on her and walked toward his door for the purpose, she assumed, of seeing her out.

He could not be serious! Or could he?

"Mr. Manners." She was exasperated to discover that her voice sounded strangled. Desperate. "Joshua . . ."

When he faced her this time, his gaze was serious and utterly uncompromising. She took two steps backward.

"There will be no negotiating on that point, Miss Cameron!" he said in a warning tone that matched his look. "It is unconditional. A kiss for each day that we are husband and wife. No more, and no less."

He was breathing hard, as though the statement itself had been an exertion. Allyn felt as though she wanted to hold on to something. But she was standing in the middle of the room, with nothing about to lend support.

"Agreed?" he demanded, startling her.

What choice did she have?

She nodded, swallowing hard.

"Agreed," she all but whispered. "But if you think that I—"

"No conditions, Allyn," he reminded her in a softer

tone, still staring at her with that blank, unsettling look. "Remember?"

"To what," she ventured in as chilly a tone as she could muster, "may I attribute this boundless generosity?"

"To the Good Samaritan in me," he replied easily, as though he intended to be insulting. "And my weakness for the fairer sex."

This was the limit. Paying a man to marry her, with money and kisses. The crowning joke, she realized bitterly, would be Sheik finishing out of the money, thus shutting out Manners's chances of collecting on the purse.

But not the kisses.

She quickly tallied. Twenty-three days until the Belmont. Twenty-three kisses. Looking at his frankly leering expression, she knew those kisses would neither be virginal nor brotherly.

"I—I think I'll go now," she whispered, looking away from him.

"Just a moment."

He put out his hand, halting her progress without even touching her. She did not think she could tolerate being in the same room with him for another moment.

"What now?"

"I'll come for you at three o'clock tomorrow," he said, his quiet baritone lacking its earlier strident mockery. "The justice will expect us at four, and I've already taken the liberty of arranging for the bridal suite here at the hotel. Remember, it must look perfectly natural, Allyn. No one must ever suspect the real reason why we need more than one room."

Allyn chuckled after a moment, amused by the irony of it.

"You knew all along that I would come to you," she remarked wonderingly, sensing that she had fallen into a carefully laid trap. She looked squarely into his expressionless brown eyes. "I hate you, Joshua Manners."

"You're becoming repetitive," he replied, sounding more bored than offended. "Please dress for the occasion tommorrow. And for God's sake, as well as your own, try to make a better actress than you will a wife. Oh, wait. There is one more thing."

She glared at him, perceiving his meaning, hoping to make herself as unattractive to him as possible. "What?"

He smiled faintly. In fact, had she blinked, she might have missed the rather attractive expression altogether. He stood before her, although she could not tell how he had come to be standing so close to her, unless by magic. His hands, strong and long-fingered, rested upon her shoulders with just enough pressure to remind her that he was a man. She shivered, and took a small step backward.

"You said a kiss," she rebuked him in a hostile voice. "You said nothing about touching. Or embracing."

He bit his lip and shook his head once, seeming to rue his regrettable omission.

"You are a stickler for detail," he murmured in a drawling, sensuous tone that unexpectedly struck her like a hot surge in her womanly parts. "We will have it your way."

He removed his hands and placed them at his sides like an obedient wooden soldier. Allyn closed her mouth tightly. She remained perfectly still, trembling inside, terrified that she might respond to him.

He touched his lips to her cheek just beside her stiffened mouth. He lingered there for a moment, seeming to test her. Please, she pleaded inwardly, realizing at once that her terror had been well founded. Please finish this. Please do this . . .

His mouth was soft, but she sensed that he kept

his strength in check as his lips parted slightly. Her body became a city of tall buildings challenged by an earthquake, or some other force of nature too great to withstand. The very tip of his tongue, only the tip, etched a burning line across the faltering lower lip of her own mouth.

She could not breathe. At last she had no option but to open her mouth and gasp for air while her heart pounded against her rib cage in loud warning. His tongue completed its tour about the outline of her lips. Touch me, she wanted to implore him. Please.

Spirals of shimmering waves relaxed her jaw at last until she could offer no further resistance. His mouth, sensing a victory, at last fused triumphantly with her own.

And he had not even touched her, except with his mouth.

Humiliated, she realized that her body had betrayed her. She found herself pressed against him. His body was hard, almost rigid with restraint. Her arms remained at her sides, and her fingers stretched out in mute supplication. The heat of him, and the faint, seductive scent of tobacco and cloves about him, was devastating. She prevented a sob from escaping her throat, but just barely. He had won this round, literally, hands down.

His kiss was gone, almost as if it had never been. Like a torturously sweet dream, of which one tries valiantly to recall every succulent detail. She was obliged to rest her forehead against his chin for a moment until she regained sufficient strength and composure to look him in the eye.

"That wasn't so very bad," he whispered naughtily, his dark eyes tantalizing. "Was it?"

Somehow, Allyn made it back to her own room, although she was shaking badly. You've done it this time, she told herself, leaning against her door as though trying to prevent someone from entering. Worried so long over marrying Bill Boland because you don't love him, and now—no. I can't think about Bill now. That subject discarded, she found another, even more bizarre one waiting to supplant it.

Mrs. Joshua Manners. The very name soured her mouth as she recalled her earlier shameful demonstration. Furiously unbuttoning her collar, she realized that he had been right. She had indeed trapped herself into this matrimony. And it was, after all, a smaller sacrifice to commit marriage than it was to die. If Bert could die for his devotion to her and to Missy, and his belief in Sheik, then surely she could endure marriage to the dangerously sensuous Joshua Manners. After all, except for the kissing clause in their agreement, it would be a marriage in name only. She cast aside her skirt and blouse and folded herself into her chair, clutching her stockinged toes.

Mrs. Joshua Manners. At once the all-too-vivid memory of his masterful kiss assaulted her. He had managed to reduce her resistance to rubble only with his mouth. She remembered their improvised scene in the alley the night before, his sinewy body pressed feverishly against her own, shielding her from the danger of Raif's men. She recalled the gentle caress of his hand on her face as he felt the bruise left by one of her abductors.

A marriage in name only? She brushed the perspiration from her forehead, acutely aware of the uncomfortable sensation in her loins with which she was, by now, all too familiar. The curse which had been with her since her affair with that common criminal Raiford Simms had ended. She thought of lying with Joshua Manners, and was shocked to discover that the idea made her short of breath and dry of mouth . . .

No. This was too much. She had loved Raif. She liked and respected Bill Boland. For Joshua Manners, she entertained only distrust and resentment. Resentment, she guessed, because he was not cowed by her perverse sentiments. Because he was one of those men who could, and did, swagger about without need for concern about his reputation. And because he alone, of all the men she had ever known, was brutally frank with her, maddeningly opinionated, and unapologetically condemning. He laughed at her. He provoked her. He dared her to debate him. Theirs would be a marriage in name only, she vowed, as long as she could hold her own treacherous animal lust at bay. The distrust, coupled with the humiliation which he had thrust upon her, would surely be more than enough to keep him at arm's length.

She suddenly realized. He had kept her at arm's length this afternoon, but that had not prevented her from wanting him, desperately . . .

She slammed the door on that alarming recollection. She no longer wanted to think about Joshua. Stretching herself out on the divan, she found Bert waiting in the wings of her conscience. She remembered their ride to Deadwood, their conversation and their harmonizing. She remembered flowers in their train car, and the scolding on the dance floor in Louisville. She remembered, with a broken sigh, that she would never see him again. She allowed herself a minute of tearless grief for her lost friend, and for the innocence that she wondered if she'd ever had at all.

Chapter Sixteen

At a quarter to three the following afternoon, Joshua's dark eyes stared across the narrow gulf to his mirror. He was unsmiling, his long fingers awkwardly hitching his tie. Dissatisfied with the first result, he uttered a curse and pulled out the knot. It offered little resistance, and he made another attempt. The new result met with his standards, and he turned his attention to his hair.

The unruly mass of frankly brown hair was uncharacteristically coöperative. Smoothing the back with his comb, he frowned at his reflection, feeling like a fool. It had not taken him long at all to question the wisdom of his frivolous addition to their contract. The feel of Allyn's mouth beneath his had been something more than he had been prepared for. He further wished he had not been so unrelenting in his interview with her the previous day.

Never before had matrimony enjoyed any priority in his life. Why was he suddenly about to embark on that mission, in the best of circumstances a precarious ship, with a woman who not only did not love him, but admittedly distrusted him? For the first time, he began to wonder just how deeply his noble streak ran. Or perhaps his romantic streak? Certainly, it was not the money which made him warm to the thought of making Allyn Cameron his wife. Then what?

A theory materialized and teased his thoughts. Was it possible, among the potpourri of sensations the hotheaded and enigmatic woman stirred in him, that love was included? Admitting only that it was a distinct possibility, he turned away from the mirror, not wanting to see the answer plainly etched in his features. Why, in the early morning hours yesterday as he had watched her sleep, had this whole scheme seemed so sane and rational? Ruefully, he decided that it was because the marriage—damage?—would not be permanent.

He finished dressing, putting on his dark gray pinstripe coat and black Stetson. He left his room and cadenced his stride to arrive on time to fetch his reluctant bride-to-be. He wondered, without any feeling, whether she would still be willing to plunge ahead with the marriage. He wondered whether she might not have disappeared, taking her horse with her. He discovered that, having already run the gamut of emotions, neither result would surprise him. He knocked on her door.

Before his hand returned to his side, he found himself staring at his bride-to-be. The initial shock subsided in moments, and he remembered to lower his arm completely.

"Miss Cameron, I have always admired your punctuality," he said lightly, with a hint of mockery aimed at himself. "And you look beautiful."

Allyn's lips smiled briefly. Reluctantly, it seemed to him. Her almond-shaped green eyes did not.

"Thank you," she murmured in reply, her voice lyric.

It seemed to him that she had deliberately selected her most magnificent gown, emerald green in color. It was an agreeable compliment to her face and figure, offering an intriguing, yet highly proper display of cleavage. A smile tugged briefly at the corners of his mouth as he allowed his gaze to admire that panorama. Their agreement, he recalled, did not specify where on her person those kisses were to be delivered. His gaze reluctantly abandoned that scene and moved upward. Her abundant chestnut tresses were swept from her face, with but a few stray curls caressing her cheek and neck. That snow-white neck, gleaming alabaster, waiting for his lips to leave their mark upon it . . . He closed his eyes tightly, then opened them wide again, meeting her gaze at last. Her self-satisfaction was obvious in her cool green eyes, but she could not know she had given life to one of his more whimsical daydreams. That realization was momentarily paralyzing. Joshua quickly commanded himself.

"You're late," she commented further, lifting an arm draped in billowing green illusion to push back one of those lucky curls that licked her throat.

"You're right," he replied, finally remembering to speak. "Shall we?"

"Let me get my hat."

He obligingly stepped in the doorway and watched his daydream reverie apply a stunning but not overly fussy piece of millinery to her neat, softly feminine coiffure. He tried to concentrate on his carefully laid plans, but could summon no other thought than that Allyn Cameron, soon to be Allyn Cameron Manners, was the most beautiful, most enticing woman he had ever set eyes upon.

"Now I'm ready."

When she faced him again, she seemed different somehow. As though a whole new personality had gone on with the hat. She wore a daring expression as well, a look of defiance and challenge. But the challenge, he suspected, was not meant for him. Rather, it seemed directed at herself.

Allyn desired to feel nothing, and three fingers of bourbon had afforded her that dubious luxury. She maintained an erect, if overly deliberate bearing throughout the journey to the courthouse, offering no conversation, and responding as briefly as possible when addressed by Joshua Manners. Emerging from the carriage at their destination, she was surprised, even alarmed, to discover three men charging the cab. They began barking questions at her that, in her inebriated state, she could not comprehend. Turning to Joshua, who had already emerged and was helping her down, she noted with some vexation that he was smiling that hateful, urbane grin of his and commenting in brief but glowing terms about their impending nuptials. At once, she perceived these unpleasant creatures to be reporters, no doubt representatives of some of the local scandal sheets. Perhaps the same ones Raif had threatened to contact. Damn Joshua, but he was clever at this game! It must be public, he had said. And soon. Before Raif could carry out his threat, she supposed.

She could say nothing to the men, not having heard their queries. But she could, and did, suffer Joshua Manners's protective embrace as he led her through their midst. She even managed to look pleased.

"That was hateful of you," she said through her smile when the gossip hounds were behind them.

"That was necessary," he reminded her.

"Of course," she sniffed. "You know best. Joshua Manners always knows—"

"Keep your voice down!" he warned in a whisper as they mounted the steps.

"Take your hands off of me!" she retorted in kind.

"Gladly."

His arms fell away from her, and for a swaying, dangerous moment she realized just how much bourbon she had consumed. She hoped, fleetingly, that he had not noticed, but her hopes were quickly dashed as he added, "An odd sentiment from one who obviously can't hold her liquor."

"I will not dignify that remark with an answer," she said with as much composure as she could muster.

"You can say that again," he muttered, opening a door for her.

Oddly, Allyn was reminded of a troublesome childhood dream in which she stood in a small room with strangers who spoke to her in words she recognized but could not understand. She remembered the fable of Dr. Faustus, who contracted his soul to the Devil in exchange for some boon she could not recall. The justice was businesslike and humorless, droning on in a relentless monotone. Two bystanders had been seized as witnesses, and they stood by like stray dogs hoping for a cast-off treat.

Joshua's arm was about her waist again, and he held her right hand in his. She stared at the justice's little book, feeling suddenly frightened: Who was Joshua Manners anyway? And why was he really doing this? Would she find, upon completion of this horrid nightmare, that she had flown, as the saying went, from the frying pan into the fire?

All at once the room was still. The justice was staring at her. The witnesses, a young man and woman, were watching her as well, and she could feel Joshua's eyes upon her, although she did not dare to look at him. They were all staring at her, waiting for something. But what? She tried to think, but her mind was blank. She felt herself begin to tremble.

There was a small, gentle pressure on her hand, and magically her trembling ceased. A response came to her, as though it had come from the squeeze Joshua had given her hand.

"I do," she said, her voice barely a whisper.

Moments later, after more words, she heard the man beside her give the same response, in a quiet but sure and strong baritone.

Then there was a ring upon her finger, a slim gold band that caught the light. She did not know how it had gotten there. She looked up at Joshua at last in wonder.

He was smiling at her, his angular, handsome features wearing an expression she had never seen in them before. She wanted to study it longer. His dark eyes compelled her, and she knew it was all over. She knew he was going to kiss her. She knew, with a sudden shock, that she wanted him to kiss her. Stunned by this unwelcomed sensation, she could only watch helplessly as his face neared hers. She closed her eyes against his approach, and tilted her chin upward, keenly aware of a sweet stab of anticipation . . .

And was crestfallen when she received nothing more than a chaste, brotherly peck upon her moistened lips. The insult was complete. Her eyes opened and she glared at him murderously. His dark eyes answered her with a hellish grin, daring her to make a comment. She opened her mouth and closed it again, common sense telling her that this was not the time. Later, she promised herself, even managing a smile at her thoughts of revenge.

"Well, Mrs. Manners," Joshua addressed her after the deed was done and they had embarked on the return journey in the cab.

She dealt him a perfunctory, contemptuous glance. "Don't you dare to call me that when we are alone," she warned him, bristling, feeling capable of all sorts of evil. "Bad enough I must endure the title in public."

"Cheer up, my darling wife. It's only for a few weeks."

A few weeks. She groaned inwardly. He might as well have said a hundred years.

"What other surprises do you have in store for me, I wonder?" she continued in a saccharine tone. "More reporters at the hotel? A grand reception, perhaps?"

"Not so grand," he said deprecatingly. "Anticipating your unsociable humor, I have arranged for an intimate nuptial dinner to be served in our suite. No doubt, however, the famous Huntington Hotel will have a few additions of its own invention."

"I detest surprises."

"That does not surprise me in the least."

Her brow furrowed as she observed him with genuine resentment. His expression, very matter-of-fact, dared her to say more. She expelled a short, hard breath and looked away, feeling her frustration fester. If only he would look hurt, or become angry, or do something that would prove she had some power over him. But she knew he would never give her the satisfaction. The cad.

The Huntington, indeed, surprised her. Upon their return to the hotel, they discovered that a good part of the staff had assembled on the front steps, and as her husband alighted and helped her down, smiling like a Cheshire cat all the while, a torrent of rice was released in a shower.

Few things could be worse, she thought, than having to smile and laugh in the face of small, hard objects being flung your way by people who obviously think they are performing some good work. Allyn picked up two handfuls of green watered-silk skirt and allowed Joshua to secure an arm protectively around her while his other hand held up his hat like a shield against the grain. They charged the steps between the columns of well-wishers, through the doors, through the lobby, and up the stairs to the door of their suite. There, Joshua relinquished his protective custody, and Allyn began brushing and plucking off the tenacious rice grains from clothing and hair. She was still so involved when Joshua found his key and unlocked the door.

"Madam," he pronounced ceremoniously, with a wave of his arm. "Your suite. I should, you're aware, sweep you into my arms and carry you across the threshold, but I will not demand you suffer that embarrassment."

"Oh, hush," she warned, feeling her cheeks grow warm at the very idea. She escaped into the room, hoping that at last the nightmare had ended.

Behind her, the door closed with a resounding bang. Allyn spun around in surprise.

Her husband leaned negligently against the door, crossing his long legs in a manner which could only be described as arrogant. Her stare traveled slowly up his lean, rock-hard form, pausing for a moment while his arms, elegantly clothed in gray pinstripe wool gabardine, crossed in front of his ample chest. Her gaze continued, reluctantly, up his immaculate lapel and collar, to his firm, smoothly shaven chin and the lower lip of his wide mouth, curled down in a derisive grin. His angular jaw tightened, and his dark, straight eyebrows lowered over his hateful, dancing brown eyes.

It seemed he waited. She endured his idle, insulting gaze, and realized she was as alone as she was going to get. He waited until she realized that she was bound to him by legal means. He waited until it occurred to her that her name was the same as his, and he waited until the slow, hot blush which had begun outside the door came to fullness in her cheeks.

With a calculated, careful gesture, he removed his hat and unbuttoned his coat. Still commanding her gaze, he roused himself from his indolent pose and shortened the span between them.

"I must apologize to you, my dear wife," he began in a light tone, but with an edge of cool courtesy, "for my behavior at the ceremony."

She allowed herself an open-mouthed stare of puzzlement, forgetting, for the moment, that he was coming very close to her.

"It really was inexcusable of me," he continued, a ghost of a disarming grin on his face, "to ignore the fact that you were waiting for a kiss. I hope you can forgive me, and accept a belated token . . . of my great esteem . . . for your beauty . . ." He trailed off in a whisper, and she found she was under the spell of his words. His arms folded around her and, still enrapt by his eyes, she allowed her head to fall back. She was helpless against the inevitable coup of his kiss.

This was no stolen kiss. Neither was it tentative. It was a bold kiss. A kiss that did not apologize. A kiss that, in fact, took what it plainly thought its due. It was the kiss she had expected, even wanted, at the ceremony. Only now, here in their suite, they were alone together. There was nothing to prevent that kiss from becoming something more . . .

Allyn closed her eyes and felt the familiar thrill at her surrender, as she had the day before. This day, however, his arms had joined the battle, and his hands freely glided across the soft, yielding chiffon on her back. He massaged her shoulder blades brazenly, even sliding one hand down to her waist, where his thumb pressed circles into her hip. His tongue dived in, taking her mouth with deliberate authority. Her mouth felt weak and gloriously swollen, like the unbearably hot place between her legs, and her lips trembled beneath his with excitement as they had only the day before in his room.

How dared he?

She wrenched herself away from his embrace, swinging a pitifully weak slap against his face. Joshua retreated a step, his hand covering the punished cheek. His dark eyes were wide with stung surprise.

"When I feel in need of your compliments," she panted, shaking, "be assured that I will ask."

She turned away from him and, not forfeiting an ounce of the dignity which had been so endangered moments before, swept out of the parlor and into her new bedroom, slamming her door for emphasis.

Intolerable cad! she thought, furious, denying the uncontrollable shivering that overwhelmed her entire body. He had caught her unawares with that outrageous demonstration. What had he hoped to accomplish by kissing her in that fashion? Certainly not the apology he had professed. Apology? It had seemed more like an affront.

Maybe it had been. Perhaps it was his way of reminding her that he knew she was not chaste. That he knew of her scarlet past, and that he was the only barrier between herself and disaster, and because of that knowledge he would make the rules. One of which being that ridiculous, not to say perilous, kissing clause.

Her cheeks were burning hot, and her heart pounded a loud, breakneck pace that rattled in her breast like an alarm. What if he were to come in there right now and demand payment in full in advance? She grew dizzy at the very thought. She breathed deeply, trying to manage herself. She sat down at the small writing desk, extracting pen, paper, and ink with badly shaking hands. The situation demanded a letter to Missy, as much for Missy's own information as for Allyn's composure.

She filled her pen and headed the paper, already seeing another perspective of the recent events. No man, she reasoned, scribbling amenities, would kiss a woman like that unless he wanted her. Unless she was desirable to him. Allyn did not delude herself: She thought herself reasonably attractive, and had past experience enough with men, if not love, to know she possessed a degree of appeal. The thought that she appealed to Joshua Manners was both frightening and, at the same time, perversely titillating. Perhaps, she mused, she could use that appeal to her advantage in her dealings with him.

No. It had not worked so far. Besides, there was something demeaning in the notion that she should use her sex as a weapon. It was certainly no better than prostitution. Perhaps it was a good deal worse: At least between prostitute and client there was a clear understanding of expectations. Between Joshua and herself, there was only distrust and dislike.

She stopped and wondered. There was dislike and distrust on her part. But what of Joshua Manners? What were his true feelings toward her? Certainly, she thought, unwillingly feeling his arms around her and his lips on her mouth again, he wanted her. She shuddered: So had Raif's men. Joshua, she recalled with fresh embarrassment, had told her on more than one occasion that she was stubborn, conceited, and cowardly.

And yet—and yet he had risked his own life to rescue her from Raif's men. He had summoned the security force to her aid at the Derby, and he had "scraped her off of the ground" in Deadwood.

He had, in short, picked up the pieces of each of her mistakes. Why? He must entertain some tender feelings for her. And if he did not, why, there were

248

ways. You have to learn to use every means in your power for your own ends. That was how Joshua himself had put it.

She rejected the thought immediately. It was only a schoolgirl fantasy, believing anyone could make a man fall in love with them. Raif Simms had taught her that much. Besides, God alone knew what mad sort of things Joshua Manners would be capable of were he really in love with her.

She wrote.

"You will find this difficult, bordering on impossible, to believe, but I have actually entered into the bonds of matrimony—here, a curiously apt expression—with your champion, Joshua Manners. I can see your smile already; however, I hasten to caution you that ours is a marriage of strictest convenience, with less than no romantic attachment and no connubial relationship. So you see to what new depths I have sunk for the sake of our colt, who, I am confident, could not care in the least . . ."

Allyn's letter went on to request that Missy not mention the event to Bill since it would only confuse things and was a temporary arrangement anyway. She devoted two sentences to that, then went on to the subject of Bert. It was difficult to write about him, for she still had to remind herself that he was gone. Gone, with no grave to mark his passing. By now, she realized, Missy had seen the telegram she had sent the day after Bert's untimely murder, and the younger woman was no doubt in a distraught state. Allyn said a quick prayer that Missy would bear up and that someone, perhaps Bill, was there to comfort her.

Bill Boland. Dear Lord. No, she would not think of Bill at all, she decided, tucking the thought of her fiancé away for another time. She went on with her letter, finding her own solace in the stream of words that issued lovingly from her pen. Writing was a way of suspending time. It enabled her to create an illusion of life, of actually participating in the admittedly bizarre events of the last few days.

Several pages and some time passed before her diligent recording was interrupted by a soft, respectful rap upon her door.

"Allyn?" Joshua's voice, lacking its characteristic mocking tone, came to her from the other side of the door. "Dinner is here."

Dinner. An "intimate nuptial dinner, to be served in our suite," his words echoed to her from earlier.

How intimate?

She completed a sentence and put aside her writing. Abandoning the desk, she paused before her mirror to assuage vanity. Steeling herself for the impending encounter, she effected a cool demeanor and entered the parlor.

Joshua was already seated at the dining table when she emerged from her room, his back to her door. He had removed his jacket, and his broad shoulders all but blocked from view the fresh-faced young waiter who stood ready to serve them with a pristine towel draped over a crooked left arm. Allyn did not like the idea that another person might be present for this meal, as it would mean maintaining the charade for an extended period of time. She was disposed to enjoying her meal in as much solitude as the situation would allow.

How to get rid of the fellow?

She took a deep breath and organized her features into a smile which she hoped closely approximated that of a woman in love.

"You may go," she murmured, sidling to Joshua's chair. She stood behind it, resting her hands lightly upon his broad shoulders. "I would like to wait upon my husband."

250

The waiter, she noticed with amusement, began to look increasingly uncomfortable in the face of her bold intimacy. Encouraged by her success, she dared to give further lie to her sentiments by kissing Joshua on the top of his head. She was intrigued by the fresh scent of his soft sable locks.

"I—" the young man before her stuttered and swallowed hard. "Certainly, Mrs. Manners," he babbled, concentrating on the assortment of silver domes on the table. "I'm sure you'll find everything you need . . ."

"Oh," Allyn, enjoying his discomfiture, said in a husky whisper. "I'm sure I shall."

Now she caressed Joshua's cheek with her right hand. Suddenly she felt his hand, warm and strong, on hers. She resisted the urge to withdraw her hand from his grasp, wondering if he could feel her pulse accelerate. The waiter closed the door behind him, and she quickly pulled her hands away and took her seat across from Joshua. She began methodically uncovering the domed plates so she did not have to look at him right away. Presently she realized that a full minute had passed and Joshua Manners had not said one word. She did look up at him and was surprised, even amused, to find him staring at her in open-mouthed astonishment.

"Why Joshua," she observed, relishing his unconcealed disappointment. "You look quite flushed. Have I indeed proven a better actress than a wife?"

She could not resist the barb. She felt she had gone some distance in the last few minutes toward settling their score, and she intended to enjoy it.

"I know you to be a woman of many accomplishments," he responded in a quiet but cold tone.

Damn him! He was never at a loss for words. She did not answer him. Instead, she began serving portions of the various foods provided, including some delightful crab dishes that were plentiful in Baltimore and had quickly become her favorites. Joshua uncorked the champagne and poured the pale gold nectar into each of two tall goblets. She set his plate before him as he replaced the bottle into its bucket. He then picked up his own glass by its slender stem and stared into it for a time. She pretended to concentrate on her dinner, but stole a glance at him, perplexed by his dark humor.

"To us, my dear wife," he said presently, lifting his glass in her direction. "Or rather, to the fool in each of us." And in a single long draught he drained it.

Allyn's appetite vanished at the bitter toast. It was replaced by a chill in the pit of her stomach, as if she had swallowed a snowball. She was not of a mind to engage him in a verbal joust. In fact, she was uncomfortably aware that some expression of gratitude might be in order. She fingered her own glass, having no taste for the beverage. She sensed that Joshua was watching her, and she could not bring herself to look at him again.

"Please excuse me." She tried to speak in a normal tone, but could manage only a breathless whisper. "I am retiring."

His low chuckle startled her into meeting his gaze.

"Hardly how I would describe you," he offered in a faintly mocking tone. He rose as she did, his sable eyes probing her in a way which made her want to run from the room.

"Good night," she murmured, aware that she awaited some signal of dismissal from him. Perhaps a kiss. He merely nodded, his expression becoming one of boredom, even disgust. She mastered her desire to run, instead walking in her best debutante gait to the door of her room. Once safely inside, she hesitated only a moment before locking the door. The loud click of the lock induced laughter from the other side, which she endured in silence.

She undressed quickly and got into bed, craving the release of sleep. Sleep, she discovered grimly, was not of a cooperative nature. Lying awake in the darkness, she became aware, suddenly, of movement in the other room. There was a crash, like the breaking of a glass. There was a light showing through the crack at the bottom of her door, a seam of dim yellow, quickly lit, and quickly extinguished. Then, unmistakably, the sound of a door closing with a bang which bespoke desertion.

Chapter Seventeen

The look of prepossessed composure Allyn had rehearsed all the while she dressed in her customary working clothes went to waste. As she emerged from her room in a too-bold stride, she knew immediately that she was alone in the suite. Joshua was not there.

The breakfast cart, obviously brought some time earlier, was still set for one, the other place having been violated by an earlier diner. Wondering where Joshua could have gone before nine o'clock in the morning, she reached for the half-empty basket of biscuits. They were cold, but still soft. He had been gone no more than an hour.

The flame under the coffee pot was small but still burning, so Allyn undertook to effect her morning nourishment. The solitude was an unexpected gift. As she debated her third cup of coffee, she was joined at last by her adventurous husband. He entered the suite without knocking, carrying a *Baltimore Sun* under his arm.

"You have eaten?" he inquired by way of greeting, settling his Levi-clad frame into the chair across from her. "Good. You'll probably lose your appetite after this."

He tossed the paper to her in a calculated gesture which propelled it accurately into her lap.

She frowned and put down her cup. She looked across at his matter-of-fact countenance with suspicion.

"Nothing you shouldn't have expected," he added helpfully. "Given the society reporters, and knowing Raif as you do."

She scowled at his double meaning, but chose not to remark upon it at this time, the paper being somewhat more important to her than further argument with him. She picked it up, curling her fingers around it like choking vines. It did not take her long to find the article and headline to which Joshua referred.

She scanned it rapidly, as if haste would lessen the sting. She perceived its import at once. The salient feature appeared to be the wedding itself, with pointed reference to Joshua T. Manners and the J.J. Mannerses of Annapolis, his family. The preceding article outlined, however, in suitable Victorian vagueness, that his new bride, a Cameron of the Philadelphia Camerons, was "of questionable character, according to Reliable Witnesses." Allyn hurled the paper to the floor with disgust.

"Damn him!" she hissed. "Damn him!"

"Easy, Allyn," Joshua soothed urbanely, folding his hands upon his chest as he rocked his chair back on two legs. "It will be simple enough to put a stop to the scandal."

"How?" she demanded. "This is so easy for you, isn't it, Joshua? It's a game. An amusement. It's my reputation, damn you!" How she despised him!

He ignored her outburst. "We simply behave like

255

the perfect couple, loving and circumspect. And I will make clear to those papers, and to anyone else, that I will brook no slanders on my wife's moral character. Actually"—he tilted her a tantalizing grin, as though he were indeed going to enjoy the whole joke immensely—"I, for one, overestimated Raif Simms."

"You are despicable," she flung at him, rattling at the bars of her invisible cage. "You are no better than he is, and I detest the thought of—of my reputation resting in your whims."

"Would you prefer leaving it to Raif's?" he countered, his words aimed to cut. He did not add, "That could be arranged," although his stare did.

For answer, she stood up, knocking her chair over as she did.

"I am going to Pimlico to check on Sheik," she muttered, glaring at him.

He rested his cheek against his fist with a tolerant look.

"I don't believe you heard me," he said carefully, as though addressing a child. "I said, 'loving and circumspect.' From now on, my dear wife, we go everywhere together."

"Oh, indeed? I wonder," she remarked coolly, "if you would dare to take me wherever it was that you went last night."

Her triumph was fleeting. He met her stare, and his frankly paternal expression changed to one of pity. Pity was second on the list of emotions she did not comprehend. Angered anew, she clenched her fists in the folds of her habit, wishing she could bury one in his face. A fleeting smile crossed his lips, as though he were aware of that wish.

"Come along, Allyn," he beckoned in a low voice. "Let's go to see Sheik."

Upon their arrival at the stables, it was evident that something was wrong. There was a small gathering of grooms and various stable personnel clustered around the colt's stall like mourners at a casket. Both Allyn and her husband broke into a run at the sight, with Joshua getting the better of the contest. Just as he had cleared away the last of the onlookers, Allyn caught up to him, breathing hard.

"Sheik!" she called out frantically. "Where's Sheik? What's wrong?"

In reply, a grim-faced groom swung open the doors of the stall to reveal the magnificent stallion lying prone in the straw. Relief, knowing that he was there, commingled with alarm as she knelt at his head with a cry.

"He took sick late last night," the watchman offered with concern. "Didn't eat. Stood real still, and then sort of—collapsed."

"Why wasn't I sent for immediately?" Allyn demanded hotly, glaring at each of the men in turn.

"It should be obvious," Joshua enjoined briefly, low enough for her ear alone as he knelt to examine Sheik's eyes. "No one wanted to disturb us on our wedding night."

Startled by his comment, she fixed her angry glare upon him, but he was going on with his examination of Sheik, ignoring her.

"Have you sent for a doctor?" she asked, turning to the grooms again after a moment, using a less recriminating tone.

The men nodded vigorously.

"About an hour ago," the watchman supplied.

"What's he been eating?" Joshua looked around at the troubled but helpless menials. One of them brought forth a handful of feed. Joshua accepted it and performed a ritual of examination, smelling, even tasting the concoction. Stroking Sheik's perspiring neck, Allyn watched her husband with expectation.

Joshua frowned, then held the feed out to Sheik's

muzzle. With a woeful look, the thoroughbred nibbled at it, then listlessly dropped his head into his
mistress's lap.

"Joshua?" Allyn looked to her husband for reassurance, but could find no consolation in his grim countenance.

The doctor arrived an hour later. He was a tired
man of undetermined age, whose most memorable
features were an ill-fitting, outdated suit of clothes
and a poor shave. He seemed nervous, his small grey
eyes darting to and fro from the concerned onlookers
to the afflicted creature. He examined Sheik, who was
less cooperative with him than he had been with his
previous examiners. Allyn stood by watching, feeling
frustrated and helpless, until Joshua directed her to
a stool.

If the doctor drew any conclusions from his observations, he gave no immediate sign. Instead, he ques-
tioned them. What had Sheik been eating? What were
his bowel habits, his behavior? Allyn supplied him
with a thorough synopsis of the animal's bodily functions, ignoring the embarrassment of the spectators.
Demonstrating no emotion, the physician brought
forth a big brown bottle from his bag.

"Colic," he pronounced in a curt way. "Give him
this. One cup to a gallon of water. Make sure he drinks
plenty of water," he further advised. "And keep him
warm."

"How long will he . . ." Allyn's question trailed off,
and she dreaded his response.

"It's not too bad. He should be up in a few days."

"But he's supposed to run the Preakness the day
after tomorrow!" she exclaimed, grabbing the doctor's
hanging sleeve.

The doctor stared at her as though she had suddenly
acquired a second head. "Not this horse."

As the man departed, Allyn felt her heart sink into

her boots. No! It wasn't fair! She heard the activity resume around her, but she could not will herself to move. It was too awful to think about. That all of her planning and sacrifices should come to this!

Joshua watched the retreating doctor with mixed emotions. He came up behind Allyn and gripped her shoulders in an attempt to comfort her. She looked to him as though she had just lost her second friend in the same week.

"Oh, I've done it this time," he heard her say under her breath with a broken sigh.

"It isn't your fault, Allyn," he answered her softly, wishing she would turn to him as she had done several nights ago in the tack room, where Bert had been murdered. She did turn to him, but not with any loss of composure. It was suspicion which distorted those lovely features.

"You don't think he could have been poisoned, do you?" she asked.

It was not an accusation. It was merely a question.

He shook his head. "What would anyone gain by killing him? Or even making him ill?" he countered, hoping to console her. "There was nothing in his feed. His water's fresh. And the watchman was here all night. No, Allyn. He isn't poisoned. Only sick."

Allyn broke away from him and went back to her horse, wearing an expression which was not lost on her husband. "Only sick." He may as well have said, "Only dead."

"Poor Sheik," she murmured, kneeling to scratch the ailing thoroughbred's forehead. "I've neglected you! Please try to get well! What will Missy say?"

She faced Joshua again, and he noticed jealously that her expression lacked any emotion for him.

"I'll be staying here with him," she told him in a tight voice, not quite successfully masking her dejection from him. "There's no point in your staying too."

Joshua shortened the distance between them, unable to resist the impulse to brush a lock of chestnut hair from her cheek. He marveled at the softness against his fingers, and he marveled that she did not pull away from him. His hand moved from her cheek to her shoulder, where he allowed it to rest.

"You've forgotten," he said dryly after a moment. "Sheik is not only your problem. No, my love, I married you for better or for worse, in sickness and in health." He managed a grin at his words, aware that he was only half-teasing. "And I'm sure tending to Sheik falls into at least one of those categories. Besides," he continued, offhand, "we have gossips to silence. Remember?"

She turned away from him, and he guessed she did not want to be reminded of that. Besides, what would it matter, he wondered, watching her sponge Sheik's perspiring body, if the horse was out of the Preakness anyway?

He worked along with Allyn all morning, sponging, medicating, grooming, and watching Sheik. If anything, Joshua thought the thoroughbred appeared worse after the medication than he had before, and he said so. Allyn sat down on the clean straw and gave him a look of weary disdain.

"Joshua, if you can't be more encouraging, perhaps you can be more helpful," she said crossly.

"Any suggestions?" He directed an inquiring look at her.

"The only thing which comes to mind," she replied, staring at her horse, "is something to eat. Oh," she added, in a tone he recognized as her best acid sarcasm. "You might try coming up with a miracle or two as well, since you're obviously displeased with the doctor's diagnosis."

Her pretty mouth twisted in a disparaging grimace.

He sighed at the rebuke, grudgingly admiring her composure in the face of this new and unexpected setback, but not surprised by it. "At your service."

He ducked out of the stable, hoping to clear some cobwebs from his brain. Allyn wanted a miracle. Perhaps, he thought, doubtful, he would be able to oblige her.

He did not agree with the doctor's assessment. He knew he had seen horses in that condition before, and it had nothing whatever to do with colic. He thought hard, raking his memory for a clue.

His pace slow and pensive, he headed toward the commissary with the grim realization that Allyn's beloved stallion would not run in the Preakness. Surely she realized it as well, but she gave no hint of the devastation she must be feeling. She just squared her narrow shoulders against the third—no, fourth disaster in a week, counting their marriage, and plowed on, never losing sight of the single purpose of making her horse the champion. There could not be another woman like her.

He debated consulting with a few trainer acquaintances at the commissary about Sheik's condition, but decided against it. Best not to start any rumors about the colt from Rapid City. There were enough flying about his owner already. Commandeering an assortment of victuals, he started back, not anxious to leave Allyn or Sheik alone for too long.

The answer, he mused, was right under his nose. Some simple thing they had overlooked.

It had been more than a half an hour since he left, but Allyn was still engrossed in the same activity upon his return. He did not have to inquire about the horse. The unfortunate animal's condition had not bettered. His mistress made no comment, so he unburdened his parcels onto an upright barrel.

"I suppose we can't expect that medicine to work so quickly," Allyn ventured in a doubtful greeting. "Still, I thought—I hoped—he'd show some improvement by now." She sighed brokenly, stroking Sheik's drooping forelock. "If only Missy were here. Or Bert." Her voice broke off with a tremor.

"Come on over here and have something to eat," Joshua urged, hoping to distract her.

She looked up at him and her forlorn expression faded to a brief, unexpected smile.

"Missy would say something like that too," she told him. "I remember how much she tried to feed me on the morning of the Steeplechase. The day I met you."

If there was a reason why she mentioned meeting him as though it was at least as important as the Steeplechase, she did not remark upon it. She fell to helping him unpack the assortment of foods he had brought, including a round of cheese, a hard, durable bread, some oranges, and a clay jug. She uncorked the last and sniffed at it suspiciously.

"What's this?"

"Elderberry wine," he replied, offering her a stool. "The best I could do. I know you would prefer champagne . . ."

She scowled at his reference to their scene on the train, cast a dubious glance at the jug, and sat down. She broke off a piece of cheese and nibbled at it.

"I'm not really hungry," she said at the end of a sigh.

"But you can't resist this perfect feast," he interjected lightly, lowering his tall, lean form to the straw floor near her. " 'A loaf of bread, a jug of wine . . .' "

He could not prevent himself from looking up at her, nor could he persuade himself to complete the verse.

She retreated from his gaze, glancing over to Sheik instead.

"You were not aware that we shared this stall with Omar Khayyam, were you, Sheik of the Desert?"

He recovered from the little spell he had inadvertently cast, not surprised that she was familiar with the phrase. He offered her the jug, which she accepted with graceful hands and raised tentatively to her lips.

It was not a good wine, he knew. It was sweet to the point of rottenness, but with a bitter bite. After two swallows, she handed the jug back to him, coughing until tears fell from her eyes. He allowed himself a chuckle, accepting the wine from her shuddering grasp.

"Shall I get you some water?" he offered, rising. "It's your only other option."

She shook her head. "City water doesn't agree with me."

"Oh."

Joshua stared at the prone thoroughbred. Seized by a sudden inspiration, he leaped up. Allyn started at his movement.

"City water!" he exclaimed in echo, preempting her question. He was filled with a sense of triumph, and he turned to her in elation. "Allyn, you've done it!"

Allyn stood too, her fine eyebrows furrowed in wonder.

"Done what?" she demanded. "Joshua, what are you—"

He felt a laugh inside of him, which he let out as he flung his arms around her triumphantly.

"All morning I have been trying to remember when and where I had seen horses in Sheik's condition before. And you have just reminded me. I don't know why I didn't think of it before!"

"Where?" She still seemed baffled, and did not protest his embrace.

"In Dakota!" he told her, holding her by the shoulders. "Every horse we brought back took sick like this after about a week. We'd try everything, but finally they'd just get better in a week or two. Then we figured it out after we bought a pony from a neighbor."

"What has any of this to do with Sheik?" She grabbed his arms and shook him ineffectually.

"It was the water, Allyn!" He pronounced every syllable deliberately. "Your horse is suffering from a change in his water!"

Allyn stared at him for a moment as though she thought he might have lost his mind. Then she brightened.

"I'll bet you're right!" she said after a moment enthusiastically.

"I know I'm right."

"But what can we do about it?" she asked, releasing him at last. "Knowledge is not necessarily power."

"It may be too late already," Joshua muttered, examining Sheik's eyes again. "To have him ready for the Preakness, I mean. But we can try. We'll have to boil all of his water, but he shouldn't drink until he looks better. Judging by his appearance, I'd say we won't have to worry about that for a while."

Before Allyn's eyes, the Marylander sprang to life. He summoned grooms to fetch wood for a fire and a tripod kettle for boiling. He seized every blanket and shook them out, draping them on the stable door like banners. He even began to rake the stall, calling loudly to the ostler for fresh hay. Daunted by this display of energy, Allyn sank to her knees by Sheik. She resumed her care of the sick animal, watching Joshua exert his most commanding demeanor, which always, she was discovering, achieved results.

Sheik's trough was dumped and scrubbed. The prescribed medicine was poured onto the ground. The straw was changed, and fresh blankets were brought. The tripod was set up and, in no time, a big black kettle of water was warming over an open fire. Yet all Allyn had done was watch as the stablehands and her husband performed all of the tasks. Even when she had tried to help, Joshua kindly told her to sit with Sheik, although she knew he meant she was in the way. Unused as she was to having a man take charge of things, she experienced mixed emotions at the arrangement. It was an unexpected relief to share the burden of this latest crisis with a willing partner, and yet she could not deny a twinge of resentment that an interloper should presume to usurp her position of authority. While Bert was alive, they had shared opinions, decisions, and work equally. At home, she managed the saloon herself.

At least, she always had. For the first time, she began to wonder what would happen to that arrangement after she married Bill. Quickly she shook off those thoughts. Better to deal with husbands as they came along, she decided. One at a time was quite enough. And this one, Joshua Manners, was proving to be as much as, if not more than, she could handle. So, as he suggested, she watched.

But she did not watch Sheik. True, she sponged the colt, and stroked him, and even sang to him. But her gaze, ever rebellious, strayed incessantly to the tall, lean, rugged frame of the man who vigorously oversaw and partook in the tasks at hand. She watched the play of muscles on his sinewy arms and the ripple of his back and shoulders, visible as his shirt began to cling to him. Fascinated, she watched his face. His dark eyes flashed like bolts of lightning as he directed the grooms in their tasks. The stark, angular lines of his profile intrigued her as he shouted brisk orders. His unruly sable hair was kept at bay by the long-fingered hand which occasionally raked through it, but there was a rebellious strand, which she longed to smooth with her own fingers. Several of the grooms had removed their soiled shirts, and Allyn found herself hoping that Joshua would do the same, although she would rather have died than suggest it.

It was nearly seven o'clock before they had any sign of the fruits of their labors. Sheik had been sipping tentatively at the new water all afternoon, and had stopped perspiring. Suddenly, shaking his massive head with a hint of the vigor he normally displayed, the thoroughbred shook off Allyn's caress and struggled to his feet amid the delight and scattered applause of his curators. Quickly Joshua grasped his bridle and felt Sheik's neck and throat.

"Fever's down," Joshua reported to all.

Allyn's heart leaped. Joshua looked her way, commanding her gaze for a moment. Then he looked away, fishing in his pocket. He pulled out a gold piece and slapped it into the head groom's hand, smiling as he said, "There's a steak dinner for all of you. You've earned it. Just bring back a couple of sandwiches for us, would you?"

The three men agreed enthusiastically, seeming more than content with the tip they had been offered. Thanking both of them, the party of men bowed out into the dusk, leaving Mr. and Mrs. Manners alone with the patient.

"Thank you, Joshua," Allyn offered, facing him from the other side of the horse. "It looks like you came through with that miracle."

He was watching her. The smile he had given the stablehands was gone. In its place was an expression she could not analyze, except that it made her feel uncomfortably warm. She at last could not endure it, and returned her attention to Sheik to mask her confusion.

"You're welcome," she heard him say in a quiet voice.

He heaved a sigh that was as big as he was and

began to gather up the blankets scattered about. Wanting, oddly, to be near to him, Allyn came around to help as he shook one out.

"You really do know a lot about horses, don't you?" she mused, taking hold of the other end of the blanket to help him fold it.

"Like you, I have many talents," he replied, joining the corners. "Maybe I'll tell you about them someday. Meanwhile, I've given no guarantee that Sheik is home free yet."

"No, but he is better. If we can get him to run tomorrow . . ." She trailed off, walking her corners to him. He took the blanket from her, covering her hands with his own. The gesture was surprisingly intimate. Her throat tightened as she looked up at him in wonderment.

"Allyn, don't get your hopes up," he warned, his eyes serious. "Sheik is a long way from healthy."

Allyn grimaced, tugging her hands away from his, pretending to be annoyed. She did not want him to guess at her treacherous feelings, that she was hoping for her daily kiss.

"You were full of gloomy predictions this morning too, I recall," she reminded him, staring at the blanket between them. "Sheik is going to be fine. He's going to run, Joshua! He's going to run!"

Where was this conviction coming from? she wondered, trying to calm her racing heart. This had nothing whatever to do with Sheik. What was happening to her?

"Listen to me!" he insisted, taking her shoulders, shaking her gently on each syllable. "Sheik is not well. He may not run. He probably won't run. I know"—his voice softened, and he stopped shaking her, but he kept his grip on her—"that you want him to run, and I know what you have been through. Honey, you have to understand."

267

"Understand?" she repeated, meeting his gaze at last. "Oh, I understand. I'm a silly woman with false hopes for a sick horse. I need a man around to take charge of things, and to keep me off balance, like Raif . . ."

Her hand covered her mouth, and a scarlet blush filled her cheeks. She had said, he suspected, more than she intended. Stunned by her outburst, Joshua did not reply. Studying her stormy, beautiful face, he wondered what else she had not said. He found, suddenly, that his arms were around her, and that her mouth, half-open with·shock, was inches from his own.

"I'm not Raif, Allyn," he heard his own voice whisper, pleading. "He's destroying you, from the inside out. Don't you see that? He's taken everything that was beautiful inside of you and turned it bitter and distrustful. Don't let him do it! He isn't worth it, honey. He never was."

She was staring at him with a strange look in her eyes, a look which both frightened and excited him. He was kissing her then. He was starved for the taste of her mouth, and for the gentle yielding of her soft lips he had come to crave so easily . . .

God, he was in love with her!

The thought made him release her abruptly. His features grew utterly slack from the shock as he met her glazed stare.

"Leave me alone," she said in a dark, trembling voice, turning away from him.

Her cold words were like a bucket of ice water in his face. He could not bring himself to reply to them right away.

"Don't tempt me," he warned at last under his breath, retreating to a far corner of the stable and slamming himself to the straw.

Chapter Eighteen

A squeaking hinge and clattering door brought Joshua to consciousness with a jolt. He pried his reluctant eyes open to the sight of the groom swinging the stable doors wide for his morning duties, flooding the place with sunlight. Shielding his eyes with a clumsy hand, Joshua sat up, and the groom called a greeting to him.

"Morning," he replied, rubbing his neck. "Have you seen my wife and Sheik?"

The man gestured to the warming track. "Working out," came the brief response.

Thanking him, Joshua lowered his booted feet to the floor. Cots and stables were not his favorite places to pass the night, but he had indulged his new bride's bizarre demand, even, he realized with tacit amusement, understanding it. As in his races, Sheik came first in Allyn's sphere. In fact, he placed second and third as well. That seemed to leave Missy, Bert, Bill Boland, and people in general—except maybe Raif— nowhere at all. Raif? Joshua wondered, arching a crick from his back. No, Raif could not possibly place anywhere, after what he had done to her. But women were a different breed altogether, and the way he had seen her kissing Raif in Louisville—no. He did not want to think about it, anymore than he wanted to recall the events of the previous evening. He hauled himself to his feet with effort and sauntered out to find Allyn and her thoroughbred.

It was a short walk to the warming track, and it was not difficult to pick out the well-favored chocolate colt, or his fair, habited mistress. They walked at a comfortable pace, like a pair of young lovers in tryst. Sheik did look much improved, but Joshua personally doubted the animal would be fit for competition on the morrow.

He waited at the rail until the unlikely duo came around to the near side again. He signaled to Allyn, who looked immediately guarded, but led Sheik over.

"Good morning," she said formally, without smiling. "Did you sleep well?"

"Well enough." He shrugged. "Considering the circumstances. You?"

She nodded in non-answer. She looked exhausted. "We didn't want to wake you when we left."

"Which was?"

"About dawn."

"You must be hungry," he observed.

"I could eat."

He beckoned her with a gesture, and they strolled to the gate. He put his hand out for the lead and she gave it to him automatically. As though she trusted him. He wondered if she was aware of that, but did not voice the question.

"Let's go back to the hotel," she suggested. "I would love a bath."

Joshua concurred. "I think the staff can take care of Sheik today."

"Wait a minute!" She stopped him, her eyes narrowing. "I didn't say that! I want to be right back here this afternoon when Sheik runs!"

There was no point to be served by arguing with her. They did return to the Huntington, where they bathed and breakfasted and did not introduce the recovering horse as a topic of discussion. Joshua did not want to start an argument, and he was sure Allyn did not want to hear his warnings. She would see soon enough that afternoon, he was certain, that Sheik would have to be scratched from the Preakness.

Nourished and refreshed, they returned to the track in mid-afternoon, about the time Sheik was due for his run. The stallion was in good spirits, greeting his mistress with a lively nod of his head, and no one protested when Allyn ordered that he be run. But Jack Riley was more than usually surly, and was slow to comply with Allyn's wishes. Riley's comments were terse and abrupt, and Joshua noticed that the sinewy little jockey cast a suspicious eye at him more than once. It surprised Joshua that Allyn endured his rude treatment without retort. He made note of the man's temperament and the woman's reaction with covert interest, wondering whether his own presence had any influence on either.

Sheik ran. He ran reluctantly and sluggishly, but he ran. Watching him, Allyn became more and more somber. His times worsened, and she signaled for his return. In a terse voice, she told Riley to take Sheik in. The man complied without answer, and a visibly deflated Allyn followed them back in silence with Joshua close beside her.

"What now, Allyn?" he asked quietly.

The only reply he received was a brief shake of her head. She trudged on in a businesslike stride, breathing hard. Her pace slowed, and he slowed with her, watching and waiting. Just when he thought she was about to cry, she swore a soft oath that only he could hear, one he'd thought only men knew. He could barely prevent himself from laughing out loud.

After they returned to the stall, he watched her pace. She had an interesting habit of bouncing her fingers against her thumbs, as though playing an invisible piano. Joshua was tired of the whole affair, though, and wanted nothing more this evening than a hot bath, a hot meal, and a soft bed. Beside him, Sheik swatted flies casually with his luxurious tail.

"You'll have to withdraw," Joshua pointed out, impatient for some kind of action.

"We still have time," Allyn muttered in reply, staring into space.

He was not certain whether she really believed that, or was simply looking for an excuse to delay her decision.

"Yes, and we still have to live," he reminded her, slapping his gloves against his leg with a sharp noise. "It's dinnertime. And I'm not about to spend another night in a stable on a cot for Sheik. Not even for Christ Almighty."

She dealt him a withering look, seeming to find resolve in perversity.

"And if I decide to stay?" she retorted, her green eyes narrowing in contempt.

"You'll look awfully silly slung across my back," he fired back wearily. "Besides, Sheik doesn't need you here tonight. You'll only worry him."

Her defiant expression told him she was thinking about the spectacle of herself being carried from Pimlico across his shoulder, wondering whether or not he would really do it. He knew his uncompromising gaze assured her that he would.

"You may be right," she agreed finally, looking away.

* * *

Behind her locked door, Allyn penned a letter to Missy that evening. In fact several. The first outlined all of the reasons why Sheik had to be scratched from the Preakness. The next two explained that he was going to run, and that everything was fine, respectively. Each of the missives found their way into the wastebasket.

Foiled in her attempts at correspondence, she went to bed, hoping sleep would release her from the terrible burden of indecision. She then lay awake for what seemed hours, staring into the dark, trying to decide the fate of the thoroughbred.

Restless, she finally abandoned all attempts at sleep and left her chamber for the common parlor. Robed and slippered, she did not make a light. She treaded softly across the floor to the wine decanter. With deft movements, she unstopped the bottle and poured a generous portion of the ruby liquid into a glass, making only a soft clinking sound as the neck of the decanter tapped the rim of her goblet.

"I could use a glass myself, Allyn."

She nearly dropped both implements at the sound of the deep, soft baritone. It was, of course, only Joshua, sitting somewhere in the dark behind her.

"You just about scared me to death," she accused him testily. "What are you doing out here anyway?"

There followed an amused silence.

"I can't sleep either," he responded. "And I don't mind the company."

She did not comment. Annoyed by her reaction to his unexpected presence, she poured another glass of wine and replaced the stopper. Two glasses in hand, she turned toward the room in time to see him lighting a small hurricane lamp.

She nearly dropped both glasses again. He was clad only in his freshly laundered blue jeans, and his bare, well-defined chest was at eye level. The increasing glow of the lamp illuminated the swarthy tone of his skin as well as the pattern of dark hair upon his beautifully sculpted pectoral muscles.

If he noticed her discomfiture as he straightened from his task, he chose not to remark upon it. She willed her legs to move forward. Joshua's unusually serious features surveyed her with no hint of mockery. She halted before him at arm's length, offering him one of the glasses she had poured. She strove to keep her eyes expressionless as they met his. He accepted the wine glass from her hand with a leisurely slowness, wrapping his fingers around the bowl until they touched hers. Through no will of her own, her hand lingered, then finally relinquished hold. She hastily retreated to the wing chair in the center of the room, curling into it like a cat.

"Do you want to talk?" he asked, his baritone soft and light.

He settled himself on the love seat and lounged carelessly. She shook her head, sampling the robust wine. Breaking her own resolve, she heard herself implore, "Tell me he's going to run, Joshua."

He did not answer her right away. He seemed to measure her with his deep, coffee-colored eyes, taking a thoughtful draught of the claret.

"What do you think?" he countered, settling his broad shoulders against the cushions with a quiet grunt.

She knew she did not really want to hear his opinion. Still, his question both annoyed and amused her, as his questions often did. Joshua Manners had his faults, but he certainly did make her think, that was sure.

"I don't know what to think anymore." She shook her head, feeling monumentally weary. "I wish my decision could be made for me."

Joshua shifted in his seat. "Would you like me to make it for you?"

She sent a tired glare his way.

"Certainly not!" she retorted, and she saw at once that his sensuous, slack mouth had widened to a grin. She realized he had been baiting her, and she smiled ruefully.

"You are hateful," she pronounced with a brief, resigned chuckle.

"So you keep saying," he agreed in a breathy version of his urbane manner. "But that's part of my charm, is it not?"

His charm. She bit her lip.

"Morgan Mellette would know more about that than I would, I suppose," she said, looking into her glass.

Across the room, she heard him issue a small sigh.

"She was Morgan Brown in Pierre," he told her, his quiet baritone unadorned. "An eligible, available widow."

He rubbed his jaw with his free hand, and his dark eyes stared into the night. She watched him, burning to know more, but afraid to ask, lest he misconstrue her interest.

"Marriage was never an option with me, and she knew it," he went on without prompting, to her relief. "Then the governor came along, and she took the chance to regain some respectability. But Morgan is like a spoiled child. She wanted, as the saying goes, to have her cake and eat it too. She can't seem to understand that I couldn't do a thing like that to my worst enemy, let alone to my employer."

His words, and his tone, were sincere. She felt a tightness deep within her breast, like a sob that wanted to surface but could not.

"Raif could," she thought aloud, then pressed her hand to her mouth in horror. The wine. The wine had loosened her tongue, and her inhibitions. And

275

her good sense. She was glad of the dim light, for in it, she might hope that Joshua could not perceive her heated blush.

"I told you before, I'm not Raif," he told her, in a voice so gentle it made her want to cry.

She got up from the wing chair and left her wine glass upon the table. She needed to compose herself, and she knew she could not accomplish that with Joshua's caressing gaze upon her. The draperies had been drawn on the tall windows, and she pushed one of them aside, pretending to be interested in the Baltimore night.

"Who are you, Joshua Manners?" she whispered to the brocaded portiere.

She felt a warm ripple of wind beside her and she knew, swallowing hard, that he had joined her.

"Joshua Manners," he replied quietly, "is a man who has traveled a long way, looking for something he's found in his own hotel room on a warm night in May."

His brown velvet baritone was as soft as the drapery beside her cheek. It made something break inside her, something she could almost hear. For an awful moment, she thought it might be her heart. There was a tender weight upon her shoulder. She was afraid to look at him, but all at once she was doing just that. She could barely see him in the darkness, but she could feel him all around her like a quilt. When she laid her head against his warm, bare chest and felt his strong arms encompass her, there were tears stinging her eyes.

"I can't, Joshua." She could barely get the words out, it hurt so much. "I can't love you. I'm going to marry Bill. I told him I would."

Joshua felt a physical pain, as though she'd kicked him in the groin. He could not let her go, for fear that the pain would double him over.

"You *can't* love me?" He managed a clear, if incredulous, tone in spite of it. "Or you don't?"

"I can't." Her voice sounded strangled, like the hiss of steam escaping from a tiny hole in a boiler. "And I don't."

"Give yourself a chance," he tried, pressing his cheek against her soft hair. "And give me the chance to show you how."

"No!"

She broke away from him and ran several steps back toward the light. She swayed, panting, and her eyes were wide with anger, and hurt.

"I am not a whore," she said in whispered outrage, her eyes astonishingly cold. "And I won't be one. Just because I had an affair with a man I loved . . ."

"You poor fool," he breathed before he could stop himself. "You poor little fool!"

He heard her draw in a hard, sharp breath, as though she had taken a punch. He wanted to say something else, perhaps to apologize, but the words jammed in his throat. She half-ran back to her room and quickly closed herself inside. Joshua was powerless to do anything but watch her.

He knew, all at once, the agony of a wild animal wounded, but not killed, in a hunt.

Chapter Nineteen

The Preakness was won. Joshua led Allyn to the winner's circle amid roaring throngs of spectators. This will make her happy, he thought. This will show her how trust is rewarded. They reached the circle, and there, atop Sheik in black and green silks, was Raiford Simms.

Joshua sat bolt upright in the pale dawn light of the parlor, where he had fallen asleep on the divan. It had been a dream. His eyes focused on a shadowy figure standing before him. At first he thought it part of another dream, but then the apparition spoke.

"Joshua!" it commanded in an urgent whisper.

It was Allyn calling his name.

He rubbed his eyes with the heels of his hands. After their brief, delicious interlude last evening, he had not been able to so much as close his eyes without seeing that look of undisguised desire in her damnably beautiful face, or feeling his arms ache for her to fill them again. He had just managed to fall asleep out of sheer exhaustion, and here she was, awakening him.

"Joshua!" she repeated, louder. There was impatience in her address.

He shook his head hard.

"What time is it?" he asked, his voice a somnolent growl.

"Six o'clock," she replied in a crisp tone. "I have to check on Sheik to see if he's going to run today."

Today. The Preakness. The mist cleared from his brain, and his eyes adjusted to the light. Allyn, he could make out, was wearing her habit and her bland, businesslike expression, betraying none of the tenderness of the previous evening. Perhaps, he thought sourly, he had dreamed that as well. No, he reflected, standing up at last. Had it been a dream, he was sure he could have effected a much more satisfactory denouement.

"Give me five minutes," he told her, ambling to his own room.

Six minutes later he returned, having taken care of his morning needs and added a red flannel shirt and work boots to his blue jeans. He found her gazing out of the window with a faraway look in her eyes. He was reminded, with a sting, of the previous night. *I can't love you,* she had said. *I don't.* He was stricken by a compelling desire to go to her and take her into his arms from behind, perhaps to brush that prim knot of dark hair from the back of her neck and replace it with a kiss . . .

God, what was the matter with him? he wondered, thoroughly disgusted with himself. She'd made her feelings pretty clear last night. Or had she? He was behind her, without a clue as to how he'd gotten there. What was this power she had over him?

She faced him with a surprised gasp, and he realized, abashed, that he had placed his hands on her shoulders. She pulled away from him ever so slightly, her features registering agitation.

"My God, you startled me!" she said accusingly, hugging her arms to her chest.

"What were you thinking just now?" he asked, his arms falling to his sides.

She sighed.

"He has to run, Joshua," she breathed, looking out of the window again. "What will I tell Missy? What would Bert have said?"

He thought of the numerous occasions upon which she had told him of his own arrogance. In spite of himself, he felt a chuckle rise in his throat.

"There's an old saying," he told her, remembering something he had heard in his youth. "About having the serenity to accept the things you can't change, the courage to change the things you can change, and the wisdom to know the difference. There isn't anything you could have done that you didn't do, and nothing you shouldn't have done that you did. It's all up to Sheik now, isn't it?"

She stared at him with a look which defied analysis.

"What?" he pressed her, curious beyond restraint. "What's the matter?"

She smiled faintly, and the sun emerged from a bank of dark clouds.

"You are a very nice man sometimes, Mr. Manners," she told him, and her voice had a ring of wonderment.

Sheik appeared to be a little improved. He had eaten, and seemed restless and glad to see his affectionate mistress. Joshua noted the attentions his wife paid to the thoroughbred, aware of a spasm of jealousy. He helped her saddle the colt and together they led him out to the warming track.

"Where is Riley?" Allyn mused, looking around in

annoyance. "He was to meet me here. How is Sheik supposed to run with no jockey?"

Joshua glanced about and, seeing no one but grooms and trainers, responded with a solution.

"Why don't you ride him?"

She met his gaze with startled green eyes. She smiled, a rakish, challenging expression he enjoyed. "Why not?"

He gave her a leg up.

"Take him slow at first," he advised. "I'll watch him to see if he shows any signs of distress."

She nodded in reply, and nudged the chocolate thoroughbred to an easy canter.

Joshua marveled at her command of the animal, as he had on at least two other occasions. What a pity, he thought, that she couldn't jockey the beast herself. He'd seen many a man in that position who had demonstrated no such skill, and far less instinct.

"He wants to run," she reported. "I'm going to let him."

Indeed Sheik was chafing at the bit. Before Joshua could nod his assent, she gave him rein and nudged him forward with a cry. The plunger sank on Joshua's stopwatch, and the horse took off down the field like a thing possessed.

It was a respectable time for a beast. Surely not his best, but certainly an improvement over the previous day. Allyn cantered him to the rail, her green eyes bright with hope.

"A minute four," Joshua informed her, unable to keep a smile from his face. "Not bad, considering the weight."

"Or Baltimore water," Allyn added, ignoring, or not noticing, the playful barb. She dismounted as he caught Sheik's bridle. "He'll run. He may not win." She glanced at the thoroughbred fondly, patting his steaming neck. "But he will run."

Joshua breathed a sigh of relief. The dilemma was solved.

"Of course," Allyn was going on, "I will want to check on him again before the race."

She walked on toward the stable, pulling her riding gloves off as she went. Joshua followed with Sheik in tow, sensing a coming storm.

"That won't be easy to do from the clubhouse," he told her, curious to see her reaction.

She halted in mid-stride and spun around, staring at him blankly.

"Clubhouse?" she echoed, as if she had not understood him. He and Sheik caught up with her as she stood rooted with shock.

"Clubhouse," he affirmed, tucking her arm into his own and leading the way. "It will be more important for us to appear at the Preakness than for Sheik to run it. You keep forgetting that."

"And you never miss an opportunity to remind me!" she retorted, breathing hard. "Sheik needs me, Joshua. I don't expect you to understand, but that's more important to me than appearing at a social event."

"Sheik doesn't need you," Joshua argued, not daring to chuckle at the sentiment. "But you don't have to be afraid of the clubhouse. I shall protect you."

"Afraid?" Her laugh did not quite sound natural. "Me?"

"Yes, you," he replied in a low tone, feeling his patience ebb. "Don't be so hard-nosed. Of course you're afraid. Anyone in your position would be. Anyone in their right mind, that is."

"Are you implying—"

"But I promise," he went on over her words, "I won't leave your side even for a moment. And I won't give anyone the opportunity to attack you. So no more of this nonsense about Sheik."

"As if I care about a—a social function!" she sniffed. "Me—afraid. And you," she fairly sneered, "protecting me. I don't know which notion is more absurd!"

Joshua felt a spark of anger ignite in him at her snide bravado. How easily she dismissed him! Disdain his "protection," would she? Wouldn't it serve her right to find out just how much she needed it?

Perversely, he nurtured that spark to an ember as they deposited the lively colt with his grooms, and his hurt pride fanned the ember throughout the ride back to the hotel. He did not help her down from the cab, and drew some small satisfaction from the sound of her feet running to catch up with him.

Through the lobby, up the stairs and to the suite, he addressed no word to her. It was not until they had gained the privacy of their rooms that he spoke.

"Be ready in half an hour," he said coldly without looking at her. He entered his own room and slammed the door with a force that tested the hinges.

Fear, he knew, was a thing which made a cornered animal turn and fight. This knowledge, however, was not enough to inspire a forgiving spirit in him. She was like a spoiled child, he reflected angrily as he dressed in his charcoal-gray pinstriped suit. A vase-hurling, tantrum-throwing, hothouse variety thorny rose. And what she needed was the wrath of God to instill the proper spirit in her. Unfortunately, gods were notoriously capricious about whom they bestowed both wrath and blessings upon. The gods, he decided, glancing in his mirror at the finished product, might require some assistance this day from Joshua T. Manners.

She was not in the parlor when he emerged. He glanced at his pocketwatch. The half hour was up.

"Aren't you ready yet?" he called to her, not bothering to mask the hostility in his voice.

"You go on ahead," came her calm reply, muffled

by the door. "I told you, I have to go to Sheik."

That was the limit. With his balled fist, he battered upon her door.

"Damn it, Allyn, come out here!" he exploded. "And if you don't come out properly dressed—"

"How dare you shout at me!" she shouted back at him through the door. "You married me, you didn't purchase me. I'll do as I please, and it pleases me to look after Sheik."

That was the last straw. Intending to give his wife a credible facsimile of godlike wrath, he thrust his booted foot into her door, tearing off the lock and rendering useless its function of protecting her honor.

Allyn was clutching the bedpost at his dramatic and unceremonious entrance, her eyes wide with astonishment, yet blazing with contempt. She was, as he had suspected, clad in her habit.

"Take that thing off," he snapped curtly, and turned his angry attentions to her closet. Rifling through her wardrobe, he chose a blue chiffon dress and threw it on her bed.

"Put that on, and make it fast. Because if you aren't out here in five minutes, I promise I'll come in here and dress you personally."

"You don't frighten me," she told him in a trembling voice, giving the lie to the bold sentiment.

"Allyn, you're a sore trial to a man," he warned as he approached her, his words quiet and deliberate. "I have tried treating you gently, reasoning with you intelligently, and shouting at you. None of these seems to convince you, so I guess that leaves only brute force."

In a lightning-quick gesture, he had her lapels in his two hands. With a sudden, sharp movement, he wrenched them apart in opposite directions as though spreading the wings of a hapless bird. The material of shirt and vest yielded, and in an instant hung about her arms in shreds. She gasped and hugged her bared arms to the lacy white camisole at her breast. But Joshua was not admiring his handiwork. Moving quickly, he snatched up the pale blue confection he had selected from her closet and found its collar. He threw it over her head, and its skirt cascaded downward like a rustling blue waterfall. Reaching underneath, he grasped the skirt of her habit and pulled until the seams gave way. By this time her habit was a memory.

When her face appeared again, it was red hot with humiliation.

"I think I can manage myself now, thanks," she retorted, her voice shaking.

"I don't believe you. And in any case, I'm not going to leave you alone in here so you can sulk and nurse your wounded pride."

He reached into a sleeve to pull her arm through.

"Don't touch me!" she hissed, trying to shake off his firm hold, failing entirely.

"That, my dear, depends entirely upon your behavior. Turn around."

His tone was not to be disobeyed. As she righted the bodice and sleeves, he buttoned the back, struggling only a little with the tiny buttons and loops. He completed the uppermost buttons, suppressing a desire to fasten his hands around her throat.

With trembling, infuriated fingers Allyn adjusted the collar and affixed a cameo brooch, wincing as she stabbed her thumb. She sucked at it savagely, aiming her darkest scowl at him. She swept past the equally scowling Cerberus behind her and selected a pair of shoes for the ensemble. No one had ever put her in her place so summarily in all of her life. She wanted to strike him but was afraid, as forbidding as he looked, that he might actually strike her in return.

Carole Howey

"You may go now," she managed, choking with rage. "This dress needs a petticoat, and I don't trust your skill in that area. I doubt Morgan Mellette wears any."

To her outrage, he laughed, a loud, hearty, infuriating demonstration of mirth.

"Why, my dear Mrs. Manners," he declared roundly, his features alive with amusement. "I do believe you are jealous!"

"You are insufferable!" she cried and, no vase being handy, threw her purse at him.

Mr. and Mrs. Joshua T. Manners arrived at Pimlico in the spectacular glare of the afternoon sun, as smiling and luxuriously contented as a perfectly matched pair of turtledoves. The adoring wife was serenely beautiful, and the indulgent husband courtly and attentive. To any but the knowing eye, and the only knowing ones present belonged to the happy couple, the Joshua T. Mannerses were the veritable portrait of wedded bliss, giving lie to the taints heretofore printed.

They held forth in a prominent area of the clubhouse overlooking the winner's circle, a location through which much of society's traffic must pass. The improvising duo was greeted and congratulated by all comers and carefully scrutinized by watchful gossips. They passed inspection with all colors flying, despite lack of rehearsal.

Allyn's beatific countenance was enlivened by her glimmering green eyes, but the only person who fully comprehended that glimmer was her tacitly bemused husband. He alone knew the glimmer was aimed at him like poisoned darts. But he had triumphed, and was complacent in the knowledge that Allyn's reputation was secure in spite of herself.

Wagering opened for the Preakness Stakes. Until

286

this time Allyn had, on principle, invested each successive winning pot right back into the ante, without question. Here in Baltimore, however, with such a staggering sum of money at stake to be lost on the chance of an unhealthy animal, she experienced no small doubt.

As the crowd gathered at the betting windows, she felt Joshua's inquiring gaze upon her. Please don't say anything, she thought, feeling tension in her jaw. Blessedly, he did not.

"My money goes on Sheik to win, Joshua," she heard herself say in a steady voice which surprised even her.

"All of it?"

"All of it."

She heard him draw in a breath, then release it. "I'll be right back."

He strolled off, and she watched him go, drawing inspiration she desperately needed from his bold and buoyant walk.

O ye of little faith, she had said to Bert, what seemed centuries ago. O ye of little faith, she repeated to herself, swallowing a lump in her throat. To even think of abandoning the champion . . .

But, oh, God, if he loses? If he loses?

"It's done." Joshua had returned from his mission.

Allyn did not look up. Her hands lay dormant in her lap, and she felt small and alone. Joshua resumed his seat beside her. She did not look at him, but she could not deny her relief at his presence. As though aware of her feelings, Joshua drew his chair closer and placed a firm, reassuring hand on hers. His hand was warm and dry. Slowly her fingers entwined about it like vines.

On the track the contestants were escorted to the starting gate. Rising, Allyn abandoned the hand she had been clutching and strained for a glimpse of

Sheik. Was he improved? Had he suffered a relapse? Was the colt from Dakota, the "dark horse" winner in Louisville, going to present a respectable accounting of himself before thousands of spectators eager to profit by any result?

Sheik was showing odds of eight to one, rumor of his illness having gotten around. The two horses chosen by the public to finish ahead of him had not competed in the Derby, so there was no telling how they might affect the outcome. Sheik was seventh from the post, not, to Allyn's mind, a favorable position. But the track was soft, labeled slow, due to much damp weather that week. And of the three races—the Kentucky Derby, the Preakness, and the Belmont Stakes—the Preakness boasted the shortest distance, a mile and three sixteenths. All of that favored Sheik.

But a Sheik recovering from such a debilitating illness?

The starting gun fired. Allyn tensed, watching the horses issue from the gate. Jack Riley kept the colt to the outside for the start, only moving to the rail for the turn to shorten the distance. By that time, Sheik had moved into fourth, demonstrating the strength and spirit he had shown in his morning workout. He did not seem overtaxed. He held that position through the turn, moving again to the outside along the backstretch.

Rounding the far turn, Sheik had pulled up to second, without having spent his energy for the final move. Coming out of the turn, Riley gave the mighty thoroughbred his head, and they surged forward to the finish line.

Even if greater glories lay in store for the three-year-old, none could be so shaming or gratifying to Allyn as the sight of his sixteen hands hurtling across the finish line a half a length in front of a worthy competitor who could only place.

Laughing, crying, wholly incoherent, Allyn flung her arms about Joshua's neck. He embraced her willingly. Even if the embrace was for Sheik's sake, he knew, it was still an embrace. A bond. It was with reluctance that he said in her ear, "Allyn, we have to get down to the winner's circle."

He did not need to remind her of what had happened in Louisville.

Unlike Churchill Downs, Pimlico's winner's circle welcomed them, with crowds of bystanders cheering and applauding. Allyn was more than a little stunned by the attention. She stared about her at the sea of faces, all of which stared back at her and Sheik. Some of them were smiling, others merely curious. She remembered Raif's threat, and wondered how many of these people had read the insignificant entry in the paper. How many of these people were here because they fancied they'd never seen a "scarlet woman" before? She faltered at the idea, hesitating as she approached her horse, who was blanketed with yellow daisies whose centers had been painted to look like black-eyed Susans.

"Go on, honey." Joshua nudged her forward, his smile encouraging and unbearably proud. She tried to smile too as she seized Sheik's bridle and impulsively kissed the steaming thoroughbred full on the muzzle. The crowd laughed and applauded more at this act, and once again Allyn shrank back against her husband. She felt his arm, like a support, about her waist.

"It's all right, Allyn. I'm here," he whispered. She wanted to hide her face in his lapel like a timid child.

The crowd pressed. She could see grinning faces of every description. Behind her was the solid presence she knew to be Joshua. The figure in miniature atop Sheik was Jack Riley. The noise was as ceaseless and as hushed as the sound of the sea in a seashell. The officials began their presentation, and Allyn could not hear their words. She saw their crinkly, smiling eyes, their lips moving and their heads bobbing. She knew then that she was going to faint, and that there was nothing she or anyone else could do to prevent it. Another soul within her cried out and pleaded with her to hold on for just a few more minutes. Frantic, but still smiling, she searched the crowd for help.

A cool, mocking pair of blue eyes met hers across a narrow gulf. A red-gold mustache twitched once and the face of Raiford Simms, but a few feet distant, smiled unpleasantly at her. Clutching Sheik's rein, Allyn at last quietly fainted into her husband's arms.

Chapter Twenty

Allyn awoke to the softness of linen and the firmness of muscle beneath her cheek. She tried to move and to open her eyes, but the effort was too great and her cushion too comforting. She heard a moan from far away.

"Shh, Aly." It was Joshua's voice, deep and soft, in her ears. "Just lie still. We're going back to the hotel. Everything's all right."

No, it wasn't all right, she wanted to shout. Sheik was in terrible danger.

"Raif . . ." was all she could murmur.

Joshua's heart slowly turned to ice. Suddenly the warm pressure of her head against his arm was a terrible burden.

Raif. Would it always be Raif, even after the grief he had wrought?

"No," he breathed, finding his voice at last. "It's Joshua. Be quiet now." Because I can't bear to hear you say his name again. He thought the last, but he did not say it.

At the Huntington, he carried her swooning form through the lobby, ignoring the bellboy, who was paging Allyn Cameron in a stentorian voice. Whoever wanted her would have to wait until he had taken care of his armful.

Their suite was stifling. He laid Allyn down on her bed atop the white lace coverlet. Her skin was pale, her breathing was shallow, and she did not move. He opened the windows and drew the shades. In the darkness, the room felt cooler at once. He shed his own hat and jacket, loosening his tie and collar as he went back to her bed. She was trying to sit up, and she fumbled groggily with the chiffon fastenings of her hat. He sat down beside her, forcing himself to feel nothing. Gently he pushed her fingers out of the way as he completed the task for her.

"What happened?" she asked him, her voice weak as a kitten's.

He removed the broad-brimmed hat from her head and tossed it to the foot of the bed.

"You fainted," he told her. "Must have been the heat. Or maybe because you haven't eaten. I'm going to order some supper, and get you a doctor. Turn around. Let me unbutton you."

Obliging, she turned her back to him. All at once she realized that she could not remember how they had gotten back to the suite, or even from whence they had come. It was a frightening sensation.

"Joshua, what's happened?" she demanded in an urgent whisper. "I don't remember—"

"What?"

His voice was so soothing!

"Anything," she admitted, feeling foolish.

Behind her, he sighed.

"Sheik has won the Preakness, Allyn. You fainted in the winner's circle, and I brought you back here."

His words brought the memory, cloudy and distant, vaguely into focus. But there was something else. Something . . . awful.

"No, Joshua," she protested, slipping her arms out of her sleeves. "There's something else—I can't—"

She stopped, aware that he sat inches away from her, and that only her camisole stood between her and his caress. His dark eyes were serious and penetrating, and there was no hint of amusement in them, or in that wide, sensuous mouth of his.

What would it be like? she could not help wondering as she watched him moisten his lips with the very tip of his tongue. She felt dizzy at the memory of that tongue teasing her lips, and she swayed ever so slightly in his direction. He took hold of her arms, the soft part just above the elbow, and held her for a moment. She dared not stir. She watched as his lips moved, but to her surprise, no sound came out.

Abruptly Joshua released her and got up from the bed, striding to the window. Disappointment stabbed her. She wanted to call him back, but she could not form the words. She heard a call, but it was a woman's voice, calling her name from outside of the room. At first she thought she'd imagined it, but Joshua turned sharply at the sound as well. There were four distinct knocks, followed by the same voice. Recognition came to her like a sudden light in a dark cave.

"Missy!" she exclaimed, forgetting her weakened state. She hastily pulled on her sleeves and ran to the door of the suite. "Missy!"

Missy Cannon's full, fair face was a study of relief and weariness. Her familiar grin was a sight that Allyn had not realized she'd dearly missed until that moment. Allyn seized the younger woman and embraced her as though she were a phantom that might, at any moment, disappear into mist. Missy hugged her in return, and Allyn felt her cool hands on her back, where the buttons of her dress had been undone.

Allyn could form no words for her complete joy at seeing her friend, and so satisfied herself by laughing and crying alternately with fierce embraces. Presently she felt Missy stiffen. Confused, she backed away from her friend to see a look of utter astonishment on Missy's pleasant, scrubbed features. She followed Missy's stare across the room to the towering Joshua Manners, who had emerged from the bedroom in his state of undress, no doubt to discover the cause of the commotion.

"M-Mr. Manners!" Missy stuttered in a barely audible whisper. "Oh—my! I'm—"

"Good afternoon, Miss Cannon." Joshua greeted her with one of his charming smiles. "How nice to see you again."

Judging by Missy's reaction, Allyn realized that her friend had probably departed Rapid City as soon as she had received the wire about Bert's death, and had not received her subsequent letters about the marriage arrangement. Dear Lord, she thought, embarrassed for her friend. What must this look like?

"Missy," she began in an exasperatingly uneven tone. "Joshua and I are—we were married three days ago. I sent you a letter expla—"

Missy's expression changed, mercurially, to one of unabashed glee. "Oh, how wonderful!" she cooed. "I told you—"

"Missy, hush!" Allyn interrupted her savagely, seizing her friend's shoulders. "It isn't like that! Be still and let me explain!"

Carefully, and without passionate embellishment, Allyn recounted the events leading to her matrimony. In the end, Missy appeared much sobered, but no less delighted. Turning her attention once again to

Joshua, she addressed him in what Allyn recognized as her best formal courtesy.

"Mr. Manners, this is most noble of you to come to our—to Allyn's aid in so selfless a fashion," she began, her gray eyes twinkling only a little. "How fortunate we are to benefit by your generous intervention."

Joshua, to Allyn's amazement, merely shrugged his broad shoulders and cast his gaze downward in a fair approximation of humility, saying nothing. She had rather expected a pompous, if not completely bogus recitation of denials of worthiness of such praise. Instead, he actually looked uncomfortable in the face of such undisguised gratitude. She felt a compelling, if peculiar, desire to rescue him from the situation.

"Joshua, excuse me, but weren't you going to see about some supper?" she inquired gently. "Suddenly I am starving. And I'm sure Missy would like something after her journey."

This stirred him into action.

"Yes, and I was going to get a doctor too," he remarked in a lighter tone, rebuttoning his collar. "With your permission, Miss Cannon, I'll inquire about a room adjoining our suite for tonight. We leave for New York tomorrow, of course. I trust you'll accompany us?"

Missy, Allyn noticed with a mixture of amusement and, oddly, jealousy, seemed completely at the mercy of Joshua's undeniable charm.

"How kind of you, yes," the young woman murmured. Joshua excused himself, and Missy turned once again to Allyn.

"Doctor!" she exclaimed in a whisper, her faint Southern drawl completely disappeared. "What's he need a doctor for? Is he sick?"

Allyn shook her head and spread herself out on the divan.

"For me," she yawned, stretching. "I fainted at the track after the race. Can you imagine?"

Missy, to Allyn's surprise, paled visibly. "You fainted?"

Allyn nodded, waving her hand. "I'm sure it's nothing. I haven't eaten all day. It was warm . . . What is it, Miss?"

Missy did not look as though she thought it was nothing. She sprang forward and felt Allyn's forehead and neck with the back of her hand, her countenance a study of concern.

"Allyn," she began, her soprano wavering slightly. "Is it possible that—that you—that you are going to have a child?"

Allyn felt the color rapidly drain from her face. It was possible, she knew. In view of events before the Kentucky Derby and occurrences since, she realized, with sinking heart, that it was entirely possible.

In fact, it was likely.

"Oh, God, Missy," she muttered, trying to think and failing entirely. "What if I am?"

Missy, Allyn knew, while giving the overall appearance of being easily overwhelmed, in fact possessed a surprisingly cool head in the face of adversity. Allyn watched with growing anxiety as Missy's expression became thoughtful and remote.

"The child is Bill's, of course," Missy began, sounding like a schoolchild in recitation. "But he may not believe that when he learns of this marriage, as he's sure to. And if what you've told me about your marriage to Joshua is true—"

"It is," Allyn cut in, with some annoyance.

"Then Joshua may be certain the child is not his. In either case—"

"In either case," Allyn interrupted again with a growing sense of dread, "I will be carrying a child with no father to claim him, and some doubt of gaining one. My God, Missy, this is really too much. What am I going to do?"

Missy tried to smile reassurance, but Allyn found the expression too painful to bear. Missy's hand was on her own, and it made her feel like crying.

"The first thing we have to do is prevent the doctor from seeing you," Missy said in a low, swift voice. "We should keep this to ourselves until we decide what's to be done. I don't suppose there's any chance you might be persuaded to remain married to Joshua?"

The idea caught Allyn off guard. She stared at Missy for a time, thinking about the import of Missy's words. Assuming it would be possible to remain married to Joshua Manners, it would mean bearing him a child that was not his own, and allowing him to believe it was. Further assuming, of course, that Joshua Manners was incapable of counting to nine.

Her stomach knotted. No. If the notion of such a falsehood was unpalatable even for a moment, it would be intolerable for a lifetime. Duplicity had never been her forte. But then, as Joshua himself had once said, one had to learn to use every means in one's power for one's own ends. She shuddered.

"I don't know," she whispered, closing her eyes. "I don't know."

"Well," Missy said crisply, after a long moment. "Bill is crazy about you. He might overlook your marriage to Joshua if we can convince him that you never—well, you know. He'd probably be thrilled to pieces about the idea of having a child of his own. Someone to pass his ranch on to. You know how men are."

"Yes," Allyn replied dryly, stroking her cheek with one finger. "I appear to know all too well."

She must have looked desolate, because Missy's brittle smile became real, and she patted her on her cheek with a reassuring hand.

"Don't be so hard on yourself," she told Allyn. "You know you can count on me, no matter what. We've always been here for one another, haven't we?"

Allyn regarded her friend with a reluctant smile. It was true, she reflected, although after half a lifetime she was beginning to perceive their relationship in a new light. Where Missy had always been cautious, she'd been bold. Where Missy had confessed doubts, she, Allyn, had encouraged risk. In all of their years together, Allyn had seen herself as the strength and foundation, and now it appeared that it had been Missy after all who had consistently provided a safe haven for her.

"Thank you, Missy," she all but whispered to her friend, grasping Missy's large, plump hand.

Missy grimaced in wry amusement. "For what?"

"For not saying, 'I told you so,' " Allyn replied with a sigh.

Joshua returned to the suite a short while later reporting the success of each of his missions.

"Supper will be brought up shortly," he informed Missy, who sat with needlework in hand, and Allyn, who had been reading a book on the divan.

Allyn still felt weak, with worry more than fatigue. Joshua must have noticed, for he inquired after her condition.

"Oh," she said, waving a hand impatiently. "I'm fine. I just need to eat. I hope you didn't bother with a doctor."

Was his scrutiny real or imagined? She could not tell. In either case she was not equal to it. She turned away from his probing stare and glanced at Missy, who shot her a warning look.

"I did." He sounded surprised. "There's no harm in letting him have a look at you."

"Huh," Allyn sniffed, putting on her best disdainful sneer. "That doctor who looked at Sheik certainly knew what he was doing, didn't he? No, I don't trust Baltimore physicians after that experience. Besides, I feel fine now. When he comes, just send him on his way."

Joshua's continued scrutiny made her terribly uneasy.

"Allyn, you fainted!" he reminded her with some amazement.

She scowled and pretended to be engrossed in her book. "For heaven's sake, Joshua, women faint all the time. It doesn't mean that they're sick or—or anything!"

She had almost tripped herself. She began to tremble, so she snapped the book closed and threw it to the floor as she rose.

"Excuse me," she said archly, sweeping past him. "I am going to dress for dinner. And I am not going to see any Baltimore doctor." Then looking over her shoulder at him with a dark expression, she added, "They're not all trained at Johns Hopkins, you know."

And she went into her room, closing the door behind her with a resounding bang.

Joshua studied the door for a time, utterly perplexed by his wife's behavior. He was in the midst of a sigh before he realized it. He flung himself into the comfort of the wing chair facing the chair upon which Missy sat, cupping his hand to his cheek and staring at the book Allyn had cast aside. He sat thus for a long while—just how long, he did not know. In fact, he did not heed the passage of time until he heard Missy speak, in a quiet tone that broke the stillness of the room like a pebble cast upon a quiet pool.

"You are in love with her."

He realized at once that it was not a question. He met her gaze and found her measuring him in some unfathomable way, her gray eyes sharp and unyielding. He was obliged at last to look away, even as his cheeks grew warm.

"Is it that obvious?" he wondered aloud, feeling exposed. He forced himself to look at her again, and was surprised by the sympathetic smile on her robust features.

"To me, yes," the young woman replied in a quiet, candid voice, a light soprano laced with a faint drawl. "I suspected your feelings in Deadwood. But not obvious to Allyn. Allyn has"—here she cast a wary glance at Allyn's door, and lowered the dynamic of her voice—"a blind spot in her heart."

"Raif," Joshua forced himself to say.

Missy grimaced, nodding her affirmation. "Allyn is a proud woman, as you have no doubt learned. That affair with Raif"—she paused, shaking her head, as though she could still not believe what had transpired so long ago—"left her in ashes. Total ruins. Of course, she never told you."

"Not in so many words," Joshua admitted, wondering at the enormous sense of relief he was feeling at being able to talk about Allyn with someone so close to her. "But it wasn't hard to guess."

Missy seemed satisfied with his response, nodding her head vigorously. "Of course, she could never forgive him now. Not with all that's happened . . ."

Joshua laughed softly, a bitter, hollow laugh. "Who do you think she called for after she fainted?"

He could have bitten his tongue for that admission, but there it was. It was the truth, after all, and perhaps it was best that he start to acknowledge it. Perhaps it was time to accept the reality that he was a convenience to Allyn, and nothing more.

Chapter Twenty-One

The first days in New York were devoted to Sheik's comfort at the stables. Allyn deferred more and more to Joshua's suggestions in these matters, resenting his authoritative demeanor while grudgingly admiring his obvious expertise in matters of security. Missy, to Allyn's bewilderment, seemed to trust completely in Joshua. The younger woman wanted to fill herself up on the sights and pleasures of New York City, and was content to allow Joshua to manage things. She scarcely troubled herself about any arrangements at all.

Invitations to Mr. and Mrs. Manners began to clutter their mailbox at the Hotel Pellier, their New York address. Allyn answered most of them with polite regrets, as there were far too many to accept. She relied on Joshua's recommendations as to which would be most advantageous in terms of promoting Sheik's interests.

Joshua himself had begun to treat Allyn with the kind of quiet, almost remote respect that she had wished for since Louisville. The problem was, having achieved this, she suddenly and inexplicably missed those unvarnished observations and provoking remarks to which she had become accustomed. He had neither demanded, nor received, any further kisses, and by Allyn's calculations, he was already several days behind. Perhaps, she thought, with no small regret, he had lost interest in her. Coupled with her secret dread that she might be with child, this sudden change in him formed a new schism in their relationship. One she felt increasingly powerless to breach.

The situation demanded drastic measures: the theater, the opera, the symphony, and shopping. Allyn's one consolation in this whole business was the profusion of fine shops, and with her recent success in the Derby and the Preakness, the abundance of funds which partnered excellently with the shops. A day did not pass when Allyn did not drag the reluctant Missy and the neutral Joshua to a succession of the establishments, where she outfitted herself in what she unflinchingly referred to as her "trousseau." Of course, while the finery was well suited to the Winter Garden and Delmonico's, as Joshua observed in his cool, unsmiling way, she would have precious little use for those sumptuous ball gowns as the wife of a Dakota rancher.

The first week drifted into the next, bringing the Belmont Stakes closer. Allyn, over breakfast, asked to be taken to the stable. She had not yet visited Sheik in his new estate. In fact, she had not seen him at all since leaving Baltimore. She realized with some amusement that she missed the beast, probably more so since Joshua had begun to treat her like a stranger.

Joshua acquiesced without argument. He did not seem even to have any interest in arguing with her, these days. Missy begged off, and Allyn, knowing her friend, understood that she was trying to help mend the fences.

The Hotel Pellier was nearly an hour from Jerome Park by cab. For that hour, Allyn introduced one topic after another for conversation, only to lapse into silence after Joshua's terse but unfailingly polite responses. Even the perfect beauty of the May morning could not brighten her dismal humor by the time they reached the stables.

Sheik, apparently, was enjoying his improved circumstances. His stall was larger and brighter, and kept clean by a veritable battery of stablehands. Two armed Pinkertons in crisp, military-looking uniforms stood watch at either end of the row of stalls, and one at the rear. The very best men money could buy, Allyn reflected, thinking of the terms which had "purchased" Joshua as her escort.

Joshua himself took his leave of her outside Sheik's stall, expressing a wish to talk with the security officials at the gate. She watched him go, glad to be alone and free of the tension she'd felt lately in his company.

"Hello, lad," she greeted the colt, entering the roomy stall where the thoroughbred stood calmly munching oats. He turned his massive head toward her and she patted his velvety neck, looking into his placid brown eyes. She wanted to speak to him, or sing to him, as she used to, but was unable to conjure the words. So much had changed in so few weeks. Where once she felt completely at home in a stable and at ease in Sheik's presence, now she felt awkward and ill at ease. She felt like an uninvited guest at a party, and worse, in her cool, peach-colored organdy dress, like one who had arrived overdressed. She had no cooing encouragement for him, and no private monologues. She was alone with Sheik. And for the very first time, she felt alone.

A quarter of an hour passed. The stable door clattered open suddenly, as if the caller had expected to find only Sheik inside. Startled, Allyn peered over Sheik's shoulder to see the little jockey, Jack Riley, whose craggy, unpleasant face changed at once to a sour expression.

"Thought I'se quit of you," he muttered in unmistakable disgust, hurling Sheik's tack to the straw floor. He placed his hands at his belt, eyeing her coldly. "What do you want?"

"I want you to remember who writes your pay voucher," she answered in as sharp a tone as she could muster in the face of such rudeness.

"You don't belong here," he snarled. "Get away from here or I'll quit."

"No, you won't," she told him, allowing herself a smug laugh. "Not when you have a chance to ride a Triple Crown winner. You are a despicable little man, Jack, but you aren't that stupid. Besides, this is New York. There are jockeys on every street corner. Better ones, I imagine, than you."

He dared to sneer at her, an altogether hideous expression at which she could not help but cringe.

"There're whores on every street corner too," he remarked in a rapier-like tone. "That don't mean I take orders from 'em."

Allyn's face drained of blood and her tongue cleaved to her mouth. For a horrifying instant, she feared she would faint. Even this common little man knew of her shame, and taunted her with it!

"How—dare—" she managed, the syllables dropping from her lips with livid deliberation. The third word, however, was lost in the sound of the stable door slamming shut. Both she and her jockey turned to see black rage in the face of Joshua Manners, who did not slow his stride to Jack Riley. Allyn watched in wordless wonder as her husband lifted Riley against the wall by his lapels with frightening ease.

"My wife would like an apology," she heard Joshua say, his voice low and dangerous. "Now."

Riley made a choking sound, and Allyn knew the man could not breathe. As terrified as she was of this rage of Joshua's, she ran up behind him and grabbed his right arm with her two hands. Riley's face, she saw, was already turning blue.

"Joshua!" she exclaimed in a trembling voice. "Please! You're going to kill him! Joshua!"

In response, Joshua allowed the man to slide to the floor, although he did not relinquish his hold on Riley's clothing.

"The apology, Riley. And it had better be good."

Allyn could imagine the uncompromising look in Joshua's dark eyes, having seen it a few times herself. She watched Riley's face, now a study of undisguised terror, as he licked his thin lips with his quivering tongue.

"I'm—s-sorry," he managed, glancing once at Allyn as though he did not dare to take his eyes off of Joshua for long.

Apparently, this did not satisfy her husband, whose grip tightened. Riley's feet once again dangled in the air.

"I apologize," Riley said louder, panting. "Mrs. Manners."

Joshua released him and he fell to the floor in a heap, like so much dirty linen. Allyn was sure that Joshua was going to kick the man, and she felt faint and nauseous at the thought. Instead, though, she heard him speak again, in that same low, chilling tone.

"I hope you believe in God, Riley," he was saying, standing perfectly still. "Because you had better thank Him every day for the rest of your miserable, misbegotten life that my wife has a kind and forgiving heart.

Carole Howey

If it were up to me, you wouldn't leave here alive."

Slowly, like a wounded animal, Riley got to his feet, backing away with a hunted look.

"If I ever hear of you talking that way about my wife again, I will kill you," Joshua promised the little man, opening the stable door. "Now get your cretinous ass out of here. And don't come back."

As though Riley might need help, Joshua seized the back of his collar and, with one hand on the man's belt, flung him far out of the stable. The hapless jockey landed, bruised but alive, and took off without looking back.

For a time, the only sound in the chamber was that of Sheik's untroubled chewing. Allyn felt as though she were suffocating, and her heart was beating like a bird's. She was compelled to watch Joshua, whose expansive chest heaved with panting, more from anger, she suspected, than exercise. Presently he looked at her, and she was equal to his gaze for only a moment. She looked down then, first at his hands, the hands which had very nearly, and with little effort, strangled Jack Riley. She found she could not even look upon them without wave upon wave of shame washing over her like a tide. She drew in a hard, broken sob, shaking all over from rage and humiliation.

"I—" she began, but her voice came out in a whisper. "Hold me," she managed at last, pleading. "Please, hold me, Joshua."

Her soft words ripped Joshua's heart from his chest. He went to her willingly, enfolding her slight, pliant body tenderly to his breast in a passionless, protective embrace, sure that it was the most important gesture he had ever made in his life.

She was not crying, he knew, feeling her awful pain as though he himself were gut-shot. She held on to the lapels of his jacket, breathing in deep, wracking

306

gasps. He stroked her soft hair and kissed it, groping for words, unable to find any that would comfort her more than his embrace. He knew, with a devastating certainty, that he loved her. Desperately. Hopelessly. More than he would have ever dreamed possible. And he knew then that, no matter what, he would stay with her, for as long as he could contrive.

"I'm sorry, Aly," he managed to whisper finally.

"You have nothing to be sorry for," he heard her say, and he knew she was mastering herself again. Her strength amazed him. "I'm the one who should be sorry. I loved him, Joshua. And look at what it's done to me. How long must I pay?"

She took another breath, as though she meant to say more. He waited. When she did speak again, he had a feeling it was not what she had originally intended to say.

"Have you ever been in love, Joshua?"

Her question caught him completely off guard.

"I—yes," he answered, hesitant. Did right now count?

She pushed herself back from his chest, but he kept his arms about her. She wore an expression of disbelief on her composed features, and did not try to free herself from his embrace.

"With who?" She sounded doubtful. "Morgan?"

He chuckled gently, hoping she could not read his emotions in his eyes.

"No. Not with Morgan. But if you're trying to make a point, I do see what you mean: to give your love, and to have it thrown back at you in so mutilated a condition that it's barely recognizable. Yes. I can appreciate what you have gone through. What I can't understand is . . ." He stopped, not wanting to go on. He let her go, turning away, hoping she would not pursue the matter. His hopes were quickly dashed with her next words.

307

"What?" She touched his hand with her fingers, and he ached to hold her again. He took a deep breath and fixed a blank expression on his face before looking at her again.

"What I can't understand," he said in as patient and disinterested a tone as he could muster under the scrutiny of those hauntingly beautiful green eyes, "is why you called his name when you fainted at Pimlico. 'Raif,' you said."

There. He'd said it at last. He prayed that he had not betrayed himself. This, he knew instinctively, was not the time. Or the place.

Her response startled him. Her hand went to her mouth and her eyes widened with terror. She was white as a ghost in moments.

"That was it, Joshua!" she breathed, grasping the sleeves of his jacket at his biceps. "That's what I couldn't remember after I fainted! Raif was there, at the winner's circle, in Baltimore. I saw him. He smiled at me, and I—oh, Joshua, I know he means to try again for Sheik! What are we to do?"

Joshua felt as though a great weight had been lifted from his shoulders, and it made him want to laugh. He did risk hugging her to him, though, saying simply, "We can handle Raif, honey," feeling as though, once again, all things were possible.

They returned to the hotel in time for lunch, and when Joshua suggested they dine in the main court, she demurred becomingly. She seemed at ease, even happy, as they perused their menus, and his heart was glad. He wanted Allyn to be happy. But more, he wanted to be the one to give her happiness. He found himself, as they chatted idly, daydreaming about her again, as he had been wont to do before their marriage. Imagining that this remarkable woman who sat across from him, sometimes serious, sometimes gay, but always bright and intriguing, was his and his alone. That no conditions had been placed upon their relationship by external forces, and that no evil threatened it from without or within. It was a dream which left him feeling regret usually, but one with which he tortured himself nonetheless.

They lingered over coffee, and Joshua signed for the check. He helped Allyn from her chair, and saw her stiffen as she rose.

"What is it?" he asked, then followed her stare across the court to the front desk.

Governor Arthur Mellette and his bold and bodacious young wife were checking in with their entourage and their trunks. Morgan was, by all appearances, creating quite a stir already among the help, as porter after porter commandeered trunks and valises and carried them off, presumably to the Mellette suite.

"How very interesting," he heard Allyn say in the light, formal tone he had come to recognize as trouble. "Of all of the hotels in New York, what do you suppose the chances were of the governor and his charming wife selecting this one? Without assistance, I mean?"

Her meaning was obvious.

"Allyn, you can't think that I—"

"Can't I?" Her eyes glittered like hard, fiery emeralds when she faced him. "What else am I to think?"

Allyn did not care to hear his reply, if he had one. Tears stinging her eyes, she forced a calm, even expression to her face, not wishing to create a scene. She walked away from him as quickly as she could. She did not even have a direction or a destination. She only knew she could not bear to be with him in that crowded dining room, watching his paramour come back into his life.

She found herself on the sidewalk outside the Pellier. There was a park bench under a shady elm, situated for waiting for cabs, and she sat down upon it, feeling utterly miserable.

How many days had passed, she wondered bleakly, staring at the traffic, since Missy had suggested she might be with child? A week? Ten days, perhaps? The child was growing. How long, she mused, until her relatively slim figure began to grow with it? She thought of Jack Riley and his horrid remarks, and of Joshua's violent response to them, and could not help wondering if the latter's reaction would have been the same had he known she was carrying Bill Boland's child . . .

She closed her eyes and lowered her head, unable to endure the blinding sunlight. She was close enough to tears as it was. She wished, all at once, that she had not made this odyssey with Sheik. Bert would still be alive. In Rapid City, she would have married Bill Boland long before she ever even suspected she was with child, and her brief encounter with Joshua Manners would have been remembered as a peculiar annoyance, nothing more. She would have been able to hold Raif close in her heart at the same time as she held Bill in her arms. She could have taken out her memories and looked at them like a pretty picture book. She would have been able to avoid life's harsh realities, and could have shut out love as easily as she now locked her bedroom door every night . . .

You are a coward, Joshua Manners had told her in a heated, charged argument so long ago. And not even a smart one at that, she added to herself. All she had been able to do was to get herself into a fix, get Bert killed, and—her hand went to her mouth in dismay—fall in love with Joshua Manners.

Oh, God, she thought, feeling a sob choke her. What have I done to myself?

The traffic outside the Pellier was increasing with the afternoon. Cabs, carts, wagons, trolleys, and a few horseless carriages. Hurricanes, she'd heard them called. Noisy, hazardous-looking things, darting about among the slower-moving vehicles like mad hornets. Frightened pedestrians hardly dared to step off of the cobblestone sidewalks in terror of being struck by one vehicle or crushed by another . . .

Would one really be killed? she wondered, a detached sense of calm overtaking her. Or would one merely be injured enough, perhaps, to miscarry?

She was on her feet. Twenty steps to cross the street, she guessed. Perhaps she would not make it past ten.

Chapter Twenty-Two

"It's warm, don't you think?" The source of the brown velvet baritone which Allyn had recognized at once was beside her, as though he had materialized from vapor. Joshua's words jarred her, and for a fleeting moment she could not recall why she was there beside the street.

"Yes," she mumbled in reply. Part of her, she realized vaguely, wanted him to leave. Part of her, a large part, wanted very much for him to stay. She continued to stare at the street, afraid to look at him. Afraid, she knew, that he would lay bare her emotions and her secrets.

"We need another jockey," Joshua said, and Allyn was glad of a fresh topic upon which to fix her mind.

"Have you any recommendations?" she asked at the end of a sigh.

"Several." He sounded businesslike, thank heaven, and she was able to pull herself together. "Do you trust me?"

He was trying to rile her, she realized, but she hadn't the will to rise to the bait.

"Is there any reason why I should not?" she asked.

"If I said no, would you believe me?"

In spite of her dark humor, she laughed. "You are impossible, Joshua. Where must we go?"

At last she felt strong enough to look at him. He was biting his lower lip, regarding her with a measuring look.

"It's no place for a lady, Allyn," he told her. "It's best that you stay at the hotel with Missy. I'll be back in a few hours, and we can all talk it over. Go on back to the suite. I think a rest will do you good."

His voice was so gentle that she wanted to curl up inside it, and his dark eyes bore no trace of merriment. She wanted to stop time so she could save that moment forever. She had never felt this way in her life, she realized. It was a wonderful, terrible feeling, and she never wanted it to end.

"Joshua . . ." Had she spoken? Was that her own voice, so breathless and light?

"What is it, honey?"

"I . . ."

What's on your mind, honey?

The past reached out of the darkness and seized her like a hawk clawing its hapless prey. She loved where she was not free to love. Bill Boland had a claim on her now. Greater, it seemed to her, than any Raiford Simms had ever had. Her mistakes had caught up with her all at the same time, and they paraded before her eyes like ribald, mocking circus buffoons. She was devastated.

"I'll see you later," she managed, and fled before he could say anything more to her that would only add to her pain.

Missy accepted the news about the fired jockey as though it was of little consequence.

Carole Howey

"Joshua will find us a new one," she said cheerfully, helping Allyn undress. "Good riddance to Jack Riley. He sounds to have been horrid, and we are well rid of him. Allyn, I've had a wonderful idea."

Allyn lay down upon the coverlet of her bed, wearing only her undergarments, watching as Missy hung up her dress. Missy, she reflected, had fallen into her old place of serving as maid to her since they had returned to city life. And she had allowed her to. She sighed, making a mental note to speak to Missy about this unusual turn of events. But just now, she was obliged to trail doggedly after Missy's mercurial train of thought.

"I'm almost afraid to ask," Allyn responded with a small yawn. "What is it?"

Missy abandoned her attention to Allyn's wardrobe and came to sit down beside her upon the bed. She folded her hands in her lap and appraised Allyn with a sharp-eyed gaze that sent a shiver down the older woman's spine.

"Tonight," Missy said in a low tone, as if afraid someone might overhear, although they were quite alone, "you must go to Joshua and—seduce him."

"What!" Allyn nearly leaped from the bed, shocked to hear such a suggestion from her ordinarily prim friend. "Missy, have you lost your mind?"

Missy neither blushed nor looked away. "He's in love with you, Allyn. He told me so himself. And I suspect you love him as well, or am I mistaken?"

Missy's instincts were, as usual, incontrovertible. Allyn felt a blush in her cheeks, and she could not deny the truth.

"Missy, what has love to do with any of this?" she demanded, lying back and staring up at the lacy canopy above her head. "I am carrying Bill Boland's child. Even if I hated Joshua, I couldn't trick him into remaining married to me. I must put

314

aside my feelings and make Bill stand by me. And if I can't—"

"Allyn, you are so hard-headed!" Missy exclaimed impatiently. "If you can't, what will you do? Give birth to a bastard, and suffer ridicule and humiliation at the hands of the people of Rapid City? People who have been waiting for years to see you brought down? How can you be so eager to throw away the best chance of happiness you've ever had?"

Missy's arguments were always strong, especially when they made so much sense.

Allyn felt a deep sigh wrack her body. "Do you remember," she asked quietly, "why I left my family?"

It was Missy's turn to sigh. "Allyn . . ."

"Do you?" she repeated, still staring into the canopy.

Missy got up from the bed and moved to the casement. "The little house on Delancey Street," she murmured, as though it were a part of a nursery rhyme. "Your father's mistress and her—their little boy. Yes, I remember."

"Then you can understand," Allyn went on, sitting up against the broken-arch pediment of the headboard, "why I can't do that to Joshua. Or the child. Or myself."

"No," Missy said firmly. "I can't. This is nothing like that. You are married to Joshua. You don't even know for certain that you are pregnant. You love Joshua. He loves you. It all looks quite simple to me. Stay with him and be happy. Or leave him and be miserable, and possibly disgraced besides. Now, there's a difficult choice," she wound up sarcastically.

Allyn could not form an argument. There was, after all, a great deal of logic in what Missy said. Premature babies were born all the time. Joshua Manners would,

315

she had no doubt, make a wonderful father. And she had no doubt that she could be happy to remain Mrs. Joshua Manners. Still, there was another option.

"Suppose," she began, crossing her legs and holding her stockinged toes, "I told him about the child? What do you think he would do?"

Missy spun on her, disbelief in her steel-gray eyes. "Now who's lost their mind? One of two things will happen if you tell him: His pride will be so crushed that he will utterly reject you, or his honor will force him to pack you off back to Bill. Are you prepared to deal with either of those consequences?"

It took a moment for the import of Missy's words to settle. Missy had very clearly outlined three different and distinct scenarios to her, two of which involved the absence of Joshua Manners from her life. The third, and perhaps most dreadful of all, involved a monumental deceit. A deceit which Allyn doubted her ability to play out. Maybe, she thought, only a little hopeful, Joshua would not react to the news in the ways which Missy had suggested.

Maybe, she thought again, his reaction would be even worse.

"I can't do it, Miss," she breathed, sensing that the dreadful time was at hand. "I couldn't deceive Joshua in that way. I know I couldn't live with that lie."

Missy narrowed the distance between them and, with a firm but gentle hand, tilted Allyn's face upward. Her gaze was uncompromising. "Ask yourself this, Allyn: Can you *not* do it?"

Allyn jerked her head away, unwilling to see Missy's grim scenarios played out in her bright, gray eyes.

The darkness of Joshua's room was like a thick, black shroud. Allyn slipped quietly through it, musing with no small dread about her coming deed. She drew her robe closely about her otherwise naked shoulders, shivering, not from any chill.

Joshua had returned before dinner with the names of three candidates for the honor of riding Sheik. He had seemed pleased by his success, and had acted more than a little surprised when she had declined his suggestion that they go out on the town, the three of them. Her heart had been too full of what lay ahead of her.

Missy had chided her later, in private, saying that everything would have been much easier if she'd had a little wine, or champagne. But Allyn wanted a clear head and steady nerves. She needed all of her wits about her, she realized, if she was to succeed.

Joshua was now asleep in his bed. She could hear the resonance of his shallow, regular breathing. It was a comforting sound. It was a sound she could even love, were it not for the contemplation of the sheer ugliness of what she was about to do to him. The thought of it turned her insides to a mass of tangled, hot metal, like the aftermath of a train wreck.

Quietly, she found the lamp on the nightstand beside the bed. Should she light it? No, she decided. She would not be equal to his scrutiny right now. It would be best if he could not see her clearly. Surely her treachery was etched in her face. Surely he would perceive her intent at once.

She paused a moment longer, wanting to watch him in innocence one final time. The metal within her writhed and twisted. She loved him, she knew. As completely as she loved Missy, and as passionately as she had loved Raif. And she was about to gamble everything to embark upon a lifetime of deceit and trickery. She was about to stain that love with the indelible print of a lie . . .

She drew in a hard, painful breath. I can't do this, she thought, her heart aching as she thought of his tranquil face in the darkness.

Can you not do it? Missy had pointed out with cold, hard-headed logic.

She sat down upon his bed, and the creak of the springs beneath jarred the catlike sleeper to startling awareness.

"Allyn!" he exclaimed, his warm baritone scarcely above a whisper, tugging at her heart. "What are you doing in here? Is something wrong?"

She swallowed hard, desperately trying to will herself to numbness.

"No," she managed softly. "I . . ."

Where had her carefully planned recitation gone?

Joshua rolled over and was soon sitting beside her on the bed.

"I—I have to . . ." She stopped again. She felt he was looking at her in the way he had several times before. The look had always made her want to run from the room before. But now she wanted a lifetime to savor it. She could not speak.

"God, you are beautiful," he whispered in the darkness, brushing the hair from her cheek with a strong hand that was unbearably gentle. The hand lingered on her jaw, and instinctively she leaned her cheek into it, starved for his touch, although she had never allowed herself to believe it until that moment.

He kissed her, his lips parted, taking her mouth in a gentle, exploring way. She was filled instantly with the sweet, honeyed foam that was want, and her hand was on his neck, holding him to his purpose. His kiss went on and on, and she allowed it to, wanting to taste him and to know him as she had not known him before. His mouth was strong and firm, and his tongue was a sweet brand that made her burn.

There was a low moan, and it startled Allyn, until she realized it was her own desire breaking the stillness. His other hand was at her collar, slipping, with a leisurely slowness that was torture, between the

318

soft chenille and her shoulder. Her robe yielded as his hand slid down along her collarbone, its way eased by the light film of perspiration which had formed at his first touch, to the soft, firm roundness of her breast. Her desire swelled as he caressed her hardened nipple with a bold yet tender touch.

He loves you, Missy had said. He said so himself. And you love him. You'll be doing the best thing . . .

Everything that was warm inside her suddenly turned to ice. She could not do this. With effort, she lowered her head, breaking the current their lips had created. He seemed to mistake her gesture, now kissing her eyes, her temple, anywhere his mouth could reach. With his other hand, he took the lapel of her robe, intending, she knew, to draw it back.

"Joshua, wait," she managed, her desire ebbing quickly in the face of the task before her.

"I've already waited so long," he murmured, his lips teasing her ear so she thought she would go wild. "My sweet, my love . . ."

There was nothing she wanted more in that tender, awful moment than to be able to answer him in kind, and to realize the promise of those lush kisses. It required all of her will to push herself back, to break the spell of their powerful desire, and to turn away from him. Tears stung the back of her eyes and her throat filled so with emotion, she thought she would choke.

"Please, don't, Joshua," she pleaded, rising from the bed to escape from him. "You don't know everything."

He was behind her, wrapping his arms about her waist in a strong, possessive embrace, burying his face against her neck.

"I know that I love you," he told her in a tone that turned her insides to a trembling mass.

Her hand went to his cheek of its own volition,

softly outlining his angular jaw.

"And I love you," she was able to whisper before she sobbed. "That's what makes it all so difficult. Please, listen to me."

His hands fell away from her, and she thought for a moment that she might fall. Swallowing hard, she turned to face him, to find him lighting the lamp on the nightstand. The room glowed a pale, ghostly gold. He turned to her again, standing but three feet distant, his sable eyes serious and expectant.

"I'm listening," he said in a terse voice.

Oh, dear God, she prayed. It had been so long since she had prayed, though, that she was unable to conjure further supplications. There followed a long moment when she could conjure nothing but the desire to be held in his arms again. But she could not ask. She must do this on her own.

And Joshua was waiting.

"I'm afraid I might be—expecting a child," she barely whispered at last, wanting to look away, but not daring to.

He blinked. His eyes widened, then narrowed. He drew a deep breath, then let it out all at once.

"Raif's?" he challenged her.

The word knifed her. She hesitated over her reply. Would it be better to lie and be thought a fool, or tell the truth and be thought a trollop?

"Bill's," she breathed, feeling her shame to be complete. "Bill Boland."

She wanted to tell him everything. How she hadn't loved Bill. How she'd been broken by Raif, and how she'd been afraid of being alone for the rest of her life. But she could see, watching his eyes grow empty of all emotion, that her explanations would be of no use.

Joshua had slipped away from her like fresh, sweet water through a sieve, and she was parched.

"Why did you come here to me tonight?" His quiet words made her tremble, and she marshaled her courage to answer him.

"I think you know," she replied in a whisper. "I'm sorry, Joshua. I didn't want to hurt you. I couldn't do it. I couldn't lie to you."

A faint smile traced his mouth, but it was not a pleasant expression.

"You couldn't lie," he echoed, and there was no mistaking the mockery in his voice. "And that's supposed to be enough? That's supposed to make everything all right?"

His words were small, sharp stones hurled with great force. She wanted to touch him. She wanted to make it right. But there was more separating them now than three feet of Persian rug. There was more separating them than there ever had been, even at the Steeplechase in Dakota. She wondered abstractly if he would kill her. She wondered if she might not simply die.

"Thank you," he went on, his tone brash and overloud, "for your concern. You didn't want to hurt me? That's touching. It really is. And I might even have believed it, had I not remembered your often-repeated avowal of hatred for me."

He paused, shaking his head with a small, bitter laugh.

"I let you do one hell of a dance with me, lady, and I can't think of one good reason why I should give you a chance for an encore."

Allyn felt her jaw sag open, and her face drain of blood.

"What are you—"

"I'm saying," he interrupted, his hands resting at his waist, "that you have a lot of fancy talking to do with your Dakota bull, don't you?"

She wanted to leave the room. She wanted to run. She thought she was running, but it was just her heart, beating like the wings of a wild, caged bird. She was still standing there with him. She was still watching him, watching both of them, as from some distance outside her own body. There was a sound like a rushing in her ears. It was, she perceived, his breathing. His bare chest, decorated with a sprinkling of dark hair, rose and fell with his rapid panting.

"Get out," he breathed, his eyes as cold as a killer's.

She was in her own room, with no idea as to how she had gotten there. She leaned against the door fumbling with the lock, cursing the tears which blinded her. She felt a sob well up inside of her, but it never broke. It sat in her chest, and in her throat, choking her. She sank to her knees, sliding down the door, and collapsed finally in utter despair.

Joshua stood for a time staring at the door that Allyn Cameron Manners had lately passed through. There was a knife in him, in his stomach. In his chest. In his gut. He tried abstractly to remember when he'd felt such pain before and found, to his vague surprise, that he could not.

He tried to move. His feet were stiff and aching, as though they had hardened to the floor. He looked down, fully expecting to find them bleeding. But they were not. They had merely turned to stone, like everything else in his body, except for his heart.

God damn her, he thought. God damn her. God damn Bill Boland. And Raif Simms. And God damn Joshua T. Manners.

The room was stifling, and reeked of failed dreams. He had to get out, or he would suffocate.

Chapter Twenty-Three

Allyn did not get out of bed the next day, or the day after. And Joshua was nowhere in evidence. Missy knew, from these two facts, that her plan had failed. She was able to make a pretty shrewd guess as to why as well. She did not require Allyn's mute depression as further proof.

On the morning of the third day, Allyn was still more deeply melancholy than Missy had ever seen her, even more than the first days after Raif had left her so many years ago. Then she had not spoken much, or eaten, but she had gone mechanically through her tasks, maintaining at least the outward appearance of normalcy. Now she neither spoke nor ate, accepting only water, and did not rise from her bed.

Missy was desolate. What had Joshua said to Allyn, or done to her? She could raise no response from Allyn when she posed these questions with quiet urgency. Allyn merely shook her head and avoided eye contact.

323

And Joshua? What had become of him? Surely the revelation had hurt him, but if he loved Allyn as he professed, he could rise above it. Or could he? Missy sighed, drawing her chair closer to Allyn's bed. She wrung out the washcloth from the basin on the nightstand and placed it on her friend's forehead. Allyn's eyes were closed and her breathing was regular, but there was no way of telling whether she was asleep or awake.

Damn Joshua, Missy thought angrily. She had often wondered what it must be like to have a real sweetheart, but if this was the best that a man in love could behave, perhaps she was as well without one.

She heard a door close, and footsteps in the parlor of the suite next door. Allyn did not stir. Missy left the washcloth on her forehead and went to see if Joshua had returned.

He had. She entered the parlor to find him sprawled in the wing chair, which he had apparently turned to face Allyn's door. His head had fallen back. His hat lay where it had dropped to the floor. His collar was open, and his tie hung loose about his shoulders. There was at least a day's growth of beard upon his jaw and his eyes were closed. His arms hung down limply from the arms of the chair.

The picture raised anger in Missy. She slammed the door behind her, taking some small satisfaction in the fact that Joshua jerked at the sound. His head came up, and he opened his eyes wide. They were glazed and bloodshot.

"You look terrible," she said without thinking.

Was he disappointed that it was only her, or did she imagine it?

"I feel terrible," he replied tonelessly.

His head fell back on the chair again like dead weight.

"You should," Missy told him. She was determined not to say anything to him about Allyn, or that night, unless asked. She sat down in the tiny Queen Anne chair beside the door to Allyn's room, sending hostile looks his way whose meaning, she hoped, was not obscure.

"Where is my wife?"

It seemed to require great effort on his part to lift his head again, but he accomplished it, and regarded her with a steady gaze.

"Why do you want to know?" Missy challenged him, every inch equal to it. "Are you going to browbeat her again?"

Joshua stared hard at her.

"She told you everything?" he asked, his voice quiet.

"You bastard," Missy breathed, unable to restrain herself. "You did, just now. Allyn hasn't said a word for two days. And if you really cared, you would have known that."

His eyes narrowed, and he sat upright. "What do you mean? Where is she?"

"She is in her bed," Missy retorted hotly, barely above a whisper. "She's hardly moved. She doesn't deserve this, Joshua. What have you done to her?"

In answer, he bolted up from his chair, nearly knocking it over, striding for Allyn's door. Instantly Missy was on her feet barring his way.

"But the baby!" he demanded, his dark brows furrowing. "Missy, she hasn't gone and—oh, sweet loving Jesus!"

He started to push past her, a look of real terror on his handsome features.

"No, she hasn't!" Missy told him, grabbing his arm roughly to prevent his further passage. "But why should you care? Haven't you done enough damage already?" she hissed at him, standing her ground in spite of his imposing presence.

"What about the damage she did to me?" His relief quickly blended to hurt. "Do you know about that too?"

"You fool!" she flung back at him. "I told her to go to you that night. I told her not to tell you about the baby, and that it would only cause trouble for both of you. But she couldn't lie to you, Joshua. Not even about something that happened before you ever really knew her! She had to tell you. Allyn is a lot of things, not all of them good. But she's as honest a person as you'll ever know."

He was stunned.

"You told her to?" he muttered wonderingly. "Why?"

"Because Allyn's happiness is the most important thing in the world to me," Missy replied with neither guile nor pride. "And you, Joshua Manners, are only important insofar as that happiness goes. If you think I wouldn't kill you to make her happy . . . I'm disappointed in you, Joshua," she wound up disdainfully. "You are not the man I thought you were."

He looked away, pretending to ignore her last comment. She knew, however, that her words had hit their mark.

"Step aside, please, Missy," he said quietly, clenching his hands at his sides.

She stood firm, glaring hard at him.

"She's my wife," he insisted, an urgency in his voice which she had not heard before. "Let me by."

Against her will, she felt a tiny stab of empathy for him. She knew, looking into his pained dark eyes, that he loved Allyn, and that it was his own sense of honor which had made him spurn her. Missy edged away from the door, cursing herself for a fool, even though she knew he could have his way without asking.

"If you hurt her again . . ." she began, hoping she sounded menacing.

"You have my word," he said gravely. "I won't."

Joshua had been unable to rid himself of the terrible leaden weight in his chest for two days, and he noticed no lessening of it as he stilled his trembling hand on the lever of Allyn's door. He knew, entering the room, that he could not bear to see her. He knew, closing the door behind him, that he could not bear to do otherwise.

The room was dark and quiet. The curtains and shades were closed. There was a still mass upon the bed in a tangle of bedclothes. He was filled with a sense of dread. Was there something Missy had not told him? Had Allyn done herself some injury after all? The thought wrenched his heart, and he found that he could not speak as he drew nearer to her bed.

She was asleep, or appeared to be so. She lay prone, her face half-buried in two feather pillows. Her dark hair was strewn about her face like blown autumn leaves and her small mouth was slack, the lips slightly parted. The memory of that awful night assailed him, but the anger was gone. All that was left was the hurt. And he could not be certain, but it seemed to him that some of the hurt he was feeling was hers, not his own. Please, God, he thought, laying the back of his fingers against her cheek. Please, let her be all right.

Her skin was cool and dry. She stirred at his touch and he withdrew his hand, watching as she turned onto her back and opened her eyes.

Her stare was glassy and vacant. He thought for an awful moment that she did not know him. He moistened his lips with his tongue.

"Allyn," he said after he found his voice. "It's me. Joshua. I—are you all right?"

He saw her eyes fill with tears before she turned away from him again.

When Allyn rose from her bed early in the afternoon, she felt paradoxically exhausted. She felt weaker than she ever had in her life, although she knew that, having not eaten in two days, she should not be surprised by the fact. Missy ordered her a meal and drew a bath for her, and she washed her hair with scented soap surrounded by gallons of warm water. The miracle of running water was a luxury she would miss living on Bill Boland's ranch.

She let out a painful, broken sigh. Perhaps, she thought, there was a great deal to be thankful for after all. Joshua Manners would gladly corroborate the story that he had not touched her during their brief marriage. Bill, she felt sure, would, as Missy had said, be delighted at the prospect of a son. All that remained for her to accomplish was the transformation of what was left of her love for Joshua Manners into loathing. And that, she thought, shuddering, should not be too difficult to do, given the pain and humiliation she had already suffered at his hands.

No. She was done with crying. She splashed water into her face, then poured a pitcher full of water onto her head. She emerged from her bath and toweled herself vigorously, wishing that she could as easily scrub Joshua Manners from her soul. She had done with love, she told herself, even growing accustomed to the emptiness inside her. In a little more than a week she would be quit of Joshua Manners, and this entire bizarre and exhausting adventure. She could shut away her heart again, or what was left of it, and become Mrs. Bill Boland.

She caught her breath suddenly, dropping her towel to the floor.

"Missy!" she called out as loudly as she dared, knowing that Joshua was in the suite parlor beyond the door.

Missy appeared from the bedroom, wearing a frown of wonderment.

"What . . ."

Allyn merely pointed at the towel upon the floor. Missy's eyes grew wide.

"You've come on," the younger woman barely whispered. "Oh, Allyn, you're not expecting after all!"

"Don't tell him," Allyn ordered curtly.

"Allyn, for the love of—"

"Your word, Missy!" she insisted, leveling a stern gaze upon her friend.

"My word," Missy echoed weakly, looking unhappy. "Me and my big mouth. Look at all of the trouble it's made already!"

Missy was near to tears. Allyn silently concurred, but nevertheless found a smile for her well-meaning friend.

"Another week," Allyn soothed her, "and it will all be over. We'll be on our way back to Rapid City together, and Bill and I will be married, and that will be that."

Her pronouncement left her breathless and numb.

Missy looked troubled. "But Joshua—"

Allyn held up her hands in interruption.

"I am erasing Joshua Manners from my vocabulary immediately after the Belmont," she told the younger woman firmly. "And until that time, he is not a topic for discussion. Is that clear?"

Missy nodded, her eyes wide as a waif's. "Are you going to the Cotillion tonight?"

Missy's question distracted her. There really wasn't any way around it. She and Joshua had accepted the invitation, as they had the Belmonts', which would take place on the eve of the race.

"Help me get dressed," she sighed in answer. "I suppose I'd better talk to—to him."

Joshua's head ached. It was a thorough, unapologetic pain, the kind that made him feel like his head might explode. It was just the sort of pain he needed, and just what he'd been working toward these last few days. It almost hurt badly enough to make him forget that his life had gone to hell.

From his slouch in the wing chair, he could reach the bourbon bottle on the table beside him. If he concentrated, he could tilt it, and pour the amber liquid into the glass without spilling too much. He talked his way through these activities in silence, pleased ultimately by his dubious accomplishment. The difficult task, he realized through the regrouping alcoholic haze in his brain, lay ahead. How to replace the bottle with a fresh one, when this one, half-empty, was finished?

He drained the glass he had just filled and wondered, in a detached, even disinterested way, if his head had actually gotten larger, or if it only felt that way. He debated for a moment getting up and going to the mirror hanging above the unused fireplace to find out. He rejected the idea. He doubted, with the shred of rationality remaining in his brain, that he could negotiate so complex a maneuver.

He set the glass down on the table, knocking it over as he reached for the bottle again. He cursed under his breath and righted the glass carefully, but did not refill it. He'd had enough. Between the pain and the thick fog in his brain, he could no longer conjure the image of Allyn Cameron Manners's damnably lovely face as she told him she carried another man's child in her womb.

The worst part of the whole lousy business was that he was powerless. He was overwhelmed by the magnitude of his failure. By the one variable in this complex equation for which he had not allowed. The fact that he still loved her beyond reason was completely beside the point. Allyn might be his wife by law, but she now belonged in a very real sense to another man.

It was over, he mused, toying with the empty glass, before it had ever begun. Allyn would return to Rapid City and her Dakota rancher to live contentedly, if not happily, ever after. And he, Joshua Manners, left in her ruinous wake, would grow old with the memory of the few brief, glorious moments when her heart had been his.

He did refill his glass then, spilling only a little. He lifted the glass to his lips, surprised at its heaviness, and drank down its contents. Through the thickening in his ears, he perceived a door opening. Through the thick glass at the bottom of the vessel he saw a blur of Wedgewood blue enter the room. He placed the glass on the table, aware of a profound relief that Allyn was no longer confined to her bed. At the same time, he felt an ache in his heart, as though she were pulling on it with a rough, heavy rope.

She closed the door behind her and took several steps toward him before her eyes met his. She let out a small gasp, as though she had not expected to see him there. He gripped the arms of the chair hard, the only thing which would prevent him from going to her and gathering her into his arms.

Let not the creaking of shoes, nor the rustling of silks, he recalled from Shakespeare, betray thy poor heart to woman.

She did not speak to him, and it was a moment before he trusted himself to address her.

"You're—better?" He managed an even tone despite his inebriation.

Her chin went up and her spine straightened like

331

a ramrod. She surveyed him with cool scrutiny.

"As if you cared," she replied, her voice low and well tended.

Her gaze went from his face, at whose expression she could only guess, to the glass and bottle on the table beside him. He wished that he had not drunk quite so much bourbon. It made him feel exposed, and dangerously vulnerable. But of course it was too late now.

"I do care," he heard himself say dully. "If I didn't care, I'd have taken you that night, then abandoned you as you slept. Or I'd have struck you, instead of punishing myself. I care, Allyn. I'll always care. And that is my curse."

Her eyes narrowed, and he knew she did not believe him. Well, perhaps that was best for both of them.

"You care," she fairly sneered, "for your pride and vanity. Like every other man."

He allowed a slow, bitter laugh. "If I had any pride or vanity, you cured me of it long before now."

She appeared to consider this, her stern gaze softening as she looked down and her tight mouth going slack. He remembered kissing that mouth, its softness and sweetness, and how it had kissed him back. He ached so then that he was obliged to look away from her.

"I've come out," she said in a less stolid tone, "to remind you that we are obligated to the Cotillion this evening."

Damn! He thought, closing his eyes and expelling a hard breath. He did not feel that he would ever be able to get up from the chair, much less shine at a social event a few hours hence.

"I haven't forgotten," he lied, rubbing his eyes with the thumb and forefinger of his right hand. "Have I failed yet in my husbandly duties? Other than in the Biblical sense, I mean?"

He mustered the courage to look at her again, and found, not unexpectedly, her emerald eyes reproaching him.

"You know best the answer to that." Her reply was low and mannered, reminding him oddly of the tone she had used on Morgan Mellette on the occasion of their last joust. He felt the bile of his anger rise at her insinuation.

"Yes," he said, feeling reckless, thanks in measure to the bourbon. "I do. And if I may say, I've been a gentleman for the most part, except for the few times when I was overcome by your many charms. And who could blame me? Not even Bill Boland, I'll bet. Certainly not Bill Boland! After all, seeing as how he himself succumbed to—"

"You hypocrite!" she hissed at him. "You dare to sit in judgment of me, and of Bill, when you yourself so shamelessly carried on with another man's wife! I wish—I wish I never had to look at you again!"

She had turned away from him, and he was glad, for he felt as though he had been cut by broken glass and was bleeding on the floor. He nevertheless felt incapable of preventing the bourbon from urging him on.

"I wish I'd sent someone else to Rapid City in April," he muttered, closing his eyes again.

Chapter Twenty-Four

A New York Cotillion was as different from a Louisville party, or even a Baltimore affair, as Philadelphia Quaker society was from Rapid City saloon life. The Biltmore Hotel, reputedly the finest in the city, played host to the event, and it was spectacularly lit with electric lights. But Allyn could not even wish that she was able to enjoy it.

She knew she looked dazzling in her newest gown, a daring affair of black lace on royal blue satin. The dress displayed her shoulders to good advantage, along with other more intriguing aspects of her anatomy. Even Joshua admired the gown, although he did not say so. She had caught him several times from the corner of her eye, watching her. She took some perverse satisfaction from that, although she did not know why.

Joshua himself looked dashing, she grudgingly admitted, in his black tails, top hat, and opera cape. Remarkably too, he demonstrated no trace of his earlier dissolution. No doubt, Allyn reflected with some bitterness, the Mannerses would cut quite an impressive swath at this important event.

She spoke little to Joshua, and he to her. There was no need. After the trial by receiving line, Allyn was taken up by an array of fashionable young society matrons, and Joshua disappeared, she assumed, to promote Sheik's interests. She was glad of the music and gaiety, the brightly colored gowns and jewels and the witty, racy, half-heard conversations. There was such a feast for the eyes and ears as to make it possible to forget, for a time, her ruined life.

The champagne too was dangerously plentiful. There always seemed to be a full glass at hand, and before long she was aware of a hum in her head, as if a swarm of bees had been released into the room. Couples began swirling about the dance floor, and gradually the conversations dissolved into the lush sounds of the string orchestra. Allyn watched, sipping the last of her latest glass of the delightful sparkling wine, feeling a familiar and unpleasant loneliness pervade her, magnified, she was sure, by the quantity of champagne she had consumed. She held her empty glass out to abandon it on a table, and would have missed the table entirely had it not been for the strong, warm hand which suddenly closed upon her own.

Her startle reflex was slowed, but some part of her that was still unaffected by the champagne realized it was Joshua beside her, guiding her reach to the table so she might avoid an embarrassing accident.

"Champagne sneaks up on you, doesn't it?" Joshua's voice was low and rich, like bittersweet dark chocolate. She turned to him with a petulant retort that died upon her lips. He was regarding her with a look of such gentleness as she had not seen upon his features in days. It made her want to cry.

It was the champagne that made it seem so, she thought at once. Or perhaps an act, for the benefit of the other guests. She could not bear either thought, and so looked away from him to the assemblage of swirling, lively color on the dance floor.

"Dance with me, Allyn," he invited her urgently. She was about to decline when he added, "We can talk, then. And I can tell you what I've learned."

Without a word, she nodded. He offered her his hand, and she accepted it, allowing herself to be led to the dance floor.

The orchestra had begun a waltz by Strauss, the Austrian whose works were so popular lately. This one was "The Emperor." She remembered it from the Medford party in Louisville.

Louisville seemed so long ago, and so very far away. Her biggest problem in Louisville had been the feud with a disapproving gentry. How petty it all seemed now.

Joshua was a wonderful dancer, although he held her a bit more tightly than would have been decent were he not her husband. She felt his chin beside her temple, and was in the midst of a sigh before she realized it. He did not speak, although he had professed to be interested in doing so when he had invited her to dance, and she did not inquire. There was a perfection about their activity which she did not want to clutter with conversation. Her eyes closed, and she felt vulnerable once again to his sensuous attentions . . .

Suddenly he stopped, although the music was going on. Allyn opened her eyes, annoyed at having been torn from her reverie so rudely. Over Joshua's shoulder she perceived the cause of the interruption at once, to her outrage.

Governor Arthur Mellette stood behind Joshua, apparently having tapped the younger man's shoulder to cut in. The governor stood a head shorter and at least a foot wider than his former operative, but not wide enough to completely blot out his frankly sensual young wife. Morgan Mellette, as usual, was drawing stares in her claret-colored silk gown, which set no standards of decency.

"Governor!" Joshua had released Allyn and was regarding the intruder with genuine surprise, if not dismay.

"I knew it was only a matter of time before some pretty young thing would get you to the altar," Governor Mellette declared by way of greeting, pumping Joshua's hand in the manner of a practiced politician. "Congratulations! To you, too, Miss Cameron—or, I should say, Mrs. Manners!" He laughed. A bit too loudly, Allyn thought. Taking up Allyn's hand, he announced, "I'd like to dance with your bride, my boy. You don't mind obliging Morgan, do you?"

Joshua looked down at Allyn with no trace of regret or embarrassment. She could not even manage a false smile.

"I promise I won't step on your toes," the governor went on, leading Allyn back into the waltz.

Did she imagine it, or had the notes soured? Arthur Mellette was prattling on in her ear about his detour to Washington, a meeting with the President, and his trip to New York, but Allyn was not listening. She could not take her eyes from the striking couple who danced together as though joined at the soul, and laughed like bold lovers. By the end of the interminable waltz, she wanted nothing more than to find a hole somewhere to which she could crawl away and die.

Morgan and Joshua appeared at their side at last, and Allyn managed to murmur her empty gratitude to the governor, even punctuating it with a faint smile. She was aware of the cat's eyes upon her, and was determined to do as little as possible to satisfy her.

They exchanged partners again with a few courteous words, and in moments Joshua was leading her into a lively two-step.

"You don't look well, Allyn," Joshua said in her ear as he led her among the dancing couples. "Are you all right?"

No, she wanted to shout, and to strike him with her fists. Instead she ignored his question and proceeded with her own.

"You had something to tell me," she said by way of a reminder. "Before we were interrupted. Tell me. Then we can end this farce. I am sick to death of it."

"We should at least stay until after dinner."

"Damn you, Joshua!" she whispered, finally unable to control her anger. "You think you are the supreme authority on matters of etiquette! You presume to show me my duty, and yet you carry on shamelessly with that—that—"

"Common baggage," he supplied calmly, adjusting his hold on her hand as he nodded and smiled to an unknown party over her shoulder. "Smile, my darling wife. You look like murder incarnate."

"Let me go! This instant!" She began to pull her hand away, but he held her tightly, hurting her.

"You expect me to understand you and your Dakota bull," he said in a harsh whisper into her ear. "But you can't allow me an old friendship. We've had our bouts, but Morgan and I were friends before we were anything else, and it's likely we'll still be friends long after this sham we call a marriage is annulled."

Friends? Allyn wondered, doubtful. Women, especially women like Morgan Mellette, did not make friends of men. They collected men the same way they collected jewelry, used them for a time, then cast them aside in favor of a new trinket that caught their eye. In a stunning moment of clarity, Allyn realized that Morgan Mellette was doing just that, although to what purpose, she could not guess. She laughed, more amused than angered by Joshua's unexpected naivete. He seemed surprised, even stung, by her mockery, staring at her with no trace of a smile.

"Morgan Mellette's tricks are apparently as foreign to you as they are crystal clear to me," was what she said to him. "For a smart man, you understand precious little about women." And she laughed again, enjoying his obvious surprise.

"What do you mean?" he challenged her, his dark, uncompromising eyebrows meeting in consternation.

She felt a surge of triumph, and dared a condescending smile.

"Smile, my darling husband. You look like murder incarnate."

He scowled at her in earnest, and she kept her delighted laugh inside.

"It would take another woman to understand," she went on, now happy to bestow smiles in abundance. "As a man, you might understand, but you would choose not to believe it. So I shall save myself the trouble of explanation, and let you learn your lesson the hard way. I've changed my mind. I'm enjoying myself immensely, and I want to stay all night. Perhaps I'll even dance with Arthur Mellette again. He's actually quite a good dancer."

Joshua was smiling again, but she could see the suspicion in those dark eyes. Having planted her seeds, she was contented to watch them take root.

But the governor and his wife did not cross their paths again. Joshua had apparently forgotten the things he had wanted to tell her, and she did not care to fix his mind upon a fresh topic. He would remember later, she told herself, eyeing him across the table at dinner, taking no small pleasure in the fact that Joshua continued to watch her with a curiosity he obviously tried to conceal.

As the company began to leave the table, a young bellboy in a red jacket appeared beside Joshua, bearing a note on a silver tray. Allyn watched as her husband traded a coin for the note. The boy bowed slightly and disappeared again. Joshua unfolded the paper and scanned it, pursing his wide mouth to a thin line.

"What is it?" she inquired, more than a little curious.

He looked up at her in surprise, as though he had forgotten she was there.

"A note," he replied—rather stupidly, she thought. That much was obvious. "From an old friend who's found out I'm in town. I'm sorry to spoil your evening, but we'll have to leave."

He was lying, and he was surprisingly bad at it. She arched an eyebrow inquiringly.

"Old friend?" she repeated in an exaggeration of the overly casual tone he had used. "Like Morgan Mellette?"

He opened his mouth to reply, then closed it, and she saw his sable eyes glimmer. With amusement, or malice? She had a suspicion that she was about to find out which.

"Even older," he told her, the faintest trace of a smile appearing at the corners of his mouth as he refolded the note. "Although not quite as pretty. Come on."

Before she could protest, he was striding off toward the doors, and she was forced to hurry to catch up with him.

It was after midnight by the time Joshua left Allyn at the suite and caught a cab to Jerome Park. By the light of the passing street lamps, he withdrew the note from his breast pocket and unfolded it, reading again:

"Red-haired man asking about Sheik. Please come."

It was not signed, which struck Joshua as a little odd, because the security guards were known by name. And there was something vaguely familiar about the scrawl, although not familiar enough for him to pinpoint. In any case, the situation required, as a former superior of his used to say, "a look-see."

Predictably, Allyn had been curious about the note, although she had tried to appear disinterested. But Joshua did not want to enlighten her, because he knew she would want to participate in a potentially dangerous situation, and because her remarks regarding Morgan's motives had provoked him more than he cared to admit, and he had wanted to return the favor. It was childish, he knew, but he did it anyway, without further apology or rationalization. He was, he decided, a rogue. But an honest one.

Morgan's tricks. What could Allyn have meant by her declaration? He kept trying to dismiss it, but she had been so sure of herself, and so mocking . . . Chagrinned, he felt his cheeks burn just thinking about it. Surely he knew Morgan better than Allyn did, although women did tend to have an understanding of one another surpassing that of men.

"Jerome Park, sir."

It was the driver, startling him out of his contemplation. The cab had stopped. It had probably been stopped for some time. With a brief curse, he got down from the coach and paid his fare. He did not bid the driver wait, nor did the driver ask. In moments Joshua was alone at the front gate, and the clatter of the departing cab quickly faded to a chorus of crickets and things of the night.

He identified himself to the watchman, who admitted him with some reluctance, owing, Joshua guessed, to the absurd hour. He asked the older man if he had seen or heard anything unusual, but the man merely shook his head, waving him inside before he closed and locked the gate again.

The night mist was damp and cool, but utterly still. By the dim, sparse lanterns patterned against the buildings like a whore's lacy lingerie, he made his way quickly and quietly to the stable area, distractedly picking apart the clues to the puzzle at hand.

Red had no doubt dogged them to New York. Joshua's quest for a new jockey had told him that much. But to what end? Surely he could not mean to spirit Sheik away, for a brilliant horse with no papers had no future, and certainly no market value. Did Allyn's former lover intend to tamper with the beast? Frowning, Joshua paused in his quest to extract a cigar from his gold cigar case and light it, hoping at last to put his distractions aside.

If he were Red, he reasoned, drawing upon his Havana as he slowed his pace to the stables, and the ploy to blackmail Allyn with her honor had failed, what would be the next step? An answer materialized like the pale gray smoke from his cigar. Red would find something else to hold for ransom.

Momentary panic struck him, and he stopped dead in the darkness. Suppose Red had sent that note himself to draw him away from the women, so that he or his associates could abduct Missy, or Allyn, or both from the suite? Joshua cursed his obtuseness and spun around, intending to return to the hotel. As he did so, he received an abrupt and unmistakable response to his theory.

Many strong hands seized him in the darkness. Cursing, he struggled against his unseen captors, until a dripping rag was thrust into his face. He knew the smell: ether! Lunging forward to break the human chain binding him, and to free himself from the insidious grip of the anesthesia which threatened to rob him of consciousness, he managed to free his gun arm.

The ether, however, had done its work quickly. Through the gathering maelstrom in his brain, he counted one, two, three men. Sluggishly he went for his gun, but a hurricane force whipped him on the left side of his face, and he was delivered to the blackness.

Chapter Twenty-Five

Allyn was angry in the morning to find that Joshua had not returned to the hotel. She spent a few hours readying her verbal arsenal for assault when he came in, but found by noon that her anger had turned to worry. She shunned Missy's attempts to distract her throughout the afternoon, electing to sit by the window, scanning the street five floors below for any sign of her husband.

By evening, she was distraught. Convinced that something dreadful had occurred, she barely nibbled at the supper Missy had ordered to be sent up. She had no stomach for it. If only she had insisted on knowing the contents of the note, or knowing where he was going! If anything had happened to him, she realized, feeling her insides knot, she would be devastated.

At nine o'clock there was a knock at the door. Allyn hurried to open it, disregarding Missy's admonishment to caution, hoping against hope that she would find Joshua's handsome, insouciant grin on the other side.

But it was not he. It was a bellboy. He handed Allyn a small package, wrapped crudely in brown paper and string. "Mrs. Manners?" he asked.

Allyn nodded mutely, shuddering with premonition. She accepted the package with trembling hands and closed the door without offering him a tip. Missy was at her elbow in an instant.

"What is it?" the younger woman demanded breathlessly, hovering like a nervous mother hen. "Open it! Open it!"

Allyn stared at the package for a moment longer, trying to rid herself of apprehension. After all, it could be anything . . . and nothing good.

At last she tore at the wrapping in a fumbling, awkward way, starting when an object tumbled out and landed on the carpet with a small thud. She gasped: It was Joshua's fine gold cigar case. She stared as Missy stooped to retrieve it. A point of white paper protruded from one end. Missy pulled it out. Allyn snatched it from her hands greedily and unfolded it.

"Allyn, what the—"

"Hush!" Allyn hissed, shaking as she read:

"My darling Aly,

"I have a man here who claims to be your husband. You know who I mean? I am prepared to make a trade. Come alone to the back gate at Jerome Park at eleven o'clock. Do not be late, and do not bring guests, as I have no love for your husband and little patience remaining."

It was not signed, but Allyn needed no signature. She crushed the note in her hand and held her balled fist to her lips to keep from screaming.

"Allyn! What is it?" Missy shrieked in her terrified soprano.

Carole Howey

"Raif has Joshua," she replied, amazed at the quiet, even sound of her voice. "He wants to make a trade. My husband for Sheik."

She faced Missy at last, and found her friend staring with a horrified gaze. The younger woman wrung her hands.

"What must we do?" Missy breathed.

Allyn knew the answer, but she could not get the words out. She felt dulled by fear.

"You stay here," she managed finally, "and do nothing. Nothing, mind you," she repeated more firmly as her resolve gained momentum.

"But what are—"

Allyn dropped the note to the floor, seizing Missy's shoulders.

"Be still and listen!" she commanded her friend, fiercely emphasizing each word with a shake. "Raif wants me to come to the stable alone. Do not follow me, and do not call upon the police. Do you hear? Bert died that way!"

Missy's gray eyes were wide. She nodded hesitantly.

"Allyn—what about Joshua?" she asked in a whimper.

Allyn felt a stab of anguish, thinking of Joshua in Raif's hands. What exquisite torments might the latter have devised for her husband's amusement? She shuddered.

"I must go," she muttered, snatching up her cloak. "I'll think of something."

But she could not. The ride to the stables was long and black, like a horrible nightmare from which she could not awaken, and she was unable to conjure a single cogent thought. Sheik for Joshua: A trickle of cold sweat edged down the small of her back. Raif was obviously unaware of the conditions of their marriage. It would surprise the Kentuckian to learn

346

that she and Joshua meant nothing to one another at this point but money and protection. It might even enrage him to learn of that one serious flaw in his otherwise perfect plan, a plan which, under normal circumstances, would have been a paragon of cruel brilliance.

Bert's murder suddenly replayed itself vividly in her mind, and a dry sob knifed her throat. Would Joshua die before her eyes as horribly as Bert had—or worse? Could she condemn the arrogant Marylander with the same stubbornness which had destroyed Bert Emmet?

Her cab jolted to a halt. She clambered out quickly and paid the driver in silence, waving him on. In minutes, she was alone. Darkness shrouded the back gate, which loomed as ominously as the dark thoughts of murder and treachery in her mind. Joshua was behind that gate somewhere.

And Raif.

She approached the gate warily, looking about. Peering into the darkness in all directions, she could perceive no sign of another human being. She waited, listening hard for any sound that would indicate that someone was coming.

Although it was June, the night air was cold. Allyn shivered, drawing her cloak closely about her throat. Her trembling did not stop, and after a minute, she realized she was shaking with fear rather than the chill. Annoyed, she willed herself to be still. Fear was what Raif wanted, she thought. She must master her fear if she was to have any hope of saving Joshua, and Sheik.

"I'm here, Raif," she found the nerve to call out, and was encouraged by the clear, deliberate sound of her voice. She dared to go on. "I hate to be kept waiting."

A pair of strong, rough arms seized her like vises from behind, pinning her own arms against her sides.

She cried out in surprise as a stubbly-bearded cheek pressed close to her own. Her unseen captor laughed, a sound which was disturbingly familiar.

"Is that a fact?" Raif's low, reedy voice taunted her. She nearly fainted from the reek of whiskey on his breath. "Come on, Aly, let's do it here, like we used to in Dakota. Josh don't need to know, and I'll bet that worthless Yankee ain't man enough for a woman like you anyway."

She wrenched away from him, sickened and mortified.

"You disgust me," she panted, facing him as she backed away. She could barely make out his silhouette against the darkness, and she was glad of it.

Raif laughed again. It was an ugly, raucous sound that split the darkness like raw gunfire.

"That ain't what you used to say," he drawled, sidling closer like some slithering reptile.

"I'm a lot smarter than I was then," she retorted. Somehow he did not scare her anymore. He was Raif Simms, itinerant ranch hand, lean, hungry, and uneducated. And drunk besides. She felt empowered by these facts, and her spine stiffened.

"Where is Joshua?" she demanded. "What have you done with him?"

Raif took a few weaving steps toward her. She forced herself to stand firm.

"Okay," he said then, sullen, almost challenging. "Let's take her to Joshua, Harry."

Allyn was chilled to the bone. A big hand took hold of the soft flesh of her arm, and she knew, without looking, that the hand belonged to Bert's murderer. The man offered no sound. He merely propelled her forward with a gesture that nearly broke her arm. She bit her lip to keep from crying out, tasting her own blood. Raif took her other arm none too gently, and the two men ushered her through the gate and along the narrow path leading to a row of stalls. Her arms ached so that she thought she would faint.

They halted finally before a closed stall at the end of the row and released her. She could not prevent a sigh. She crossed her arms, massaging them with her hands.

"Open it, Harry," Raif snapped.

"I ain't your damned slave." Harry's impertinence had a warning sound to it. "Or hers either. Let her do it."

"You have such remarkable taste in friends, Raif." She could not resist a taunt as she deftly worked the bolt.

Suddenly she felt warm steel beneath her right ear, digging into her neck.

"I hate a sharp-tongued bitch," Harry remarked casually.

"Not now, Harry," Raif soothed the man in a silky tone. "You can cut it out of her later. First she has some papers to sign. And maybe one or two other favors to do us. Don't you know, Harry, this is a lady? She has a nice evening planned for us, I'll bet. Don't you, honey?"

The knife was withdrawn. Allyn did not answer. She felt a strange detachment from the circumstances, as though part of her knew this awful thing was happening but another part of her refused to believe it. With effort, she pulled on the door until it swung wide. Presently her shoulder caved in from a blow from behind, and she stumbled into the dark stall. With effort she got to her feet, giddy with pain.

The illumination of a lantern dimly lit the small area. A few feet away, Allyn perceived a form on the floor. As another lantern was added, the light grew brighter and she could see that the form was Joshua, lying in a rumpled heap, a condition which eliminated any guesswork as to how he'd been treated.

She did cry out then, unable at last to contain her dismay. She knelt beside him, turning him gently onto his back. He had no jacket, no tie, and no hat. His white shirt was torn, soiled, and spotted with dried blood. His eyes were closed, and he appeared to be unconscious. His face was puffy, and there was an untreated cut slowly oozing blood above his left eye.

She called his name, touching his cheek with her fingers. His skin was cool, and for an awful moment she thought he might be dead. But even as she drew in a hard, quick breath, she saw his lips move in a soundless whisper which she could not decipher. Her small relief was torn from her as someone grasped her arm. She was jerked roughly to her feet with a deft twist designed to inflict blinding pain.

"Look, but don't touch, Aly." It was Raif taunting her, his Southern drawl dripping poisoned honey. "First I get my horseflesh. Then you get yours."

She could not speak. The burning pain seared across her back in unrelenting waves.

"Let—let go," she breathed in a pleading gasp.

Raif laughed as though she were a favorite joke. He released her and she fell to her knees, holding her arm gingerly. It took a moment for the pain to subside enough for her to gather her wits.

"Raif," she panted softly, steadying her voice as she watched Joshua lying motionless in the straw, "you have finally overplayed your hand."

"What?"

Allyn got to her feet again, willing the small room to stop spinning. She faced her abductors with as cold a stare as she could muster, and took a deep breath before going on.

"We outfoxed you in Baltimore," she told him, taking some pleasure in his bewildered expression, "after you murdered Bert. I married Joshua as protection against your threat. And it worked too. Even you believed it. You've gone to a lot of trouble for nothing."

Raif's hard, handsome features, while not registering total comprehension, did narrow with suspicion.

"What are you saying?" he demanded, taking hold of the soft flesh of her upper arm with a bruising grip.

"Don't you see?" she managed, hoping he could not hear her heart hammering in protest. "We didn't marry for love. We married to foil your plans. Your new threat is really no threat at all."

Raif released her. His stare was hard and measuring. She felt a chill, but forced all emotion from her face as she returned the stare boldly. Raif's features suddenly relaxed. Then he laughed. She cringed at the sound.

She had not succeeded.

"No threat?" the Kentuckian repeated, in a faint imitation of her imperious tone. "Then why'd you run out here like a bitch in heat? Why'd you whimper like a whipped puppy when you saw him? Honey, I think it's more of a threat than you'd care to admit."

She watched in mute wonder as he produced a small packet of papers from the inside of his shirt.

"Here they are. All nice and legal. All you got to do is sign 'em."

There was no laughter in him. He was deadly serious as he held them out to her. She regarded them with a chilling sense that she had, at last, come to the end.

"I am damned if I will sign anything over to you," she said then, folding her arms across her chest.

Harry took a step forward, a look of menace upon his rough features. Raif stayed him with a firm hand, not taking his eyes from hers.

"Honey, you just stand there a minute." Raif's tone was mockingly gentle and considerate. "Just rest yourself. And you think about bein' a young widow. Take your time. Joshua ain't goin' anywheres, and neither are we. Harry, get those other lazy bastards in here."

Harry, dispatched upon his errand, departed, looking impatient. Allyn stared at Raif across the narrow gulf separating them, trying to comprehend how she ever could have loved him.

"Raif," she tried again. "This will never work. Even if I sign those papers, I'll tell the Commission that they were signed under duress. It will be tied up for years. I can see to it that you'll never make a penny out of Sheik."

Raif drew in a breath, but was interrupted as Harry returned with two other men whom she did not recognize. Raif's expression became one of triumph.

"She wants to be a widow, Harry," he said loudly. "Oblige her."

Harry stepped forward, apparently pleased that some action was being taken at last. Allyn's legs weakened beneath her.

"Raif!" she exclaimed desperately, trying to think. "Not even you could be so callous, so unprincipled, that you'd execute—"

"Me?" Raif's exaggerated innocence was chilling. "I'm not going to kill anyone, am I, Harry? Why don't you let Mrs. Manners in on our little plan?"

She forced herself to look at the man, whom she already knew to have murdered once. He took her by the hand and pulled her roughly toward Joshua, then put his own gun in her hand, forcing her fingers onto the trigger. He trained the muzzle toward the man on the straw, who had just begun to stir.

Through her horror, the irony of the situation mocked her. Joshua had married her weeks ago to protect her from Raif's threats. Now it seemed that by marrying her, he had placed his own life in her hands.

"Red, I must say I'm impressed. What a hell of an idea."

She started. Joshua had sat up, and even now was rubbing his eyes with the heels of his hands.

"Shut up," she said to him in a terrified whisper. "And stop being clever!"

Joshua looked at her, beyond the barrel of the gun poised inches away from his face. His dark eyes were surprisingly alert and radiated calm. She thought of the times when she had wished for a gun, or some other weapon, in her hands as they'd sparred verbally, wondering if this was God's punishment for her pride and her anger. She found she could no longer meet the gaze of the man with whom she had daily exercised her resentment. The man who had, for weeks, been protecting her in the best ways he knew how.

In moments, as Harry's fingers pressed inexorably upon her own, Joshua Manners would be dead. His blood, like Bert's, would be spattered upon her soul.

"Give me the papers," she begged softly, avoiding Raif's grin of triumph. Harry loosened his hold, and she breathed again, a small sigh of relief. They were safe, for the moment. She had neither condemned Joshua, nor damned herself. She heard a quiet breath escape her husband, and saw his jaw tighten as he regarded Raif intently. What could he be thinking? Whatever it was, she realized with a terrible sense of foreboding, it was going to be trouble.

Raif held the papers before her face. She accepted them, watching from the corner of her eye as the two men whom Harry had brought in hauled Joshua to his feet. He appeared none too steady, and she hoped he would not try anything foolish.

"I was half-hopin' you'd go ahead and kill him." Raif sounded almost wistful in his cruelty. "I've hated that yellow Yankee bastard from the first minute I saw him. I'm surprised you could settle for him after what we had. It must've been quite a comedown."

He laughed, but it was a forced laughter, a bitter, hollow sound. She felt Joshua's gaze upon her, and she could not look at him. She might have guessed that Raif would subject her to this kind of humiliation. But she had endured too many insults from the man to cause her to dignify this one with a response.

"No answer?" the Kentuckian went on as she unfolded the rumpled papers. "Can't expect one, I guess. A wife owes her husband the duty of loyalty. Even a worthless one. Here's a pen I borrowed from Joshua, honey. Sign these quick so we can have a proper good-bye."

She felt his bold, insolent hand slide along her arm to her shoulder, and she drew away from him, shuddering. She made no move to sign the papers. Three feet away, and a little behind her, she saw Joshua shake off his guards and felt the charged current of his stare aimed at Raif. All at once she realized that Raif was afraid of him, and that he'd been trying to provoke Joshua into some kind of action as an excuse for violence. She was filled with a dreadful sense of déjà vu.

"Let Joshua go," she all but whispered to Raif, no longer caring how frightened she sounded. "I'll sign anything. I'll do anything you want, after I see Joshua walk out of here. Alone."

"Don't make any bargains for me." Joshua's voice was hard. "I'm not leaving here without you, Allyn."

With those vehement words, Joshua took a meaningful step toward them. Instantly Harry's .45 appeared, leveled at Joshua's chest. Raif merely seemed amused.

"I was wondering when you was gonna come out from behind her skirt," Raif sneered, hooking his thumbs in his belt.

"Joshua, don't!" Allyn warned, staying her panic. "It's what he wants! Can't you see that?"

"You let your woman order you around like that?" Raif went on, gaining momentum. "You're even sorrier than I thought. Maybe Allyn just wants you outta here so's she and me can renew old acquaintance in private."

Raif slid his arm about her now in a show of rough intimacy. She could not prevent a gasp from betraying her terror. Joshua made another sudden move, but was seized by the two men who had gotten him to his feet. Harry still held the gun on him, but seemed in no hurry to use it. Raif had placed himself between her and Joshua, and was now pulling at the buttons of her dress with a lazy, insulting hand. She tried to push him away, dropping the pen and papers, but he pulled her hand away, twisting it behind her back with an excruciating jerk.

"What's the matter, Aly?" he breathed, sliding his free hand under the collar of her dress. "Are you afraid he'll see what kind of a woman you are? Or are you afraid to find out what kind of a man he is?"

Then he buried his face against her neck, and the touch of his lips made her blood run like ice water. Anger supplanted her fear. She closed her eyes and brought her knee to his groin with a swift, hard motion.

Many things happened at once. Raif fell to the straw, bent double, screaming like some fearsome wounded beast. She watched as Joshua swiftly pushed one of his restrainers onto Harry, whose attention had been momentarily distracted, and jammed his elbow into the other's ribs, temporarily handicapping the three men. Faster than thought, he seized her forearm and pulled her, running, toward the door.

Suddenly Joshua fell to the floor with a grunt. With a cry of dismay, Allyn turned to see that Harry had taken hold of Joshua's leg and was holding him down.

"Get out," Joshua gasped to her, the wind apparently having been knocked from him. "Go! Go!"

The very suggestion appalled her. Instead of running, she pulled at Harry, although he was twice her size and panic had rendered her maddeningly weak.

Raif's men had not been gentle before, but now they were savage. One of the men seized her from behind in a vise-like grip which she was powerless to break, and she watched helplessly as Harry and the other man battered upon Joshua. The scene was compellingly horrifying. Miraculously, Joshua did not lose consciousness, and as Raif rejoined the living, he barked out an order for the beating to stop.

The men obeyed, as though they had grown bored with their play. Harry returned to Raif's side, leaving the other two men to hold a considerably subdued Joshua. It was only after he was certain Joshua was held fast, Allyn noticed grimly, that Raif dared to approach the taller man. She watched, immobilized, as the two men glared at one another, making the air between them crackle. Joshua panted hard like a caged animal, the expanse of his chest straining at its human bonds.

"Now that's what I call love." Raif's compliment was a taunt. "Protecting your lady that way. Tell me, how you gonna protect her now, Josh? Curse your goddamned Yankee hide for interfering!"

On the penultimate syllable he exploded a punch into Joshua's midsection, following through with his whole formidable body. Allyn cringed at the very sound of it, and cried out, watching helplessly as Joshua bent double at the sudden force. She felt sick. Raif returned his attention to her with no sign of amorous intent, however mocking.

"Sign them damn papers! Now!" he ordered her, and Harry retrieved them from the floor where she had dropped them. It took him a moment longer to find the pen. She snatched the papers, trying to still her hands, which were trembling violently. She scribbled her name several times.

"Let him go, Raif." She was pleading, but she did not care anymore. She only wanted to know that Joshua was going to live. If she had to beg Raif, she knew, she would beg him.

"I'll let him go," Raif promised her darkly, grabbing the documents from her at last. "I'll let him go straight to hell!"

As if on cue, Harry drew his hunting knife from its sheath with an ominous sound like wind through a narrow tunnel, holding it underhanded, as if he intended to filet his victim. Before Allyn could think, she reached out for the knife with her right hand. Her fingers wrapped tightly around the razor-sharp blade like a sheath of flesh. The would-be murderer pulled back hard on the weapon and Allyn's fingers burst apart, spouting blood like a grisly fountain.

There was no pain. She stared at her hand, fascinated and repulsed. Raif's men forgot about Joshua for the moment, watching the gruesome spectacle. It was just long enough for him to seize one of the lanterns from the wall beside him and bring it down upon the head of one of his guards with a force that might have killed the man. Kerosene ignited and a ribbon of gay yellow flame danced to the floor of the stall, setting the damp straw to a slow, smoky blaze. Allyn watched Joshua use the same lantern on Harry, and Bert's murderer fell onto the small fire, extinguishing it.

Allyn felt a lightness, as though she were floating above the room. There was no feeling in her hand at all, or in her body, only a sense of calm and serenity. She was no longer a part of the ghastly events around her.

Joshua, conversely, felt as though he had just come into the world through a long, dark abyss. Having eliminated the threat of half of the Simms contingent, he found renewed strength from his success and delivered a strategic kick to the third man. The man doubled, and Joshua followed up with an ax-like swing of his joined hands to the fellow's jaw. Turning quickly from this deed, he discovered with sinking heart that even this had not been enough.

Raif had Allyn by her hair and held his own knife, a Bowie design, poised across her neck, leaving an ominous shadow like a slash. Allyn's head was back. Her eyes were closed. For all he could tell, she was unconscious, or already dead from loss of blood. Her maimed, gory hand hung limp and useless by her side, and her entire skirt was stained a macabrely patterned red with her own blood. Joshua stared in horror from the travesty of a hand to the blade pressed to her neck.

"Red." He forced a calm into his voice which he was far from feeling. "She's bleeding to death!"

Raif's hand tensed upon the knife, and Joshua dared not even breathe.

"She'll bleed even more from the throat, Josh, just you watch! Now get those papers over here! Quick!"

Joshua did as he was told, aware that there was no chance he could prevent Raif from killing Allyn if the Kentuckian chose to do so. That knowledge was a bitter pill, but he swallowed hard and hoped. Raif snatched the papers from his outstretched hand and dragged his captive to the door with him. Raif seemed to have lost his taste for taunting him, escape being, he assumed, the important thing. With one hand, Raif shoved the door open, still holding Allyn close.

"I'll give your regards to Morgan," Raif said, then deftly threw his knife at Joshua, who only dove away in time. When Joshua looked up, he saw that Raif was gone, and that Allyn lay prone before him on the straw.

Joshua felt an icy hand grip his heart, and he went to her. He turned her gently onto her back, willing himself to think. She had already saved his life. Now it was up to him to return the favor, if he could. With only one lantern the room was considerably darker, but he knew that was not the reason why he was having difficulty seeing. He pressed his ear to her sternum. She was breathing, and her heart was beating a slow but steady pulse. His relief was quickly tempered by his examination of her injury. Carefully he uncurled her fingers, which had closed upon themselves for protection.

It was a travesty of a hand, a gnarled and bloodied mass of tangled flesh and tendons. He'd had some experience with wounds, but nothing that had prepared him for the devastation wrought by the hunting knife. Disregarding his own aches and injuries, he tore off the sleeve of his already ragged shirt. As he wrapped the material around her hand, she spoke, startling him.

"Go after Sheik," she murmured like a half-drowned kitten. Her eyes were closed. He could not be sure that she was actually conscious, but he knew she needed a doctor. In answer to her request, he lifted her easily into his arms and carried her out of the stable and into the cool June night.

Chapter Twenty-Six

Allyn was warm, surrounded by softness and the scent of yeast. Yeast? Definitely yeast. And something else. . . . She sniffed. Charcoal. She dismissed the odd combination of odors. It felt good just to lie still. In fact her body felt so heavy, she thought it must be an impossible feat to move it. When she persuaded her eyes to open, she discovered she was in her own room at the Pellier, with only the golden sunshine of afternoon for company.

Fragments of memory came to her like pieces of a disassembled puzzle. She examined each piece separately, not up to reassembling the whole just yet. Joshua on the floor. The sheaf of paper. The lantern. The knife. Her hand ached suddenly, as if the memory had given life to the pain. She raised her hand and found that she was bandaged from her forearm to her fingertips in pristine white gauze. The sight made her realize that time had indeed passed since the nightmare.

But how much time? And had the nightmare ended?

She called out to Joshua twice before any sound actually issued from her lips, and the first sound was a laughable attempt, even to her. She tried again, and her last effort brought not Joshua but Missy into the room, her brow puckered into a frown of motherly concern.

"Where is Joshua?" Allyn asked, hoping to preempt Missy's inevitable flood of solicitous questions.

"He's not here!" Missy exclaimed, as though surprised that Allyn would ask. "What—"

"Missy, I need answers, not questions. Tell me first: What day is it?"

Friday," Missy answered promptly, fluffing Allyn's pillow. "Friday afternoon. Joshua brought you back late Wednesday night, and we sent for a doctor. Joshua changed his clothing—he looked as though he'd been in a cat fight—and then he went out again before the doctor even got here. All he said was that we shouldn't leave the rooms, and we shouldn't allow anyone in except for the doctor. He hasn't been back since. Allyn, what happened with Raif? How did your hand get like that?"

Joshua had gone after Raif. Relief mingled with apprehension as Allyn thought of the palpable hatred which characterized the two men's relationship. She did not want to think of the two meeting one another alone on a battleground. More than a day had passed since then, a day in which she had remained in limbo. And Joshua had not been heard from. She was chilled. This was not good.

Allyn drew back the covers resolutely and sat up. Blackness gathered quickly in her field of vision, but she closed her eyes and willed it away.

"Help me dress, Miss," she said to her friend. "We have to go to Jerome Park. I'll tell you everything on the way."

Missy protested, with the argument that Joshua had charged her to remain at the hotel, but Allyn wanted none of it. The Belmont Stakes was to be run the following day, she reminded the younger woman. Sheik's ownership might be open to question at the moment, but as long as there was a chance that Sheik would run for the C-Bar-C, they must go ahead on the assumption that he would.

"But what of the ball?" Missy reminded her anxiously. "You're not still planning to go, are you?"

The Belmont Ball.

Allyn settled back into her pillows, closing her eyes. If the Joshua T. Mannerses did not make an appearance at the event, it would give rise to all sorts of rumors. Having accepted the invitation, Allyn was compelled to attend, with or without Joshua. Through sheer accident of timing, she was forced to obey Joshua's wishes for the moment.

"Yes, I'm attending the ball," she breathed, acutely aware of her weakened state. Her hand began to throb, or perhaps it had been throbbing all along, and she had not noticed it before. It felt as though small demons were prodding her fingers with dull, hot needles.

Missy pressed the back of her hand first against Allyn's cheek, then her forehead. Her lips were pursed.

"What if Joshua doesn't return?" Missy asked quietly. "What then?"

Allyn drew in a sharp breath. She did not want to consider the possibility that Joshua would not return. The very thought made her feel ill.

"He'll come back," she said, half to herself. "He has to come back."

She told Missy about the events of that night, recalling some of them herself for the first time. Something came to her that she had not thought of before, something that puzzled her. Raif and Joshua seemed to

362

know one another. She said nothing to Missy about it, but the notion plagued her. If it were true, then why had Joshua not said something about it before? Several answers occurred to her, none of them comforting. The most persistent, devil-inspired of these was that Joshua had been, from the very beginning, part of an elaborate and inscrutable scheme to con Missy and herself out of Sheik.

No, she told herself firmly. It had not been a scheme that had mangled her hand. It had been a knife. A knife that would have killed Joshua Manners.

But where was Joshua now?

By eight o'clock that evening Joshua had still not returned. He's not coming back, a mocking voice inside Allyn taunted as she examined her reflection in the full-length mirror. Her emerald-green taffeta gown was an exotic confection. Her pristine white gloves covered not only her bandage, but came up over her elbows almost to the drop-shoulder sleeve of the dress. Missy had cleverly altered the fingers of the right glove to accommodate the bandages while revealing no hint of injury. In fact, she could almost forget the injury entirely. Its pain was inconsequential when compared to the ache in her heart.

Joshua Manners had carefully nurtured her to this very moment, that naughty voice inside continued. He'd intended that she be repaid in full for each cut and abrasion she had dealt him since they'd met by abandoning her to the ruthless jaws of New York society to suffer ridicule and humiliation. Or perhaps he was exacting revenge upon her for her pregnancy. The pregnancy that did not exist.

None of these things, she knew in her heart, was worthy of Joshua. But that did not prevent her from thinking them nonetheless.

"I have to go," Allyn announced with a brisk confidence she was far from feeling. She met Missy's anxious stare, hoping to convey that assurance, but could not muster a smile. "Just tell Joshua, when he comes back, where I've gone. He'll understand. And try to get word to me at Belmont mansion."

Missy looked desolate. "I should go with you," she blurted out in a piteous tone which pierced Allyn to the core.

Allyn straightened, imagining a steel rod sliding down her spine. She could almost feel the hardness of it, and the cold. It was enough to drive away the tears behind her eyes.

"Don't worry, Miss. I'll be fine. You stay here and wait for Joshua."

She patted Missy's cheek with a gloved hand and fled the room, feeling, as she closed the door behind her, that she had walked blindly out over a void.

The Belmont mansion was the jewel of Fifth Avenue. Through her window Allyn could see all of the carriages ahead of her along the street, lined up like petitioners before royalty. The glow of the street lights added to the air of gaiety, and the distant music of a string orchestra mingled with the sounds of laughter and conversation of guests as they debarked and proceeded inside the house. Several times Allyn debated ordering the driver to turn around to return her to the Pellier. Each time she resisted.

At last the footman swung open the door to her conveyance. The man could not mask his surprise at finding her alone. Indeed, he poked his head into the cab and looked about as though someone else might be hiding inside. Allyn mustered her most arctic imperiousness, and the footman, not equal to it, merely closed the carriage door and waved the driver on.

The main entrance hall was a large, opulently appointed room, with pink Italian marble floors and a high, coffered ceiling, paneled in Chinese silk brocade. In a smaller home, it could have served as a ballroom. Allyn offered chilly nods and perfunctory smiles to the unabashed stares she received. She could almost hear the remarks whispered behind gloved hands: unescorted? Where is her husband? She edged about the room, carefully avoiding pockets of newly arrived guests, keeping her head up and her eyes straight ahead.

Before long, she felt an ache at the back of her neck, as though someone were drilling into it with a dull metal bit. At the entrance to the ballroom, she caught a glimpse of the receiving line. It looked rather as she imagined a firing squad might, except that its members used smiles instead of rifles.

It was not a drill bit boring into her, she realized all at once, rooted to the spot. It was the stares of all of those around her.

Strength failed her at last. She could not do this. Joshua, her husband, was missing. Possibly hurt. Maybe dead. She could not face these people without knowing the truth.

She wanted to leave, but her feet were frozen to the glossy pink ice beneath them. In another moment, the people around her would begin to notice that something was wrong. If she could only will her feet to move!

She felt as though she were suffocating in a small space. She watched as a line of guests moved in an undulating way, like a big snake, to the receiving line. Their collective movement fascinated her, and she was compelled to watch as one by one they disappeared into the ballroom. Her gaze then rested, quite suddenly, upon the tall, lean, impeccably dressed Joshua Manners, who was smiling as though he had been watching her for some time.

Relief washed over her like wave upon wave of warm sunshine after a Dakota blizzard. She felt momentarily faint. A huge sigh filled her until she smiled.

Joshua was safe and whole and, except for a small plaster over his left eye, looking as though he had not a care in all the world.

She wanted to kill him.

She watched his approach, hypnotized by his familiar, arrogant gait that fell just short of a swagger. He made his way through the thickening crowd, never once taking his eyes from hers, until he stood so near to her that she could feel his warmth. His sable eyes absorbed her, and his grin made her want to ruffle his hair, which for once was neatly trained. He offered her his arm.

"My dear Mrs. Manners," he said to her in an intimate tone which made the rest of the room disappear. "Shall we?"

The very sound of his voice coaxed tears into her eyes, but not out of them. She accepted his elbow and fell in step beside him as they made for the receiving line in an unhurried fashion.

"Joshua, are you all right? Where have you been?" she murmured under her breath, maintaining her smile. It was easier to smile now, and that pain in her neck had vanished. She felt something warm on her gloved hand, the one she'd slipped about his elbow. Looking down, she noticed he had placed his other hand there on top of her own. It was so possessive and so lover-like a gesture that she never wanted to have her hand back.

"Were you worried?" he countered, and the surprise in his voice made her look up at his face in anger.

"Worried!" she cried in a furious whisper. "How dare you ask such a thing! I've been frantic! You were almost killed that night, or have you forgotten?"

Joshua did indeed look as though he had forgotten. In answer, he raised her good hand to his lips, pressing a kiss onto her fingers, a kiss that burned, even through her glove. A tingle teased the base of her spine.

"So were you," he replied softly, still holding her hand near to his face. "I almost couldn't believe it when Missy told me you'd come here. But then I remembered you holding on to Sheik for dear life in Deadwood, and I thought, 'This is Allyn Cameron we're talking about.' Excuse me: Allyn Cameron Manners."

He kissed her fingers again, and her face heated.

"Joshua, you're causing a scene," she murmured, as out of breath as if she had run all the way from the Pellier. Looking about her so she did not have to look at him, she could see the crowd in the foyer increasing. No one paid them any attention.

"How so? Has it become unfashionable to acknowledge one's wife in public? You are still my wife, remember?"

His voice had that light, urbane quality she used to find so irritating. She did look at him, not only because she wanted to. Something about his tone compelled her. She was disconcerted by the glint in his dark eyes, which was not so much unpleasant as it was bewildering. Was he mocking her or—or wooing her? The thought that he might indeed be flirting made her blush all the more, and she found herself staring at his cravat.

"After that night," she ventured, hoping her vague reference was not too obscure, "I would have thought you might not want to be reminded of that fact."

She felt his fingers on her chin, and in a moment she was looking into his deep, penetrating eyes.

"You thought wrong," he said simply. She swallowed hard. She felt a thrill. She felt awful.

"Don't toy with me, Joshua," she warned him softly. "I couldn't bear it."

"Allyn," he breathed, urgency in his whisper. "I . . ."

He looked about himself, as though reminded that they were not alone.

"Let's not air our linens here," he said in a lighter tone, tucking her hand once again into his arm. "We can talk after we've been received."

The receiving line was the gauntlet through which all comers had to pass before entering the ballroom. It was comprised of nearly two dozen Belmonts, lesser and greater, young and old, by birth and by marriage. Allyn could not help but admire Joshua's ability to charm them all. Mrs. Pemberly had been right, she reflected, recalling that grand dame's confidences about the Mannerses and politics. Joshua was a born campaigner. Unlike most politicians in her admittedly limited experience, however, he possessed both honor and sincerity along with his charm.

She loved him so much it hurt.

After carrying out their social obligation, Joshua again took her arm without a word, leading her purposely through the dazzling ballroom, past dancing couples who moved about the floor like glorious pastel and black shooting stars. There were not one but several pairs of glass doors fifteen feet high leading to the patio beyond, and they were open to admit the cool night breezes of late spring to a room that would soon have need of every breath of air it could muster. It was to one of these that Joshua guided her, and the contrast of the moonless June night outside to the bright room behind them was numbing.

Allyn hugged her arms to her chest against the unexpected chill. Somewhere beyond the smooth granite of the patio wall, roses were blooming. She could not see them in the dark, but their aroma was as faint and delicious as the first words of love spoken in an uncertain whisper. The warm pressure of Joshua's gentle hands upon her bared shoulders sent a familiar tingle from the nape of her neck to the very base of her spine. In a moment, to her astonishment, it was his lips she felt on her neck, and his warm breath sent unexpected ripples of delight coursing through her.

"Joshua!"

She meant to reprove him, but the whispered exclamation sounded more like encouragement, even to her. Certainly Joshua seemed to take it as such, turning her toward him with firm but gentle hands. In the light from the ballroom, she could see his features. His dark eyes wore an unbearably tender expression.

"We've had a lot of bad starts," he began, his baritone a hoarse whisper. "But somebody, or something, keeps putting us back together. You saved my life at the stable, Allyn. The Indians say that if you save a life, that life belongs to you. Why did you take hold of the knife?"

Allyn felt as though she had struck a wall of glass at a dead run. That was what this was about! This gentle, lover-like performance was nothing more than a response of gratitude. The idea choked her. Gratitude, she knew, was a close kin of pity, and no relation to love at all. She suddenly could not abide his touch.

"Instinct," she replied dully, trying to hold back the crippling disappointment from her voice. She stepped backward and could no longer look at him, electing instead to survey the scene in the ballroom. "Reflex. I saw Bert die that way. To be honest, I did it without even thinking." She stopped herself from going on, feeling the pain of her discovery grip her reason. She mastered herself, and continued in a slower, more deliberate way.

369

"Now tell me. What of Sheik, and those papers I signed?"

She was so overwhelmed with devastation that she did not even hear his reply. All she could hear was the sound of his voice, and the orchestra, and the sea in her ears. Her vision blurred.

"Allyn!" His exclamation corralled her attention at last, and she had to look up at him, silhouetted against the light from the ballroom. "You're crying!"

She mastered an urge to strike him.

"Joshua Manners," she managed, her voice quiet and shaking. "You are either the most insensitive man I've ever met, or the most stupid!"

She could not bear to remain there with him a moment longer, amid all of the brightness and gaiety of the Belmont ballroom. She turned from him and ran, toward the darkness. Toward oblivion. She heard him call after her, but she did not answer. She did not stop until she could no longer breathe, and her heart ached in her breast. She had no will left to keep her from sobbing.

Joshua felt as though he had been instantaneously transported to a foreign country where he understood nothing and where no one understood him. Stupid and insensitive? He had never thought of himself as either. But then, he reasoned, he had not a woman's perspective. There was obviously some monumental misunderstanding taking place, but who misunderstood whom? Hurt, mystified, he started to follow Allyn, but was halted in mid-stride by a familiar mocking voice.

"Joshua! Playing 'Hide and Seek' with your wife?"

Morgan Mellette emerged from the shadows like a black widow spider in ebony taffeta. A huge, vulgar array of diamonds glittered at her throat and in her hair. She wore a complacent, knowing grin that

Joshua ached to wipe from her face.

He wanted to go after Allyn, but he had some words for the governor's wife as well. Most of them would have to wait for a more convenient time.

"Not now, Morgan," he breathed, turning away from her again.

"You know, I'm surprised," she went on, the dynamic level of her voice a notch higher and its timbre a shade harder. "I never took you for the type to dance to any tune a woman cared to name. But then," she added, "I never imagined that you could be satisfied with such as Red's leavings."

Joshua faced her again, and she drew back, alarm on her features. In some bitter amusement, he realized that his desire to kill her must have been evident.

"He seems content with mine," he offered matter-of-factly. "For the moment."

She drew herself up. "I'm sure I don't know what you are talking about," she huffed, but did not meet his gaze.

"And I am sure you do," he replied, curbing his anger. "But save your explanations. I have no use for them, and you may need them later."

He left her, reining in his desire to extract Raif's plans from her, by force if necessary.

He had to find Allyn.

Chapter Twenty-Seven

Allyn heard heavy, running footsteps on the gravel path behind her. She had not gone far, and there were cunning little lanterns hung from poles along the route so that such as she could not lose their way. Perhaps, she thought, if she were very quiet . . .

"Allyn."

Her hope vanished. It was Joshua, and he was not even out of breath. Well, he hadn't had to run in stays and pumps.

"Go away," she breathed. She could not look at him. Her chest ached from running, from crying, and from having a broken heart caged inside it.

"I can't go away," he told her, barely above a whisper. "I already tried that once, and I came back. I couldn't go away again if I wanted to. And," he added with a small, hollow laugh, "I sure don't want to."

His words were like pebbles cast upon a still lake. She risked a look at him. He stood inches from her, yet in the dim light of the colorful yet virtually useless paper lanterns she could barely discern his features. Thus she could gain no clue from his expression.

"What are you saying?" she demanded, grabbing his sleeve with her good hand.

"I'm saying," he began, taking hold of her arms, "that you've had my heart on a ball and chain since Deadwood, when you called me Governor Mellette's lackey. I'm saying that Bill Boland or no Bill Boland, baby or no baby, you're not getting rid of me that easily."

His face neared hers, and it was all she could do to turn her head away from him. She wanted his arms around her, and his lips against hers. But she wanted to be sure this time. She could not bear to make the same mistake again.

"That's what you say now." She tried to sound aloof, but her voice sounded small and faint in her own ears. "But when the gratitude wears thin—"

"Gratitude!" His interruption was as startling as his whisper was harsh. "You think I—Allyn Cameron Manners, you are without doubt the most aggravating, most hardheaded . . ."

He paused. Allyn could not prevent herself from looking at him. He seemed like a general, marshaling his forces for a second assault. His gaze, even in the darkness, commanded her.

"Damn pride," he breathed, and she did not know whether he meant his own or hers. "You have me so turned around, I can't even think anymore. You've gotten into my system, like a drug, or a poison. I've never felt more terrible, or more wonderful, in my life. I love you, and I've loved you for so long I can't remember what my life was like before I met you. I can't imagine my life without you. But if you can't forgive me, or if you don't think you could love me, tell me now. I need to know, Allyn. I can't go on like this anymore."

Carole Howey

His words were like a distant, roaring surf, and for a dizzy moment she thought she might faint. He was her only support, the only solid mass in a world which had turned suddenly to jelly. His arms were around her, so strong and warm she never wanted to leave them.

"I . . ." Was that her voice, so breathless and weak? "I can love you, Joshua," she said, touching his cheek with her good hand. "I can. And I do. Oh, I do . . ."

He took hold of her hand and held it to his cheek, his mouth widening slightly at the corners.

"Then let's go home, Mrs. Manners," he whispered in a mockingly proprietary way. "We have some long overdue business to transact."

"I've lost count of the kisses I owe you, Joshua," she confessed, sliding the tip of her finger to his slack and sensuous mouth in the darkness.

His rumbling chuckle warmed her.

"We'll settle our accounts presently," he assured her, and it became her dearest wish.

Joshua made their excuses to the Belmonts, claiming fatigue on both of their parts. Allyn could not help but think that they knew he was lying, for she could see the fever of desire on his face, and could feel her own desire written in crimson on hers. As Joshua comandeered a waiting cab out in front of the mansion, she remembered something else she needed to tell him. She waited until he had helped her inside, and the footman had secured the door behind them.

"Joshua, I—"

"Shh," he ordered her, sitting beside her in the darkness, pulling her close in his arms. "Don't talk, now. Don't say . . . anything . . ."

The restraint she had sensed in his previous kisses had utterly vanished. His mouth was strong and hungry, drinking from hers as from a deep artesian well.

She yielded to him gloriously, relishing the exploration of his tongue and his teeth. She felt a carnal sob linger in her throat as his hand slowly, slowly found her breast, straining against the material of her dress as though she would burst. Under the layers of clothing, her nipples tightened, and his caress became confined to that. His fingers alternated between gentle and more urgent manipulations of that most deliciously sensitive portion of her being.

He left her lips, and she uttered a muffled cry at the abandonment. In an instant, however, he had pressed his face against the swell of her bosom that adorned the front of her gown. The heat of his mouth seared her flesh. Her loins responded with a throbbing which shook her entire body, and yet left her wanting more of him. Her hands were in his thick, dark hair, holding him there.

"Joshua," she uttered in a tortured whisper. "Joshua, Joshua . . ."

His answer was to move both hands downward, past her waist, pulling at her skirt. He gave up on that admittedly daunting mission, contenting himself with finding the outline of her hips and thighs, and pressing his hard, fevered body against hers until it hurt.

But it was a thrilling hurt.

When the carriage abruptly jerked to a halt, he pushed himself away from her, breathing hard. Allyn, temporarily thwarted in her desire, could barely compose herself before the driver opened the door to let them out at the Pellier.

They did not speak as they made their way to the suite. Allyn did not trust her voice, as all of her sensibilities had concentrated in but one or two areas of her body. Joshua fumbled with the key, and Allyn offered a brief prayer that Missy had already retired for the evening. She knew she was not capable of rational thought, or of explaining everything to Missy just then.

The suite was dark and still. Joshua took her firmly by the hand and led her to his room. She followed, her anticipation building with every step. Inside, he closed and locked the door and lit a small lamp on the table beside the bed. He stood for a moment, watching as the small light filled the room with a dull golden glow. When he looked at her again, she felt the potency of his love in his bright, dark eyes. She caught her breath.

"Come here," he entreated, beckoning her with his arms outstretched.

She went to him willingly, reaching for the lapels of his jacket.

There was fumbling and giggling and more kissing and sighing, and presently they were in Joshua's bed. The urgency in the carriage had been replaced by a languid slowness. They were alone, together, with nothing, not even bedsheets, between them. They had all the time in the world to enjoy one another, and their love. Allyn lay upon her back, allowing herself the pleasure of the anticipation of what was to come. Joshua, beside her, had propped himself up on one elbow, regarding her with an undisguised appreciation which made her tremble.

"My God, you are one beautiful woman," he breathed, tracing a line with his finger from her neck just below her left ear to a small, raised mole just above the nipple of her left breast. "And this mole is mine. May I have it?"

His activity had made her suddenly short of breath. She nodded quickly, swallowing. She studied his face as he stared at the mark, and she felt raw, undulating waves inside her as he gently circled it with the very tip of his finger. He lowered his head slowly and his dark hair glistened, beckoning her fingers. His lips touched the mole, and her hand tightened in his hair, massaging his head, holding him to his delightful task. His attention to the mark had the effect of making her breast shudder with jealousy at being ignored. As if in compensation, his hand cupped that tender swell of flesh. He worked it between his fingers gently as though acquainting himself with the feel of her, and with the very gestures which made her quiver and sigh with pleasure.

His mouth closed over her nipple, and the caressing hand moved slowly along her side and across her hip. Sucking upon her hardened, aching nipple, he pressed his hand against her femininity, gently searching with his fingers for the swollen, tender place within.

She was wet with wanting him, and she cried out softly as her loins released their warm, welcoming fluid for him.

He was above her, his arms like pillars on either side of her shoulders. She crooked one leg around his, then the other, pulling him toward her. His manhood found her at once, entering with long, slow strokes that she felt even at the very base of her womb deep inside her. With each practiced thrust she cried out, calling his name, or parts of it. Suddenly the room was very bright, and his movement became more urgent. In an instant, his body shuddered and came down upon hers with a delicious pressure which triggered another explosion of bright darkness within her. She was his. She was, at last, Mrs. Joshua Manners.

Joshua rolled over, pulling her with him so he could remain inside of her. She had whispered his name over and over, like an incantation. He felt bewitched. Charmed. He was entirely wrapped up in her, enmeshed in her being. He was her slave, and he wanted never to be free of her.

He held her so tightly that he wondered she did not cry out, but the only sound she made was a deep, shuddering sigh as she slid her bare leg over his.

"Joshua," she murmured, rubbing her cheek against his shoulder. "Will you love me always?"

"Always," he said firmly, cherishing the warmth of her all around him.

"Like that, I mean," she amended in a teasing way.

He felt a chuckle rise in his throat.

"I don't like to be too predictable," he told her. "I have one or two other ideas I may want to try out. If it's all right with you, that is."

"When?"

God, was he hard again already?

"How about right now?"

He wanted her again. His joy in her was like a freshwater spring liberated after a millennium of imprisonment in rock. She had awakened some part of him that had always been there, but had been dormant until this night. All of his actions, and every event of his life, had been but a prelude to this night. From this night on he was born to the world. Nothing mattered to him anymore except that she loved him.

Allyn had wanted to tell him she was not pregnant after all, but that could wait. She forgot everything presently but his kiss and his touch. Something had happened to her, something strange and wonderful. Aside from the fact that her body felt charged by his very touch, she felt as though her soul were reaching out to his through every pore of her skin. In a quicksilver flash of white-hot light, his soul met hers in the narrow space between them, which was really no space at all. It was an awesome sensation, for when her soul receded, like the drawing back of a curtain, it seemed not only to have carried a little of his back

with it, but to have shared some of its own essence
with him as well.

"I wasn't supposed to fall in love with you, Joshua
Manners," she remarked softly after it ended again,
caressing his cheek with her good hand. "I didn't plan
to. And I certainly never wanted to."

He chuckled, and the sound reverberated pleasingly
in his chest as if in a cathedral.

"Mrs. Manners, you are a shameless flirt," he
declared in mock rebuke, stroking her arm with a
strong, lazy finger.

She felt a giggle rise in her throat. God, how good
it felt to laugh! How good everything felt!

"Would you like me to flirt with you?" she teased
him, tracing the outline of his jaw.

He grinned at her.

"No," he replied firmly. "It would probably kill you.
And it would certainly kill me."

Involuntarily, she shuddered. He very nearly had
been killed, and so had she. The memory of that awful
episode made her cling more tightly to the reality.

"I'm sorry," he said quickly, sensing her dismay. "It
was a bad joke, wasn't it?"

Her injured hand, which she had very nearly forgotten about, began to throb again.

"I'm being silly," she answered, trying to shake the
sense of dread his words had invoked. "I should be
happy that the event hasn't robbed you of your somewhat irritating sense of humor."

"Another of your many endearing qualities," he
declared, nuzzling her cheek. "You don't pile on a
lot of empty compliments."

"Heaven forbid that I should contribute further
to your already elevated opinion of yourself!" she
retorted fondly. "How sad for you that an annulment
is now out of the question!"

His ensuing laughter startled her.

"Annulment!" he exclaimed, and she quickly shushed him. "Annulment!" he repeated, more quietly. "Do you still believe I ever had any intentions of granting you an annulment?"

Perplexed, Allyn sat up and found the coverlet, drawing it about her shoulder. He reached for her good hand, massaging it with a hint of devilment in his dark eyes. Before she could ask what he meant, he went on.

"It will probably surprise you to learn that you never even had to marry me in the first place," he confessed in a tender voice. "In Baltimore, Raif was working for Mellette. I could have wired the governor as soon as Bert told me about the blackmail attempt, but I made the mistake of believing that Raif wouldn't stoop to murder. Besides, I couldn't let on that Bert had told me about you and Raif. After that business, it was too late. I could still have blown the whistle on Raif, but with the murder, the whole scandal would probably have ruined you and Sheik anyway. I wanted to help you, but I knew you'd refuse if I offered. It had to work out so that you would come to me. Then once you did, I knew you would have to agree to just about anything I suggested, so of course I suggested the marriage."

"Of course," Allyn interjected, wondering why she was not the least bit angry with him.

"Of course," he echoed, pulling her close again. "What more logical assumption upon which to base a proposal of marriage?"

"Oh, only love, perhaps," she replied, exaggerating her response. "I've said it before. Joshua Manners, you are not to be trusted."

"Not for a minute," he agreed, laughing again. "Especially not when the truth sounds more like a lie. You must admit, my love, you would never have believed me had I chosen that moment to declare myself to you."

"I suppose not," she conceded. "Still, it seems a drastic measure."

"Drastic times call for drastic measures. What surprised me was that you never seemed to suspect my feelings at all. Did you hate me that much?"

"No," she confessed to him. "In fact, I think I was even a little in love with you already."

"Only a little?" He was teasing.

"Well, you were maddening. And I had no idea . . . I mean, for all I knew, you were just another mercenary preying upon the misfortunes of others. I was afraid that you—well. You know."

"I should have told you," he all but whispered. "Even if you didn't believe me, I should have told you over and over again. Maybe then you would have believed me. Maybe then you wouldn't have had to take that knife . . ."

"Don't, Joshua," she urged him, placing her bandaged hand upon his chest. "This isn't your fault. You mustn't think that."

"What did the doctor say?" he asked, and she could tell he was not persuaded.

She sat up again and presented the hand to him, noticing dark stains at the joints of her fingers through the bandages.

"Deep cuts," she pronounced. "They still open and bleed when I move my fingers. Missy's packed them in some awful-looking black stuff, and changed the dressing several times. I never saw the doctor, but Missy said he told her that if . . ." She paused. She did not want to think about what the doctor had warned, but she knew Joshua must be told. She bit her lip and plunged on stolidly. "If gangrene sets in, I will lose my hand."

She watched Joshua draw in a sharp breath.

"My God," he whispered, catching hold of her wrist, pulling her close again. "We'll just have to make sure that doesn't happen, won't we? I still can't believe you grabbed that knife. I don't think I'll ever forget the sight."

Allyn lay with her head upon his chest again, listening to his accelerated heartbeat, surprised that she herself could barely remember the event. The present filled her sphere, and not even the specter of further mutilation could mar her present happiness.

"To more important matters," she said in a proprietary way. "The papers. The ones Raif made me sign . . ."

"All here," Joshua affirmed. "Raif left me a trail I could follow in my sleep, and I slipped in and relieved him of the documents while he was, uh, otherwise occupied."

Allyn sighed with contentment.

"She's a fool," she said.

"Who?" Joshua was undeniably startled.

"Morgan," Allyn replied, lifting her head again to fully enjoy her husband's surprise at her knowledge. She was not disappointed.

"How did you—"

She could not prevent a laugh.

"It was a hunch, which you just confirmed," she told him, sliding a finger across his lips. "I knew she was up to no good that night at the Cotillion. And of course that's why the Mellettes chose this hotel. She needed to spy on us for Raif. The poor fool. I could almost feel sorry for her."

Joshua did not comment. He was thinking about the Cotillion, remembering Allyn's mocking remarks and the note. He suddenly realized that the handwriting which had seemed so familiar belonged to Morgan Mellette. She had obviously tried to disguise it, but she had written him enough notes for him to be able to recognize the slant and the abbreviated flourishes. Morgan was more deeply involved with this plot than he had previously thought. And the governor? Joshua had his doubts. More than likely Raif was using the governor's resources, one of which was Morgan herself, with the intention of selling Sheik to the highest bidder once he procured the beast. And Raif, along with Morgan, was still at large . . .

" . . . Joshua?"

It was a moment before he realized that Allyn had asked him a question.

"What? I'm sorry. I was woolgathering." He effected a light banter, unwilling for the moment to share his grim thoughts with her. "What were you saying?"

"I'm insulted that your attention could wander with me in your arms," she chided him with a reproving look, then kissed his throat. "I asked when you contrived this matrimonial scheme of yours."

He was pleased by her interest.

"It occurred to me the night Bert was killed, while you slept in my room. I very nearly gave it up when I found that you'd gone by the time I got back. But when you came back to ask my help, I knew I had you. You know, you are a very frustrating woman, my love."

"Say that again," she murmured in an inviting tone that sent a ripple of desire through his body.

"You are a—"

"No, the last part."

"My love," he whispered, and her mouth closed over his.

The first explosion split the headboard inches above them. He heard Allyn cry out and Joshua seized her, rolling on top of her with a quick movement.

"The papers, Manners!" Raiford Simms's enraged tenor was a staccato mockery of his usual drawl. "Where are they? I want them! Now! No, don't move," he went on as Joshua slowly lifted his head from Allyn's shoulder. "It'll only be a little harder to find them after I kill you both. Don't tempt me!"

Joshua searched Allyn's terrified face and felt her slender body shudder beneath him. Her pleading green eyes commanded his gaze and her lips parted to form a single, soundless word:

"Bluff."

"Now, Manners!" Raif barked.

Joshua responded to her suggestion with a slight shake of his head. He dared not risk the enraged Raif making good on his threat. As if to confirm his belief, another shot hissed past them, closer. Allyn gasped, closing her eyes tightly.

"In my coat," Joshua replied in an even tone. "Over there on the floor."

"Don't move," Raif snarled again, his voice dark with skepticism.

Joshua listened to the soft, shuffling sounds of Raif's search, wondering if the conscienceless intruder would give them the chance to get the papers back this time. The rustle of paper against cloth signaled the success of Raif's mission. Joshua felt Allyn's fingers dig into him, and soon his shoulder was sticky with blood from her reopened wounds.

"You two have made more trouble for me than that damned nag is worth," Raif continued, sounding satisfied despite his words. "And I can't think of one good reason to give you the chance to make more."

Three more shots fired.

"Joshua," Allyn sobbed softly.

A fourth shot ricocheted harmlessly off the ceiling above their heads.

Chapter Twenty-Eight

Allyn did not immediately realize that she was un-
harmed. The room settled into an eerie silence, a
silence which hung in the air like a noose swaying in
a light breeze. She looked up at Joshua, whose puzzled
expression told her that he too had been untouched by
the bullets. Slowly he eased off of her. As he cleared
her field of vision she saw Missy standing in the open
doorway to the parlor. Missy was not looking at her.
She was staring at the floor.

"Missy?" Allyn ventured, sensing that she was calling to her friend from across a greater distance than
the breadth of the room.

The younger woman met her gaze. Her eyes were
like gray cat's-eye marbles. She looked strange, even
frightening. Her mouth was drawn into a thin, tight
line.

"Missy, what—what happened? Are you all right?"
Allyn tried again, fearing the answer.

"Never better," Missy declared in a sharp, strident
tone. "He's in Hell now, where he can't bother you

anymore. By God, I feel wonderful!"

Allyn sat up, and Joshua with her. Allyn noticed the gun in Missy's hand, half hidden by the folds of her robe. She seized her own robe from the floor and covered herself with it as she rose quickly and went to Missy's side.

Raif was indeed dead. He lay in a heap upon the floor like so much dirty linen. His skin was already white and waxy. The gun with which he had threatened her and Joshua still rested in his slack fingers. His blue eyes, once piercing, were glassy and vacant, staring into oblivion. A cord of blood issued from his mouth and the back of his brown coat was stained in three places with dark crimson, where Missy had shot him.

Allyn knew she should feel something for the human being who lay upon the floor, but she was aware only of profound relief, and that Raif's blood was the same color as Bert's had been. She placed her bandaged right hand upon Missy's shoulder, and the younger woman offered her the gun she had used. Wordlessly, Allyn accepted it. The barrel was still hot.

"A common burglar," Allyn heard herself say.

"He was common, all right. And a burglar," Missy declared emphatically. "He robbed you of nearly four years, Allyn. And he took Bert's life. I'm only sorry I wasted three bullets on him. One would have been enough. And I should have fired it the day he came to the C-Bar-C."

The authorities were prompt and courteous. Allyn remained at Missy's side hoping to ensure that her friend would not, in her strained state, blurt out anything which might be either embarrassing or incriminating.

Joshua proved to be a superb actor. Indeed, Allyn

reflected fondly, watching her husband manage the investigation, the stage had lost a star when Joshua Manners elected to pursue another career. After answering the few questions put to them by the police, Allyn retired with Missy to the latter's own room to try to rest, hoping at last to put the specter of Raiford Simms behind them forever.

Later that morning, the Saturday *New York Times* reported—on the third page, Allyn noticed—the incident which had troubled the Mannerses and their guest, Miss Melissa Cannon of Rapid City, South Dakota. A random act of burglary perpetrated by an unidentified assailant, the article said. The police had agreed that the shooting was clearly a case of self-defense. Joshua had handled the mechanics of that coup, and Allyn felt nothing but satisfaction at the outcome.

Saturday afternoon at Jerome Park was fine and warm. Allyn accepted the sympathies and good wishes of all who came forth to their camp in the clubhouse, and Joshua remained fixed at her side. Missy, as Missy was wont to do, kept herself apart from the attentions lavished on people. She concentrated instead on Sheik, bestowing all of the attention upon him that she could from the clubhouse.

Sheik. Bless him, thought Allyn, he was the only one of them who had not been affected by the machinations of Raif Simms. He looked as spirited and eager, parading to the starting gate at the hands of his new jockey, as he had in Rapid City two months before at the Steeplechase. And the crowds! The fickle crowds which had so despised the colt in Louisville and even in Baltimore had, here in New York, taken him to their hearts and made him their favorite at eight to five. From the grandstand to the clubhouse, the name

Carole Howey

on everyone's lips was that of the chocolate colt from an obscure little ranch in Rapid City, South Dakota.

The odyssey was finally over.

Allyn sat down as if the impact of that realization had knocked her down. Her mission was completed. Her purpose for the last two months had come, at last, to this verdant, noisy place. Sheik would fulfill his destiny and go on, with Missy, to greater glories. She could not deny the regret which accompanied the pride she felt for Sheik, and the joy she felt for Missy. Nor could she deny the sudden emptiness and nearly overwhelming sadness. Sheik, and Missy, no longer needed her.

A soft rush of warm wind told her that Joshua had taken his place beside her. Gently, as though sensing her humor, he touched her hand. She could not help but smile at him. His feelings were plainly written in his indulgent expression. But not even love of him, a love so hard-learned, could compensate for this strange new emptiness.

The feeling, she realized suddenly, was not unlike some of the sensations she had experienced shortly after she'd found that she was not pregnant after all. Dear Lord, she thought. I've forgotten to tell him about that! Later. There would be time. They had all of the time in the world now.

"Here we are at last," Joshua commented, so low that only she could have heard him.

She gave his fingers a squeeze. He understood. He always had, and he always would. That, at least, was a comfort.

"Allyn! Quickly!" There was no urgency in Missy's words, merely a childlike excitement. "They're entering the starting gate!"

Allyn obeyed Missy's command, moving forward to watch. Joshua joined them, saying nothing. An unusual circumstance for him, Allyn thought. Per-

388

haps it was because there was nothing to say in this long moment, which was an undeniable milestone in all of their lives. She linked her left arm in Missy's and her right in Joshua's and watched the field of ten erupt from the starting gate.

The Belmont Stakes was Sheik's from the outset. Like a thundering, mad warlord he pounded the track into submission beneath unrelenting hooves, crossing the finish line an undisputed champion.

The shock of the finale rendered Allyn momentarily devoid of emotion. Missy, however, seemed to possess more than enough enthusiasm for the three of them, taking turns hugging her and Joshua, at once laughing and weeping.

"Come on, Allyn!" she shrieked, pulling Allyn's sleeve. "The winner's circle! I want you—and Joshua—there!"

"You go on, Miss." Allyn had found her tongue at last, feeling the warm comfort of Joshua's hands upon her shoulders. "After all, he is your horse. My job is done."

Missy laughed, shaking her head. "Says you!" she retorted, tugging with greater urgency. "Your job is just beginning. Yours too, Joshua!"

Joshua's hands fell away from Allyn, and she was compelled to follow her jubilant friend through the throngs, bewildered by the younger woman's remarks.

Joshua started to follow, but caught sight of Governor and Mrs. Mellette and their retinue, not far from where he stood. Morgan, he noticed, seemed pale despite her rouges, and sat closer to her husband than he had ever known her to before. As though his stare had attracted her attention, she looked up suddenly, her black eyes widening as her gaze locked into his. He started toward her, but stopped himself. Whatever danger she might have once posed to him, or to Allyn, or Sheik, had died along with her lover.

I can almost feel sorry for her, Allyn had said. And indeed so could he.

He stared at her a moment longer, and he realized that no words need pass between them ever again. She was as much a part of the past as Bill Boland, thousands of miles away, or Bert, or Raif, who were both dead. Joshua forgave her, and let her go, knowing that, secure in his paradise, he did not need to compound Morgan's hell.

Sheik, sweating, wore a yoke of white carnations. Allyn chose a position to his left, keeping her camouflaged injury from view, while Missy grasped the stallion's bridle on his right, lifting his head so the photographer could flash his picture. Allyn tried to remain obscure as the distinguished member of the Belmont family brought forth the traditional silver cup and the winner's purse. Missy doggedly took her arm, determined to make her share in Sheik's triumph.

Allyn could not help but smile, in spite of her numbness. The elder Belmont was saying something. She tried to concentrate, but could not, so she merely smiled and nodded, and accepted the cup offered to her. She watched Missy accept the purse, noticing for the first time the tears flowing freely from her friend's eyes. It was that sight, finally, that released her own emotions. She embraced Missy, overwhelmed by her joy and her loss.

"He's your champion," Allyn whispered, choking. "You're on your way, Missy."

"He's your champion," Missy corrected her, hugging her in return. "Yours and Joshua's. My wedding present."

Heedless of her injured hand, Allyn seized Missy's shoulders, pushing her back, stunned.

"Missy, you're mad! I won't allow—"

"You can't prevent it!" Missy told her, her hands

390

on her hips. "It's all quite legal. And I'm determined to have my way. It's something I learned from you, you see!"

Allyn wanted to shake her, but there was such love in Missy's voice and expression that she could not bear to.

"Sheik is yours, Allyn," Missy went on, low enough for Allyn's ears alone, seeming to ignore the crowd of reporters and others all about them. "In a way, he always has been. I trained him, sure, and Bert . . . but an animal knows who he belongs to after all. There'll be other Sheiks for me and the ranch. I've no doubt of that now. And—oh, Allyn! I'm so happy for you and Joshua! He loves you so much, you know!" Missy's eyes filled with tears again. "Just promise me that you'll retire Sheik to the C-Bar-C when his career is over!"

Missy drew back, leaving Allyn with Sheik's bridle, the cup, and a throng of inquisitive reporters pressing her. Sheik snorted. With amusement, no doubt, Allyn thought wryly.

"What's next for Sheik, Mrs. Manners?"

Allyn began to understand that these people were looking to her as Sheik's owner. She grasped the stallion's bridle more tightly.

"I—we haven't any plans as of yet," she heard herself say with a confidence which surprised her. She suddenly wanted Joshua very much.

"Grand National's in June," someone quipped. The reporters and nearby spectators laughed at the reference to the famed steeplechase to run in England in a few weeks.

"His first race was a steeplechase, as you know," she defended the colt. "He'd be ready for it. But I'm looking toward Saratoga." She was pleased that she was handling this so well. She glanced at Missy, who nodded in approval.

Carole Howey

"The Travers?"

"Probably," she replied, craning her neck to find Joshua. Where had that man gotten to?

"Will Mr. Manners allow you to continue racing him?" still another reporter wanted to know.

The question amused her.

"Let him try and stop me!"

The cluster of reporters and onlookers laughed, to her surprise. This was going so well! But where the devil was Joshua?

"Mrs. Manners, do you believe that Sheik is the fastest horse in America?"

"He's the fastest horse alive," she proclaimed in a louder voice, standing a little straighter. "And the smartest."

"There's talk of a match race with the Canadian champion on turf. Any comment?"

"Gentlemen, there is only one champion, and . . ."

Joshua appeared alongside of her, and he accepted Sheik's bridle from her, covering her hand with a squeeze at the same time. She looked up at him, and her gaze was locked helplessly into his tender one.

"Mrs. Manners?" the reporter prompted.

"Sheik is ours, Joshua," she whispered to her husband. "Yours and mine."

"There is only one champion, and what?" the reporter persisted.

Joshua shook his head, not moving his tender gaze from hers.

"Sheik is yours, Allyn," he told her, his voice low and unbearably gentle. "Yours alone. And you're mine. Alone."

Many voices shouted, but Allyn did not heed them. She was in Joshua's arms again, her lips demanding to be satisfied with his kiss. He met the challenge, and she thrilled to the flush of victory and the ecstacy of surrender.

To the Reader

Thoroughbred racing enthusiasts and horse lovers will know that, until 1930, the Preakness and the Kentucky Derby were run on the same day, and the Triple Crown did not come into being until after that time. I hope that I will be forgiven for taking such a liberty in the interest of the narrative.

Respectfully,
The Author